BITTERN ISLAND

James Conroy

For information, or to order additional copies, please contact:

Beacon Publishing Group
P.O. Box 41573 Charleston, S.C. 29423
800.817.8480| beaconpublishinggroup.com

Publisher's catalog available by request.

ISBN-13: 978-1-949472-27-1

ISBN-10: 1-949472-27-1

Published in 2021. New York, NY 10001.

First Edition. Printed in the USA.

Dedication

To Helen,

Writing is hard work, loving you is easy and came to me naturally. You had me from the very start. Thanks for the devoted follow-through. All my love, all my life.

To M. & L.,

As always, you both prefer to remain behind the scenes. I appreciate that and owe a great debt. No doubt you will remind me, often! Friends for life.

CHAPTER ONE

"I want rent saw," said my customer.

Regarding him over my coffee mug I asked, "What kind of saw?"

"Power saw. *Ya.* Power." His accent was heavy.

"Still doesn't help me." I flipped pages of my catalog. "I've got circular saws, jigsaws, saws-all. What do you want to cut?"

My assistant Rolando Tobar came in with logs and kindling. He went to the pot-bellied stove and prepared a fire. The stranger watched him.

"Wood," the man said. He turned back to me. "I cut wood."

"What kind of wood?"

The fire sputtered. Rolando closed the grate and left the room. My customer was average height, stocky, with a dark mustache.

"Tree limbs." He used his hands to form a six-inch circle. "*Dis tick.*"

"Then it's a chain saw you need." Finding the page, I turned the catalog around for him.

He examined the picture. "Good. You have *dis*?"

"We have everything at All Island Rental."

"I take."

Rolando came back with a broom and began sweeping the shop. From underneath the counter I extracted a three-part rental form.

"I need your driver's license," I said in my shopkeeper's voice. "How would you like to pay?"

He produced a wallet. "Cash." Out came the license. "How much?"

"Twenty-four dollars for the day. Do you have a can of gas?"

"A *vat*?" He did not understand what I meant.

"Gasoline," I repeated. "Petrol. The saw is gas-powered. Takes a half gallon to run it for about two hours."

"You got also?"

"Full can, five dollars."

"I take petrol," he agreed.

I filled out the rental agreement. He looked like the man pictured on the license. Ruddy face and flat nose over the mustache with close-cropped salt and pepper hair. I was renting a saw to Janus Martin.

"Twenty-nine even," I said.

I turned the papers for his signature.

Mr. Martin put a twenty and ten on the counter. He signed the contract in scribble.

I rang the sale on the register and plucked his dollar change. The form had white, yellow, and blue pages. The white, with his dollar change, went to Martin. I called Rolando and handed him the yellow copy that served as our requisition slip. The blue went in a drawer under the register.

Behind the store were four barns, red in contrast to the beige cinderblock store. These were my storage sheds. Rolando was gone a few minutes. Martin and I did not speak in his absence.

My assistant hoisted the saw and gas can onto the counter. Martin came forward for the gear.

"One more thing, Mr. Martin," I said.

"*Vat* now?"

"There's a warning label on the saw. You're supposed to wear the goggles supplied when using it. If you don't, I'm not liable if you have an accident. It's in the fine print of the agreement. All tools must be used in accordance with the factory recommendations."

"Fine print," Martin muttered.

Clutching the can in one hand, he picked up the saw with the other and left my shop.

Rolando went to the window and reported Martin drove a late model Jeep.

"Strange *hombre*," Roland said. "Seen him before?"

"Nope. Must be a summer rental."

"In February? Where'd he say he was from?"

I took out the contract and scanned the particulars. "Michigan. Hubbards Lake, Michigan."

"You'd think a guy from a lake in Michigan would know something about saws."

"Hubbards Lake is just a name. It doesn't mean anything. After all, Los Angeles isn't a city full of angels."

"Ever been to LA, boss?"

"No."

He laughed. "Then you wouldn't know."

I conceded his point. Rolando helped himself to coffee then moved the pot from the hotplate to the stove.

"I heard the weather report," I said. "Storm's headed our way. They say it's a big one. Better tune up the snow blowers. They're bound to go."

"They been tuned since November," Rolando said. Most winters Bittern Island gets hardly any snow.

"Check anyway."

"What'll you be doing?" Between us it was not impertinent.

"I'll check the portable generators."

"Think it'll be that bad?"

"Been listening to the weather since four this morning. If we're getting a hard blow this season, this is it."

"What the hell you doing up at four in the morning? *Cristo*, Karl. It ain't like you got cows to milk," Rolando said.

I dismissed his question with a shrug. We finished our coffees and went to the chores.

The blowers were in barn "A," denoted by the painted letter over the door. My work was in "C." It felt about thirty degrees and the sky was gray with clouds rolling northeastward. Snow always came out of the southwest over the water.

The shed had a padlock securing a crossbeam. I undid the lock with my key and slid out the beam. A lightbulb dangled from a rafter. The room smelled of oil, tar, dirt, and straw.

All Island Rental stocked four generators. After checking their fuel levels I started each up. They chugged a few moments then reached steady rhythm. Fumes filled the room. I shut them down. The smell never bothered me. I worked around machinery my whole life. What you could not smell was lethal.

The barn was full of machines and tools for rental. There were posthole-diggers, pumps, table saws, paint sprayers, and rototillers. One shed, "B", was crammed with folding chairs, tables, and canvas tents with poles and rigging ropes for outdoor parties. Each summer caterers rented these for Island shindigs. It was easier than hauling their own from the mainland.

I heard Rolando fire up one of the snow blowers. Moments later he revved another one.

Aside from the prediction, some muscle in my gut had a twinge. It would snow all night. It would snow like the devil. Southeast off Rhode Island, Bittern Island was dead in the storm path.

I turned out the light and rebolted the door.

Gravel separated the barns from the store. Halfway across, I heard a rifle shot from the crest to the northeast. These glacier-formed ridges split the Island in two. They are covered with brush and squat, sturdy trees. Another shot echoed down to me.

McCallum, I thought. Dan had a wife and six hungry kids. He must have expected the worst and been stocking up fowl. A bad storm would cut the ferry service for days. Dan's hunting was illegal but no one would bother him. "Live and let live" was Bittern Island's motto.

When I reached the back door of the shop I heard my radio. The station was switched from all weather to Country-Western. From the smell of tobacco, I knew my visitor.

"Hey, Karl," Gunner Hogan said between puffs on his pipe.

"Hey yourself, Gun. Want coffee?"

"Helped myself." Gunner lifted his metal cup, like one from a mess kit. Hogan always carried a backpack filled with the cup and tobacco and odds and ends he found washed up on the beach. He pointed the cup at the window. "Gonna be a hard snow. That's a fact."

"Don't I know it. Anything you need, Gunner?"

"Coffee's fine. Knew Rolando would have a pot of Latino brewing."

Gunner sat on a stool beside the stove. Even in that position you realized he was a large man. When his butt was on the stool, his head was above the stovetop. Reddish-gray hair flowed in ringlets down the sides and back of his head. Sometimes he shaved, sometimes not. Gunner Hogan was a man of moods.

"Remember the last blizzard?" he asked. "Eighty-six it was, no seven," he corrected himself.

"Eighty-eight," I said, remembering well.

"Judith was alive. Wasn't she?" He meant my late wife.

"Yes. Died that summer."

"She was a good one, Karl. Damn shame."

Rolando came in and I fetched us both coffees. Gunner held up the tin and I topped it off. From his pack Gunner took a silver flask and splashed whiskey over his brew. He set the familiar container with its "82nd Airborne" crest on the floor beside his boot.

The shop door opened and in blew a frigid blast of air. The wind was suddenly blocked by a figure cradling a chain saw. It was Martin.

"No work," he complained.

I bade him come in and relieved him of the saw. Going behind the counter I set the saw on top. I checked it was filled with gas and oil. Holding the blade a safe distance over the counter, I yanked the starter cord. With my thumb I pressed the safety button and squeezed the trigger with index finger. The chain whirred and I released the trigger. It stopped with a mild buck.

Martin came around the counter uninvited. "How you do that?"

"See this?" I pointed to the red button that was the primary safety feature of the saw. Martin nodded. "You have to depress and hold it with your thumb. Otherwise the trigger won't start the blade."

Martin grunted. "Ah, damn. Safety switch. I understand."

He thanked me with embarrassment, collected the saw, and left the store muttering to himself.

"Be lucky he doesn't hack off a limb of his own," Gunner said.

"Or somebody else's," put in Rolando. "You sure he's from Michigan?"

"According to his ID," I said.

Gunner scoffed. "Didn't sound American."

"*Si. Pero.* You think I do?" Rolando kidded him.

"American enough for me." Gunner picked up his flask, reached out and dabbed whiskey into Rolando's mug.

I switched the radio back to the weather out of Providence. It was snowing in Delaware, tracking up the Atlantic coastline. Airports in Baltimore and DC were closed.

"Staying open all day?" Gunner asked me.

"Sure. Some Islanders will take precautions. We've got at least six hours before she hits."

"What else you want checked?" Rolando asked.

"The space-heaters," I said. Wet firewood and loss of power would put them in demand.

"I'll go with you," Gunner volunteered. He guzzled his coffee and followed Rolando.

I went to the back porch and fetched more firewood. It was eleven o'clock in the morning. The sky was grayish-white like the underbelly of a whale. The temperature had dropped since I went to the barn.

On the northeast tip of Bittern Island is the community of Daretown, a collection of bungalows in the lee of the dividing ridge. Boarded up half the year, it comes to life in April, grows in May, is vibrant and raucous June through August, expires during September and by October empties again.

The lively period accounts for most of my business. When repairing winter damage, summer residents used All Island rather than lugging equipment from the mainland.

West along the coast from Daretown is a bluff. On its crest is a lighthouse. At the base is Gracetown. Grace, as we call it, is the only real town on Bittern Island. The majority of year-rounders live in Grace and it comprises most of the Island's commerce. Along with the harbor's fishing fleet, it has a general store, gas station, and a pharmacy that is also post office and public library. The town has three restaurants and two taverns. Only one of each open year-round.

Grace is port to the ferry that serves the Island from Narragansett. Since we cannot afford helicopters, it is pretty much our lifeline.

Rolando and Gunner came back. They stomped their feet and rubbed their hands by the stove. Gunner produced his flask. Rolando and I declined.

"Then I'll be on my way," Gunner said. "Got to haul in some wood myself. Gonna need a lot of it."

"You can take one of the heaters," I said.

"Thanks, I'll be fine. See you men when we've dug out."

Gunner shouldered his pack and waved as he went out the door. Watching him from behind you noticed his right-legged limp and soft dragging of that foot. From the front, his sheer size made it hard to detect.

The phone rang. I answered and took an order for a kerosene heater from a family in Gracetown. I promised delivery within the hour. No sooner had I hung up than it rang again. It was Pat Lawler, owner of the general store. Pat wanted a generator. His deliveries had come from the mainland and he did not want to lose refrigerated goods if the power failed. I said it would be along directly.

Rolando and I went to the barns and loaded the equipment into the All Island pickup. He offered to bring back lunch from Grace and I pressed some cash into his gloved palm. He started the truck and headed out along the gravel. Past the last shed he turned up onto the road called Mariners Path.

As I watched him the wind gusted up. A cold blow was driving from the southwest. It was the edge of the storm line.

Beyond the road and over the ridges a plume of black smoke rose to catch the wind. The dark column billowed out at the lowest point visible. Something was on fire near Walls Head. What it was I could not tell but there was not much over there except my father's old plant. The ridges blocked my view with their sassafras trees.

Rolando made two more deliveries that afternoon. He reported the fire I had seen was the abandoned fish processing plant at Jacob's Cove on the windward side of Walls Head.

"Didn't your father have something to do with that place?" he asked as we closed shop late in the afternoon.

"One of the original partners. Ancient history. Long before you came. Been vacant for years."

The clouds were lower. Wind whipped down the alley between the shop and barns.

"Why don't you take the truck?" I offered Rolando. He lived further from the store than me.

"You sure, boss?"

"Don't thank me. You'll have to dig it out in the morning instead of me."

He laughed and thanked me anyway.

My friend climbed into the pickup, wished me well and drove up to the road.

It was getting dark. No moon and no stars twinkled through the clouds and haze. The air dripped moisture as if it were humid. This evening's moisture was cooling rapidly and felt strange. It had tension the way water must right before it freezes. Walking home I felt invisible ice crystals sting my cheeks.

As I hiked west the ridges began to fade. Between hillocks I saw curls of smoke still rising from Jacob's Cove against the dull sky. Ribbons of black raked by the wind stretched northward trailing out over Rhode Island Sound.

Fires, not storms, are the bane of Bittern Island. Unless contained by volunteers with rudimentary equipment they burn until burned out. If the population is threatened, fireboats are dispatched from Narragansett or the Coast Guard stations at Castle Hill or Block Island. Summoning them is determined by Bittern Island's Fire Warden. No effort would be mounted to save the abandoned fish plant. It would char and fall in on itself extinguished under a blanket of snow.

I live in a house hand-built with stone foundation and wood frame. Fieldstone chimneys rise at each end. It lies in the nave of two outgrowths of rock that combine to form a common bluff at the back of the house. Beyond the bluff, dunes roll toward the Atlantic Ocean a hundred paces from my back door.

In good times I had been offered handsome money to sell. Some years back a law hit the books prohibiting sales except to the State of Rhode Island. Despite the State's long-term plan for the Island, the thought of selling never occurred to me.

I set a fire in the kitchen before removing my coat. Then I brought in more wood from the back porch. Through the crooked elbow of rock I could see the ocean. Huge whitecaps appeared to stop in mid-roll to lick up at the sky and then collapse. Clumps of dune grass lay flattened by the wind along the shore.

Back in the kitchen I stripped to my long johns and made a pot of tea. Rolando's lunch was still heavy in my stomach. I pulled the light chain over the table and sat down. If the power did not go out the storm would not be bad. But the power always went out. I fetched my portable radio and then two oil lanterns from the pantry and set them unlit at opposite ends of the table. Working the radio dial all I caught was scraps of music and chatter. No signal held for more than seconds. The rest was static. There was an old television in the parlor that only received two mainland stations on a clear night, so I did not bother.

I make tea strong like a Russian, but not as potent as Rolando's coffee. He always returned from the mainland with beans native to his homeland of Guatemala. Once he gave me a bag. I brewed some but it did not taste the same as when he made it so I gave back the rest as not to spoil it.

Lunch had come from the one year-round café in Grace that was owned by another Hispanic American, but not of Guatemala.

Don Ostros, the *"don"* referring to "sir," was from Nicaragua. How he afforded to stay open all year was never my concern. During Rolando's excursions to the mainland he scoured *bodegas* of the Latino communities and returned to Don Ostros's *cantina* with delicacies, for which he requested a fair price with a modest profit. The arrangement suited the Don and provided variety to his menu otherwise restricted to rice, beans, and the meat or fish of the day.

Gusts of wind gathered far away and whooshed over my house. I went to the front door and looked out. Snow was falling. Light from the doorway caught fat, wet flakes a glistening second before they disappeared below my knees. Within moments my hair was icy and my shoulders powdered.

The first hour a foot of snow fell on Bittern Island. Another six inches came the second hour. Later it was up and over my porch. I shoveled a path several times to keep ahead of the accumulation. Snow whipped in every direction. My world seemed inside a white trembling bubble.

For the rest of the evening I kept a fire blazing in the parlor and read by oil lamp when the electricity failed.

Judith loved a good fire. Summers we made campfires in sand holes in the dunes. We fell asleep there wrapped in each other's arms and did not wake till dew penetrated when the fire expired. We awoke stiff and achy but happy, clothes pungent with woodsmoke.

It was after eleven when I climbed the stairs for bed. I had shoveled three times. The snow last measured twenty-nine inches.

Upstairs was a hallway with a bathroom in the center. Left was my bedroom. On the right was the studio, Judith's studio. I had done a lot of work on that room for her, including cutting two skylights in the roof so she could work in natural light.

Carrying the flickering lamp I pushed open the studio door and went inside. Holding the lantern in front of me I looked at the ceiling. The two skylights were white with snow like blank canvases attached underside the roof. In the center of the room were her easel and paint table with its jars of brushes, tubes of paint, and cans of oil. Scrupulous when she worked, she left her palette on the table scrubbed clean, ready for her next session.

The easel was empty. No work in progress when she died. In the blinking lamp glow its struts appeared as masts of a fragile sailboat bobbing at anchor during a lightning storm. In one corner, stacked on edge, were assorted canvases, all stretched, bleached and ready. The opposite corner had two wooden crates, one atop the other. Inside were her paintings. The ones she had not sold. Judith never allowed me to hang her pictures in our home. That was not what they were for, she insisted, without clarifying the point. I still respected that quirk years after her objection could not be heard.

Retreating from the studio I closed the door and went to my bedroom. Finally peeling off the thermal underwear I wore all day, I slid under the comforter and extinguished the lantern.

Relentlessly wind penetrated every crack and joint where air could seep. It was as if fierce spirits dashed to escape. Unafraid of spirits — my father had seen to that — I fell asleep.

CHAPTER TWO

"This is Papa and Mama at Grandpapa's house near Kiev." My mother had a stack of old photographs she kept hidden. This was the first time she had shown them to me, and she had made me promise I would not tell Papa.

I squinted at the faded black and white picture. "That doesn't look like Papa."

"He had black hair then. And he did not wear a beard."

When I looked closely I could tell by the eyes of the man. They were piercing, yet brooding, just like Papa's. The man wore a suit and tie. Very straight, shoulders back, chest puffed where the tie disappeared behind his vest.

The woman next to him was my mother. Her long dark hair was shorter in the picture, cropped close to her cheeks and temples. But the face unmistakable.

"Kiev," I repeated the sound. "Where is that?"

"Russia. Far away."

"Do you have pictures of Papa's boat?" I was anxious to see more. These were the first photos I ever saw in our home.

"He did not have a boat."

That was odd. Papa always had a boat. It was his work. He fished the waters off Bittern Island. Wasn't Kiev on Bittern Island? Wasn't Russia some point or cove I didn't know because Mama said it was far, maybe on the other side of the Island?

"Then how did he fish?" Maybe Mama had forgotten some of the story. The pictures were old and she had not been well.

"Papa wasn't always a fisherman. No, *ditina*, not always."

"What did he do if he didn't fish?" It was all he did for my six years.

"You must keep a secret," she whispered. Mama put her arm about my shoulder and drew me close. "You must promise with all your heart."

"I promise," I almost shouted.

"Shh, I believe you." She stroked my hair. "Papa was a soldier. He was a brave soldier. But you must never repeat that, not even to Papa. He has good reason for you not to know. I only thought it time. There is so little time."

I was too excited to listen. "Do you have a picture of him in his uniform?"

"No, *ditina*. It was not like that. He was a special soldier. Papa only wore his uniform at great occasions of State." I had no idea what a great occasion of State was. "Or he wore it for me," she added in an unfamiliar voice.

I was disappointed. I only knew Papa in his sweater and slicker he wore fishing, or his tee shirt in summer. And there was the robe he wore when he read and smoked his pipe and came to breakfast wearing the one day of week he did not fish.

"So what are the other pictures?" I pouted.

"There is another of me. I'm wearing sort of a uniform, though certainly not a soldier's."

Mama moved the Kiev photo to the side, revealing another picture. It was of a young girl.

Behind the faded gloss the girl's face was fresh, exuding energy and excitement. Dark hair was pulled back from the face and gathered in a knot on the crown of her head. Strips of lace bordered the head and features, ending with a ribbon tied at her throat. The girl's arms extended up in arcs above her head, fingertips of each hand barely touching.

I stared at the photograph. What should have been a billowing dress ended abruptly at her thighs to reveal sculptured legs that narrowed to crossed ankles pedestaled on arched, slippered feet. The feet intertwined so perfectly they touched the floor in one tiny point.

I did not see my mother in this picture.

"Who is that?" I whispered.

Mama sighed. "That's me, *ditina*. I was sixteen."

"What are you doing?" My eyes remained fixed on the figure.

"Dancing. Oh, God, how I could dance, *ditina*."

Mama explained ballet. You told a story with movement, wonderful music rising from the orchestra pit. She had left Kiev and gone to live somewhere called Moscow when not much older than I was at that moment. The fortunate one of a hundred young girls, she was singled out by masters after a rigorous selection process. She felt lucky to be sent away by her parents. Sent away to Moscow to study dance.

"What story is this picture?" I asked.

"*Romeo and Juliet* by Sergei Prokofiev. I danced Juliet." The memory made her voice full despite her illness. "This was opening night at the Kirov Theater in Leningrad. A marvelous affair. Stalin attended. Such splendor."

My mind was overwhelmed by so many strange names and images. My body shuddered from excitement.

"Enough, *ditina*," Mama said. "We must put these away before Papa comes home. Another day we will look at more. Go wash up while I start supper. Papa will be home soon. Remember. This is our secret. You promised."

I renewed my pledge and went as told. Mama put the pictures in her secret place. When I returned they were not to be seen again. Light-headed and enthralled, I went to my chores setting table and fetching wood. I felt infused with a brooding, remarkable new vision of life. That there was music and dance; stories that needed no words. And there were times men dressed in secret uniforms that had the hypnotic name "great occasions of State."

At supper I must have looked flushed. Papa felt my forehead.

"Is he sick?" he asked my mother.

Mama put her hand to my head and then my neck.

"No, Kurt. I don't think so," she said. "He's had a busy day. He's tired and fighting it. Wants to be strong like his Papa. Such a help he is to me."

Papa was satisfied. "That is good. You need rest."

Except for touching me the conversation was as if I was not in the room.

"I feel bad," Mama confessed. "I rely on him too much. When I'm better he should play more. He's a baby."

"We are not babies long, Galina," Papa said, calling Mama by name. "Soon he learns to fish. Now he must go to bed."

Accustomed to my cue, I laid down my spoon and stood at my place. Papa pushed his chair back and beckoned with his arm. Up close he put both hands on my shoulders and kissed me on the forehead.

"Done, and well done, my son. But I will not read to you tonight. You are tired and must go to sleep," he ordered. "Kiss Mama and off you go."

Indeed, I was exhausted. Moving like a zombie I walked into mother's embrace.

She kissed my cheeks. "Good night, *ditina.* Sleep well my little *khlopchik.*"

When I left the kitchen Papa's voice turned gruff. "Don't call him that. I've said it's dangerous to speak like that in front of the child. What if he repeats it? He starts school in a month."

As I climbed the stairs I heard Mama agree not to speak the language in my presence. Later I learned it was Ukrainian.

At the top of the stairs I heard them lapse into the strange tongue. Though not truly strange, for in its forbidden realm I was Mama's *ditina.*

Soon I started school. The facility was on the mainland, necessitating a round-trip sailing. Nine school-age children lived on Bittern Island. Five of us had boat-owning fathers. As the school district did not recognize the Island, these men shared our transportation. Due to weather and seas, we missed days our parents considered too rough for us to cross.

I learned my last name was Hoffmann. Mama taught me to spell and print it. Owing to Papa's reading to me, I was considered one of the brightest pupils in the First Grade. They judged my reading skills at a Third Grade level.

Geography became my favorite subject. At first I was confused because I thought the places Papa read to me existed. Where were Camelot, Sherwood Forest, the pirate islands of Robert Louis Stevenson? Papa explained the distinction between fact and fiction, reality and myth. No gods dwelt on Mount Olympus though their stories were important to know.

That prompted a question that took Papa by surprise.

"Where are we from?" I asked while he selected a story to read me.

"What do you mean?"

"I mean what country? Sean in school says his parents come from Ireland. My friend Sal is from Italy. Where do we come from?"

Papa laid the book on my bed. He stroked his beard contemplating the ceiling.

"Your mother and I are from Germany," he said at last. "Hoffmann is a German name."

I was confused but said nothing. Papa seemed uncomfortable and I still wanted him to read. But what happened to Kiev and Moscow? Then I remembered it was a secret and I had given Mama my word.

A few weeks later I went shopping with Papa in Gracetown. Mama was sick and too weak to go for groceries. In the general store we went to the butcher counter. A rotund man with red face and pointed mustache stood behind the case of meats. Papa addressed him in a language I had not heard before. It sounded harsh and seemed to come out of his mouth in chunks. The butcher smiled to hear it and responded in kind.

The next day Mama was still in bed and I made her tea. I recounted the exchange for her.

"That was German," Mama explained. "The butcher's name is Mister Ziegler. He is from Stuttgart in Germany."

"Are we from Germany?"

"We are if anyone asks." I was surprised by her sudden sternness. "That is Papa's rule."

"But we're really from Kiev," I teased, wanting to change her mood.

"Not precisely," she admitted reluctantly. "I never should have said anything, you naughty boy. Papa's rules have purpose. You must obey them."

"What about Moscow? What about Russia?" Wickedly, I knew she had not the strength to dissuade me.

"You are a terror, *ditina*." Then she smiled.

"I want to know."

"Very well but remember your promise."

"I swear. Tell me."

Mama closed her eyes an instant and raised her frail arms to place her hands on my shoulders.

"Listen closely. You might never hear this again. I was born in Kiev. This is in Ukraine, part of

Russia. Your father was born in the north. His parents lived in Tallinn. That is the capital of Estonia. Estonia is also part of Russia. Do you understand?"

"I'm not sure."

"Consider it this way, *ditina*. Ukraine is like Rhode Island. Estonia like California or Maine. They are separate but part of the same. Like the states of the United States. We speak differently and have local customs, but we are part of something bigger, something stronger than all the parts."

"Then why do we say we are German?"

"It makes us safe."

"And because Papa speaks the language?"

"Goodness no, Papa speaks nine languages. It was his job."

I assumed the job was not fishing but soldiering. Mama was tired and I stayed quiet while she fell asleep.

Papa did a strange and wonderful thing that night. Even if I did not yet realize it, he knew my mother was dying. The doctor had come by many times. Bottles of medicines were by her bed. She had spent a week in a hospital in Providence. Now she was home.

From his truck Papa unloaded two large boxes, large for a little boy. He set them by the stairs. In a pledge of conspiracy Papa winked at me and put a finger to his lips. I nodded my head.

From the first box came a device similar to one we had at school. Carrying it, Papa ascended the stairs, careful to make little noise. He entered their bedroom where my mother was sleeping.

Downstairs again, he selected some packets from the second box and led me up the stairs by my hand. At the top he pushed down gently that I should sit on the top step. Once more he winked. Then he entered the bedroom.

It was quiet for some moments. The door was open a crack. As I waited a lone violin note drifted out to me. Before it faded it was joined by a flute and then a horn and a chorus of strings. The music was sublime.

Mama awoke to the overture of Tchaikovsky's *Swan Lake*. I am certain she smiled. The next two weeks our house was full of music from ballets, operas, and symphonies. I may have imagined it, but Mama's health and spirits brightened with the music.

Papa was not a man likely to give presents. His was a stolid and reserved countenance. And we were poor. There was always food. But fishing earned irregular income. Some seasons good, others bitter. The markets for fish were as capricious as the sea. Money from prosperous months needed to be stretched through barren ones. And Papa's boat required yearly outfitting, maintenance, and petrol to power to the fishing grounds, the markets on the mainland, and home again.

It was the economy governing our lives that made Papa's gifts of a second-hand record player and a case of albums such a sincere act. Years later when I fought with myself to hate him, I remembered the pleasure it brought to Mama, and relented.

We were not a religious family. Bittern Island had only one church and that was Episcopalian. We attended service on Christmas and Easter only, and that was for social reasons among fishermen and their families. I never learned to pray.

So Papa's words to me that Friday in November were strange and empty. He had not gone fishing though the late fall had been bountiful. He stayed in the bedroom playing records until noon. I sat at the kitchen table and did my arithmetic lesson since I was not in school. Chopin and Puccini drifted through the house.

I sat upright in my chair when the music stopped in mid-strain. In the silence I heard Papa descend the stairs, each foot slow and heavy.

Into the kitchen he came. His face above the gray beard was pale and emotionless. He could not bring himself to look at me let alone touch me. The voice that came from his mouth was hollow the way wind is hollow heard from long away.

"Your mother is dead. There is nothing you can do but go to your room and say a prayer."

Toward evening men came. One of them asked me if I wanted to see my mother before they moved her. I could not bring myself to do it. They brought a stretcher upstairs. A while after they brought it down and took Mama away.

Her remains were cremated on the mainland. She returned to us in a wooden box with brass corners. Papa and I took it to the highest point on the Island, a ridge ending above the ocean at the east end. Papa opened the box and poured the contents into the wind. Ashes rose and swirled in a cloud. Some landed amid rocks, the holly trees, the plums, and sassafras roots. More were carried out to sea. If the beach roses had been in bloom I would have sailed one after her.

As we walked home Papa touched me for the first time in days. He put his hand on my head.

"You were a good son to her. Done, and well done. Toward the end I know that was not easy. Perhaps it will be easier now. As easy as it is hard. And it is always hard."

CHAPTER THREE

Fishermen rarely need timepieces. Day is not measured in hours but sun and shadow on water, the height of waves, and the direction and force of wind. I went to the window and wiped a patch. It was black outside. The light from Gracetown Lighthouse swung over my house and I saw the snow had stopped. I figured it to be about three-thirty in the morning.

Lamp in hand I went downstairs. On the porch was the outline of the path I had dug several times with eight inches of fresh powder on top of it. The screen door brushed this back.

I held the light up and stuck out my head. At the left edge of the porch was a drift as high as the house's soffit appearing as a continuous wall. Ahead, the porch seemed not to end but roll into a bleached plain to the extent of my light. No road visible, only lapping waves of snow toward the ridges across the way in the last of the starlight. Stars meant the storm was gone.

Despite the serenity of the scene, a shiver quivered down my spine. Occasionally morbid of nature, I felt if death was like this it would not be bad. A quick stroke of absolute cold followed by a numbed melding with this blue-blank nothingness lasting forever. No memories, no faces, neither joy nor pain, only endless empty sea in the dream of a sleeping God.

In the kitchen I made tea. Radio reception was clear. The weather report came in for a quarter past four.

The storm had tracked across Rhode Island Sound and up Narragansett Bay. Newport, Warwick, and Providence got three feet of snow before the storm pushed into Massachusetts. A textbook Nor'easter, the storm brought high tides in its aftermath. Categorized as the worst New England blizzard in forty years, it surpassed the one I remember in eighty-eight.

After an oatmeal breakfast I set to some chores. More shoveling, cleaning the fireplace and stove, lugging in firewood. The sun came up dazzling the landscape. It hurt to look at the snow for long. No point in opening All Island Rental yet. Nobody could get to it. I settled down to read and the morning was passing quietly.

Deep in my book a noise distracted me. It came again, louder. A cough, a sputter, then a gunning motor sound. The pulse reminded me of a chain saw. Closer and clearer, the cadence of pistons. I turned to the window but it was snow-caked. Then the staccato ceased with a cough. A few seconds passed before a loud knock on my door.

"Karl? You home?" came a voice. "It's Archie. Open up. It's damn cold out here." More rapping on the wood.

I opened the door for Archie Bealer and then caught sight of something behind him in the snow.

"What the hell have you got there?" I said.

"Oh, that," he muttered. "A snowmobile. It's all that will get you around on a day like today."

"I wasn't going anywhere. What brings you out my way, Constable?"

Archibald Bealer was Bittern Island's elected and paid peace officer.

"Got any coffee going?" he asked.

"I can in a minute."

Bealer removed his gloves and blew into his hands. He followed me to the kitchen as he shed his blue official Constable coat. A little over six feet, same as myself, Bealer had a red face due to a combination of cold and his whiskey fondness. One of his eyes had a slight tic. When he was agitated, it made you think he was winking at you. He took a seat while I made the coffee.

"Where did you get that thing?" I asked.

"The snowmobile? Picked it up at auction in Providence. You should rent them at your shop. They're fun once you get the hang of it."

"Not likely. This is the first decent snow in years. Never pay for themselves in rentals. I'll stick to basics."

"That's all anybody does around here. Basics. You know?" It was not really a question. His eyes roamed my kitchen. First time for him in my home. Like every room, except the studio, the kitchen was crammed with shelves loaded with books. "You read all these?"

"Some of them twice."

I poured us both coffees. Bealer drank his with both hands, revealing a slight tremor. Gunner Hogan was occasionally the same way. Bealer was much worse.

"Want something to better warm your bones, Constable?"

Bealer was silent a moment, concentrating on holding his mug steady. "If you got something, that would be grand."

I fetched a bottle of whiskey and glass and placed them on the table. So as not to watch him pour, I busied myself feeding wood to the stove. I heard his long first gulp. When I turned around he was pouring another. I waited until he finished that one too and then sat down.

"Checking up on me, Archie? Must be. After my house there's only snow, sand, and ocean."

My home was on the western end of the Island's south side. Beyond it were only marshes, dunes, and the beach.

"You don't need checking." With the liquor, the New Yorker was coming into his voice. "Everybody knows you do all right by yourself."

"There's all the coffee and whiskey you need at the Sea Witch." That being the year-round bar in Gracetown where Bealer was a regular. An Islander name of Sweeney owned it.

"There will be when Sweeney digs her out," Bealer said. "Now she's got a six-foot drift up over the door. Whole town is damn near immobilized. That's why I got that little buggy. Knew I'd need it some day. Hell. I ain't used half my yearly budget in the seven years I've held office."

"That's why you got re-elected."

The constable job was a four-year term.

Bealer half-chuckled to himself. "Probably. But I keep the crime rate down."

Now I laughed. "Crime rate? Bunch of frat boys drunk on Labor Day Weekend. That's a Bittern

Island crime wave. And if they were Islanders, it wouldn't even be a crime."

Constable Bealer got serious. "I look out for my own. That's why I've come."

"What's the problem?"

"Been a fire in Jacob's Cove. Ben Marshall checked it out first. The old fish plant is gutted. He knew it wasn't worth saving."

Ben Marshall was Fire Warden on Bittern Island. He was also Harbor Master in Gracetown. Not many Islanders sought elected office. It conflicted with our "Live and let live" philosophy.

"Wasn't a hazard," Bealer went on. "The cove is wasted space anyway. Spring comes we'll haul away the debris. Maybe build dockage for pleasure craft."

"Nobody's going to sink money into the Island and you know it. They just want us to die off or move off."

Our State Legislature prohibited re-sales on the Island. After the deadline you could only sell your property to the State which had a long-term design on Bittern Island. But a grandfather clause respected family lineage. A home could be willed down the family. If no blood relative wished to carry on, it had to be sold to Rhode Island.

"They got themselves a wait," Bealer said. He poured another drink.

"You still haven't told me why you're here."

Bealer ran both his hands through his mussed gray hair. Then he rubbed his eyes. "Found a body down there this morning." He looked at his glass, not me.

"Whose body?"

"Damned if I know. Hell, if I hadn't done twenty years on the force in New York, I probably would have missed it. Burnt beyond recognition. Whole place is a mess. Completely burned. Then the snow came and made a mountain of mush out of it. Ever smell a fire?"

"Sure."

"I mean a real fire. A building fire. One where people lived like the tenement fires we have in the City."

"I guess I haven't."

"I have. Plenty. And firemen would call us if they found a body that looked more than burned."

"More than burned?"

"Not killed by the fire," Bealer explained. "Sometimes they'd haul out a corpse with a bullet hole or a meat cleaver wedged in its head. Murder case, so we'd be called in."

I nodded, understanding.

"Never forget that smell." It prompted a sip of his whiskey. "It's like you took a hunk of rotten meat and threw it in your fireplace. First you get a whiff like there's a nice steak on the grill. Then it goes foul, putrid foul and you swear you'll never eat porterhouse again."

"Jesus, Archie." I poured some whiskey into my empty mug. "That's disgusting."

"Yup. That's why you don't forget."

My drink went down in a single gulp. It burned and I let it.

"I was investigating the scene. Doing my job," Bealer was saying. "Figured Marshall would make a report and so would I. Then I smelled it. Christ. It was Twenty-Third Street all over again. My first one. You never forget that smell."

Bealer drifted in his mind a moment. His hands had ceased trembling. He came back and said, "I moved some crap around and found the body. The clothes are burnt right into the skin so you can't tell which is which. Hair and face are gone. Need a Medical Examiner from the mainland to identify this one."

"That'll take time. Storm's probably shut everything down."

"That's why I'm here. I need your help."

"What kind of help?"

"Preserving the evidence. If I leave the body I'm afraid some debris will crash down and bust it up. Worse yet, a lot of what's left is leaning out over the water. A strong wind might blow it into the cove. Flood tide will swallow it up and wash it away. Can't let that happen."

"You think this is a murder," I said.

"Yup."

"How come?"

"Because of this." He produced an object wrapped in a red bandana. He placed it on the table and gingerly unwrapped it. Revealed was a ten-inch knife. It was blackened with soot but I distinguished the slotted handle from the blade.

"Found it wedged up in the ribs," Bealer said. "If I had to guess, and I'm good at this stuff, it was in the poor bastard's heart. But I can prove a lot more with a body than I can with a murder weapon. There's men in Attica State Prison threw a gun or knife in the East River. All I needed was a victim and some sharp lab boys. We need to keep that body. Karl, you've got to help me."

"What do you want from me?" I really did not want to hear his answer.

We bundled up and then, with me behind Bealer straddling the snowmobile, we roared off to All Island Rental. I had to dig out the shop door to get the key to the shed. Grabbed a lantern as well. We trudged through waist-high snow to shed D. Dug that door out too.

Holding the lantern I led Archie Bealer as we selected what was needed. We took a roll of plastic sheeting and a canvas tarp. Two coils of rope were added to the pile we made at the door. Next came a bucket and a shovel.

The last item was actually a pair. I forgot I had them. Never rented them out. Judith bought them at a garage sale on the Island though they were old and wooden and not of much use. Still Judith insisted. The family having the sale was desperate for money. I teased her anyway on our way home.

"What do you intend to do with a pair of dilapidated water skis?"

"And I suppose you need a single shoetree. Plan on losing a leg?" she countered.

I have no idea what happened to the shoetree. But the skis finally had purpose.

Using rope I made a bundle of our supplies and crude sled out of the skis. Bealer and I hauled it around front and secured it with more rope to the tail of the snowmobile.

"Take it slower this time," I warned Bealer. "The added weight might pitch us around."

"Roger." Bealer revved the engine and took us off in a wide arc.

We headed back Mariners Path through the snow. It went easiest when Bealer used the rut we cut going to the shop.

Before reaching my house Bealer came to a halt and pointed to a low section of ridge.

"I think we can cross there. It will save time."

Before I could object he swung the nose of the snowmobile that direction. We plowed through drifts at the base of the ridgeline. The handmade sled bobbed and swayed behind us. At the crest was a narrow gap and we glided through it.

Bealer braked and we skidded to a stop. The northern half of Bittern Island lay shrouded below. Beyond I could see Rhode Island Sound. Huddled down the slope was Gracetown. Smoke curled from chimneys but not a soul could be seen. Right was Daretown. Snow on the roofs there lay thick and even, for there were no fires in the houses. My tailbone ached from the mobile as it broke through drifts and slammed down on the other side.

"Nice and quiet," Bealer said over his shoulder. "So much the better."

Down from the ridges we glided onto Quilin Road. Like Mariners Path on the other side, it was a wavy ribbon of snow. Bealer veered left. The ground on the north side of the Island is higher and rockier than the south. Our view was unobstructed. Bright sunshine played like fire on the water. It felt odd to be so cold.

The snowmobile dipped, then again, and kept nose down as if tracking a scent. From Walls Head we descended the rim of Jacob's Cove, following a path off Quilin into the belly of the cove. One side had the decaying moorings no longer in use. One of those abandoned slips had been my father's where he docked his boat, *Galina.*

"Here we are," Bealer called in the wind. "Hold tight. This could get dicey. There's debris all over."

He throttled back and we sledded up a small rise to the entrance of the plant. There should have been a wooden gate but I supposed it had burned away. Charred wood rose all around as if guiding the way in Hades. Bealer brought the machine to a stop.

"Come on," he said and pointed. "Over that way."

We got off and untied the bundle from the skis. Bealer picked up the sheeting while I slung the rope over my shoulder and carried the tarp.

Bealer took me through the remains of the plant. Steel fish vats were empty and blackened. Tables for chopping and filleting also survived although stained and seared. The ice machine shell, long scavenged of parts, was bent and burnt.

"Here he is, poor bastard," Bealer said. He held up his arm for me to stop.

The awful smell came to me. I gagged but fought it down. Archie stepped aside for me to see. It could have been a burnt log. One end was the head, blackened, featureless, not the grotesque skull I expected. An arm jutted out, its hand melted into a mitt. The legs appeared as one charred trunk of tree ending on one side in a burned boot.

"Might as well get started," Bealer said. "Do as I tell you. We've got to disturb him as little as possible."

"Nothing will disturb him."

"It's evidence. Be careful."

We rolled out layers of sheeting. As we lifted, bits of him, or his clothing, fell away. We wrapped the body lengthwise, then across, then lengthwise again. With my pocketknife I cut rope to secure the covering. Then we rolled the package onto the tarp, wrapped it up and tied it off with more rope.

It was a surprisingly light bundle we carried back to the sled. Much slower due to our fragile cargo, we crossed the ridge, descended to Mariners Path and on to my house.

A few yards from the house we dug a mock grave in the snow. In the hole Bealer tamped the bottom and sides. I filled pails that we used to whitewash the base and sides of the house with water and lugged them to the gravesite. The water turned to ice, forming a snug vault. We laid in the body, covered him with snow, and applied more water to seal it in ice.

"That should hold him a few days," Bealer said. He was sweating under his heavy clothes.

"Should hold him until spring."

"We'll have this solved before then."

"We?"

He did not answer, suggesting instead we go in the house and have a drink.

Inside we shed our bulky garments and I stoked a fire in the stove while Bealer fetched the whiskey and glasses.

"I wonder if he'll go back," Bealer said after his first swig.

"If who'll go back?"

"The killer. Then he'll know someone's got the body. That should shake him up."

"Who'd be that stupid?"

If nothing else, Bealer was a wise, old city street cop. "You'd be surprised. Besides, one thing is certain. Since the storm there's been no ferry. The killer is still on the Island."

CHAPTER FOUR

Men were in the room with my father. I was sent to bed and no reading that night. Their voices rose to my bedroom. It was too much for me to sleep. Never had there been company in the house. I crept down the hall to listen.

"It's always been this way, Kurt," someone was saying, calling Papa by his name. "You haven't been here long enough to realize."

"So the longer I live, the dumber I get," Papa said.

A scuffle erupted. When it grew still I heard the front door slam.

"Ray's a hothead," a voice said. "He'll come around. What choice has he?"

The men mumbled. A third voice urged my father to speak.

"Friends and brothers," Papa said, "it's a hard life we chose. But it is our life. What we make of it is how we shall be measured as men. Who among you has more to lose than I? I came here a foreigner. My wife is dead three years. The boy grows. He needs clothes and food same as your children. My boat needs petrol. There is insurance to pay. I am one man with a son. What happens to him when I cannot sell my fish? When my fish do not bring me the value of my labor?

"Many of you fought the Fascists. And what did it get you here at home? Not every despot wears a brown suit or salutes with a stiff arm. Nothing starts on a grand scale. It starts with subjugation of a neighbor. Subtle at first, insidiously subtle. You must watch for it. They hurt his business. Mock him in his church. Tell lies about him. Believe me. I have seen this," Papa said.

"Everybody knows you came here to escape, Kurt," a voice said. "You were lucky to get out of Germany when you did. Still, it must have been easier since you're not Jewish."

Papa interrupted him. "It wasn't only Jews. The State had many enemies. There were gypsies, liberals, intellectuals, and communists also."

"Politics," a voice complained. "I'm sick of politics. We are fishermen, not statesmen. This is about fish. I can't sell my fish at a fair price. It's those money hungry bastards in Newport and Portsmouth. They are starving my family."

The voice that had requested my father speak said something.

"My brother lives in Boston," he began. "He says I must be doing well. His wife goes to market and can't afford swordfish, tuna, or cod. They buy mackerel because it's cheapest. He wants to know what I'm doing with all the money I'm making."

The image brought a cheerless snicker from the group.

"Money is its own politics," Papa said. There was a murmur of agreement. "Excuse me while I check my son."

Hearing that I scampered down the hall to my room. By the time Papa came I was pretending to be asleep. When he put a hand on my head I inadvertently opened my eyes.

He was not surprised.

"You were listening?"

"I couldn't help it," I said.

"I will calm them." Papa kissed me on the forehead. "Do you know what we were saying?"

"A little. You can't get money for your fish. You want to do something about it."

"Shh, you're right. This is serious. You must never speak of it outside this house. Not to anyone. Some of the men who own the fish market have children in your school. They must not know we think like this. Do you understand?"

"Yes, Papa."

"Good. It is our secret. You know how to keep a secret?"

"Yes. Like we didn't come from Germany."

Papa raised his hand from my head. His eyes went blank the way I had seen when he scattered Mama's ashes. He set his hand down gently, and bowed his head to me.

"That is correct, son. We will talk about that soon. I promise. Go to sleep."

For the first time I can remember Papa kissed both my cheeks just like Mama.

Weeks later a stranger came to the house. Papa expected him. They shook hands. Papa introduced him as Mr. Chandler, an old friend. After I shook Mr. Chandler's hand Papa instructed me to go out and play. As I went out the door I heard Papa say, "Thank you for coming, Colonel."

I went to the swing in the yard and commenced to pump my legs. Soon I was topping the swing's arc and falling backwards to the other extreme, my mouth wide open in excitement. Only blocks from the sea, the air was salty. A raging thirst came on.

I tramped to the kitchen for a glass of water. Papa and Chandler were in the parlor. They were arguing.

"I gave you what you wanted and asked for next to nothing," Papa was insisting.

"You gave us what you had, Kurt. There's a difference," Chandler objected.

Without getting my water, I moved closer to hear better.

"And Galina," Papa ranted, "she was almost killed. She never danced again."

Chandler's voice grew stern.

"Major Viljandi, need I remind you? You chose the crossover point. You said you knew the schedule of patrol boats. I never liked sea routes. It should have been through Berlin as I suggested. As always, Major Viljandi had his own way."

I heard my father's real last name for the first time.

"Berlin?" Papa shouted. "I had no business in East Berlin. That would have been suspicious. Especially for Galina. We were watched. You Americans love Berlin. Of course. You have all those troops on the west side of the Wall. Safer for you. Riskier for us. In Finland you could not throw your weight around."

"This isn't getting anywhere," Chandler said. "There is no undoing the past. But you and I, Kurt? We're even. I did what I said I'd do. How can you ask more? Besides. We're older now and don't matter much anymore. Why not let it be?"

I heard a chair move, heard a familiar stride, knew my father was pacing.

"How can I let it be? The Combine is crushing the fishermen of this Island. They drive down the price of our fish and raise their own. It cannot go on."

"It was never our intention you wind up on this godforsaken Island. Again, you had your way."

"If I listened to you," Papa said, "I'd be a minor clerk in some company rich with defense contracts shuffling papers. You might as well have shot me."

Chandler afforded Papa a crude laugh. "Be that as it may, the United States government does not regulate the price of fish. That is why we call it an open market. It is our nature to be competitive. You communists, I realize, employ different methods."

Chandler's tone had a smug quality. Papa stopped pacing and addressed it.

"Competition I know. This is my point. We fishermen want to compete."

"What have you done?" Chandler sounded alarmed.

My father explained. His voice grew stronger as he spoke.

Papa and his friends wanted to open their own fish processing plant on Bittern Island. Instead of taking their hauls to the mainland and accepting the going price of the processing Combine, they would clean and prepare the fish themselves. Afterwards they would go directly to the retailers, bypassing the corrupt markets that paid little and charged much.

When Papa finished there was silence. It ended when Chandler said, "My God, Kurt, you're still a socialist."

Papa laughed from deep in his chest. The sound filled the room and then the whole house. It was exhilarating to hear. Exhilarating for me, not Colonel Chandler. He spoke harshly to cut off Papa's laugh.

"We won't give you a penny. It's ludicrous. The government does not finance private enterprise. Besides, what would we get in return? You have nothing to offer. You've played your hand. It bought freedom for you and Galina. The slate is clean."

"A slate is never clean," Papa said in a low voice. "Otherwise it is not a slate. What is written is wiped off so something else may be written."

"What the devil are you saying?"

I heard Papa regain his chair. He savored the moment with a deep breath. Here is my father the soldier, I thought.

"This war," he said calmly, "the one you call the Cold War. It goes on without end. Secret warriors parry and retreat. I know it well. It is a global game of chess. But what pieces you can not capture, you must seduce."

"Come to the point," Chandler said.

"Do you read *Life Magazine* or *Time*?"

"What?"

"Look around," Papa said. "Look at me. Look into the eyes of my son. Go to the place where we spread his mother's ashes. Come watch them give pennies for my fish. Eat soup with us more water than stock. This land of plenty. I'll tell it to anyone who will listen. You know they will listen. For this I betrayed my country. I ask you. How many defectors will you seduce with pictures of this?"

Chandler let out a whistle that ended in a curse. "You bastard."

"In this business, everyone is a bastard. You," Papa added, "know better than most."

I sneezed and quickly ran to turn on water in the sink.

"Karl? Is that you?" Papa called.

"Yes, Papa. I'm getting a glass of water," I called back.

"Come in here when you're done. I want you to say goodbye to Mr. Chandler."

Chandler's face was grave as he shook my hand treating me to a stiff nod.

"I'll see what I can do," he told Papa. "You'll hear from me."

"Don't take long," Papa warned him.

Chandler's eyes roamed the room, taking in all the shelves piled with books. Some were books Papa read to me. Many others he read only to himself. Those were the ones I hoped to read.

"You should have been a teacher, Kurt," Colonel Chandler said as he put on his hat.

"I prefer remaining the student. There is always much to learn."

Chandler made a strange face, turned, and left.

"Is everything all right?" I asked Papa.

"I believe so. We shall see."

Two weeks later Papa took me to the Post Office in the town's drugstore and retrieved a letter. The next day we ferried to the mainland and went to a bank.

At the bank my father talked a long time to a stern man in a three-piece suit. When they finished, Papa gave him the contents of the envelope. The banker lent Papa a pen to sign the back of it.

Things got very busy on Bittern Island after that day. There were more meetings at our house. Visitors came with papers. Papa took me to Jacob's Cove where men drove machines pushing sand and driving pilings.

We started going to church. Papa said it was a form of "solidarity" to do so.

The processing plant opened ten months later. There was a ceremony. The minister from the Episcopal Church blessed the endeavor. There was a party at a *cantina* owned by a man named Ostros. Ostros was a foreigner like Papa and invested in the plant.

In the morning the fleet went out as usual. In the afternoon they returned early. Without having to make the voyage to the mainland, they motored into Jacob's Cove to unload their catch.

It went on like that for a year. But as my father once said, there is a tide that is no tide but the will of men. Go with it, swim against it, or drown. Papa had already swum against such a tide. Yet he refused to go with it.

First came the State inspectors. These well-bribed men issued summonses. Next came union organizers with placards and threats. Finally the retailers were intimidated into boycotting Bittern Island fish regardless of price.

By that summer the Combine won. Bittern boats started to the mainland with their hauls. The Island's processing plant ceased to function. There were no fish to process and even if there were no place to sell them.

In a cruel gesture, the Combine bought the plant for a penny on the dollar so it could sit and rot empty as a reminder.

Papa never spoke about it. Nor did other fishermen on Bittern Island. They fished their boats, took what the Combine paid, and times were hard for several years.

In the 1960s things got better. State and Federal authorities investigated the Combine. There were indictments. Papa knew the names and faces of the men led into courtrooms on the front pages of the newspapers. If he felt satisfaction, he never said so.

It was the decade ending my youth. I grew up, physically and mentally. I had Papa's passion for literature and by high school was reading two and three books a week along with my regular studies. My task was easy with the thousands of volumes Papa had accumulated over the years and libraried in our house in Grace.

Melville's *Moby Dick* and Hawthorne's *The Scarlet Letter* gave way to Faulkner and Upton Sinclair, F. Scott Fitzgerald, and John Dos Passos. I spent one summer when not fishing reading everything written by John Steinbeck.

Often when I perused the shelves, having finished one book and in pursuit of the next, Papa would reach up to a shelf, snatch one with a finger and flip it to me.

"Read this," he would say. "It's time."

I discovered Tolstoy and the plays of Chekhov.

"Done, and well done," Papa always said when I reported a work finished. He would quiz me on the book and we would discuss it.

But all the reading in the world was not changing anything. And that, I decided, was the problem.

During the last weeks of senior year I spent a lot of time on the mainland. My friends and I were old enough to power our parents' boats across the Sound.

One Saturday night four of us went to the movies in Newport. Afterwards we wandered down by the docks and one guy produced a bucket of iced beers and another a bottle of whiskey. We sat on the pier and drank and sang and told lies until we fell asleep under the stars.

In the morning we awoke clammy of clothes and dry of mouth. We hustled to our boat and headed back to the Island knowing we were in trouble.

Trouble waited on the dock at Bittern Island. I could make out my father pacing while we were a hundred yards out. Other fathers were there too, and one guy's mother which embarrassed him beyond mention.

The adults waited while we tied up taking undo time securing lines.

"Karl," Papa called down from the dock.

"Yes, Papa?" I tried to sound nonchalant but it did not work. Papa was not a violent man and I did not fear rage like some of my comrades. But I did fear his shame.

"You come home now. This nonsense is done."

I nodded and climbed up to him on the pier, shivering and sweating all at once.

"Are you hurt?" he asked.

"I'm all right."

"Then enough. We go home."

He turned on his heel and walked away without another word. I heard the other boys' folks cursing and yelling at their sons. Not Papa. He simply left and, after hesitating only a second, I followed.

We ignored each other the rest of the day. At supper that was impossible. Papa laid down his spoon after his bowl of stew.

"So? What is the matter?"

"Nothing is the matter," I said. But I could no longer hold back. "Nothing is anything in this goddamn place. You made us our own little gulag."

A flash of color stained his weather-beaten face. He moved his chair back abruptly and I thought he would stand, but instead both his hands came off the table and trembled over his bowl. He swallowed. He blinked. He lay his hands down.

"So," he said, gaining control. "On top of everything else you've been reading Solzhenitsyn without consulting me."

The moment passed. There was everything and nothing to say. We were poor fishermen on a poor Island. For me there would be no cars, no college, no weekend ski trips. There was only the sea, the sun, the sea, the bitter cawing of birds, the sea, the knife-edge sting of dune grass thrashing a bare shin as I ran, ran in every direction only to find the sea.

"What will you do now?" Papa asked. His voice was full of resignation. He was asking a man's question of another man. Papa was taking my measure and ready or not I had to summon up the mettle.

"I've decided to join the Army."

For a second his body went limp; the features in his face drooped. I had never seen Papa like that. I was suddenly struck by his age.

"Is that so?" He rose from the table, clearing his bowl and cutlery.

"Yes, it's what I want. I'm going to volunteer."

As Papa sat down I got up with my own dish. I started to wash but Papa called me back to the table.

"Sit, Karl. Come sit down."

I did as he said.

"You thought carefully about this?"

"Very carefully, Papa."

He slapped the tabletop with his palms. "Then I think this is a good thing. You will make a fine soldier and make me proud."

Papa stood up and I did too. He came around the table, embraced me, and kissed both my cheeks. I returned his hug. He broke my embrace and held me at arm's length.

"Go fetch the bottle," he said. "The time has come we have a drink together. We will drink soldier to soldier."

CHAPTER FIVE

"*Madre de dios*," Rolando gasped. "Put where?"

Archie Bealer and I returned to All Island. Rolando had a fire in the stove. He tramped across the ridge through the snow and opened shop. I recounted Bealer's and my project of the morning.

"You shouldn't have done that. It's a matter for *la policia*," Rolando said.

"I am the police," Constable Bealer said.

Rolando was not impressed. "You're a traffic cop on an Island with no traffic. You should have called the State Police. The weather's clear. They could fly in by helicopter."

"He has a point," I said to Bealer.

"I thought of that, but the crime scene was unstable. We might have lost everything," he explained to Rolando. Bealer turned to me for affirmation. "You were there. Tell him."

"It was a hell of a mess," I described for Rolando. "What's left is shaky. I think one strong wind and it's a goner."

"No matter," Rolando said. He got the coffeepot off the hotplate and set in on the stove. "You guys are in over your heads."

"How come you came to work?" I asked to change the subject.

"To rob a snow blower and make my fortune."

"You might have something there." The robbery remark he did not mean. "If nobody can get to us, maybe we can get to them."

Bealer interrupted us. "Got any whiskey around here?"

Rolando ignored him. He said to me, "I was thinking of Don Ostros's place and maybe the Sea Witch. We could do Lawler's store. Hell, we could plow all of Main Street. What you think?"

Main Street in Gracetown is little more than a wide sidewalk. Rolando's idea had merit. If not for revenue, it was a community service.

"What about the whiskey?" Bealer said.

"We don't keep any at the shop," I finally answered him. I was considering Rolando's idea.

"There's one problem," Rolando said.

"I'll say," Bealer said. "There's no damn whiskey."

I cocked an eyebrow at Rolando to explain the problem.

"How do we get the blowers over to Grace? I barely made it over the ridge on foot. There's no road passable."

"We have the snowmobile. We'll tow them like we towed the body."

"That's why you're the boss."

"No way," Bealer said. "That's an official police vehicle. You can't go operating a snow removal business with it."

"Let me put it another way, Constable," Rolando argued. "There's no whiskey here but there's cases of it at the Sea Witch. *Comprende?*"

Bealer licked his parched lips. "Well, if it's a community service…"

Rolando and I did not wait for him to finish. We had work to do. We took the snowmobile around back to the sheds, where I reconstructed the makeshift sled.

Two blowers were too much to haul in one trip, so I lashed the first one to the skis. Bealer insisted on making the first crossing. Rolando and I did not have to guess where to drop him.

"You take the first run with him," I told Rolando. "Drop him at the Sea Witch and leave the blower out front. Then come back and get me and another blower. You think you can drive this thing?"

"Back in Guatemala, I had the only Harley in my country."

Constable Bealer needed no prodding; he had the vehicle revving. Rolando saddled up behind him and the two roared off, towing the swaying blower behind them.

Though the sun was bright, I was damp to the bone. Inside the shop I helped myself to coffee, hung my peacoat by the stove and settled in to wait.

It was after noon when I heard Rolando gun the mobile around the back. I waited until he came into the shop and poured him coffee. He warmed himself by the fire.

"How did it go?" I asked.

"Not bad once you get the hang of it. It bucks but it gets you there."

When he finished his coffee we started out on the second crossing after I tied up the blower to the back of the snowmobile. Rolando handled the vehicle well. If anything, he drove faster than Bealer. I hung on tight.

We pulled up in front of the Sea Witch where the first blower sat idly.

"Archie inside?" I asked.

"No stopping him. I thought he'd break down the door. Thank God Sweeney was inside and let him in."

Rolando and I started the blowers and formed an offbeat conga line proceeding down the sidewalk. After two passes we were in the street. As the way cleared shopkeepers and residents poked their heads out to thank and encourage us. Sweeney came out with brandy to fortify us. Don Ostros promised us dinner on the house.

It was dusk when we finished and the center of town was clear. The roads in and out were still packed with snow, but you could get around the village.

We parked the blowers behind the Sea Witch and went inside. Sweeney served us more brandy. A couple of patrons had come in since the way was cleared. There seemed a cheerful attitude among the assembled, which excluded Constable Bealer. He was passed out at one of the tables, head down, hand clutching a half-glass of whiskey.

Don Ostros came in and renewed his offer of a free dinner. We thanked Sweeney for his hospitality and followed Ostros across and down the street to his *cantina*.

The day's work left us famished. The cook made us steaks and rice and beans. We washed down the meal with beer and settled back to belch and drink coffee. Ostros joined us at the table, serving the coffee himself.

"That was a marvelous display of industry," Don Ostros said.

"The meal was great," I said.

Ostros laughed. "Not the eating, *mi amigo.* I mean the plowing. I thought the town would be choked for days."

Rolando sipped his coffee in contemplation. I felt more talkative.

"It's not like your business thrives in winter."

"I do all right," Ostros said. "I get by."

"That's what we all try to do. Sometimes we get lucky."

"In my country we say a man makes his own luck. Unless, of course, he has caught the eye of the Evil One."

Out of the corner of my eye I saw Rolando discretely make the Sign of the Cross. I had always known him to be superstitious.

"Then what difference does it make?" I asked Ostros.

"In what manner?"

"Two men work hard with good luck. One of them is taken down by the Evil One. The other one lives a happy and prosperous life. Which is the better man?"

Don Ostros smiled but said nothing.

A child appeared from the kitchen, a small boy maybe three years old. He ran across the room to Don Ostros. Ostros turned in his chair and scooped the child up in his arms. The child was babbling and Ostros spoke softly to him in Spanish while stroking the lad's hair. When the boy was calm Don Ostros took a chocolate candy from his pocket, unwrapped its foil, and placed it in the child's hand. The youngster popped it into his mouth and kissed Ostros on the cheek. The Don kissed him back and placed the child back on the floor. In a flash the boy ran back to the kitchen.

Don Ostros sipped his coffee and looked at me. "Life is more simple than you make it, *Señor* Hoffmann."

"How so?"

"I don't always carry the chocolates." Then he laughed.

"It is getting late," Rolando said. "Thank you for dinner, Don Ostros."

"Yes, thank you," I added.

"Then I bid you *buenos noches*," Ostros said. He stood up and shook hands with us.

Rolando and I crossed the street back to the Sea Witch. Constable Bealer was no longer at the table. I asked Sweeney where he went.

"His wife came for him as usual. He woke up babbling about frozen bodies. It's no use when he gets like that."

Rolando and I had a nightcap.

"Come on," Rolando said. "I'll give you a ride home on the snowmobile."

A three-quarter moon hung high over the ocean. Rolando stopped at the top of the ridge as if deciding which way to go.

"Are you okay?" I asked.

"You feel it? It's getting warmer."

Without waiting for my reply he throttled the engine and took us down to Mariners Path and on to my house.

The next morning at first light my phone rang. That usually meant the power had been restored as well. I had been awake almost two hours and not bothered to check.

"Where the hell is my snowmobile?" Archie Bealer demanded.

"Rolando said he would leave it behind the Sea Witch."

He calmed down a little. "All right. The power and phones are back on."

"I noticed."

"We got work to do, Karl. I'm about to call the State Police. I don't know how long it will take them to get here, but they are going to want that body. You didn't mess with it, did you?"

"Don't be ridiculous." Then I remembered Sweeney's remark Bealer prattled drunken stuff about frozen bodies. "Who did you tell about this?"

"Nobody. Why?"

"Because that's not what I heard. You shouldn't drink so much."

There was silence on the other end of the phone.

"So?" he asked at last. "Are you going to be home when they get there?"

"If I'm not here, I'm at the shop. You and Rhode Island's Finest can dig it up for yourselves. I'll leave the shovels on the porch if I go to the store."

"They'll want a statement from you."

"I've told you where to find me."

"I guess that's okay. See you later." He hung up.

For the first time in what seemed like days I took a shower and shaved. The hot water heater chugged and sputtered and was not much good. No matter. I was wide awake.

In the cupboard were some corn muffins but they had gone stale. I threw them in the trash. I was not very hungry anyway after Ostros's big dinner.

Something on the top shelf caught my eye as I went to close the door. I reached up and snatched it. I must have known it was there and forgotten. It was a cardboard tray of three vitamin bottles wrapped in plastic. Judith had been younger than I, and she insisted I take vitamins to keep up with her. It was our joke. She took a daily regimen herself. I turned the package over in my hand.

STORE IN A COOL DRY PLACE

I put the package back on the shelf. It made me think of something.

"I don't always carry the chocolates."

Outside the snow was melting at a furious pace. As Rolando had noticed last night, it was getting warmer. By estimation, I thought at least twenty degrees warmer than when the snow was fresh. My boots made sucking sounds as I hiked through it to the shop.

Rolando was there when I arrived. So was Gunner Hogan. Rolando was fresh and clean-shaven too. Gunner was same as always.

"What's this about murdered bodies in Jacob's Cove?" Gunner greeted me. "And you carting them about like Army plebes kidnapping Navy's goat?"

"If that's what you know, then you know as much as me. The State Police are coming over to figure it out."

"You mean the great New York sleuth is unable to solve the crime?" Archie Bealer bored everyone with tales of his career. "Who is our departed Islander?"

"That's the question. Can't tell from the corpse. Burnt beyond recognition."

"Christ," Gunner muttered. He took a slug from his flask. "I seen that in 'Nam. Never forget a sight like that." Another pull of whiskey.

Unlike Archie Bealer, I had never seen Gunner Hogan drunk. Maybe I had never seen him sober for comparison. Despite his frequent neglect of the subtleties of hygiene, he always appeared in control of himself.

"He ain't one of us," Rolando blurted out.

"What do you mean?" I asked him.

"The dead guy. He can't be an Islander."

"How do you figure that?" Gunner asked.

Rolando stuck out his mug, first pointing at me, then Gunner. "You two guys are the closest thing we got to hermits on Bittern Island. And you're both accounted for. Anybody else would have been missed by now."

Rolando was right. He lived with a woman in Gracetown. Even Archie Bealer had a wife. Aside from Gunner and myself, everyone else on Bittern Island had somebody more than most of the time.

The three of us reflected on that and then Gunner asked, "Remember?"

I was already headed to the counter. I pulled the blue slip from the drawer.

"Janus Martin owes me a chain saw."

CHAPTER SIX

Basic training at Fort McGuinn was similar to life on Bittern Island. I rose early. Calisthenics and drills, like fishing, were physical. Food was basic and bland. I went to bed early and tired.

When not drilling, I was bored. I missed my books. There was little time to read. When there was time, the Fort library had a skimpy selection and the PX only carried magazines and comic books.

One word was heard daily, many times, in varying contexts. It was shouted on the rifle range. The word was intoned solemnly during Company meetings. It served as greeting among veteran soldiers at McGuinn. At night in latrines, recruits and draftees said it with fear. The word was the name of a place. The place was Vietnam.

Basic lasted eight weeks. The men in my squad learned to march, salute, field strip an M-16, rappel walls, hurl grenades, recite a litany of military codes, and keep our boots shined.

Near conclusion of training we were barraged with aptitude tests.

"Private Hoffmann," my platoon sergeant, a massive Floridian named LeVance, called. "Front and center."

It was Thursday morning and a rare one. Most of the platoon had the day off with the exception of those pulling guard duty or KP. I was in my bunk daydreaming after morning chow.

I hopped out of the bunk over Kevin Slade, a city kid from Chicago, and marched down the line to where LeVance waited.

"Present, Platoon Sergeant," I said.

"At ease, soldier," LeVance snapped. "In my office."

I followed him into his office. It contained a cot, desk, and two chairs. Such a small room for so large a man. He directed me close the door.

LeVance pointed. "Take a seat. Relax. You ain't fucked up. Yet," he added.

LeVance sat behind the desk, took a folder from a drawer and laid it closed between us. Nothing was said while he extracted a cigar from his pocket, gnawed the end, spit into his wastebasket, and fired it up with a lighter.

"Consider yourself lucky, Hoffmann?" he asked through a cloud of smoke.

"Not especially, Sarge," I said warily. LeVance took relish in stomping a recruit by drawing him into an exchange and exposing the guy's lack of knowledge with respect to the Army's method of accomplishing tasks.

LeVance chomped his cigar. I had not taken the bait and he was disappointed.

"Basic training is over," LeVance said. I already knew that. A graduation exercise was scheduled for Saturday. "That means you're a soldier, Hoffmann. You ain't a good soldier, but you ain't dog shit either." He opened my file. "I see you enlisted instead of being yanked by Selective Service. Enlistment can mean anything. Maybe you're too dumb to make a living in civilian life. Thought the Army might give you a ride and teach you something."

I said nothing and he continued.

"Or maybe you got some high school chippy," he said and paused to scan the file, "in Rhode Island pregnant and thought this might put distance between you and her pappy. Then again you might be John Fucking Wayne who ain't had a serious shave yet. What about it, son?"

"Ever lived on Bittern Island, Sarge? I have, my whole life."

He was going to smile but he plugged it with his cigar. He looked at the file. "Ever lived in Wakulla, Florida?"

"No, Sarge. Never heard of it."

"And I never heard of Bittern Fucking Island. But I know the score." He picked up a sheet from the file. "Says here you've applied for Advanced Infantry Training and then you want a crack at Jungle Warfare School."

"Correct, Sarge."

"Mighty ambitious, but all the same, there's someone visiting the Fort I want you to meet. It came down from the old man himself. His name is Captain Ryder and he is here on a recruitment exercise. Had your name at the top of his list. He'll see you at Company HQ at 0930. Put on fresh utilities and go on over, boy."

"Thanks, Sarge."

LeVance bristled. "Don't be thanking me. Do your duty. Keep your nose clean and your head out of your ass. And I'll promise you. You won't live out your days swatting skeeters on Butternut Island."

LeVance closed the file and I did not correct him on the name for my home.

"Dismissed, Hoffmann. Now get the fuck out of my face."

For the second time that morning I showered and dragged a razor over my cheeks and chin, even if LeVance thought that was a waste of time, then lathered and washed up. At my bunk, I dressed in a crisp set of camouflage utilities. My boots were already polished to perfection.

"Got a date?" Spade called. He was in his bunk reading a comic book.

"Sarge wants me to meet someone at HQ."

Slade pretended to spit. "Oh, shit. Sorry for you, man."

"What the hell are you sorry about?" Slade's twisted logic always amused me.

"We draw a stand down today and then you're called to HQ. Only two explanations for that. Either somebody saw you whacking off and ratted you out to Sarge, or your mother died."

"I told you, my mother died when I was a kid."

"Damn. Then it's a pecker-pull for sure." Slade tossed the comic to the floor and rolled onto his side. "Should have done it in the shower like the rest of us."

Captain Ryder was none of Slade's business so I let him have his fun. Slade was a draftee, not a volunteer. His displays of vulgar humor were his manner of coping with fear. Slade was convinced he was Vietnam-bound.

Fort McGuinn was nestled in the Blue Ridge Mountain foothills. Beyond the perimeter the land was green and sprouted trees like I had never seen. The climate of Bittern Island and the sweeping winds stunted most varieties of growths. Not so for the hills and swales of West Virginia. The soil, when you nudged it with your boot, was rich and dark and soft.

Walking over to Headquarters I could smell the earth like the first morning I got off the bus eight weeks ago. Smell the earth. Smell the sky. Smell a piece of ground that had not been touched by the ocean in a billion years. It smelled like living, or what I thought life ought to smell like.

"Private Hoffmann reporting as ordered for Captain Ryder," I said to the corporal on duty.

"Captain Ryder." The soldier repeated and checked a roster. "Room Six. Up the stairs, third door on the left."

At the top of the stairs I swung left and knocked on the door with the correct numeral.

"Yo. Enter," a voice called.

I pushed the door open, stepped inside, caught sight of a pair of collar bars on the man across the room and came to attention saluting.

"You must be Hoffmann." He acknowledged the salute. "At ease. Come in. Grab a seat."

He appeared in his mid-thirties. Not as tall as I, he was broader, more compact. Before I reached the chair he stuck out his hand.

"Captain Ryder."

The Captain's grip was firm. He released quickly and indicated the chair again. Ryder moved behind a desk and sat down facing me.

There was a pipe smoldering in an ashtray. Ryder picked it up and rekindled it with a lighter. He eyed me up and down through a cloud of smoke as he tamped the bowl. I was familiar with the procedure having seen Papa do it as he read by our fireplace.

A sheet of paper was on the desk instead of the customary file. The Captain moved it to the side, sliding it with one hairy-knuckled hand. His face seemed almost as wide as his shoulders. The nose had been broken once. Ryder's hair was short, black and curly. Black bushy eyebrows hooded his calm eyes. The broad face and taut jaw reminded me of longshoremen I had seen along Rhode Island's waterfront when Papa and I unloaded fish.

"How do you like the Army, Karl?"

"I like it fine, sir." I was dying to know who he was, what he was about, and what he wanted. I asked nothing. That was a military courtesy you learn quickly. Never ask officers a question unless directed to do so.

"Tell me about yourself: where are you from? What does your father do? What are your plans after the Army?"

"I'm from Rhode Island, sir. A little island off the coast called Bittern Island. My father is a fisherman."

Ryder raised his hand. "Stop right there." He laid down his pipe. "You've got to tell me this. You live on an island. Your daddy is a fisherman. Probably done your share of fishing with him. Seems you spent your whole life surrounded my water. How come a kid like you didn't join the Navy?"

He had me stumped. It had never crossed my mind. I almost blurted out that my father had been a soldier. I checked myself. It would not do to go into that. This guy, I figured, was going to offer me something. I did not want to ruin my chances.

The officer waited for my answer. In my limited experience, a rare quality in an officer.

"Well, sir, you're right. I've been on the sea all my life. When not on it, never out of sight of it. Not until I got on the bus to come here. I guess I wanted to try something different in my life."

Ryder picked up his pipe and pointed the stem at me. "I like that, Hoffmann. New experiences, a change, a look at the unknown. That is exactly what I'm looking for in a soldier."

"Pardon me, sir?"

He put the pipe down again. Ryder clasped his hands in front of him on the desk. "Do you know what I do?"

No clue, but a bunch of possibilities crossed my mind. He was Special Forces doing covert operations. He was Army Intelligence running agents. Nothing made sense. What did a seasoned officer want with a recruit barely out of training? His camouflage outfit, except for bars of rank, bore no insignia denoting his purpose.

"No, sir. I have no idea."

The Captain chuckled. He stood up, grabbed his hands behind his back, turned and looked out the window. When he spoke, the words came over his shoulder without his turning his head.

"I build things, Karl. I build things all over the world."

Captain Ryder turned around, leaned forward and placed his palms on the desk.

"I'm with the Army Corps of Engineers and I think you should be one of us."

Not knowing what to say, I smiled stupidly. Ryder ignored it.

"There are two kinds of men in this Army. You're the other kind," he said cryptically. "I believe you know how to use your head for more than dodging bullets."

How he arrived at that was beyond me. Maybe it was the aptitude tests. There had been hundreds of them. Maybe it was my Fitness Reports filed by LeVance. Ryder was not going to say. He reached down and turned the single sheet of paper around and pushed it over to me.

"What do you say, Private? I'm short on time. You want to join us?"

His enthusiasm was so infectious, I came to my feet. "Count me in, sir."

"Fine. Sign the transfer request. You move out at 0500."

Move I did. The next morning, along with recruits from other platoons, I was choppered to an air base. There we boarded a transport plane for Clarkston, Kansas. I missed my graduation. When the Army wants something, it wants it now.

It was August. Kansas was hotter than West Virginia. It was also flatter and browner. About a hundred newcomers arrived that week. We were formed into platoons. The only thing I discovered we had in common was that we were all enlistees with four-year hitches, no draftees in the company.

Over the next two and a half months I learned how to drive bulldozers, steamrollers, road graders, and operate cranes and derricks. When not at the controls of one of these I was taught to weld steel and splice wire. Basic drafting was taught so we were able to read blueprints. Our company built things and tore them down or blew them up. It was an incredible period and I was having the time of my life.

Graduation came in October. The season changed. Kansas wheat and corn were harvested. The men of my company were issued certificates, shoulder patches, and our orders.

More than half the men were sent to Southeast Asia. Vietnam to build bases, bridges, airfields, and when destroyed by the enemy, rebuild them. Thailand where construction was underway to support B-52 strikes against North Vietnam. A few men drew stateside duty while others went to the Philippines or NATO bases in Europe. My orders were for South Korea.

All of us were granted a two-week furlough before reporting to our assignments. A transport was headed to New York where the Corps of Engineers was building artificial reefs to protect the shores of Long Island. I hitched a ride.

After a confusing day in New York City I boarded a train the ticket agent assured me stopped in Kingston, Rhode Island. From there I thumbed rides to Narragansett. The ferry took me home.

Papa was surprised to see me.

CHAPTER SEVEN

To say Rhode Island State Police are a competent and dedicated group of men and women would be an understatement. They are an intense and highly devoted cadre. In crisis their courage is resolute and selfless. In tragedy they are renowned for compassion, just short of fault. But like cops everywhere, they have no sense of humor on the job. Police work is serious business.

Rolando and I had a busy morning. The two snow blowers we left in Grace were rented out by phone. The two in stock were promised for delivery as soon as Rolando could find a passage through the hills to retrieve the pickup from his house.

The weight of snow collapsed some roofs of sheds and chicken coops. Soggy men and women tramped into All Island Rental to contract for saws, drills, jacks, and lanterns. Each was welcomed with hot coffee and hearty words that, what the hell, we had survived.

In the afternoon a convoy of Jeeps and a two-ton truck slogged its way out of the west along Mariners Path. Rolando and I stood at the door as if watching a parade. The lead vehicle, a military-style Jeep, stopped in the road before us slinging up slush. Out came Constable Archie Bealer and three uniformed men.

Before they reached the store Gunner Hogan came up behind us and peered between our shoulders at the posse.

"Mind if I slip out the back?" he asked me.

"No problem. Go ahead."

Gunner clapped me on the back then retreated through the shop. Whatever his anxiety with respect to police he did not say and I did not ask. He was a friend and that was what counted.

"This stuff is turning to goddamn soup," I heard Bealer curse. He led the troopers up to the steps. "We'll be flooded by tomorrow."

As he came up I could see he looked like hell. Bealer's eyes were bloodshot and he had missed a few patches shaving. The troopers in contrast were immaculately groomed.

"This is Colonel Devon of the Rhode Island State Police," Bealer said, stepping aside to allow the officer to face me. The Colonel removed a glove and stuck out his hand.

"Karl Hoffmann," I said shaking the hand. "And this is my business associate Rolando Tobar."

Devon shook Rolando's hand.

"Why don't you come inside?" I invited.

As the men doffed their coats and hung them near the fire Colonel Devon introduced the remaining troopers as Sergeant Lee and Trooper Johnson.

"Do you want to bring the rest of your boys in?" I asked Devon. There was a second Jeep and a truck manned with troopers.

"They're all right," Devon responded curtly. "We won't be long. I want to get the body to our forensic morgue as soon as possible."

"So you found it okay?"

"Thank God we wrapped it good," Bealer said. "In this slop it would have turned to Jell-O."

Devon cleared his throat for attention. "Be that as it may, Constable, it should never have been disturbed in the first place. I thought you were cop enough to know the procedure."

He asked me, "How did you get roped into this adventure, Mr. Hoffmann?"

I laughed. "Everybody comes to All Island Rental,"

Colonel Devon did not laugh. "Any idea who the victim is?"

"Well, sir, my partner here has deduced he's not local by the process of elimination. So I have a fair idea."

"Who?" Devon and Bealer asked in unison.

I got the rental agreement out of the drawer and briefed the cops on the transaction between Janus Martin and myself.

"You never told me about some guy and a goddamn saw," Bealer shouted. His eye tic started flickering.

"I never made the connection. We were too busy sledding all over Kingdom Come and burying bodies."

"I'll take that paper if you don't mind," Devon said. If I minded I am sure it made no difference.

He did not actually take it. The sergeant named Lee stepped forward with a plastic bag. Lee gingerly took the contract from my hand and slid it into the bag.

"Do you know where his vehicle is?" Devon pressed on.

"Nope. Haven't seen it. But I'll bet it's still on the Island."

"So would I. I'll order aerial reconnaissance to locate it. The snow has melted enough."

Devon informed us that formal statements would be taken soon. For the present he wanted to get the body and the presumed murder weapon back to the mainland for analysis. A special police ferry had brought him and his entourage to Bittern Island. Devon wanted as expediently to get back.

"Have you searched the processing plant?" I asked.

"Why? Do you know something about that too?"

"No, I was only curious."

"We haven't searched it yet, but I've posted some troopers to seal it off as a crime scene."

Devon was finished with me. He and Bealer and the other troopers left and rejoined the convoy on Mariners path.

"You were awfully quiet while they were here," I said to Rolando.

"What you think? I'm like Gunner. Cops make me uneasy."

"You two have been living on this Island too long."

Later that afternoon Bealer's prediction came to fruition sooner than he suggested. Melting snow was a problem. Calls started to come in for pumps. All Island had a variety of them. That was not the problem. The problem was still transportation.

All my customers that morning had braved the elements on foot to get to my store. They left with implements they could carry. A four-hundred-pound pump and forty feet of three-inch hose was a different matter.

"I'm going to get the truck," Rolando said. Perhaps he was frustrated by our inability to service customers. Or maybe he was just bored.

"You think you can make it?"

"What the hell. We're not getting much done without it."

"You should have hitched a ride with Archie and the Colonel. Their transports drive through anything."

"Not me, boss. They'd have stuck me in the back with old dead, soggy Martin. Not me."

"You're so damn superstitious."

He stopped zipping his coat and asked, "What are you talking about?"

"Don't kid me. I saw you cross yourself when Don Ostros mentioned the Evil One."

Rolando grabbed the zipper of his coat again. He turned sideways as if struggling with it. Rocking back and forth he turned around. With his back to me, I am sure he blessed himself again. Facing forward once more, the zipper was at his throat.

"You shouldn't talk about stuff you don't know about," he said.

"Sorry. I was only ribbing you."

"Let it go."

"Done."

With hat and gloves on, Rolando went to the front door. "If it can't be done, I'll call you from town."

"Good luck."

"*Si*. That too." He went out the door leaving it open behind him.

I crossed the room and stood in the threshold. Rolando was making good progress in knee-deep slush and then turned into the rut cut by the State Police truck. Of course, that had been a big truck with thick tires made to go through anything. All we had was a puny pickup.

The sun was bright and there was a fresh breeze out of the southeast. The breeze, not the sun, was cause for the rapid melting.

Starting midway between Africa and South America, the Gulf Stream caresses the islands of the Caribbean and swings north at Cuba to run up the East Coast of the United States. Miles at sea southeast of Bittern Island the Stream turns again. There it merges with cold currents coming down from the north and fades out. Before that happens the last warmth of the once tropical waters rises, the way heat always rises, and is picked up by the prevailing winds. Every East Coast fisherman knows how it works.

The effect now was a temperature well above freezing. No freeze, no snow. Bittern Island was in the natural process of making climatic adjustment. We Islanders would have to adjust ourselves accordingly.

Closing the door I turned and headed back to my stool behind the counter. I kept some books under there and I thought I might read while I waited.

I grabbed my copy of Jack London's *The Call of the Wild* that seemed appropriate. I had read it twice before. The first time was for high school

English class. The second was my winter stationed with the Corps of Engineers in Korea.

Snow and ice, I thought, thumbing the book. Snow and ice. All that cold whiteness spreading endlessly. I closed my eyes and imagined the tundra. Here and there a mountain of ice poked up through the flatness, bright on one side, shadowed the other. It plays tricks on your eyes. There is a whiteness that is so white it is almost blue. I have seen this in the deep cold. White and blue. White becoming blue. White, blue…

And yellow.

That was it. There were three copies of the rental agreement Janus Martin signed for the saw. Martin was given the white copy as his receipt. The blue was my accounting paperwork, and I surrendered that to the State Police. But the yellow copy was our inventory record.

In each of the sheds a clipboard hung from a nail inside the door. When we removed something we hung the yellow ticket there until the item was returned. Only then did I dispose of the yellow copy.

On the clipboard in shed A hung the yellow inventory sheet with the carbonized copy of Martin's signature. Without a coat, but clad in boots, I went and got it. Jack London went back under the counter.

Coming back I heard a distant whump, whump, whump. Four years in the Army identified the sound for me. It was the whirling rotors of a helicopter. Either the Coast Guard was on a mission, common for a maritime community, or the State Police had begun their airborne search for Janus Martin's truck.

I placed the sheet of paper on the counter and peeled off my boots. The fire was burning low but the room seemed warm enough. Maybe it was me. I felt excited like I was hoarding some precious bit of contraband.

Standing at the counter, I copied Martin's professed identity onto the paper. When I was done I folded the yellow sheet, opened the register, and stowed the paper under the cash drawer. My surreptitiousness amused me. Perhaps it was Rolando and Gunner and their misgivings about the police. Then again, I had a few of my own. One time in New York City I had been detained and interrogated by the cops. Judith and I lived there in the early days.

Either way, with no reason at all, I felt better secreting it.

CHAPTER EIGHT

"You did not write much," Papa said.

"I'm sorry. There was so much going on and so much to learn."

My father nodded his head; he understood. We were sitting in the parlor, fire in the hearth, mugs of tea, dusk outside in early November. Papa peered into the flames a long time.

"A part of me thought you would never come back."

"That was not how I meant it."

He dismissed it with a wave of hand. Standing up stiffly, he fetched his pipe and tobacco from the mantle. He filled and lit the pipe.

"Tell me about this Corps of Engineers."

As the fire crackled I told Papa about basic training in West Virginia. How Captain Ryder had come to select me. What it was like when I moved to Kansas. Last I told him I was posted to South Korea.

"Not Vietnam?"

"No, at least not for now."

"That is well. No good will come of that war, son. No good for America, the Vietnamese, the Chinese, or the Russians. It's a quagmire the Army, if not the politicians, should have known better about after Korea in the fifties."

"I'll go if I'm ordered, Papa."

"Of course you will. That is what soldiers do. That is what we've done for centuries. If it were any other way we would not be soldiers and there would be no Army."

We lapsed again into silence drinking our tea. Papa finished his pipe.

"Go upstairs and hang up your uniform," he said. "Put on some of your old clothes and I'll make supper."

"I thought I might take you out. When I got off the ferry I saw Don Ostros's *cantina*. Looks like he fixed it up some. Why don't we go there?"

"*Casa Ostros.*"

"It has a name? It's still the *cantina* to me. What do you say? Dinner is on me."

Papa shrugged. Then he stood up. "All right. Let me change my shirt."

He crossed the parlor to the stairs. I had not seen him for months and noticed several changes in him. His hair and beard were still thick and gray. But thinning of his face made his cheekbones more pronounced. The once timber-like arms seemed narrow where they protruded beyond his cuffs. He mounted the stairs slower than I remembered.

I never went to change my own clothes.

"How was the fall fishing run?" I called up to him.

"Better than we predicted. It won't be such a hard winter after all. New markets open all the time. They fly our fish around the country while it's fresh. Can you imagine that?"

He came down wearing his best blue shirt and a pair of gray trousers. I went to help him on with his topcoat and he allowed me.

It was a short walk to the restaurant in the chilly night air. We did not speak until we were inside and seated by the proprietor, Don Ostros himself. The *cantina* had about thirty tables, only half of which were occupied. There were seascape paintings on the wall and one of the Gracetown Lighthouse. There was a general bustle to and from the kitchen but the place was clean, cozy, and had wonderful smells.

"Perhaps a drink, gentlemen?" Don Ostros proposed.

Papa looked at me and then at Ostros. "Vodka neat."

When Ostros looked at me I ordered the same. I had never drunk vodka before. Papa's only liquor in the house had always been whiskey. The last bottle I remembered had been the scotch with which he proposed my farewell toast before basic training.

The drinks came in frozen glasses each filled with three ounces of the clear fluid.

Papa lifted his glass to me. *"Za vasehe zdorowya ee droozeew."*

I touched the rim of his glass and we both drank a third of our measures.

"Is that Russian?" I asked.

"Not exactly."

"Estonian?"

Papa smiled and chuckled.

"Well?" I pressed.

"It's from your mother. An old Ukrainian toast."

I asked him what it meant.

"It doesn't translate quite literally. 'Here's to our health and friends, may we have ample of both.' That's close to it."

We finished our vodkas and when Ostros brought menus, Papa ordered more.

"This round is on the house," Ostros said. "We are proud of our men in uniform." He put a hand on my shoulder. "God bless America."

"God bless America," I said.

Papa raised his glass but said nothing. When Ostros walked away we studied our menus.

"This place is expensive for Bittern Island, especially off-season," Papa said.

"I've got almost six months pay in my pocket. Let's have a good time and forget what it costs."

Papa had slightly parted a curtain. One that had only parted narrowly once or twice in my whole life. Six months ago he had toasted me, "Soldier to soldier." Now his salutation was in Ukrainian, my mother's tongue, the language of *ditina* in my childhood. I was peeking through the curtain, but still only peeking.

Finished with the vodka we dined on mutton chops with fried potatoes and drank beer. There was music, but not so loud that we could not talk in comfort. Papa told me he might sell his boat. It was getting too much for him and he was not earning enough to hire a crew.

"What will you do?"

"I will do what old men do. I will watch the boats go out and watch them come back. I will drink more whiskey than I should."

"Will you be all right? I can send some money every month." He seemed to age right at the table.

"Not necessary. But thank you. I have made provisions. Things will be fine."

We ended the meal with brandy. Don Ostros presented the check and I paid it with thanks for his hospitality. He invited us back.

At home we were full and tired and went to bed.

In the morning Papa, already up and dressed, greeted me in the hallway as I went to the bathroom.

"You snore."

I was embarrassed. "I'm sorry. I should have closed my door. Did I keep you up?"

"Not really. I don't sleep as much as I used to. I only thought you should know. Better to hear it first from me than the woman you bed."

I was shocked. Then I laughed. Papa had never spoken of such things to me. In all the books I devoured I had second-hand knowledge of love and sex. From barracks life I learned more. I lied with the best of my buddies on that score.

"I've made breakfast," Papa said. "Come sit with me after you wash up."

That was how we spent my two-week furlough. We went to Ostros's *cantina* twice more and were treated well. Walking on the beach we collected driftwood for our fires. Nights we sat in the parlor reading, playing chess, sometimes with Papa listening to the radio. I offered to buy him a television but he was not interested.

The last night before I was to catch the ferry to the mainland we had supper at home. Papa made a chicken, very spicy and very good. Earlier he sent me to the store for wine. I made rice to go with the chicken. After dinner we cleaned up together.

When the dishes were dried, Papa sat back down at the kitchen table. "Fetch the whiskey and sit with me."

I went to the parlor and got the bottle and glasses from the cabinet. Setting the glasses down I poured equal measures. Papa spoke before I sat down.

"There is a present for you. It's in the cupboard. Bring it here."

Doing as told I found a small box wrapped in brown paper and tied with twine in a "water knot" only a fisherman might tie. I put it on the table and took my seat.

"It is for you," Papa encouraged. "Open it."

"I don't know what to say. We've never been much for presents."

"True. But there should be at least a few times."

Not presents, Papa had given me hundreds, thousands of books in my life. The books were issued to me as assignments. I read them. He asked questions. We discussed. As opposed to school, it had been my real education. That and the reality of being a fisherman's son, motherless, on a fisherman's Island.

"So?" Papa said impatiently. "Open it."

I pulled the box in front of me. When the knot was untied I folded back the paper. Inside was a black box. I lifted the lid.

Within the box were a black-lacquered fountain pen and a bottle of ink.

Papa sat upright and waved his arms at all the books around us. They were in every room, even on high shelves in the kitchen.

"You can write like them," he said and lowered his voice to add, "or you can simply write to me."

"I don't know what to say, Papa."

"Precisely. That is why you now have a pen. To sit and think about what it is you want to say and then write it down when you're ready. Go put it in your room with your bag. Come back and we'll have one drink."

Upstairs I slid the pen box into my duffel bag. Everything was set for my leaving.

In the kitchen Papa had drunk his shot of whiskey and was pouring another. I sat down across from him.

"There is one more thing." Papa wiped his mouth with his handkerchief. "It is for you and we shall not discuss it. Understand?"

"As you say, Papa."

He reached into his shirt and pulled out an envelope that had been next to his heart. The white envelope had turned yellow with age. He laid it on the table in front of me. I picked it up, turned it over. It was not sealed, had never been sealed. I inched my fingers below the flap and folded it back. The contents slid out on the table face up in front of me.

"*Romeo and Juliet*, The Kirov Theater in Leningrad, 1948," Papa said. "That is your Mama, Galina."

My fingers trembled as I picked up the photograph. It was as fresh in my memory as the day she first showed me in secret.

"She's beautiful," I said.

Papa sighed. "Ah, yes. The most beautiful woman I ever saw."

I completely forgot his order not to discuss the matter. "Why did she not dance in America?"

No immediate answer came. When I looked up a light had burned out in Papa's eyes. He grabbed his glass and drank his shot.

"She was sick. Don't you remember?"

"I remember."

"Well. You may have that picture. It's all I have of her but it should be yours now. Go on. Put that away too. Then one more drink before bed."

In the morning I caught the ferry. Papa walked me down to the wharf.

He kissed both my cheeks. "Be careful. Remember to write."

Promising to do both I kissed him in return. As the boat pulled out from the slip I looked for him but saw he had not waited on the pier. It was still dark and biting cold.

From Narragansett it was a train ride to Boston. I reported to the Corps Field Office and received my transfer papers. A bus took me to Clement Field where I boarded a C-130 transport. The aircraft carried enough tonnage of equipment and men you had to wonder it got off the ground. We made six stops en route so it took two and half days to reach South Korea.

I landed in Seoul in the dead of night. Bittern Island got cold but Korea made that seem tropical. Eleven of us from the plane were formed up and marched to a Quonset hut to finish the night.

Crossing the tarmac I could feel the snot freezing in my nose. Though the hut was heated, we all climbed into bunks fully clothed.

Next morning we were fed and hustled over to the Quartermaster's Depot and issued arctic-rated clothing including parkas with imitation fur collars and hoods. We looked like a mission to the South Pole out of *National Geographic*.

A Korean winter morning is different from what we were accustomed to stateside. The sun rises pale and shimmerless. It stays that way all day. The world seems shrouded in vapor similar to haze over water.

Half-ton trucks took us on an hour ride to Porsamhung, a village surrounded by a huge Army camp. The north side of camp was the edge of the demilitarized zone separating North and South Korea, approximately the Thirty-Eighth Parallel of latitude. There was no landscape to speak of. Aside from miles of gray snow and gravel roads, the terrain was a composite of huts, concrete, and barbed wire. Porsamhung was a fortified position defending the South.

At least, it appeared fortified to me. The Army had a different evaluation.

After a terse welcome the eleven of us new Engineers were assigned to units. I drew a wall-building crew. A ruddy-face Irishman named Captain Connors commanded my company. My platoon had a Black sergeant named Miller.

Connors and Miller may not have been the most soldierly of Army-types, but they knew heavy construction. Our job was to lay steel, surround it with huge wooden formers, and fill the formers with concrete covering the steel. Being the new kid, referred to as "FNG" for "fucking new guy," I was given the dirtiest detail. Assigned to the master carpenter I was handed a hammer and bag of nails. Eight hours a day I nailed up the boards that comprised the formers. When the cement dried, I pried them loose and tore them down.

The work was a steady pace. Fifty feet of wall erected each day. From a center starting point we came east one day, west the next and then east again. We labored five days a week with weekends off. Occasionally we pulled guard duty just to remind us we were in the Army.

When not building there was little to do in Porsamhung. My superiors demonstrated the diversions of choice. Connors drank himself blind each weekend. Sergeant Miller gambled. Seemed like everybody owed Miller money from crap games, poker, or the pools he ran on the games broadcast over Armed Forces Radio.

I drank my share of beer on Friday nights and Saturdays. Sundays I kept mostly to myself. Each Sabbath morning I wrote a letter to Papa with the pen he gave me. As weeks went by the letters got longer. The pages filled with anecdotes about other guys, descriptions of the terrain and weather, and references to literary works we both had read.

At the PX I ordered books. One was *The Call of the Wild* by Jack London. Though I read it in high school, this seemed the perfect spot to lie in my bunk and imagine prospecting for gold, trapping animals, and feeling desperate to keep warm.

Bittern Island

By the fourth week I received a letter from my father. Never before had I read anything written by him. His penmanship was precise and his style surprisingly florid. Papa related bits of news from Bittern Island, then launched into an essay on the state of global affairs. He wrote of politics and philosophy as I imagined a professor might were I corresponding with a chaired Ph.D. from a university.

The correspondence continued. He decried the Vietnam War, convincing me the mail was uncensored coming into Porsamhung. In answer to my constant query he asserted his health was fine. In some letters the penmanship seemed forced, taut to the point of vibrating like a musical string. When I mentioned this, he dismissed it quoting the lateness of the hour it was written.

In March I compared our construction project to the ill-fated French Maginot Line. If Hitler's panzers could breach those fortifications, surely the North Koreans could hurl bombs and rockets over my wall. Papa advised me to keep that opinion to myself, as a good soldier does not criticize his superiors. But I should feel free to write him about it all I wanted.

The Corps of Engineers built that wall into spring and summer. By the start of fall we were erecting bunkers for heavy guns and troop concealment. In Southeast Asia, I wrote my father, the fighting was brutal and personal. But in Korea I was building a Tower of Babel to the gods of war. The gods in Porsamhung seemed disinterested.

That year I made corporal. Captain Connors, hungover and foul-breathed, bestowed the honor. Then he did me a favor.

"The Corps is putting together a unit stateside for a special operation. I think I can get you in. What do you say, Hoffmann?"

"I would be grateful, sir."

He snorted, "No, you won't. Ten minutes out of here and you'll forget we exist. This is nowhere, son. And you know it."

The truth rated a salute.

CHAPTER NINE

While Rolando Tobar went for the truck, I dialed Information. I asked the operator for the area code of Michigan.

"Which part of Michigan, sir?"

"I'm not sure. A place called Hubbards Lake."

"Let me see what I can do."

While I waited I could hear her humming to herself.

"Found it," the operator said. "Hubbards Lake would be area code six-one-six."

I dialed Information again using the Michigan area code.

"What town or city please?" came a recorded voice.

"Hubbards Lake."

There was a pause then the monotone, "What listing please?"

"Martin. Janus Martin."

A few seconds and a live person came on the line.

"I don't have a listing for a Janus Martin," he said.

"You mean it's unlisted?"

"No, sir. Not unpublished, it doesn't exist. There is no Janus Martin in Hubbards Lake or in any six-one-six area code."

Somehow I was not surprised. I thanked the operator, hung up, and called back. From a different operator I got the number for the Michigan State Department of Motor Vehicles.

When I rang the number a clerk identified herself and the Department.

"I'm trying to verify an address from a driver's license."

"We are not allowed to do that."

"You don't understand. This guy hit my car and left the scene of the accident."

"That is a police matter, sir. Take it up with them."

Click.

I was not about to lie to the Michigan police. Besides, I was convinced Janus Martin was not from Michigan regardless of what his license said. Was there even a Janus Martin to begin with?

My opportunities were exhausted. Turning over the sheet of paper I wrote down everything I could remember about Janus Martin. Sooner or later the Rhode Island State Police would want a description in my statement.

Middle-aged, I wrote first. Heavy accent; maybe German or Eastern European would be my guess. There was his thick black mustache and a roll of fat over his belt. He also did not know how to use a chain saw. Black leather coat, but no hat or gloves. That was it.

Over my shoulder I heard the back door open. That was followed by heavy footfalls on the wood floor. Every other one dragged a little.

"I take it they're gone," Gunner Hogan said behind me.

"They took the body for an autopsy."

"You tell them who we thought it was?"

"No reason not to."

"So you can bet they'll be back. Ain't this a mess? First we get more snow than Alaska and then there's a body under it."

Gunner helped himself to a few hunks of wood and shoved them into the stove. He closed the grate and took off his hunting coat. He looked over at me, my pencil hovering above the paper on the counter.

"What are you doing?" he asked.

"Silly really. I tried to get Martin's phone number. It doesn't exist. Then I tried to verify his driver's license without success. It's probably a fake. Now I'm scribbling down whatever I can remember about him."

"Why would you want to do that?"

"I'm sure the cops will ask." Then I threw down the pencil. "Because he's got my damn saw."

Gunner shook his head and chuckled. I started to laugh also. We both knew it was not about a McCullock chain saw. Gunner stopped laughing and took his customary stool by the stove. He rubbed his coarse chin and looked up at me.

"Why do you suppose he was down at the plant in the first place? That's where you should start. You think he set it on fire?"

"No. There'd be no reason for him to burn it down. The person who set the fire was trying to cover Martin's murder."

"I'll buy that. But why was he there in the first place?"

"Who said he went there? Maybe the killer took him there after he murdered him."

"I doubt that." Gunner pulled out his flask and took a swig.

"We're surrounded by ocean. You can dump a body anywhere. No, Karl, Martin was killed in Jacob's Cove and there was a reason for that fire."

"To cover the murder," I repeated.

"Nobody goes there. The body wouldn't be found for weeks, months, maybe never. Why call attention to it? Naw. Somebody wanted to burn that place to the ground."

Once again I heard the whump, whump, whump of a helicopter. It grew louder as it passed over my shop. Then it faded.

I looked at Gunner. He was staring at the ceiling wide-eyed and pale.

"You okay?"

He recovered in an instant and took another drink. "I hate that freaking noise."

The phone rang. It was Rolando. He said he made it home and was sure he could get through with the pickup. The call was to see if I needed anything.

"Bring back some food. Gunner's here too. And see if you can rustle up a bottle of whiskey."

Rolando promised he would and hung up.

"That whiskey for you or me?" Gunner asked.

"All of us."

"What are we having? A wake for Martin?"

That made me laugh. Gunner was a morbid creature like myself. Maybe it was life. Or maybe the winter. Maybe it was the Island.

"I don't know," I said. "Yet I don't think there will be much grieving for Janus Martin."

"That's what is wrong with you and me."

"What do you mean?"

"We can't grieve any more, Karl. We can't grieve." He added something else. "Maybe we don't give a shit anymore."

Gunner stood up slowly and limped over to the counter. He put the uncapped flask in front of me. I picked it up and took a long slow drink.

The snow continued to melt. By the time Rolando arrived with the truck, tops of bushes and outcrops of rock were visible on the ridges. Melted snow was cutting crevices in the hill like troughs to carry it down.

Rolando brought plenty of food. A loaf of fresh bread, cheese, a tube of salami, smoked fish, two six packs of beer and the whiskey I had asked for.

"How are the roads?" I asked him.

"What you think?" He flipped the top of a beer can. "Anything ain't under snow is under water."

"Any trouble in town?"

"Not yet."

Gunner opened a beer for himself. He cut a hunk of salami with his jackknife and chomped it. "Not to worry, gentlemen. We are an island. Been here millions of years. Know why? The topography. That big spine running smack down the center. If there's one thing this old Island knows how to do, it's shed water. That's why she's still afloat. The storm was the quirky part. Now the old girl is doing what she does best."

"It can still be dangerous," Rolando said.

"I suppose," Gunner conceded.

That reminded me of the pumps we had to deliver. We ate quickly to get back to business. I had a beer and my friends their seconds. What remained we put in the refrigerator in the back room.

Gunner opened the bottle of whiskey. "Can't forget the Irish wake."

"*Que*? What's he talking about?" Rolando asked me.

"Don't get him started. Just have the drink with him."

Gunner rinsed out our mugs and filled each with several fingers of liquor. As we picked them up Gunner raised his higher. "The Lord giveth and the Lord taketh away."

"How does that apply?" I asked.

"Never trust the kid who owns the ball," Gunner said. "If he's winning, he's always the first one who has to quit and go home to supper."

Whatever that meant, we drank.

"Besides," Gunner added. He pointed his cup at me. "You've lost yourself a chain saw."

We finished our drinks and Rolando and I went to load the pumps into the pickup. The machines were on wheels but we needed the pulley winch to hoist them onto the flatbed. We loaded the winch to take along. Gunner helped with the hoses.

"You wait here and mind the shop," I said to Gunner. "I'll go with Rolando to help in town."

"Count on me," Gunner said.

Rolando drove. We turned up Mariners Path and east through the water and slush. We crossed the ridge fighting water on the way up and nearly carried with it on the way down.

None of the houses in Grace had basements. Some had root cellars, but that was all. The problem was drainage where man had contravened what nature ordained. Alleys between shops and houses cut off receding water creating pools. They needed to be drained before rising to door level.

We delivered the pumps and helped get them set up and running. By late afternoon several customers started to string lights and lanterns to monitor the pumping through the dark.

"We're done," Rolando said. The last pump was throbbing and gushing water safely out the opposite end of the hose.

"One more stop."

He gave me a puzzled look. "We're out of pumps, boss."

"There's something I want to see again for myself."

"What would that be?"

"Jacob's Cove. Take me over that way."

Rolando shrugged and got behind the wheel. We sloshed up Main Street and turned west on Quilin Road. The sun was low and red in the distance beyond the Island.

I pointed. "Over there."

"I know the way." Rolando nosed the pickup onto the path.

"Stop. Stop the truck," I shouted. I jumped from the cab. "This is it. This must be the reason."

On the sides of the dirt road were wooden pillars that had supported a gate to block the way. The crossbeam logs that formed the gate were nowhere in sight. I examined the post to my right. Midway up its shank was the joint for the crossbeam. Only the stub of the beam protruded from the post;

the rest had been cut away. Probably with a chain saw. Across the path I inspected the other post. It bore a similar cut. I had missed them when Archie Bealer and I recovered the body. They were beneath a drift of snow.

"What did you find?" Rolando called.

"The reason Martin needed a chain saw."

Up the path from the Cove walked two figures. One of them called out, holding up his hand like a traffic cop.

"State Police. Stand where you are."

Rolando turned off the engine. In the dusky light I made out their uniforms as they approached. Water was running across the path. Beyond them I could see glistening ribbons of water running down the sloping sides of Jacob's Cove.

"What are you fellows up to?" one of the troopers asked. He was a large man with a jolly face protruding from his parka hood. "You're not allowed here. This is State Police business."

"Sorry, sir," I said. "Just being nosy."

While I spoke, the other trooper went to my truck and read the name "All Island Rental" off the side. He eyed Rolando in the cab.

"They look okay. Truck's got some gear in the back," he called to his partner. "Let's move them on their way."

There was a sharp crack, like a shot. We all flinched. Another cracking noise, longer and louder. A series of creaks and a sustained groan rose up from Jacob's Cove. We heard the sound of water splashing. Rolando leapt from the truck and stood beside the trooper.

More cracking. Then a sound like wind in a long tunnel. Loud splashes as heavy objects struck the water. We all looked in the same direction.

The dark twisted hulk of the processing plant shifted forward on its foundation. It leaned and appeared to sway. Roof timbers sagged, then caved in. As one mass, one disintegrating, braceless mass, the plant came apart, pieces falling headlong into the water of Jacob's Cove.

"I'll be damned," I said. "Bealer was right."

"What?" the trooper next to me demanded.

"Only it wasn't the wind. It was water from the melting snow."

I was staring in amazement at the rubble left of the foundation.

"What are you talking about?" the trooper shouted.

"It was Gunner who was right. This old Island takes care of herself."

The State Police did not detain us, but they ordered us out of the area. The big guy fetched their Jeep from down the path and radioed in about the collapse. Rolando and I drove back to the shop.

Gunner Hogan was sleeping on top of the counter. We woke him. I told Rolando he could keep the truck another night as long as he dropped me home. We told Gunner about the plant before he left. He was most interested in the fence posts.

"Proves my point. Martin wasn't taken there dead. He broke in. Then someone killed him."

CHAPTER TEN

Stateside I thought I might visit Papa. That was not to be. Routed through Chicago, I was flown to a base in Florida. My flight was met by Military Police. I was ushered onto a bus with other guys. We were all Engineers. None of us knew where we were going.

The bus barreled through a moonless night for hours. Then we stopped.

"On your feet," a sergeant bellowed. "File out. Follow the MPs. Stay in line."

The MPs had white helmets and flashlights. They marched us single file through trees, a barbed wire gate, and into a compound. Sentries in battle dress guarded the gate.

We came to a row of tents and counted off by tens. Each group of ten was assigned a tent. Inside we found bedding. As you are wont to in the Army under such circumstances, we went to sleep.

They got us up at 0430 for cold showers and C-rations. Afterwards we marched to an assembly area and a colonel addressed us.

"My name is Colonel Markham. Welcome to Camp Sinclair. We're not on any map. This is a classified installation. Keep it that way.

"As you get to know us and each other you will find there are two types of soldiers here, Engineers and Signalmen. From that you may conclude our purpose, build and communicate. That is all you know. You will be told more when you need to know."

I stole a look around me. We were under a camouflage net in a clearing between groves of trees.

My group of thirty had swelled to ninety or more. As Markham indicated, some soldiers bore the patch of the Signal Corps and the rest of us Engineers.

"At this point I'll turn the briefing over to Captain Sanchez."

A slender olive-skinned officer took Markham's place. He read a prepared statement.

According to Sanchez we would undergo three weeks of testing and training. Some of us would not make the cut. Men eliminated would be reassigned. Whatever we learned and did here, was to stay here.

Sanchez introduced a burly sergeant named Cominsky.

Cominsky read off names assigning us to squads. Seven men to a squad. We formed up in lines at the edge of the clearing. There was an identical composite to each unit. A squad had four Engineers, two Signalmen, and a lieutenant. When the roll was done we marched off to separate areas.

The rest of my first day at Sinclair consisted of paperwork. I filled out dozens of forms, all detailed and personal. Not only did they require my family background, the questionnaires asked for everything I had done since baby steps. What were my grades in school? Did I belong to any clubs, sports teams, school or community activities? How many girls had I dated and their names? Did I travel much? What states and countries had I visited? It went on and on the whole day.

The second day was physical. It began with a five-mile run. That was followed with calisthenics. Then we ran an obstacle course. After lunchtime chow we were issued packs and marched in the blazing sun. The day ended with a three-mile run.

Physical preparation lasted the first week. Run, do pushups, run more. At morning chow, I saw our ranks were shrinking. One guy from my squad was cut. We did not know why and did not ask. There was a reshuffling and we were down to six units, always the same configuration; four Engineers, two Signalmen, an officer.

The second week was different.

Monday morning my unit loaded a helicopter and flew to a remote location. As the sun came up, I sat in the chopper's bay and saw the Everglades in the distance. Our pilot skirted the edge and set down. When we were out he flew away.

Our officer, Lieutenant Sutterman, gathered us around him. He was a young Californian out of West Point.

"Here's the deal, men," he said. "An aircraft will shortly deposit a mess of gear. You will recover and assemble it."

From his map case he took a large folded paper. It was a blueprint.

"This, gentlemen, is a COM-TACH."

The Army has many acronyms and it does not help to know what they stand for. Things are simply their acronym.

"Once assembled," Sutterman explained, "we are a self-sufficient radio station. With it we can transmit, receive, and jam the crap out of anybody else.

"You Engineers are expected to put this equipment together. That includes building the tower and getting the generator hot. You Signalmen are to wire the radio and get us on the air on a frequency I'll designate. Any questions?"

One of the Signals guys had a few. Sutterman responded knowledgeably.

Sutterman's final remarks were, "Once recovery is affected you have fifty-five minutes to accomplish the whole task. My job is to observe and time you."

With that Sutterman walked to a tree, set his butt on the ground, and leaned back against the trunk. The rest of us huddled over the print studying the components.

At 0830 we heard the drone of an aircraft. A pair of parachutes billowed. Their payloads hit the ground simultaneously. We were on them like an NFL player on a fumble.

The fifty-five-minute job took two hours and ten minutes. Sutterman tried to be encouraging as he clicked his stopwatch.

"Not a bad first whack. You'll do better this afternoon. Break it down."

We were flown out, fed, and choppered back. Our second attempt was an hour and twenty-eight minutes.

By Wednesday afternoon we were below the fifty-five mark three times in a row. Then came a new twist. The squad was issued M-16s and taken to the firing range. Not only would we erect a radio, we would defend it.

My shooting prowess was low side of adequate. Guys ribbed me about it. I tried it one eye open. I tried it both open. It did not matter. I was a lousy shot.

Sunday morning Sutterman sent for me. I found him in the Operations tent seated beside a folding table. Papers and files littered the table.

"Grab a seat, Hoffmann," Sutterman said. Normally his voice had the edge of eagerness. This time it was flat. I sat down on a folding chair.

"You're out of the program." He seemed relieved to get it over in short order.

"I don't understand, sir. Why?"

He opened a folder. "You're one of the smartest guys in the outfit. But you can't shoot worth shit, Corporal."

"I'm the worst in the squad, maybe the outfit, but my scores are passing. I was never proficient with guns, even in basic training. But I passed."

Sutterman scoffed. "Guns? Cowboys shoot guns. In the Army you fire a weapon. You can't even get the jargon straight. You're out. Pack up."

"No offense, Lieutenant, but I want to hear it from the Colonel."

"Shit," Sutterman said. "That's your right. Won't make any difference, but you've got the right. Go back to your hooch and I'll see when he can see you."

"I appreciate that, sir." I did not want to blow this assignment. No more Korea for me. Like Connors said, that was nowhere.

In my tent I lay on my cot thinking and waiting. The Army was okay. It taught me skills other than fishing. I also learned to drink and had gotten laid for the first time in Seoul. Except for missing Papa, it was not bad.

Sergeant Cominsky came. He made it plain I was wasting the Army's time. I followed him to Markham's billet.

"What's your problem, son?" Markham asked.

Not expecting a clear opening I launched a defense of my capabilities. When I was done he shook his head.

"It's out of my hands, Corporal. Far as I was concerned you seemed A-Okay. You were dropped by Washington. Level-Three security checks were done on all men. A hammer dropped on you. It happens. Maybe you banged a Vietnamese gal in high school. So you're a Marxist by injection. That's how they see shit like that. Don't worry. You'll finish your stretch just fine somewhere else."

"I've got to know." I was out of line.

"What, soldier?"

"Beg your pardon, sir. I mean I'd like to know the facts, sir. I don't want to be buried on a technicality. I was thinking of staying in the Army."

"That so?" It must have impressed him.

"Absolutely, sir."

"Let me see what I can do. I can't promise anything. I'll delay your transfer order forty-eight hours. That's all the slack I can cut. In the meantime, you're to stand down."

The next twenty-four hours, except for chow, I spent on my cot. Another bed was brought in for the guy who replaced me. The squad treated me like a leper. I wrote a long letter to Papa not mentioning my problem. Cominsky returned the letter to me.

"Take out the Florida crap. This base is classified. We postmark the mail in Saint Louis."

The assignment was so sensitive they were censoring our mail and rerouting it.

Tuesday morning I had a visitor. I was alone in the tent reading.

"You Hoffmann?" the stranger asked.

"Yes, sir," I replied out of habit.

He was not in uniform. Tall, clean-shaven, crew cut, dressed in chinos and polo shirt. He sat on the cot next to mine.

"My name is Fargo. Jake Fargo."

He extended his hand and I shook it.

"What do you want?" This time I dropped the "sir."

"Not me, my friend. You're the one that shot up a flare. What's your problem?"

"Are you Army?"

He shook his head in the negative.

"CIA? FBI? NSA?" I persisted.

"What difference is it? You've got questions. I'm here. Make the best of it. This is the only chance you get."

Considering my plight, I took the chance. I detailed my predicament. Dropped from the unit, regardless of what they said, would hurt my record. Fargo listened without questions. When I finished he stood up, crossed the tent, and stared out the open flap. He spoke with his back to me.

"Don't you know?"

"Know what?"

He turned around.

"For Chrissake, Hoffmann, your parents were Soviet defectors."

"I know." I looked at the floor. "We never discussed it. I swear."

"You think that makes a difference?"

"I do. My parents defected. Doesn't that say something?"

"Nothing is that clear." Fargo came back to sit on the bunk.

"You think I'm a communist?" I asked.

He laughed. "Hardly."

"So what's the fucking problem?"

"Your father is the fucking problem."

"He's an old man."

"So much the worse. Age brings its own perspective. It's not like he found the land of plenty. As you may not be aware, he's pushed buttons in his time."

"Tell me all of it, you bastard."

Fargo stood up again. "Let's take a walk."

After being cooped up so long, I agreed. Outside the sun filtered through some palmetto trees. A path led to a dry creek bed. We walked down in the creek on the silt and flat stones.

"Your father is an enigma," Fargo began. "I imagine he is even to you."

"Do you know my father?"

"I've never met him, but I know of him. The files never close on anyone who comes over from the East. First there was the control agent. The guy who brought him through it."

"That must be Chandler."

Fargo looked sideways at me as we walked the creek. "Chandler's dead. He's a legend. Chandler brought over some of the biggest we ever got."

"I'd like to hear about my father."

"Calm down. Just thought you should understand how it is."

The creek bed petered out where a dirt road had been compacted by steamrollers. Across the road we saw the chain and wire of the camp's fence line. We walked the road.

"Once we get a bird through, that's what we call them, birds," Fargo said, "they're turned over to debriefers. After they've given us what they've got we set them up and their life begins here in the States. Each case is assigned a handler. A handler provides assistance and monitors a bird's progress. Routine reports are filed; that never ends. Anything suspicious is checked out. Otherwise, it's routine fifth level surveillance. If we don't hear anything, we don't go looking. You with me so far?"

"Yes. Now can we talk about Major Viljandi?"

Fargo looked at me a moment. The day was growing very hot. Stains of sweat were forming in the armpits of his shirt. He took hold of my elbow.

"Let's sit under those trees." He pointed at a cluster of palmettos. "It's too damn hot."

We left the road and walked to the grove, then sat down with our backs to the trees. Fargo lit a cigarette. He drew and exhaled twice, the smoke hanging in the breezeless air.

"You sure you want to do this, soldier? It will go in my report."

"Damn your report. My career is in the tank because of this. The Army will ship me back to Korea, or Greenland, or some other useless place. All my life it's been a secret. I picked up bits here, a bit there. I never stood up to Papa, except when I told him I was joining the Army. I never had the guts to confront him about his past. Now that past is jerking me over. You're damn right I want to know."

Fargo grunted, squashed out his cigarette and flicked it away.

"Major Kurt Viljandi was an officer in the Soviet Army. Like every other able-bodied Russian he was drafted to defend the motherland against Hitler's tanks. The son of an Estonian fisherman, he seemed eager to advance in the service. He was bright and brave. Officers took notice of him."

I knew he was reciting a file from memory. I said nothing, hoping my silence would prompt him on with it. After a pause he continued.

"The campaign along the Eastern Front was bloody. By the second winter there was a critical lack of leadership in the field. An opportunity for the young Viljandi. He was pulled from combat and sent to officer's training in Moscow. He took some abuse there."

"Why?"

"It's no different anywhere you go. People are people. Ask any Black man in your outfit. They're in, but it's not the same. That's not fair. We're not proud of it. But it's the way it is for the present."

"What are you talking about?"

"The heart of the Soviet Officer Corps were true Russians. Others were regarded suspiciously and contemptuously. That included Estonians, Lithuanians, and a couple of other former independents amalgamated into the Soviet Union," Fargo explained. "As one of the so called 'lesser-Russians,' it was difficult for your father. Yet he graduated top of his class."

I pushed away from the tree and lay on my back staring up at the sky through the leaves. The heat of the day seemed gone. I imagined a raw Russian wind spiraling down from the Urals. I pictured a young Papa, ramrod straight, accepting his commission.

Fargo lit another cigarette. "His brains saved his life. The High Command noticed his record and decided against sending him back to the Front. The Russians had plenty of guys with guts. Intelligence was in shorter supply. The smartest were already in high positions or prison. A bright young officer, combat tested, was something to be cultivated.

"There was more schooling for Lieutenant Viljandi. His Estonian stigma seemed vanished at last. He absorbed everything they threw at him. A natural ability for languages emerged. Several were taught to him. Next came practical training. In Vologda he was instructed in every phase of radio communications."

"What about the war?" I said.

"The war ended. The war with Germany at least. But another war, one without artillery, without infantry, without bombing, was beginning."

"So Papa went into the spy business. Was he KGB?"

"Kurt Viljandi was not exactly a spy. He didn't even like the KGB. Nobody did. He was Intelligence, but a soldier first and last."

Assigned to Army Intelligence, Fargo recounted, by then Captain Viljandi set up, monitored, and graded communications centers up and down the borders of his country and into the satellites of Hungry, Poland, and East Germany. The objective was to intercept and decode NATO radio transmissions. They listened to ships and planes. They netted frequencies of ground units, missile bases, and civilian traffic that might be diplomatic communiqués. The technology was improving daily. And Papa was rising in rank and Party connections.

Captain, then Major Viljandi was a frequent guest at ceremonies, conferences, and parties. Though courted by his superiors, he was advised to dress in civilian clothes since you could never be sure who else might be attending for a covert purpose.

One night after the opening of the ballet season, Viljandi's life changed.

It was not the champagne or vodka in ample supply. It was not the proximity to ministers, generals, and Politburo members. Neither the medals he received nor his ability to travel freely within the country and its satellites turned his head.

It was the eighteen-year-old Galina who had danced the lead in *Swan Lake* and was accepting praise after her performance. The room seemed to vanish in Viljandi's eyes. He saw her and only her cradling a bouquet of roses and coyly pretending to sip champagne.

Nothing. Neither the grueling life of a fisherman's son on the Baltic and the Gulf of Riga, nor the pounding of artillery and whistle of bullets in combat had prepared him. He was a prized Estonian pup in the den of Russian wolves. Witty, wary, and never afraid.

The champagne in his mouth turned to vinegar. The vodka refused to numb him. Every pleasure he ever had or imagined lost its allure in the gleam of the ballerina's eyes.

"Tell your heart to beat again and for God's sake put your tongue back in your mouth," a senior officer chided. "You're pathetic, Viljandi."

"How do you know all this?" I asked Fargo.

"As they suspected, we had our people there."

CHAPTER ELEVEN

The snow on the bluff behind my house was gone. As the sun came up birds of the Island appeared in the dunes. There had been none for days. I saw gulls and pipers and bitterns, the heron that named the Island. You can walk right by a bittern in tall grass and never notice it. The bird straightens out its long neck and sways like a reed. The bittern's color blends it into the landscape to escape detection.

From my kitchen window I watched the dunes to spot bitterns. It was easier than usual. The grass was wet and heavy which bowed it down. The stalk not bent was a bittern.

I do not sleep much and the previous night even less than normal. Restless and edgy I made an excuse to go to the studio. Maybe the snow was too heavy on the skylights? With a ladder I could brush it away. But I did not bring a ladder with me.

Upstairs, down the hall, then standing by the closed door. From the roof I heard water running off the eaves. I opened the door. The room was bathed in light, strong natural light streaming through the skylights. The snow had melted. They were clear. I stared at the floor looking for damp spots. The seams held watertight. Those panes had been an effort to set right. Probably the finest piece of carpentry I ever did.

In the center of the room I stood beneath the skylights in the light. Light so white and warm it was like a magnet to the spot. The kind of light Judith treasured to paint by in the mornings. In front of me stood the empty easel.

Closing my eyes I heard her fussing with the cap of a linseed oil can. When it gave, she let out a sigh. She began humming as she selected tubes of paint and squirted dashes of color onto the pallet.

"Are you watching me?" she asked without turning around.

"Yes."

"Why?"

"Because I like to." I could sense her smiling to herself.

The phone rang downstairs. I opened my eyes to the light and the empty easel, and shut the door behind me when I left.

"Karl? It's Archie."

"No more escapades, Archie. I'm through being deputy. You could have gotten me arrested for moving that body. Let the State Police handle it."

"I am. That's why I'm calling. They can't find the truck."

"What truck?" Part of me was still upstairs watching Judith paint.

"Martin's Jeep. Are you awake? What's the matter with you?"

"I didn't sleep well."

"Shake it off. Colonel Devon and his crew are coming back."

"I figured they would. It is a murder investigation. You were a cop; you know the drill."

"I'm still a cop!"

"Calm down. You know what I mean."

"They're calling a town meeting. Devon called a few minutes ago. He ordered me to get everybody assembled at Saint Andrews at noon today." Saint Andrews was the Episcopal Church in Gracetown. It was also the largest building on Bittern Island.

"Can he do that?" Since the Army, I distrusted anyone who gave orders.

"It didn't sound like I could question it. I think we better do as he says."

I felt a headache coming. Bealer's voice was echoing out of the phone and ringing in my head.

"All right, I'll be there."

"That's not why I called. The Church is big enough but we're going to need some tables and chairs. You think you could bring some?"

"Who's footing the bill? You?"

"Charge the State Police. It's their show."

"Never mind."

"Another thing, Karl?"

"What?"

"Round up Gunner Hogan and bring him along. Nobody ever knows where to find that crazy old rummy."

I thought to myself: and which one aren't you? I said, "Fine. I'll see if I can find him."

Constable Bealer hung up. I was about to call Rolando Tobar when I heard gears grind outside my door. I opened the door and he was leaning out of the pickup.

"Thought you could use a ride to work, boss."

"Perfect timing. We've got a big rental this morning."

"Who's the customer?"

"The State of Rhode Island."

"Huh?"

"I'll explain on the way." Funny, my headache was gone.

In the pickup I related what Bealer said.

"Can the State Police do that?" Rolando asked.

"Damned if I know. But if nobody objects I guess they'll put it off."

"Sound more like the country I come from."

"I wouldn't break out the red kerchiefs and carbines if I were you."

"No joke, *amigo*. This shit always starts small. An incident here, a meeting there. It all adds up."

"This is about the murder of a stranger. It's only a matter of convenience for the cops."

Rolando let me out in front of the shop. While I got the keys he pulled around back.

Tables and chairs were in Shed B. Rolando parked by the double doors. The alley was still a muddy mess as I tramped back. I undid the padlock and lifted the crossbar. Rolando pulled the right door open. He stopped midway and muttered something unintelligible to me.

"What?" I asked.

He cocked his head to the side at the half-open door. I looked into the shed. There was a gleam reflecting in the otherwise dark interior of the barn.

"Aw, shit," I cursed.

Six feet into the shed was parked a black Four by Four.

"Is that it?" I asked Rolando. He had seen Martin's truck from the shop window.

"*Si*. That's it."

"Aw, shit," I said again.

We stood there dumbly side by side.

"What are we going to do, boss?"

"I don't like this."

"Me either. But what are we going to do?"

"For the moment, we're going to do what we came to do. Let's load the truck."

From the shed we took a half-dozen folding tables and two dozen chairs. Once they were loaded, we covered them with a tarp and tied it down.

Before closing the shed we stood beside each other staring at the black vehicle.

"What are we going to do?" Rolando asked a third time.

"I don't know."

"If you tell the cops they'll be all over this place like hound dogs."

"I've nothing to hide."

"Everybody's got something to hide. And if they don't, it's nobody's business anyway. You rented the guy a saw. Listen to me, *compadre*. You tell about the truck and you're a suspect. They find no other suspect and you're guilty by default."

"It's not supposed to work that way."

"Who am I talking to? Ain't you shoveled enough shit in your life?"

That made me mad. But not at Rolando.

"It's a set up," I said.

"The cops won't see it that way."

"You're probably right."

"So let's bring them the tables and chairs and be done with it."

After slamming the heavy doors I dropped the beam in place and padlocked it.

"Let's go," I said.

We got in the truck. I drove.

A short time later we pulled in front of Saint Andrews on Main Street in Grace. A group of adults and some children were milling around the Church. Attached to the Church was a parish hall and community center. The Island held parties and dances there on the Fourth of July, Halloween, and other holidays.

Archie Bealer came over to the truck, acting in charge.

"Set up in the hall," he barked.

"Who does he think he is?" Rolando asked me under his breath.

"He's having the time of his life."

"Asshole," Tobar muttered.

We recruited some men to help unload and hauled the furniture inside. Bealer was giving orders to everyone on how to arrange the place. Rolando and I ignored him and went back outside. We stowed the truck in an alley and walked down Main Street to the Sea Witch. It was a little past eleven a.m.

Despite the hour the tavern was crowded. The buzz of conversation was all about the investigation. Seated alone at the end of the bar was Gunner Hogan. Rolando and I made our way down to him saying hello to folks we knew, which was pretty much everyone. When Gunner saw us he signaled the bartender and three shots of whiskey appeared. Rolando and I reached for our drinks.

Gunner raised his glass. "I'm finding me another Island. Fuck 'em all."

"Fuck 'em all," Rolando and I said in chorus. We downed the shots and ordered beers.

Over the noise of the bar I heard the horn of the ferry coming into dock.

"I guess the cops are here," I said to my friends. "They're not wasting any time."

"They're eager," Gunner said. "It's going to be a party of Pin the Tail on the Donkey."

"How you figure that?" Rolando asked him.

"Because we're the tails," Gunner said. "Since Martin got killed, ain't no Islander been off this rock heap. It's a process of elimination until one of us is secured to the mule's butt."

We were on our second beers when Archie Bealer burst through the door.

"All right, everybody," he shouted over the crowd. "Time to get started. Move over to the Church."

Men and women started filing out. Bealer walked over to the bar where Sweeney had a double shot of rye whiskey ready for him. Bealer downed it in one gulp and wrapped his knuckle on the bar for a refill. Sweeney obliged.

Having drunk that one, he wiped his mouth with the back of his hand, looked up and saw us at the other end.

"Didn't you guys hear me?" Bealer yelled. "I said get going."

"Asshole," Rolando muttered again.

We finished our beers and left the Sea Witch leaving only Sweeney and Bealer behind.

"Sweeney won't leave until Archie does," Gunner said. "Archie would help himself if left alone. Nobody trusts that old flatfoot."

Rolando pointed. "There's my wife. I'll see you guys later."

Rolando walked down the street to a petite Hispanic woman who was not really his wife but might as well have been. They had lived together six years. On one of his excursions to the mainland Rolando returned with her and that was it. Her name was Esperansa. She worked for Pat Lawler in the General Store.

Everyone funneled through the door of the hall. Inside was a State Trooper recording each person's name as we passed. Six tables were set up in lines of three at opposite ends of the room. Behind each table sat a uniformed trooper. I saw Colonel Devon across the room. He was holding a microphone.

"Please take a seat," he said on the PA system. "When your name is called go to the table with the officer who called you. This won't take long. We appreciate your cooperation."

The room filled up quickly; everyone was seated on a folding chair. Every person I knew on Bittern Island was there and I knew almost everybody, at least on sight. There were a dozen or so children and two infants held by their mothers. The commotion of settling in subsided and the room got quiet.

"When's the show start?" a gruff male voice shouted. It brought a few snickers.

"This is not a show," Devon said into the mic. "This is a murder investigation."

Each of the six troopers at the tables, one by one, called a name. Married couples were called together. They took chairs across from the officers. Devon moved from table to table monitoring the interviews. The rest of us waited.

"Karl Hoffmann," a trooper called. I went over to his table. As I sat, Gunner Hogan's name was called on the other side of the room.

"You Hoffmann?" the trooper said.

"Yes, sir."

"Do you have some ID?"

I produced my Rhode Island driver's license and laid it on the table in front of him. He examined it and me. He handed it back. Colonel Devon came over and took a seat next to the trooper. My assigned interviewer deferred to his superior but took notes.

"You knew the deceased, Janus Martin?" Devon started.

"I rented him a chain saw. You know that."

"Why did he need a chain saw?"

"He said he had some wood to cut."

"Did he say what kind of wood and why?"

"No."

"And you didn't ask?"

"It was none of my business. The guy wanted a saw. I rented him one. That's how my business works."

Devon changed gears. He directed me to give the recording trooper a full description of Janus Martin. I described him as he appeared in my shop including the heavy accent.

Devon interrupted. "What kind of accent?"

"Maybe German or Slavic."

"And the vehicle he was driving?"

"I didn't actually see it. It was parked outside and I never checked." Grudgingly I added Rolando had seen it and told me about it.

"Are you aware the driver's license he showed you was fake?"

"Looked real to me. If you say it was fake, it must have been. I guess you checked it out."

"Ever seen a Michigan driver's license before?"

"Can't say I have. But I do see some from other states. Mostly it's people who rent here for the summer. A lot from Massachusetts and Connecticut, occasionally New York. Once I got one from Canada."

Colonel Devon reached down to the floor and lifted a briefcase. He opened it and extracted a file. He put the file on the table and returned the case to the floor. When he opened the folder I recognized the rental form.

"How did he pay you?" Devon asked.

I pointed to the form. "It says right there. Cash."

"And you never saw him again until you recovered the body with Constable Bealer?"

"Not exactly."

"What do you mean?"

I recounted how Martin had returned when he did not know about the safety switch. I left out that Gunner Hogan was there as well.

"Every time I ask something you add something else, Mr. Hoffmann."

I only shrugged.

"And that's the last time you saw him alive?" Devon asked.

"Yes."

"Then you never got the saw back."

"I suppose it's in the truck you can't find."

"How do you know we can't find it?"

"Archie Bealer told me. That's why you're here."

"I'm here to find a murderer."

"Yeah. That too. Good luck. And if you find it, I'd like my saw back."

CHAPTER TWELVE

Jake Fargo had pull. He produced gate passes and suggested we have a beer in town.

"I didn't know there was a town near here," I said.

Fargo laughed and said it was ten minutes away. He led me to a late model Chevy. We drove out the gate past armed sentries who scrutinized the passes. The dirt road turned to gravel and then tar. A few miles along we came to a town. It consisted of a gas station, dry goods store, and a roadhouse bar. Fargo parked in front of the bar and we went inside.

An old man in a baseball cap stood behind the bar. Jake and I were the only patrons. We ordered drafts and sat at a rickety table. Mosquitoes buzzed near the open door.

I picked up where Fargo left off. "So they were introduced?"

"The senior officer, a lieutenant general, did the honors. Your mother addressed the young major in French. It surprised her when your father replied in the same language."

"He speaks eight or nine languages."

"I know."

He went on to explain how the affair between the two had flourished, as the ballet toured Leningrad, Stalingrad, Warsaw, and Budapest. Papa, with his privileged papers, met her in each city. He became the envy of brother officers as he courted the beautiful Galina.

"Envy is the root of treachery," Fargo said. "And love can be distracting. Russia, as you imagine, is different. Fortunes turn and no one is loyal to anyone else. It's their biggest problem."

Major Viljandi had a young captain as aide. As Viljandi's star rose, so did the junior officer's. But the captain was always in the shadow of Viljandi's larger star.

"Your father had the experience to deal with it; unfortunately his attention was captured by the ballerina."

"What happened?"

"He was set up."

It happened in Murmansk. Papa inspected a radio intercept base monitoring American and British ships in the North Atlantic and the Norwegian and Barents Seas.

The inspection lasted three days. At the conclusion Papa made a complimentary report to the base commander. The next morning he was in Moscow to file a copy at Army Headquarters, but more importantly to make the Bolshoi's production of Minkus's *Don Quixote* with his lover in the role of Dulcinea.

Papa never made the ballet.

Freshly arrived Papa was summoned by his commander, General Federov. Federov was blue-blood Russian and Papa the only Estonian on staff. No Lithuanians or Ukrainians on Federov's staff either.

Major Viljandi presented himself as ordered. Despite the commander's distaste for mixed ethnicity in the Officer Corps, Viljandi had been a feather in the General's cap. The young officer was accustomed to deference. Not this time.

Federov barked harshly, demanding a copy of the report. Papa surrendered it. With Viljandi at attention the General sat and read it superficially. When he finished, he tossed the report at Papa.

"Go to the map, Major. Based on your findings give the position of the lead American carrier in this sector as of thirty-six hours ago."

Papa took his papers to the tactical map on the wall. Consulting his notes he took a grease pen and marked an X. Viljandi put down his report and faced his commander.

"Are you sure?" Federov asked.

"It's what the intercepts tell us."

Federov stood and walked to the map. With a rag he erased Papa's mark. Taking the pen he drew another X several hundred miles north by northeast of where Papa had placed the ship.

"At least your aide pays attention. Otherwise the Soviet Navy and Air Force would be shadowing seagulls."

"I don't understand," Papa said.

"The code, Comrade Viljandi. The Americans have changed their code. You missed it completely."

General Federov took a different report from a drawer and slapped it on his desk.

"Captain Stasov has provided the correct positioning." Stasov was Papa's aide.

"How could you possibly know all this?" I demanded.

"It's what we do, Hoffmann," Fargo said smugly. "And we do it better than anybody."

"Because of this mistake my father defected?"

"Not exactly. Many things happened at the same time. Your father was transferred to Bukhara near the Afghan border. Your mother fared better. After a KGB security check she went on tour. She danced in Paris, London, Montreal, and Stockholm. She became the rage of the ballet world. She dined with premiers and kings. Her affair with the disgraced Viljandi seemed a thing of the past. But the KGB did not know her heart."

My father, Fargo explained, obtained a two-week furlough after months of petty duty. He made his way to Kiev, my mother's home. Galina was waiting for him. So was Colonel Chandler.

The offer was a one-shot deal. Chandler would get them out but they had one day to decide.

"My father was that well regarded?"

Fargo put down his beer and looked at me. He was not about to spare me.

"Your father's career was over. He was an outcast within the Army. He was learning nothing new in a technological field that was changing daily. It was your mother Chandler wanted. She was a prize on the scale of Nureyev and Barishnakov. Unfortunately, she would not leave without Kurt Viljandi."

"She never danced here in the States."

"I know," Fargo said sipping his beer. He waited for me to ask.

"Why?"

"She was nearly killed in the escape. Chandler always brought his birds out through East Berlin. He had contacts on both sides of the Wall. Your father objected and not without reason. He was a pariah in his own Corps. If discovered in East Berlin, his proximity to freedom would be suspicious and he'd have been arrested. After the blunder most of his travel passes were revoked.

"Germany was out of the question as far as your father was concerned. He proposed a water crossing from Estonia to Finland. Chandler protested. Your father insisted. He knew the terrain, knew the waters, and he had the radio frequencies of the patrol boats. It was Estonia to Finland or he was not going. And if he wasn't going, Galina insisted she was not either.

"Chandler was stymied. He was under pressure from Washington to pull it off. They wanted Galina dancing at Lincoln Center by the start of the season. Short of time and against his own judgment, Chandler agreed to the escape route."

On the pretense of visiting his family with what was left of his furlough, Papa went home to Paldiski where the Baltic Sea spilled into the Gulf of Finland. Chandler showed up with Galina two days later.

Most Estonians did not appreciate their annexation into the Soviet Union in 1940. They labored with a dream of regaining independence. Owing to that, Papa and Chandler needed little effort procuring a boat to sail to freedom.

They were past the island of Naissaar, in open water, when the gunboats of the border security forces began pursuit. Viljandi knew the radio calls but that was not the problem. Unbeknownst to him, the boats had recently been outfitted with radar.

"It was an almost perfect operation," Fargo said. "At the limit of their range one of the gunboats opened fire with a deck gun. The first shell fell short. Before turning for home, her skipper ordered one more shot at the escape boat. You know anything about ordinance?"

"A little."

"Old artillery men will tell you. There's an angel in one shell and a demon in another. You never know which until you fire."

"What does that mean?"

"The load can vary. The last round fired by the gunboat was a demon. It carried a third farther then the one that fell short. Before it splashed into the water and detonated, it grazed the transom of the boat carrying your parents and Chandler," Fargo said. He began fingering the handle of his empty beer mug.

"But they made it out alive," I said.

"Yes, but not before a blown bit of transom, a heavy hunk of sharp, jagged wood imbedded itself in Galina's spine."

"Oh, my God."

"They made the coast of Finland. The Finnish doctors, helped by a U.S. Navy surgeon, did a remarkable job on your mother. With time to heal, therapy, and exercise, they were convinced she would walk again."

"What about dancing?"

Fargo looked at me incredulously. He shook his head indicating I missed the obvious.

"I don't know much about ballet, but I can sure as hell tell it ain't easy. For the artist, it's probably demanding and cruel. The muscles in your mother's back, though surgically restored in part, would never be toned to that level again. The doctors were satisfied she could walk."

We sat at the table in utter quiet for some minutes.

"Let's get the hell out of here," I said.

Fargo threw some cash on the table and stood up. Outside the Floridian sun blazed above the dusty road of the town. Sitting in the car I felt sweat gather at my collar. Fargo felt it too, wiping perspiration from his forehead with a handkerchief.

"I hate Florida," he said.

"You've got to finish."

Fargo continued as we drove back to camp.

Major Viljandi was debriefed. What the Americans already suspected was confirmed. He brought nothing new to the table. Months as an outcast had cut him off from the information coveted by the West. The interrogation became banal and handled by junior agents. Mama was recuperating at a nearby private clinic financed by Chandler's masters. Fargo would not tell me the location. There were no press conferences, no welcoming reception by America's ballet community. For Chandler and his cold warriors, the operation was a bust.

After the debriefing, Papa was given a job with a telecommunications company saturated with defense contracts. The contracts were not classified. Neither was Papa's job. With a new name and new papers, father was relegated to lab technician writing reports on frequency tests. He was bored and furious. At night he went home to his mending Galina and a drab cramped apartment.

"Then he made a strange request," Fargo said. "He had done the research on his own time in the library. Your father asked to be set up with a fishing boat and small house on a little island almost nobody ever heard of."

"Bittern Island."

"The same."

"And they agreed?"

"Of course. It seemed perfect. According to Viljandi, by then Hoffmann, it was all he wanted. On the other hand, it got him out of the way. Way out of the way. Exiled to an isolated island where the Major assured his superiors he could be self-sufficient. It was more than perfect. It was ideal."

His car was passing through the gate of Camp Sinclair. Again the sentries were persistent about the passes. We were let in. Fargo parked by my tent.

"I appreciate all this info," I said. "But what has any of this got to do with me? I'm a soldier in the United States Army. Why should any of it affect my career with the Engineers?"

Jake Fargo looked out from the car window at the trees and barbed wire. He thinks he has said too much already, I thought to myself. The Army is not expansive in its explanations. Then again, Fargo was not Army. He was from that community where they did things differently.

"The Cold War is heating up," he said, not looking at me. "I don't just mean Vietnam. God knows we've got problems here at home. You don't have to listen hard to hear communism knocking on our back door."

"Cuba?" I asked.

"We pissed on Castro's campfire during the Missile Crisis."

"What then? Where?"

"That's classified, soldier." Suddenly Fargo was out of character from the man I had been with most of the day. "Get out of the car. Pack your gear. I've got your travel papers in my glove box."

I did as I was told. Jake Fargo came into the tent while I stuffed my duffel.

"It ain't your fault, kid," he said.

"Whose fault is it?"

"I guess you could blame Chandler. But he's dead."

"Why him? He brought Papa out."

"No he didn't. He brought your mother out. Your dad was along for the ride because Galina insisted. But before Chandler passed his birds on to new handlers he wrote a report. In that report he advised we never completely trust Major Viljandi. The whole thing had gone sour. Matters as they were could be ripe for discontent and disillusion. And that was a breeding ground for more dangerous inclinations. Chandler was issuing a warning against your father."

I slammed my duffel to the floor. "You're all a bunch of bastards."

"Interesting choice of words under the circumstances. Don't you think?"

"Fuck you."

"Everybody's fucking everybody every day. I merely keep the scorecard. Are you ready?"

I hoisted the duffel and slung it off my shoulder. "Where am I going?"

"Germany, I think. Or it might be Turkey. I'm not sure. Does it matter?"

"Evidently not."

"But first, you're going home."

CHAPTER THIRTEEN

When the police finished with us Gunner Hogan and I walked over to Don Ostros's *cantina*. We invited Rolando and his wife to come but they declined.

At a table near the window we were served beers and given menus. The beer was cold and my throat so dry it seemed to go down in one effortless flow.

"You needed that," Gunner said.

"A few more wouldn't hurt."

He shrugged his shoulders and one of the waiters came over and sized up the situation. He fetched us two more beers.

When Gunner did not look at his menu I said, "If you're not going to eat, we could go over to the Sea Witch."

"No, I'll stay awhile. Maybe I'll feel like eating. Right now I want a whiskey."

Gunner ordered his drink when the waiter brought our beers. I stared out the window at Main Street. People were still milling about in front of Saint Andrews. Some drifted in the direction of the Sea Witch. Others shook hands and parted. After a while the State Troopers started exiting the Church. Colonel Devon was not among them.

Don Ostros poked his head out of the kitchen a few minutes later to assess the crowd.

"Join us for a drink," I called to him.

Ostros crossed the room slowly. He nodded recognition to patrons at several tables as he passed them.   One fisherman I knew named Carlos scrambled to his feet and shook the Don's hand.

Ostros let his hand be pumped and guided Carlos back into his chair with a hand on the man's shoulder.

It was then I noticed how crowded the restaurant had become. Our waiter appeared with a chair for his boss and set it between Gunner and myself. He returned a moment later with Gunner's whiskey.

"I'll have some wine, Joaquin," Ostros instructed the waiter. "There is an open bottle in my study. That will be fine."

Joaquin gave a slight bow and disappeared.

"All this police activity must be good for business," I said to Don Ostros.

Ostros only smiled and waited for his wine. It came directly, one full glass and the bottle set down beside it.

Ostros raised his glass and toasted. "To the police. They come and they go. It is better when they go."

"Here. Here," Gunner said.

"I'll drink to that," I joined them. I wanted to ask Ostros how his own interview went but decided against it.

As we set our glasses down the room grew quiet. The waiters serving seemed to vanish. Around the tables conversation ceased, glasses stopped clinking, and cutlery was laid flat. A light was switched on in one corner of the room, the brightest illumination in the subdued *cantina*.

Into the light stepped a young man with a guitar. He sat down on a chair and strummed the strings.   As the music floated, a young woman stepped into the light to stand by his side.

Out of the corner of my eye I saw a smile bend Ostros's lip. Then my attention went back to the girl. She could have been a young woman or an older teenager. Her hair fell beyond her shoulders, straight and black, covered partly from crown to shoulders by a gold and black *mantia*. The girl's eyes were round and wide and as black as her hair. A small face was below the eyes, tiny nose, mouth unseen until she opened it.

When she opened it, she sang. The guitar music faded to background. The voice had met it, conquered it. At first melancholy and pained, the song grew strength and elegant poise. The woman's hands, clutched at her heart, parted and spread. She lifted them as if imploring an embrace and then turned them confident and defiant.

The words in Spanish meant nothing to me. Yet I could not escape the captivation of the song's intent. When she ended with broad bold tones from deep in her lungs, her head was back, arms apart as if she could raise the ceiling.

The room came to its feet clapping, calling, whistling appreciation. The rafters were vibrating with our demonstration when the singer bowed once and exited into the kitchen.

The common noises of the *cantina* returned. There had been a moment and then it was gone. Waiters appeared carrying steaming dishes and served the tables.

"Magnificent," I said to Ostros. "What a voice."

"Who is she?" Gunner asked.

Ostros dismissed it. "Someone who works for me."

The smile came back to the Ostros's lower lip. He covered it with his glass and drank some wine.

"Have you gentlemen ordered?" he asked.

I told him not yet. He said there were excellent marinated steaks this evening. Also crabs fresh off the first boat out after the storm. I was feeling hungry.

A teenage lad came from the kitchen and politely begged Don Ostros's pardon. Ostros listened to him and then explained to us that his presence was required in the kitchen. He excused himself with a promise to return.

With Ostros gone Gunner grew restless. "Do you mind if I don't stay?"

"Are you feeling okay?"

"Sure. It's not that. I'm not very hungry. The smell of all this food is starting to get to me. I'd be better off at the Sea Witch."

"I'll come with you."

"No, stay and eat. I know you're hungry. Besides, you don't want to offend Don Ostros. He's sitting at your table. You wouldn't want him to come back and find us both gone. You can join me later."

It was true: I did not wish to offend the owner of the *cantina*. I told Gunner I would see him later for a nightcap.

Gunner finished his whiskey and beer. He rose, steady as ever, and with his soft dragging limp left the restaurant.

Don Ostros returned.

"Everything all right?" I asked.

"Quite all right, my friend." As he sat down he saw Gunner's glasses cleared away. "*Coronel* Hogan not joining us for dinner?"

"He doesn't each much. His diet is a little blander than your cuisine. No offense, he's not entirely well."

"Poor man." Ostros raised his glass of wine in a silent toast.

We drank. Ostros drained his glass and refilled it from the bottle on the table.

"What shall we eat?" he asked.

"I'll leave that to you."

Only raising an eyebrow, Don Ostros summoned our waiter. He spoke to him in Spanish and the young man took no notes. The waiter withdrew to the kitchen.

People were finishing their meals and leaving. Many paid respects to Ostros as they headed for the door. From the window I saw it was dark outside. The tables to either side of us became empty. Another bottle of wine was brought, this time with a glass for me. Ostros and I made conversation about the storm.

The wine was heavy. It stayed on my tongue after I swallowed. It reminded me of the song of the young woman. How the sound of her filled the room like smoke. Beautiful but indistinct before it vanished.

"How did you fare with the State Police?" Ostros asked. We had exhausted our comments about snow and flooding.

"Better than I expected since I met the victim and helped Archie Bealer move the body."

"How did this come to be?"

As we sipped our wine I recounted my renting the saw to Janus Martin. Then how Constable Bealer enlisted me to move the body so it could be preserved.

"How about yourself?" I asked. "Did they bother you much?"

Before he could answer our dinners were served. Large broiled marinated steaks heaped with a pile of red and green peppers sautéed in sherry wine. We ate some before he addressed my question.

"The *policia* always wish to annoy me." He paused for a sip of wine. "I suppose I am accustomed to it now."

"Why bother you? You run a small *cantina* on a small island. What's it to them?"

The question was no doubt naïve. Even so, Ostros did not embarrass me. He laid down his fork, folded his hands on the table and looked directly at me. I put down my fork and gripped my wineglass without lifting it.

"People, successful people, successful people from my country," he explained with a shrug, "the authorities always think we move drugs. It is inconceivable to them that we could make more money than them otherwise."

"Do you?"

"Do I what?"

I lowered my voice. "Do you move drugs?"

Ostros lowered his voice as well. But he did not lower his eyes from mine.

"Of course I do, my friend. As they all know, there is no other way. No way they will allow. Besides, I am a pathetic fisherman and an even worse cook. So I have my business and mind my business. They, on the other hand, are poor at business and mind everyone else's."

Finally I lifted my glass and took a long swallow. Two things came to mind. Ostros must have noticed something in my face for he let me ponder these in silence while he resumed eating.

In the early days of the fish plant, Don Ostros had invested money in it. He even imported some of the labor. How much he invested and lost I did not know. Papa and he always treated each other with respect. That was all I knew.

And there was Rolando Tobar. He was more than my employee. Rolando was an associate and friend. Were these so-called foraging trips to the mainland part of Ostros's drug business? It seemed too coincidental to discount. I was surprised. But I was not sure if I was hurt by it or not. My thoughts came back to the table and my host.

"I had no idea," I mumbled.

"Why should you? As I said, *amigo*. I mind my own business."

"You helped my father."

"Your father was a fine man. He almost made it in a world where he was not meant to succeed. A foreign world, as foreign as it was to me when I came here. But that, *Señor* Hoffmann, was a long time ago. Things were possible then. Opportunities more plentiful."

"I don't think so. They crushed him like a shell into sand."

"Excuse yourself and ask forgiveness of his memory. That is a judgment you have no right to make. No son ever does."

"He was a proud and stubborn man."

"You're not?"

"I've lived in the shadow of his choices my whole life. Even when I set out on my own, he was always there."

"So why are you here on Bittern Island? Is it to face him, yourself, or to merely give up?"

"It hasn't always been that bitter."

"Ah, your wife. Still you remain, despite it all. Is that not a form of pride?"

The door to the *cantina* opened and in strode Colonel Devon followed by one of his officers. They waited to be seated at an empty table across the room from us. Devon looked over at us. Ostros did not turn to meet his stare. Ostros went on with his dinner. I did the same.

When supper was ended Ostros ordered Fundador for both of us. The fiery Spanish brandy was served in small snifters. Coffee was brought.

"A heavy meal," I said.

"Is that a compliment?"

"Oh, you mean the food? The food was excellent."

Don Ostros smiled and his eyes brightened in the dim light of the *cantina*. He toasted me with his brandy.

"You are a complicated man, *mi amigo*."

"Not really."

"Is that so? Then why didn't you tell the *policia* about the truck in your shed?"

It was my turn to smile. "When it comes to Colonel Devon, sometimes I don't have the chocolates."

Ostros seemed satisfied.

"We will talk another time soon."

No check appeared at our table. I took my cue and rose to shake Don Ostros's hand.

"I'm looking forward to it." Then I went to meet Gunner at the Sea Witch.

CHAPTER FOURTEEN

The civilian airliner I flew home from Florida landed in Boston. From there I took a train to Providence, Rhode Island. Down Route One I hitchhiked to Narragansett. I wanted to call Papa ahead of time but managed not to do it. The last ferry of the evening crossed me home to Bittern Island.

I walked up Main Street of Gracetown and when I entered my house the lights were out and the fire in the parlor burned to embers. Papa was asleep in bed, his wheezing audible to me at the foot of the stairs.

Deciding not to wake him I went to my room, stripped to underwear and crawled into bed. Old smells of the house along with creaks and moaning pipes lullabied me to sleep.

"Karl, you're home," Papa shook my shoulder to wake me. "You didn't call."

From under the covers I said, "It was short notice. Only found out yesterday."

"You're home for the holiday?"

I remembered Thanksgiving was a few days away.

"I'll be here." Getting out of bed, I kissed him on the cheek. He was still too surprised to return it. "They've given me two weeks leave."

"Get dressed. I'll put on coffee."

"All right, Papa. Be down in a minute."

We were not emotional people but there was no mistaking his pleasure.

My clothes were still in the drawers and closet. After a quick wash I pulled on a sweater and jeans and headed down to the kitchen. Papa had a fire in the stove and the smell of coffee filled the room.

"Mmm. They don't make coffee like that in the Army."

"No one makes coffee like a fisherman." Papa took the pot from the stove and poured two mugs. "When did you get in?"

"Late last night. Too late to wake you so I went to bed."

"How are things in Korea? You haven't written me in weeks. Is everything all right?"

"I wasn't in Korea, Papa. At least not in the last two weeks. The Corps sent me to Florida for special training."

"Florida?" It was both a question and statement of surprise.

"Somewhere near the Everglades. It's a secret camp for a classified operation." I did not give a damn about the warnings not to talk about it.

"A secret camp and you get leave for Thanksgiving?"

"Not exactly." I sipped my coffee. He waited silently, patiently. "I've been dropped from the assignment."

I expected a "why?" but it did not come.

"They're planning a covert operation somewhere. I'm sure it's not Vietnam or even Southeast Asia. There's plenty of Engineers there already. It must be something else."

"The world is a mess. Who knows what the bastards are cooking up."

He did not ask so I plain said it.

"Papa, they dropped me because I couldn't pass muster on the security check."

Papa's eyes dropped from my face to study his coffee mug. Behind him through the window I saw the first light of morning. From down in the harbor I heard a boat toot its horn. A deep silence followed.

Papa scoffed at last. "Rubbish." He shot his arm out to the side as if swiping an insect or dismissing a lie, a blatant filthy lie. "You are no security risk."

"They don't see it that way." There was nothing to be excited about. It was over. The Army had made up its mind.

"Did they tell you why?" Papa asked.

"Yes, Papa. They told me everything."

Papa straightened in his chair. As he sat back, his shoulders, stooped with age, seemed to square and rise. He held his head high with his bearded chin thrust forward. Eyes clear, wide, defiant.

"You have nothing to be ashamed of."

"I'm not ashamed. I'm not ashamed at all. I was confused, but I'm not anymore. I am disappointed. But not disappointed in you. I'm as good as any man who wears the uniform."

"Indeed you are."

"It's their problem, not mine." The Viljandi blood was pumping in my veins.

"That's the spirit."

It got quiet in the room. There was a presence, but it was mute. What was not to be did not matter. What had been only mattered if I let it.

"Did she really dance that well?"

The clear eyes dimmed into memory. He was not looking at me though his face was directly across the table from my own.

"There was none like her. And never has been since. Your mother could walk on air, the very air."

Later that afternoon we walked to the gusty hilltop where we scattered her ashes years before when I was a boy.

"Galina," Papa called into the wind. "Our son has come home. He is a man now. I tell him we are very proud."

The wind seemed to hush a moment. Surely I only imagined it.

Walking home Papa asked, "What will you do now?"

"It's not like I can leave the Army. There's two years left on my hitch. The orders are cut. I've been transferred to Germany. Probably be there a year and then God knows where they'll send me."

"Believe me, son. God doesn't care one way or the other."

"Is that the old Bolshevik coming out?"

He took it in good humor with a throaty laugh.

"You're from good Estonian stock. Don't forget that. The lands of your parents won't be communist forever. It is a system doomed to fail. The seeds of its destruction are buried deep. But they are there. And it's not about Vietnam. And it's certainly not about some wall of garbage in Berlin. It's about the human spirit."

"Did you read that somewhere?"

Papa stopped walking. He turned toward the water beyond the windswept dunes.

"No, son. I learned it at sea."

We walked home.

The days we spent together were pleasant. We talked for hours about books, philosophy, politics, or whatever we cared to discuss. There were hours, not nearly enough, for reading. November was mild that year affording us long walks along the beach and over the docks of the harbor.

Thanksgiving we had dinner in the *cantina* of Don Ostros.   It was not turkey, but the roast veal was excellent, and we ate and drank too much.

Every morning we walked to the pier to buy the newspapers sent over on the first ferry of the day. At breakfast we read them and occasionally discussed a news item.

"Sly bastards," Papa said one morning. His face was behind the wall of his newspaper. "The sly conniving bastards."

I put my paper down. "What have you read?"

"It's not what I read. It's what I don't read but know from experience."

"What are you talking about?"

Papa folded the paper and put it down. His tired eyes behind his reading glasses twitched mischievously.

"First you tell me. What were you training for down in Florida?"

"We built compact radio stations air-dropped to our location."

"And?"

"When I left we had started weapons drills in defending them."

"Ponder this. If you were going to seize a country, what would you do first?"

"How would I know? I'm with the Engineers."

"Think, Karl. You were training for it."

"I guess I'd attack the army bases and put as many out of commission as I could in the first strike."

"Yes. That would be necessary. Unless?"

"Unless what?"

"Suppose the army was already on your side. Imagine a junta and you're only a facilitator for the military."

"Then I would seize all communications until the government was overthrown and the new power installed."

"Precisely." He slapped the tabletop with his palm. "No radio, no television, no anything until the task is complete. Then, at your pleasure, you restore communications and announce the new government. By then it's too late for the public to do anything to impede your efforts. It's already over."

"You think the United States would participate in something like that?"

Papa cocked an eyebrow at my naïveté. He turned his paper around on the table and slid it over to me. I looked down at the article's headline.

MARXIST ALLENDE ELECTED PRESIDENT
OF CHILE

Papa said, "The U.S. government won't stand for a Communist entity in South America. They fear their precious dominoes will collapse on them. Latin America is vital to the defense of the region."

"You think we'll intercede in Chile?"

"I'm surprised it hasn't happened already. It would have been easier before the election. They did not move quick enough. But move they will. Mark my words."

The old cold warrior was right. It made sense. Cuba had been exporting communism to its neighbors for over two decades. Each attempt had been thwarted by direct or indirect measures by the United States. Chile was something else entirely. Doctor Salvador Allende, an avowed Marxist, had been democratically elected.

"So we would rather back a military dictator than a communist," I said.

"Nixon would back the devil himself before a Marxist."

"I'll be damned."

Papa laughed. "No you won't. You won't be there. You're the son of a Soviet officer. You're a security risk. What a bunch of arrogant pathetic bastards they all are."

"What about your theory of the triumph of the human spirit?" He had been so passionate during our walk home from the crest.

"I said it would come. I didn't say when."

"Not for some time I imagine."

"Unfortunately, I believe you are right." He retrieved his paper and folded it. "I'll make us some breakfast."

The two weeks were over before I knew it. It was time for me to report to my new posting in Germany. Seems I posed no security threat in that theater. Even Papa, the pragmatist, thought it ironic.

Europe was reasonably stable if you discounted the student riots and the terrorist Red Brigade. No doubt I would wind up building posh Officer's Clubs and base latrines.

"You're learning a trade," Papa said. "Make it count for yourself. The independent fisherman is a thing of the past. You'll do better. I know you will."

On the wharf by the ferry he kissed me on both cheeks and made me promise to write more. I took the pen he gave me from my pocket and waved it in a gesture of commitment.

"I love you, Papa."

"I love you, son."

The ferry captain sounded his horn. It was time to shove off. From the deck I watched Bittern Island recede into the morning mist. Papa stood on the dock until we were out of each other's sight. He did not wave, nor did I. He simply faded like a cloudy sunset.

I never saw him alive again.

Word reached me in Betzdorf, Germany, where I was building barracks for NATO troops. Papa died in his sleep and was not discovered for several days. Solitary in old age, he was only noticed when the newspaper boy realized he was not coming by the ferry for his morning paper. Papa was found in bed. An old Victrola was spinning soundlessly by the bedside. The record on the machine was Tchiakovsky's *Swan Lake*.

It was spring when I came home to tend to matters. Within thirty days I had packed up everything, all the books and my belongings, donated his clothes to the Salvation Army, and put the rest in storage. The house I sold to a young fisherman and his bride along with most of the furniture.

On the last day I took Papa's ashes to that same hilltop and watched them blow away. This time the beach roses were in bloom. I gathered a handful, walked down to the beach, and threw them beyond the waves.

CHAPTER FIFTEEN

"What about Martin's truck?" Rolando asked. It was the day after our interviews with the State Police.

"It's all right where it is for the moment."

Rolando opened shop and I had just arrived.

"I had dinner with Don Ostros last night," I told him.

"And Gunner?"

"He begged off at the last minute. It was only me and the Don."

The coffee was ready. Rolando poured mugs and moved the pot from the hotplate to the stove. I waited for him to ask. It took a few minutes while he added wood to the stove.

"So? How was dinner?"

I pretended to laugh. "The food is always good at his place."

Rolando frowned. "Did you tell him about the truck?"

"I didn't have to. Isn't that the damnedest thing?"

"You think he killed Martin?"

"He didn't say that he did. The Don merely asked why I hadn't told the police about the Jeep."

"If he didn't kill Martin how would he know about the truck?"

"I thought you might have some ideas on that score."

Rolando regarded me over the top of his mug. The eyes in his head grew smaller until they were tiny dots focused on me over the counter. I put down my mug and sat on the stool. Rolando slowly put his mug down too.

"What else did you talk about?" he asked.

"Oh, that. Yes. He told me about the drugs."

"Were you surprised?"

"I was at first. Then it made sense. I had not thought about it. Maybe I didn't care. In fact, I don't care now. I only wish that damn Jeep wasn't in my barn. He shouldn't have done that without my permission. Perhaps he figured I owed him because he once helped my father."

"He did?"

"Ostros put up money for the fish plant. He lost out with everybody else when the Combine crushed it."

"The Don does not like to lose."

"Nobody does. But that's ancient history. We were having a nice chat and then Colonel Devon came in with one of his men."

"What did the *policia* want?"

"Nothing, they came for dinner like everyone else."

I detected a wave of relief cross Rolando's face. He picked up his coffee again.

"Anything you want to ask me, boss?"

"Not especially." His business was his business. Rolando did for me what I paid him for and on top of that he was my friend. "Unless you've got an idea what we can do with the truck."

"When things settle down, I'm sure it will be taken care of."

"Did you know about it? Did you know about it before we went to get the tables and chairs?"

"No."

That was a relief. I had always trusted Rolando Tobar. Now I still could.

The phone rang. One of my clients in town was finished with the pump. A second call referred to the same matter. I promised to pick them up before the end of the day. Another call came in from the custodian of Saint Andrews. The furniture could be removed any time.

"Sounds like a full day," Rolando said.

"We'd best be at it."

We took the pickup into Grace and collected the pumps and hoses. The sun was out and the streets were dry. People had returned to normal routines and the ferry arrived and departed while we went about business. The only thing that seemed out of place for a blustery day on Bittern Island was the State Police vehicle parked in front of the Sea Witch.

With the pumps all loaded we went into the tavern for a beer. Two troopers were seated at a table drinking coffee. Sweeney tended bar.

"How's it going, Sweeney?" I asked and ordered beers.

"Slower than yesterday. The 'Inquisition' was good for business."

"I've heard something good comes of everything sooner or later."

"Brought you some business too." Sweeney must have meant the furniture I supplied.

"Only if I get paid."

Sweeney jerked his thumb at the troopers. "Take it up with them."

"Ever see a cop pick up a tab?" Rolando said.

Sweeney and I laughed though it was not meant as funny. I looked over at the cops who were oblivious to our conversation. One of them brought their cups over to the bar for a refill. He was tall and broad and looked like a Swede with his blond hair and cream skin. The other trooper, still at the table, was Black and just as large.

"What time does he come in?" the blond trooper asked Sweeney.

Sweeney poured the coffee and then looked at his watch.

"Any minute now. Second stop of the day. Like clockwork." The Sea Witch's door opened and Sweeney said, "Should be Archie now."

Constable Bealer entered the tavern. He came straight to the bar and Sweeney waited for him with the bottle of rye. No words were exchanged while the bartender poured and Bealer gulped it down. After the first one, Bealer held the second drink in his steadying hand and surveyed the room. His gaze came to rest on Rolando and me for a second but he said nothing. The big white cop had gone back to his table and Bealer shifted his eyes to the officers.

Bealer drank his whiskey, brought the empty glass down hard on the bar, slid it away from him, and walked over to the State Troopers and sat down.

Rolando and I drank our beers. Sweeney washed some glasses. The three men at the table were in deep conversation. We could not hear their words.

Suddenly Bealer said in a whiskey-bolstered voice, "You better have a search warrant. Don Ostros is no fool. He'll know his rights."

The Black trooper, who I could see by turning toward Rolando, produced a piece of blue paper from inside his tunic. He showed Bealer and put it away.

"Be back in a minute," Rolando said. Without giving the impression of having to hurry, he headed out the door.

"I've got to hit the can first," Bealer announced. He got up and walked to the back of the bar where the restrooms were located.

Sweeney poured another shot and put it down at that end of the bar. Then he drew me another beer. When Bealer came back he lingered at the far end long enough to gulp his drink. The cops left their seats and the three of them headed for the door. Before they got to it the door opened to admit Rolando Tobar who passed by the officers unconcerned.

"This ought to be fun," he said to me. "Wish we could watch."

"How so?"

"Don Ostros left for the mainland on the ferry this morning."

"That doesn't mean anything. They have a warrant. Ostros doesn't have to be there for them to use it."

"I know. The thing is that nobody left over there speaks English. Archie doesn't know any Spanish. You think the other two know any?"

I laughed. "You're right. I'd love to see that."

We finished our beers.

"Come on," I said. "We still have work to do."

We took the loaded truck back to All Island and returned the pumps to their shed. Another trip to

Grace followed to retrieve the table and chairs from the Church. The custodian was a big help and I slipped him a few dollars.

Outside Shed B I could feel myself hesitating. I was thinking: Wouldn't it be great if it was gone? The whole mess would be over with. I opened the lock and dislodged the crossbeam. Rolando grabbed half the door and swung it open. The afternoon sun, low behind Rolando, streamed through the doorway. The black truck was there, hunkered down in the center of the barn like some giant beast brought to its knees, dying.

Rolando read my mind. "You was thinking maybe she be gone."

"It would have made life easier around here."

It was pointless to dwell on that, so we set to unloading the furniture into the shed.

"Close the door while I turn on the light," I told Rolando when we finished. As he swung the wooden door into place I yanked the cord of the overhead bulb.

"What are you going to do?"

Without answering I went to the worktable in the corner and found a pair of old cowhide gloves and put them on.

"I'm going to see what's inside."

"Maybe you better not. This doesn't concern us."

"The hell it doesn't. It's on my property. Either we call the police or check it out for ourselves."

"No *policia.*"

"Agreed. So what are we waiting for?"

Apparently nothing. Rolando fetched his own gloves from the bench and joined me by the driver's side door.

Reaching forward I grabbed the handle of the door and depressed the latch. It gave way and I swung the door open.

"Get the flashlight from the bench," I said. The overhead light up by the rafters was not enough to see the Jeep's interior.

Rolando found the torch, turned it on, and handed it to me. I shined it into the cab at the driver's seat. One half of a seatbelt lay limply across the cushion. Raising the beam I saw the passenger seat: empty as well. Leaning into the vehicle I pushed my head past the steering column and shined the light backwards. A set of keys, one wedged in the ignition, dangled motionlessly. Before removing them I did a quick scan of the floorboards on both sides of the center console. They were empty. I removed the keys from the column.

"Find anything?" Rolando called over my shoulder.

"Not yet. I still have to check the glove box and console."

Uncomfortable the way I was, I withdrew from the Jeep and climbed into the cab to sit in the driver's seat. The glove box was locked but I found the key on the key ring. The hatch of the box flapped downward when unlocked. I reached in and extracted a handful of folders. Placing them on the passenger seat I examined them with the flashlight.

"What have you got?" Rolando asked.

"Maps. A whole bunch of maps. He's got Rhode Island, Massachusetts, New Hampshire, Vermont, and Montreal, Canada. There's also some rental papers." I scanned the forms quickly. "This Jeep was rented in Montreal."

"I guess he doesn't have a map of Michigan."

A quick probing with the light revealed nothing else in the glove box.

I put the maps and forms back in the box and secured the hatch.

The console was locked too. The same key opened it. I shined the light down into it. It reflected back at me. I reached in and pulled out a half-pint bottle of cheap whiskey. Putting it down on the passenger seat I reached back in to retrieve an identical bottle, only this one was empty. I put it with the first one on the seat.

Only one item remained in the console. I withdrew it gingerly. My Army training flashed a moment and I turned it over in my hand to check the safety was engaged. It was a semi-automatic handgun. My guess was a 9mm. I put the gun back in the console, slid the bottles over it, and snapped the cover closed.

Turning around in the seat I played the light around the back bay of the Jeep. There they were. A McCullock chain saw and a gas can were next to each other on the floor of the bay. Beyond them was something small and dark and rumpled in the corner by the hatch door. I could not tell what it was so I got out of the truck.

"The saw is in the back. And there's something else."

Rolando followed me around to the back of the Jeep. I worked the key in the latch and pulled the gate wide open and lifted the rear windshield in its frame. The object was in the corner to my right.

"It's an empty satchel," I said as I took it out. It was black leather with two handgrips at the top. The size was approximately eighteen inches long and maybe ten in girth. A zipper ran the top length of it.

"Open it," Rolando said.

After handing him the flashlight I unzipped the bag. Pulling the handles apart, I spread it wide open. Rolando shone the light inside.

"Not completely empty." He reached his gloved hand inside and withdrew a flat crisp one hundred-dollar bill. Rolando held it under the flashlight and examined it. "I'm no expert, but I think it's real."

"There was a gun in the console."

Rolando swallowed and pointed his flashlight down at the rear bumper of the jeep.

"Check this out," he said.

I looked at the license plate of the vehicle. It confirmed the rental papers. The tag was issued by the Canadian province of Quebec.

"You covered a lot of miles, Mr. Martin," I said to the truck. "And for what?" I reached back into the truck and lifted the gas can. It was empty. I turned to Rolando.

"What about the saw and can?" he asked.

"Better leave them. I think they are supposed to find them."

He held up the C-note. "What about this?"

I took it from him and put it back in the satchel and returned them to the Jeep. Then I closed and locked the hatch.

"They'll make something of all this," I said.

"They? Are you referring to the police?"

"I guess so. Whoever killed Martin got what he wanted. This is a hunk of flotsam. I'm sure he wishes the tide had taken it back out."

"But the storm screwed his plan."

"Assuming he had a plan. The killing might have been spontaneous."

"So why stash the Jeep here?"

"Because it's private and out of sight. The lock is a joke. Any kid with a penny nail could pick it."

"This was no kid."

"You're right. By the way. Where do you suppose Don Ostros went?"

"Boston, I'd guess."

"Why Boston?"

"Because he has a home there."

"How do you know?"

"I've been there."

"Oh."

I put the starter key back in the ignition and closed the Jeep door. After dousing the light we locked the shed and went across the alley to the shop.

"Damn glad most of the snow is gone," Gunner Hogan startled us. He was seated on the stool next to the stove. The customary pipe protruded from his jaw and the flask was open on the floor by his boot. "I'm not one to judge, but you boys look like you've seen a ghost. Christ! I don't look that bad. Do I?"

"You look fine," I assured Gunner.

Rolando went over to him. Gunner lifted the flask and offered it. Rolando accepted and took a drink.

An idea came suddenly to mind.

"Can you watch the shop for a day or two, Gunner?" He had done it for me before.

"Sure I can. Where are you fellows off to?"

"Boston," I said.

Rolando looked at me then took another slug of whiskey.

CHAPTER SIXTEEN

My tour in Germany lasted a year. The land was beautiful and everybody loved GIs. I read Hegel, Schopenhauer, and Nietzche and walked the forests. The following summer I transferred again. By fate, I ended my career with the Corps of Engineers by the ocean.

On the shore of Long Island, New York, the Corps built jetties to stem erosion. The jetties I came to love. They reminded me of home on another island. There was something about working with big rocks and setting them just right as waves pounded and seagulls jeered.

Tangentially, I got interested in sculpture. My crew was billeted in Far Rockaway. When not with my buddies in the towns of Long Beach and Atlantic Beach, I went to New York City and prowled museums. There I saw what could be done with stone and marveled at it.

At an art supply store I bought clay and attempted to mold something. The something was never right and I abandoned the effort. I bought a sketchpad and pencils. Roaming the beaches I scratched renderings of lighthouses, jetties, and birds. One night I burned them in a fire we lit on the beach while we drank and listened to the World Series.

Drunk, I stumbled to the barracks and lay on my bunk. Sleep did not come. Slowly I sobered up. Then I remembered what I used to do those lonely Sundays in Korea.

From my duffel I got my fountain pen and writing paper. Sitting on the bunk I wrote Papa a letter. By the time the guys rolled in, it was seven pages long.

In the morning I bought a notebook like students use for exercises. On the inside cover I taped the letter to my dead father and wrote on from there.

That winter while the jetties grew, the notebooks multiplied. From Papa's rambling letter I moved to short stories and what I thought was poetry. At bookshops I purchased Hemingway and Raymond Carver along with the poetry of Ferlinghetti, Ginsberg, and Merwin. Despite years immersed in literature, my writing was sophomoric and imitative.

When my duty to country was done I had no idea what was going on in my life.

"End of the line, soldier," said the Lieutenant mustering me out of the service. I had reported to Fort Hamilton in Brooklyn to draw my papers. "Your country thanks you."

I threw up one last salute and signed my name.

The subway took me from Brooklyn to Manhattan. I got a room at the YMCA. The room was clean and I did not know what a soft bed was so that was fine too.

The newspapers were all about Chile. Papa had been right. With U.S. support, the Chilean military seized power. Allende, the Marxist, was killed in the coup. The junta was preceded by a blackout of communications. The boys from Camp Sinclair had done their job.

Even with back pay to carry me for a while, I wanted a job. Mornings I followed leads from the classifieds. Afternoons I spent in the library or museums. Despite my lack of talent, I still loved sculpture and started to study paintings. I bought books and went to exhibits.

Around the corner from the Y was a pub. I went there some nights. Often, I brought my notebook and went off in a corner. When not in that mood I could be enticed into games of pool. It was a blue-collar crowd with talk of sports and support for our military in Vietnam.

"When did you get out?" an older man asked as we shot eight-ball.

"Two weeks ago."

"See any action?" It was what everybody wanted to know.

"Not really." Hell, I did my time. How I spent it was the Army's choice.

"Done your time then you done your duty, kid. Did mine in Korea."

"That's funny. That's where I was."

He laughed. "No shit?"

"No shit."

"They should have listened to MacArthur. The commies would know we mean business. Fucking politicians. Except for Nixon, they're all scumbags."

I drove the eight-ball into the corner pocket for the game.

He stuck out his hand. "Hank Stodder."

"Karl Hoffmann."

We shook and walked over to the bar. Hank owed me a round for the game.

"Work around here?" he asked.

"No. I'm holed up at the Y until I can line something up."

"What can you do?"

"Anything," I boasted. "I was in the Corps of Engineers. I can drive a pay-loader, weld steel, splice cable, and a hundred other things. Just need a job doing one of them."

"No shit. Ever work with sheetrock?"

"I can cut it, hang it, tape it, and spackle."

"Careful. That's different Locals. This is a Union town."

Over another beer Stodder explained how it works.

"My Local frames out space and screws up sheetrock. Another Local comes for plastering. We don't step on their turf and they don't stomp ours. We all work. Got it?"

"I got it. Doesn't help me. I'm unemployed."

"A vet like you shouldn't have a problem. You need a godfather."

"A what?"

"A godfather. Somebody in the Union, meathead."

"I don't know anybody in New York. That means I'm fucked."

"You know me. Don't you, dickhead?"

"You'd do that for me? We just met."

"Nothing's free in this town, kid," he winked. "Get the idea?"

He explained without my having to ask. Every Local member had one free ticket to get his son into the Union. It was a tradition and guarantee. Hank and his wife were childless. His ticket into Local Six was for sale.

"Are there any openings?" I asked.

"A few. But there's no time to dick around."

"How much?"

"Three large."

"Three hundred?"

"What? You born on fucking Pluto? Three thousand cash, kid."

I had that much cash in a sock in my duffel at the YMCA.

"When?" I asked.

"I come here Sundays to watch the game. You show with the dough and I'll waltz you into the Hall on Monday."

"What if they don't take me?"

"Christ! You was born on Pluto. Some of that money is to make sure."

We shook on it and I promised to see him Sunday with the cash.

I walked around to my room. Between socks and underwear I had about eighty-five hundred dollars hidden in my clean laundry. In addition, there was a few grand in a bank in Providence I set up after the sale of the house on Bittern Island. I counted out three thousand and put that sock into a pants pocket hanging in the closet.

"Karl, you in there?" a voice called. It was Pete Franco. Franco and I checked into the Y the same day. We had stumbled into conversation waiting for our room assignments.

"What's up, Pete?" I called.

"I've got a gig downtown. Want to come along?"

After stowing the duffel I opened the door. He stood tall and lanky in jeans and oversized sweater. Hair fell to his shoulders, tangled and stringy. A wispy beard covered his chin. By his side was his guitar case.

"Got a job already?" I asked.

"It's a fill-in for one night. Maybe it turns into something. Who cares? You listen to music. We have a couple of beers. Maybe we score some weed and get laid."

"That's the second best offer I've had tonight."

"Yeah? What was the first?" A slight glaze in his eyes made me think he already smoked some grass.

"A job of my own," I said. "I'll tell you on the way. Let me grab my jacket."

My only coat was the green fatigue jacket I was issued in the Army. I had removed its stripes but my name was stenciled above the pocket and the insignia of Engineers was sown to the shoulder.

The club was underground in Greenwich Village. We went down a concrete staircase that was flanked by handrails. At the bottom stood a Black man with arm muscles stretching his black tee shirt. Franco introduced himself to the bouncer.

"Don't know you," the bouncer said. "And the group ain't here."

"I'm the sub," Franco said. "Billy Watts can't make it. They called me to take his place. I wanted time to tune up, feel out the place, warm up to the acoustics."

"Okay," the man said. He pointed at me. "Who's this guy?"

"My manager," Franco said. "We might make a deal after this."

The bouncer snorted. "Yeah, right." He eyed my jacket. "That yours? Or did you buy it in a surplus store?"

"It's mine, dickhead," I said. "See the name?" I pointed to HOFFMANN over the breast pocket. "That's my name. Got a problem?"

"No problem, brother." He grinned. "Got one of my own."

He stepped aside in the stairwell and allowed us to pass into the club. The joint was dimly lit. A bar took up one wall. Directly across from it was a rickety-looking stage. In between were tables and chairs. The air was stale with beer, tobacco, sweat, and marijuana.

"My kind of place," Franco said. "Let's grab a beer."

There was one couple seated at the far end of the bar. The guy was middle-aged, about forty. Beside him a jean and tee shirt clad redhead no more than twenty. They watched us then turned back to the bar. The bartender watched us too, hands on the bar, a towel straddling his shoulder.

Franco ordered for both of us. "Two drafts."

"No drafts." The bartender wiped a spot in front of us. "Bottles only."

There was a Christ-head tattoo on his right forearm and a dagger on his left. He appeared short behind the bar, but not like he would not be trouble if trouble was what you ordered.

I put some money on the bar. "Pair of Buds then."

He grunted, fetched the beers, and served them without glasses or coasters.

"What time does Mick usually get here?" Franco asked the bartender.

"Mick who? I don't know no Mick."

France was not put off. This was New York City. "Mick Fraser. I'm here for the gig with him. Billy Watts can't make it."

"Billy okay?"

"He will be after he makes bail."

The information satisfied the bartender. He stuck his hand out at Franco.

"Clyde."

Franco shook Clyde's hand and introduced me. This time he left off the manager routine.

Clyde pointed at Franco's guitar case. "You better be good. Billy's a favorite around here. You play steel slide on that thing?"

Franco laughed. "I'm from Louisiana. We invented steel slide."

"Show me what you got," Clyde said.

Franco took a slug of beer then pushed away the bottle. He put his case on the counter and took out a steel string Gibson. From his pocket came a pick and a four-inch metal tube. He slid the tube over his left pinky, propped himself on the stool and fitted the guitar into his lap.

"What's your pleasure?" Franco asked.

"'*Been Straight Too Long*,'" Clyde said.

"Good, Lordy," Franco cooed. "Loves me that one," he said sinking into bayou homespun. "Bobby Mike Hill wrote it in prison."

"So you heard it. Can you play it?"

Franco stroked the first chord and twanged the final string. A fast progression was strangled as the steel barrel on his pinky worked up the neck of the Gibson. As the chords changed the pinky slid back down the neck and Franco started to sing.

"Been straight too long." Two chords. "Been straight too long." Two chords. "Been straight too long, oh baby, you know I'm surely bent by now." Two chords.

"That's enough," someone barked.

The older guy from the end of the bar had come over.

"People pay to hear music in my club," he said.

"Sorry, friend," Franco said. "I was only dispelling some concerns."

"Never mind. Mick will be here soon and get you set up. In the meantime, put that guitar away. The crowd plays the juke box until the first session. I got a piece of that action. So don't be putting on free concerts."

"You're the boss."

The man introduced himself as Roy Butler, owner of the club. Franco introduced me.

"This place got a name?" I asked Roy.

"Bottom Blues," Butler said. "The bottomest of the blues in the Big Apple. It gets any bluer and it's church music and you're going in the ground."

"Amen, Brother Roy," Franco added in his down-home voice. Butler was taken with my friend's posturing.

"We like our whiskey neat, our women dirty, and our music blue," Butler said as if reciting the motto of Bottom Blues.

Roy bought us a round and returned to his girlfriend whom he neglected to introduce. She was busy. Busy rolling the biggest, fattest joint I had ever seen, not that I had seen many.

The club filled up and the jukebox started to blare. Mick Fraser came in and Butler brought him over to Franco. I met him too but Fraser was not interested in me. He led Franco away to a back room as Pete called back that he would catch me after the set.

With my next beer I ordered a shot of Jack Daniel's. After a while Roy Butler went to the back room. The redhead stayed at the bar. Twice I saw her looking at me. Each time I gave her a half smile and looked away. There was no point starting trouble.

The room went pitch black for an instant. A spotlight came on, pointed at the stage. Into the light stepped Roy Butler. Drink in one hand, cigarette in the other, Butler introduced the band, "Blue Through," featuring Mick Fraser.

Six men came out on stage. The spotlight widened. Fraser and Franco had guitars. There was a piano player, a bass, and a drummer. The last guy had a sax and a horn.

Pete Franco fit right in with the group. In the fourth number he had a guitar solo that drew applause. Then Fraser let him sing a number. Franco turned on the Cajun charm. Right before the break Fraser introduced the band members. He referred to Pete Franco as "filling in for Billy Watts."

During the break Franco joined me at the bar. He walked over, acknowledging some compliments from the crowd on the way and slapping palms. He quickly downed the beer I had waiting for him and ordered a Jim Beam.

"How'd I do?" he asked.

"You stole the set."

"Naw." He gulped some bourbon. "Just the new guy. A curiosity."

"Cut the bayou baloney. You know you were good."

Franco smiled. "I must admit, it felt like I had it there for a few licks."

I ordered my next Jack on the rocks. Mick Fraser came over and clapped Franco on the back and had a drink with us. So did the drummer and bass player. The remaining two had women in the audience and spent the break with them.

Pete Franco led off the second set with a vocal. In the next tune he had a blues harp solo that had the place crazy. Just before the last number Fraser made the introductions again. This time Franco was, "On vocal, lead guitar, and mouth organ, Blue Through's own Pete Franco." There was no mention of Billy Watts.

With the live music over for the evening the crowd thinned out. The lights came up, the band was in the back room, and I sat with my back to the bar cradling my Jack Daniel's in my lap.

"Your friend's good," said a female voice suddenly near my ear. It was the redhead. She wore bell-bottoms and a Muddy Waters tee shirt. Butler was in the back with the band.

"The crowd seemed to like him."

"What's your name, soldier boy?" She was staring at my jacket and seemed stoned and drunk at the same time.

"Karl." I looked at the empty stage, not her. "I'm not a soldier anymore."

"What do you play, Karl? Or do you just sit by yourself looking big and cool and macho?" she teased with a slur.

"Where's Roy?"

"In back with the band. He's really too old but he can't help himself. Just can't give it up."

I did not ask to what she was referring. It did not matter.

"After a good gig the boys loosen up and mellow down," she said. She swayed a little. "Sometimes cocaine, sometimes acid, depends where their heads are at."

"Why aren't you with them?" I regretted asking it immediately.

"It's a musician's thing." Her eyes rolled. "That's why Roy's so pathetic."

Time to cut this off.

"Listen, lady." I turned to her. "I'm here for Pete. He's my brother-in-law. I always cover his first gig at a new club. Then it's back to my wife and kids in Queens. So if it's okay with you, I'm going to mind my business and drink my drink."

"Aren't we on a short leash." Something was gone from her blurry eyes. She backed up slowly, maintaining command. It might have worked, but she nearly fell over a stool. She caught herself, turned, and went back to the end of the bar.

"Smart," Clyde said. He replenished my drink. "I liked the part about the kids."

I raised my drink. "When you see a freight train coming you got two choices."

He poured a shot of vodka and raised it to touch my glass.

"Toot, toot," Clyde toasted.

CHAPTER SEVENTEEN

The sea was choppy on the ferry ride. Rolando and I stood on the upper deck with the pickup hunkered down on the deck below. Brenton Point came into view across Rhode Island Sound.

"You sure you want to do this?" Rolando asked. He had to cup his hands to his mouth so I could hear in the wind.

"I've known Don Ostros all my life. It's too late for me to fear him."

Rolando nodded that he understood.

"Do you have any reason to be afraid?" I said.

"We do business. This is true. My fears lie elsewhere."

"This isn't going to be the Evil One again. Is it?"

He crossed himself and kissed the finger. "You've got superstitions of your own, *amigo*."

Rolando was right; call it what you will, everyone was a jumble of superstitions, faiths, guilts, or regrets. You lived with them or in spite of them. It was the choice you made and lived with the consequences.

"Let's go below and get coffee," Rolando said.

"You go and bring me one. I want to stay up here."

Rolando shrugged and retreated to the gangway for the galley.

The wind lessened and the water calmed as the ferry eased past Castle Hill in the channel between Newport and Jamestown. The bow swung starboard as the captain pointed her at Fort Adams.

Rolando came with coffees. We sipped as the skipper nudged into berth at Fort Adams State Park on the spur of Newport. We had to shuffle the pickup off and on to let others get their cars to disembark.

The ferry pulled out, came about, and churned under Newport Bridge in Narragansett Bay. The course took us by Portsmouth, Prudence Island, Bristol and Pawtuxet. It was dusk when we made port in East Providence.

I drove off the ferry and followed the signs to the highway.

"Ever been to Boston?" Rolando asked.

"Sure. I lived there for a while with my wife."

"You like it?"

"As cities go, it's better than most. But my opinion probably has more to do with Judith than the city."

"How did you end up back on Bittern Island?"

Ignoring the question I asked him to find a map and flashlight in the glove box. Rolando got them and shined the light on the map.

"What am I looking for?" Rolando asked. "Besides Boston."

"Route Forty-four to Twenty-four. It's been a long time."

"Why not head over to I-95?"

"I'm thinking of an alternate route. Everybody uses I-95. Do you know another way?"

"Why would I?"

"Because you've done work for Ostros."

He switched off the flashlight. We drove about a mile further in silence.

"Forty-four's coming up," he said. "You'll see the sign."

"There it is," I said seconds later.

"Stay right. It swings hard around."

The ramp veered sharply as Rolando had warned. We took it fine down to the highway.

"The alternate route," he said. "Why's that important?"

"If they find the Jeep back home in the shed while we're gone, we're going to be suspects in a murder case. I'd rather be back in Rhode Island if that happens. I don't want the Massachusetts State Police to pick us up on an alert from Devon. We'd spend a couple of days in lockup until they did the extradition paperwork."

"When did you start thinking like that?"

"It must be in my blood."

"Yeah, right. You're a fisherman's son."

I chuckled to myself. "You'd think so."

"You're getting very weird on me. What the hell is the matter with you?"

"We're both finding out stuff about each other maybe we'd rather not know."

Our headlights reflected off the remnants of plowed snow on the side of the road. A sign came up for Twenty-four and I took the exit northbound. The next sign put Boston thirty miles ahead of us.

"My father's name was not Hoffmann," I said. "It was Viljandi. He was an officer in the Soviet Army. But he wasn't Russian. He was Estonian. And my mother was a great ballerina from Ukraine."

"*Increible*," he muttered. "So how come you were raised on Bittern Island?"

I gave him an abridged version of events, as much as I could fit into the forty-five-minute ride to the Boston City line. Rolando listened and said nothing.

Twenty-four ended at U.S. One and the geography came back to me. I swung the pickup past the Blue Hills Reserve and saw the first signs for Logan Airport.

"Where does Ostros live?" I asked.

"East Boston. Near Putnam Square. Know where that is?"

I remembered. "Across the harbor."

Taking the Callahan Tunnel we crossed under Boston Inner Harbor to emerge on the East Boston Expressway.

"Are we going to just drop in on him? I don't think that's wise," Rolando warned.

"You're right. It's getting late. There are plenty of motels by the airport. We'll stay over and see the Don in the morning."

I detected a sigh of relief from my partner.

We selected a motel on no particular basis except it looked homey, no brash neon signs about lounge entertainment. We checked in, got a double room, and went to a diner recommended by the motel clerk.

Back in our room Rolando watched a medical drama on television and then the news. I read *Appointment in Samarra* by John O'Hara which I had grabbed from the shop before we left.

"We should call him," Rolando suggested. He switched off the TV.

"Not tonight," I said. It was past ten. "We will in the morning. You're right. We shouldn't simply drop by."

In the morning I asked Rolando for the Don's Boston phone number.

"Let me do it," Rolando insisted.

"Why?"

"There's a code we use in Boston when calling the Don. It lets him know we're safe. That we're not followed or on the run. If that were true, he'd send someone to meet us."

"Amazing."

"No. Business. Very serious business."

"He doesn't seem like that on Bittern Island. I mean I never detected any cloak and dagger, password stuff."

"Everything is different on the Island, different for everybody. And who are you to talk of daggers and passwords, Comrade Viljandi-Hoffmann?"

I would have laughed but the first thing he said struck some nerve of mine. Everything *is* different for everyone on Bittern Island.

"Make your call," I said.

How different would Don Ostros be here in Boston? Should we not have come? Wasn't I the one who told Rolando I had known Ostros too long to fear him?

Rolando spoke Spanish to whoever answered. A brief conversation went back and forth. Rolando wiped a bead of sweat from his forehead.

"*Señor Hoffmann esta aqui, Don Ostros. Nosotros vengamos tambien.*" He listened. More conversation. Then, "*Bueno, muchas gracias, Don Ostros.*" Rolando hung up the phone.

"He says he is glad we've come," Rolando said. "The Don looks forward to meeting us at his home. No need to stop. He'll have coffee and breakfast waiting."

"Always the host."

"Are you nervous?"

"I had a twinge there a minute ago. It passed. I'm okay with this."

"Did you bring a gun?"

"Of course not. I don't even own a gun. You know that."

"Good. That's what I told him."

Rolando drove when we left the motel. It was raining and traffic was heavy with morning commuters. Off the Expressway, we went through a commercial part of town. I heard a foghorn moan somewhere. It reminded me of home. We came up on apartment buildings and townhouses. Past Putnam Square the single houses appeared, their lights still lit in the dim morning.

Still the foghorn in the distance. Home. I was really going to see a friend. Someone I had known all my life. Everyone is different on Bittern Island. And different away from it?

We turned down a residential street of modest but immaculate homes. Tudors were interspersed with Capes and the occasional ranch. Driveways had Cadillacs, BMWs, Saabs, and Volvos.

My associate pulled into a driveway. We parked behind a black Lexus. I knew that Lexus had never been on Bittern Island.   Rolando shut the motor.

"Does he live alone?" I asked.

"Most of the time. He has a daughter but she's away at college a lot."

"Any staff?"

"Do you mean housekeepers and butlers or bodyguards and button men?"

"The man told me himself that drugs are his business. I imagine that requires protection."

I asked the question because Ostros had inquired of Rolando if I was armed.

"It's low key when the Don is in Boston," Rolando said. "This is more for his banking and private interests than his other operation."

We walked up a cobblestone path to the front door. The bell was answered by a plump woman with gray hair pulled back in a bun.

"*Buenas dias, Señora* Navarro," Rolando said courteously.

She smiled and with a hand motion invited us into the home of Don Ostros.

The woman led us down a hall past a parlor where a fire crackled in the hearth though the room had no occupants. Another intersecting hallway must have led to the kitchen. The smell of coffee and bacon drifted from there.

We came to a sitting room at the back of the house, which also had a fire burning in a fieldstone fireplace. The back wall was a phalanx of windows floor to ceiling. One could see the sloping yard running down and away and ending in some holly bushes, boxwoods, and yews. Rising from the snow-covered lawn were an ornate birdbath and feeder and several pieces of sculpture scattered here and there. Here the snow had not melted, despite the rain. The overall effect was one of serenity, a placid accord that was visible but indistinct.

The housekeeper bade us sit and, according to Rolando, for my Spanish is weak, offered coffee that we accepted. As she left another door, further to the right, opened and Ostros entered elegantly and quietly. Elegant because he was not as I had ever seen him before that moment. He wore black leather riding boots, mirror-shined, that came up to his knees. Deep burgundy corduroy pants came out of the boots to end at his waist secured with a wide belt of similar leather. A black turtleneck covered his broad chest and rolled up under his chin. A burgundy leather vest completed the wardrobe.

And I had never seen him so coifed and manicured. We Islanders are neither meticulous in our grooming nor genteel in our dress. Don Ostros, in his Boston study, appeared like a nineteenth-century squire who had been attended by menservants after a morning hunt. Every hair on his head lay flat and lacquered. As he crossed the room I caught a whiff of heavy, though not unpleasant, cologne. It was a blend of spices and humus and nuts and seemed appropriate for the gentleman outdoorsman at his leisure.

"My most welcome friends," Don Ostros greeted us. He extended me his hand and then to Rolando. "Please come sit down."

He led us to three chairs by the fire and we all sat.

Señora Navarro entered with a tray of coffee and Ostros instructed she take our coats and hang them someplace warm. We stood and passed her our jackets. She left with them as Ostros poured coffees.

"Breakfast will be ready shortly," Ostros said. "*Señora* Navarro will summon us. She takes excellent care of me."

"I apologize for the intrusion, Don Ostros," I said.

He stopped me with an upheld hand. "No guest in my home is ever an intrusion."

"I meant only the short notice."

We sipped our coffees. The brew was similar to what Rolando made at the shop.

"I am aware we have matters to discuss," Ostros said. "Perhaps this is the best time and place to do so. Bittern Island is, after all, a small island. I think that lends an unnecessary aura of intenseness to discourse. It was wise of you to come. And very much a decision your father would have made. That being the case, there is something you wish to ask me?"

I came to the point. "Why did you stash Martin's truck in my shed?"

Ostros sipped his coffee. I thought I heard Rolando choke on his own. Ostros regarded him for a second with a benign smile. Then his eyes came back to mine.

"Curious first question," he said. "Surely you would have rather asked why I killed Janus Martin. Is that not so?"

"I don't know that you did. Either way it's none of my business. What is my business is the Jeep in my barn. You admitted knowing about it so I assume you know how it got there."

"Correct."

"Why me?"

Don Ostros pondered this a moment. "Bittern Island is quite unique. Very suitable in some ways for certain requisites in my life. But it can be abruptly unsuitable in other aspects."

He elaborated. "There is of course the limited access. This feature works for me and against me depending on circumstance. It's more so the *punta* weather that irks me," he said, using the Spanish word for *whore*. "It turns on a man suddenly, unpredictably."

"We all knew the storm was coming."

Ostros laughed. "I'm an educated man, Karl. I have degrees from the University in my country. I do not admit that as explanation. The truth is I do not watch television, listen to the radio, nor even read newspapers. I let fate, or its *punta* counterpart, do as they please. I tend to my own business. Occasionally, my intentions and theirs collide. Sometimes it is for the best, sometimes not. But neither has imputations toward the other. We are separate, nonkindred forces."

"Your degrees must be in philosophy."

He laughed again, a humble laugh that made his head nod involuntarily.

"I am very much like the American mailman. Neither snow nor rain and so forth," his voice trailed off.

"And Martin's truck?"

Ostros collected himself a moment. Clearly he was fond of his own orations, but it was time   for business. The business of a murdered man's vehicle secreted on my property.

"When your father died he owed me a favor I had yet to collect, nor even sought to collect. But a debt is a debt. It has been written that he who dies pays all debts. That may be true. I've yet to learn it for myself."

"What did my father owe you?"

"That was between him and me. However, in a moment of extreme circumstance with few alternatives, I thought I might prevail upon the honor of the son in the sake of a respected memory. But so we are forthright with each other, I will tell you this. Before the harassment started, the Combine sent men to kill your father. They had singled him out as the ringleader. I found this out by accident. There was no time to warn Kurt. I acted swiftly. The emissaries of the Combine were dispatched, their bodies never found. Your father did not learn of it until much later."

"Don Ostros, I know you as a man of your word. If a debt has been fulfilled, I am grateful to have fulfilled it."

Don Ostros watched my eyes.

"And what now?" I asked. "I still have material evidence stowed in my shed."

Ostros nodded in sympathy. Then his eyes gleamed mischievously.

"It is fortuitous that you have come, my friends." He spread his arms to encompass Rolando and myself in a paternal gesture. "As we speak, the miscreant motorcar is being removed. The fortuity is that you both are not there should this diversion come to someone's attention. Denial is often as worthy as truth."

"How are you going to do that?" Rolando asked. It was his first utterance since greeting Ostros.

Ostros ignored the question. "I hear *Señora* Navarro coming. Breakfast must be ready."

CHAPTER EIGHTEEN

Hank Stodder took me to the Union Hall. By week's end I was working a renovation job. There was more than carpentry to learn in my trade.

"The job is spec'd out," Stodder said. "We're on eighteen."

We rode the freight elevator up. Hank gave me instructions on the ride. It was seven in the morning on a Thursday.

"We frame and sheetrock three offices today. Not two and not four. The pace is worked out by the shop steward and foreman. If you see a guy in shirt and tie, that's the GC, General Contractor. If he asks you anything say you don't know. Tell him to see the foreman. You with me?"

"Got it." It was a little embarrassing. Six other men rode with us.

"Who's the fucking virgin?" one of them asked Stodder. He wore a green hardhat.

"His name's Karl. It's his first day. I brought him on and he's a goddamn vet. Don't fuck with him."

Green hat backed down. "Okay by me."

A couple of guys mumbled their names and the youngest shook my hand. We jerked to a halt at eighteen.

"What do I do for tools?" I asked. All of the men wore tool belts for hammers, razor knives, snips, measures, and screw guns. My question made them laugh.

"You don't need tools yet. But buy a couple every payday because sooner or later you will," Stodder said.

"The only tool you'll need is your back," green hat said.

Off the elevator I was brusquely introduced to the shop steward and foreman. The steward was an Italian named Farino with a big honest grin. A man named Clark was foreman. I knew he did not grin much.

"Get this kid a tin," Clark barked. He ignored my attempt to shake hands.

A tin turned out to be a hardhat not made of tin but rubberized plastic. Farino got me one. While I adjusted the straps to fit, the steward made a note on a small pad.

"You owe me for that. See me payday," Farino said.

"Thanks."

"All right, ladies," Clark bellowed. "Cut the chit-chat and knock some rock."

It sounded like the Army. Rock was short for sheetrock. Rails were aluminum studs. Easy to cut with snips, pieces screwed together with fasteners driven by screw guns. By the end of the day I had not seen anyone use a hammer. Yet every man except me carried one. It was the symbol of the trade and carried with pride.

Green hat was right. I used three God-given tools all day, my hands and back. I was assigned to carry sheetrock and rails to crews erecting their quota.

"Coffee," Farino shouted. It was nine-thirty and we rode the lift down to a waiting coffee truck.

"Lunch," he called at noon.

Both times, I noticed, it was custom to stop immediately. Lay down the rail you were cutting. Withdraw your razor from the rock half-cut.

Some guys brought lunch in metal boxes. They sat up on eighteen or on the garden wall of a park across the street. The rest dispersed to local delis, pizzerias, and bars. There was a Blarney Stone Pub a block from the site. Stodder headed there with a couple of guys and I went along.

We ordered sandwiches at the steam table and sat at the bar. All the guys ordered beers, a few of them with shots of whiskey. I ordered a Coke.

"You sure this guy's a vet?" one carpenter challenged Stodder.

"Leave him alone. It's his first day." To me Stodder said, "It's okay to have a beer at lunch. But that's it. Clark and Farino don't want no lushes on the job."

He seemed oblivious to the two fellows doing shots of whiskey.

We were back on the job at exactly one o'clock.

Two-forty-five the crew started to clean up. Heavy tools were returned to gang boxes and locked up. Ladders were lashed to upright beams with chain and padlocked.

"Time," Farino bellowed at three on the dot.

The men started for the elevator.

"I thought we worked till four," I said to Stodder.

"We took a short lunch."

"No we didn't."

"Listen, Karl, we knocked out three rooms per crew. That's the deal."

I shut my mouth and rode down to the street. My back was aching and my hands were stiff and sore. Stodder invited me for a beer.

"I'll pass," I said. "I feel like an old man."

Stodder laughed and said he understood. He promised I would get use to it. On my way home I stopped in an Army-Navy store and bought a pair of work gloves. Back at the Y I took a shower as hot as I could stand. I felt tired and achy. But I felt good. I had a job.

That week I worked Thursday and Friday. Friday was payday. Right before lunch Clark handed me my two-day paycheck.

"There's a check-cashing truck downstairs during lunch," he said. "They charge a fee but you get cash."

I saw it was mostly the younger men who used the service. A van with a side window and armed guards was pulled to the curb. I passed it by and stuck my check in my wallet.

Across the street Farino sat on the park wall eating a hero from his pail. I told Stodder to go to lunch without me. He shrugged and led his buddies to the Blarney Stone. I crossed the street.

"What do I owe you for my tin?" I asked Farino.

"Fifteen."

I took cash from my wallet and handed it to him. He laid down the sandwich, took out his notepad and crossed off my name.

The job lasted eight weeks. In addition to sheetrocking offices, we hung drop ceilings. Other trades came and went as we progressed to the nineteenth and twentieth floors. I met plumbers, electricians, steamfitters, and painters. Each did his job according to the plan. The plan was not a blueprint, at least for us. The plan was what was agreed between the foreman and the steward.

With a paycheck coming in I found a studio apartment on East Fourteenth Street and moved my belongings from the Y. On Canal and Delancy Streets I bought used furniture, a television, plates, cups, glasses, and cutlery.

One weekend I took the train to Providence and retrieved a bunch of books from storage. I spent the whole Saturday afternoon rummaging through stuff I had packed and stowed away after father died. In a copy of Maugham's *Of Human Bondage* I found the photograph of my mother. I brought the photo back to New York.

I looked up Pete Franco and we tore up the Village on a Saturday night, hitting most of the blues clubs and getting too drunk to notice the ones we missed. Franco crashed at my place and in the morning we went to Chinatown for breakfast.

"Haven't seen you much. What do you do when you're not a hardhat?" Franco asked. He took a bite of egg roll waiting for my answer.

"I write a little." He was the first person I ever told.

"No shit? What do you write?"

I shrugged. "What I feel like. Stories, poetry, stuff like that." The admission embarrassed me.

"I'd like to see some."

"Why?"

"That's how a guy gets ideas. I've been writing songs myself. Once in a while I try one out on a gig. Nobody knows it's mine. I slip into it during a lull and see how it goes down."

"What's your point?"

"You and me. You shag some lines. I'll lay in a few licks. Maybe we got something."

"I don't write that kind of poetry."

"Ever try?"

I admitted I had not tried it like that. After breakfast Pete went and fetched his guitar. He was still at the Y. In my studio we drank beers, Franco smoked weed, and we played around with some lyrics and tunes. None of it was good but we agreed it was a start. Franco went home high and happy humming a tune he had composed.

In the morning I reported to the Union Hall. All the guys from the office renovation were there. We signed the log noting our seniority date and waited to hear our names called.

There was plenty of work and we all hooked up by the end of the day. It went on like that for two years. One spring I wound up with Costa Construction Company doing a job for Columbia University uptown. It was a huge contract and large crew. We worked in three different buildings at the same time. I was assigned to a detail in the School of Art.

Classes were in session, which meant we shared elevators, sidewalks, and local eateries with students. I liked working at the University. It was the first time I was ever on the campus of an institution of higher learning. Several weekends I came back to campus and explored the library.

Newer guys came on the job since I joined the Union. I was no longer the packmule. It was my chance to do real carpentry. Following Hank Stodder's advice I had accumulated all the basic tools over the years.

One day the electricians shut the power off while they connected a transformer. The elevators did not operate and we worked under box lights strung from leads hooked to a generator. Some of the guys thought it a pain in the ass but I found it kind of fun.

When I got back from lunch the juice was still off. Floor tiles were being laid in the lobby so I had to go around the back of the building and find a stairway to go up five floors. Halfway up, the passage was blocked by four men lugging a table saw coming down. I opened the fire door and stepped into the hallway out of their way.

"There's two more behind us," a worker informed me.

"No problem. I'll go around the other way."

Emerging from the stairwell I found myself on the fourth floor. It was a part of the building I did not recognize. Trying to get my bearings I started down the hallway. Coming up on my right was a large room with double wood doors. The doors had glass in the top half. I peered into the room.

Forming a large circle was a group of easels. Each easel had a canvas secured in clamps and covered with a paint-spattered cloth. I pushed the door open a crack. The air inside smelled of oil and paint. I had an urge to go in and look around. Better not, I thought. I was already late from lunch owing to the detour. The Costa foreman was strict. He would dock my pay for sure.

I was about to release the door when something stopped me. From out of sight within the room, music started to play. It was a single violin commencing a concerto. A young man walked to the center of the room clad in sweatshirt and sweatpants. He stood in the middle of the easels. Raising his arms he stretched toward the ceiling then doubled over to touch his toes. Erect again, he removed his shirt to reveal a thickly muscled chest and broad shoulders. The man's smooth skin was hairless and gleamed in the auxiliary lighting as if he had smeared on body oil.

Turning to be on my way I was stopped again when a woman's form came between me and the half-naked man. She had her back to me but I saw her reach out and uncover the canvas on the easel before her. In her left hand was a pallet dotted with globs of paint.

Beyond her I saw the model strike his pose. One arm was up with his hand behind his head, elbow thrust forward. The other arm was stretched straight out as if reaching for something, his long fingers pointing. Then I realized his pants were gone. He was naked in the stone-like depiction of a god.

I looked at the woman. Her head nodded with the music as she mixed paint on her palette. The scene captured me. The chalky smell of paint and linseed oil, the teasing violin, the inadequate lighting that produced long shadows mesmerized me into staring at her back and up her neck where lustrous waves of reddish blond hair fell forward on her shoulders as she bowed to her work blending the colors.

She felt my stare. Slowly, deliberately, and without a hint of surprise, she turned. Wide green eyes that seemed to glisten in the soft light regarded me with what I could only surmise was amusement.

"Are you coming in?" she asked.

I opened the door wider, speechless and gawky.

"I reserved the studio for the afternoon." Her eyes dropped to my tool belt. "You don't have to work in here. Do you? Are you bringing back the lights?"

"No, no," I stammered. "I'm lost. Can't seem to find my way. Don't know where…"

She laughed softly, sincerely amazed at my predicament.

"That's all right. You sound like ninety-five percent of the student body. Everybody here is searching."

"I'm sorry I disturbed you." I reached up and removed my hardhat out of courtesy.

"A polite construction worker. I thought there had to be one."

"Go back to your work. I'll find my way."

The model coughed behind her. We looked at him and back at each other.

"Does this bother you?" she asked coyly.

"What?"

She laughed again. "A naked man in the room. I'll bet you don't see that in your line of work."

"The Union frowns on it. And of course there are the safety issues."

The model yawned loudly. We did not look at him this time.

"Is that Vivaldi?" I asked, jerking my head toward the source of the music.

"I'm impressed. Do you like it?"

I nodded.

"What else do you like?"

"All kinds of music: opera, jazz, blues, Motown. But I always come back to classical."

She stepped aside revealing the canvas on her easel.

"How about art? Do you like it?" She pointed a brush at her painting.

"Very good, in a Fauvist sort of way. Reminds me of the Blue Rose group." They were Russian artists in the early twentieth century that experimented with primitivist style.

"You certainly are the Renaissance man, Mister?" she leapt for my name.

"Hoffmann. Karl Hoffmann."

"Judith. Judith Valenti. And if you want to stay on my good side, don't call me Judy."

"I'd like to call you Judith," I summoned courage to say. "I'd like to call you Judith very soon."

Being late I was docked an hour's pay. Small price for the phone number in my pocket.

CHAPTER NINETEEN

Trusting Don Ostros seemed the best option. He said the Jeep would be gone and I believed him. We ate a breakfast of fruits, pancakes, and bacon   in the dining room of his Boston home. Paintings lined the walls, mostly modern, but one was of a soldier with sash and sword of an earlier century. When the meal was over the Don lit a slender cigar and looked out the window at the yard.

"Dreary weather," he said. "Sometimes I think this winter will never end. It reminds me of a winter in my youth. My father hid us in the mountains when troops came. They stayed in our village the whole winter. We lived in the mountains. Food was scarce and it was very cold. They sent patrols to find us. Many times we could not light a fire for fear the soldiers would see smoke. My baby sister died. She was four years old. We buried her up there in the mountains."

Ostros's voice grew faint telling his story. Rolando and I sat quietly listening.

Ostros coughed to clear his throat or banish the memory. His eyes lingered on the window where he had seen the past come back like mist across the snow.

His reflection confused me since earlier he discounted weather as being no concern to him.

"Why did you kill Janus Martin?" I asked abruptly. I had promised myself I would not ask.

"I never said I did." He turned from the window to me. "No, my friend. My years as a *pistolero* are long gone. Now it is all business. Martin proved unbusinesslike and dishonorable."

Roland excused himself to use the bathroom. I doubt he needed to go. He was uncomfortable hearing Ostros talk of such things. There were things a man need not know. For myself, it did not matter.

"Why the fish plant?" I asked Ostros. "Is that part of your business too?"

"It is deserted and convenient. I have run many boats through Jacob's Cove. One too many, I would suppose."

"Your boatmen must be good. I've never heard of anyone seeing a craft at the plant since it closed."

"They're good if they want to stay alive. Many people want to interrupt my business."

"Like Colonel Devon?"

"Among others. In truth, the police are the least of my concerns."

A dog started to bark wildly. Ostros cocked his head toward the sound. He stood up.

"Rolando has wandered. I must go quiet the dog. He's trained to deal rudely with people he is not expecting."

Ostros left the room unhurriedly. He was a man in control of his environment save for the weather that he professed to ignore but which had depressed him. In his absence I stared out at his snow-covered lawn with its odd statuary. The piece closest was a male and female pair facing each other at the top. From the necks down the bodies twined and blended until there was only one form secured to the base. It could have been alabaster. The base was green marble. Raindrops struck the faces, rolled across their cheeks, and fell to the marble like tears. No passion was in the hewn faces, nor joy or grief. Their eyes were carved wide open as if in abandon or disbelief. If the artist attempted love, he neither felt it nor showed it. Were tragedy the motif, he could not fathom it. The couple stared at each other wide-eyed, clinging, because there was nothing else.

Rolando entered followed by Ostros.

"He's harmless once he gets to know you," Ostros assured Rolando. "You should see him in a thunderstorm. He whimpers like a baby."

Ostros offered more coffee and we accepted. I fetched my cup and returned to the window. Another sculpture, farther off, drew my attention. It was the winged body of a bird but the face of an animal, a panther or leopard. The stone was gray with deep dark furrows where the chisel had bit it. It was mounted on a steel pillar. The wings were open and full as if having glided into perch but hesitant about staying.

"What do you think of my garden?" Ostros asked me. "You should see it in the spring when the flowers start to bloom."

"I can't imagine it in any other landscape than the way it appears right now."

Don Ostros joined me at the window.

"It's like one huge canvas with tiny details here and there with excruciating exactness," I said. "It reminds me of the beach in winter with one piece of jagged driftwood exposed at low tide."

"You have a poet's eye."

"No, I don't. It's there and that's how it came to mind."

"All the more reason you should see it in its varied seasons."

"That won't happen, Don Ostros. We both know it."

Ostros put his hand on my shoulder in a paternal gesture. I felt nothing.

"Since the matter of the Jeep is resolved," I said, "there is no reason for us to further intrude. Thank you for your hospitality."

Ostros let his hand fall off my shoulder. I turned and put my cup on the table. Rolando came to his feet.

"When will you return to Bittern Island?" I asked Ostros.

"A day or two, three at most. I have some business here in town."

"Take care of yourself. There will be others."

"I have come to expect that in my life."

"All these years, there are still nights you can't light a fire on the hill. Is it worth it?"

"Sometimes, my friend. I'm sure you'll agree that life is only a sum of sometimes."

I nodded not to agree but because it was true.

Rolando and I took leave. I looked back just once as we followed the housekeeper. Ostros was smoking his cigar and staring out at his lawn. His face was impassive, stoical. A piece of stone hammered and shaped into something no artist cared to explain. I could still not imagine the springtime.

I backed the pickup out of the driveway.

"That was weird," Rolando said. "I've never seen him like that."

"Like what?"

"You and him talking that crazy shit. Do you believe that stuff about your father owing him a favor?"

"It doesn't make a difference. The matter is concluded to his satisfaction and mine."

Rolando was still restless. He squirmed and fidgeted in his seat. We were on the highway before he spoke again.

"Who are the others you mentioned?" he asked.

"Friends or associates of Janus Martin. When they find out he's dead, they will come. They will come to kill Don Ostros."

"He should stay in Boston."

"He won't."

"I suppose not."

"He may expect your support." In some capacity, Rolando worked for Don Ostros. I just was not sure how exactly.

"He'll have it. What about you?"

"The Don and I are even. He said as much himself. He will not expect me to fight his battles with him. He won't even ask."

"Lucky you."

It was dark when we caught the ferry home. Esperansa heard the truck pull up and opened the front door of their home. She stood in the glow of the light behind her and waited for him.

"Will you check the shed?" Rolando asked.

"No. It's gone."

Esperansa waved at me and I waved back. She wrapped her arm around Rolando and led him into the house. I put the truck in gear and drove over to

Main Street. The rain had stopped. A quarter moon was high and the stars were clear and bright. I parked near the Sea Witch and went into the tavern.

It was midnight but a half dozen men hung on drinking. Archie Bealer was at the near end of the bar, Gunner Hogan at the far end. Bealer was drunk and did not notice me pass him. Gunner said nothing until I took the stool next to his own.

"Any problems at the shop?" I asked.

"Naw. Business as usual, rented a rug shampooer to Oscar and a power washer to Lenny," he said, naming two Islanders.

"Everybody is cleaning up from the storm. A little mess is good for business."

Not a curious man by nature, Gunner never asked about my trip to Boston. I sipped a whiskey letting the liquor warm my damp bones.

"Any more police around?" I asked. I signaled Sweeney to give Gunner one on me.

"Just that drunk at the end of the bar." He jerked a thumb at Bealer. "If the killer ain't at the bottom of a bottle, he'll never find him."

"I guess things are back to normal."

"Yeah. Whatever the hell that is."

"Come on. I'll give you a lift home."

"You go on. I'm fine for a while. My car's out back."

"Thanks for minding the store."

Gunner waved it off as nothing. I rose to go. Bealer's head was on his arm and he was sleeping. According to routine, his wife would be by to guide him home.

I drove out of Gracetown and up, over, and down the ridge to Mariners Path. A van passed me going the other way toward Grace. I did not recognize the vehicle which held two men behind the windshield briefly captured in my headlights. They looked straight ahead ignoring me.

Unattended for two days, my house was cold. I set fires in the kitchen and the hearth in the big room. As the heat rose I shed most of my clothes, took a blanket from my reading chair and curled up on the floor in front of the hearth.

The fire danced and crackled and its glow was warm on my face. Very shortly I fell asleep and did not move until morning.

Awake before sunrise I poked and fed the fires and opened the kitchen door to look out toward the sea. The rain and melting snow had cut deep rivulets into the hills. Stars were still out. I pulled on my peacoat buttoning it to my throat. Stepping across the porch I went down the steps and crunched into the sand.

Behind me I smelled the woodsmoke from my fires. In front I smelled the sea. I walked toward the gap in the dunes, a shallow valley that rose and divided the two mounds of sand. The predawn was clear and windless. Climbing the gap I came to stand at the crest and saw the ocean spread out on the other side. In the stillness the breakers seemed as solid objects being moved despite themselves. When they curled and crashed there was no spray, only roiling foam that rolled up the shoreline unfolding as a flat glistening mirror of the sky.

In the east the faint glow of morning caused a dim halo on the horizon. At first it was round and tight; I watched it slowly broaden and flatten, the light stretched to the extreme of my vision. In that same direction I spied a low laden freighter churning north against the backdrop of yellow and gold.

My eyes dropped to the beach spread before me. An old faded marker buoy still dangling a hank of shredded net had washed ashore in the night. Two gulls pecked and poked the fibers determined one last scrap of bounty came ashore with it. After a moment they cawed and flapped their wings in disappointment. They did not leave. What prize there was, was theirs.

A rustling commenced in the grass to my right. Careful not to move I turned only my head in its direction. A pair of bitterns sauntered on the top of the dune beside me. They waddled in concentric circles on the crown of the dune. In summer they would move further inland to the marshes and ponds. Their foraging is not as indiscriminate as the gulls. Bitterns do not eat dead things or the scraps of men. They do not beg. They do not harass. Unlike the seagulls, they are never separate from their environment. They blend in color and motion into grass.

One of the pair spotted me and stopped stock-still. Its mate, sensing the change, did the same. Their slender necks went erect and straight. The tiny heads were like the seeded bulb of a reed. In the absence of wind they remained still.

I turned away from them and started down to the beach. The arc of sun crept over the horizon. I put my back to it and walked west. A few hundred yards along was a small inlet protected on each side by bluffs of rock and sand. Water through the inlet fed the salt marshes at the base of the Island's ridgeline. A path followed its course near where I stood. As a boy I used to come here summers and catch snappers by the pailful with only a small hook soldered to a silver spoon-like lure. Papa would scale and gut them and fry them in a pan. They were sweet and meaty and as much fun to eat as they were to catch.

Once I showed Judith how to catch them. She had never fished before in her life. We caught dozens between us and she was giddy with our success. I cleaned them right here on the beach. We cooked them on an open fire using sticks of driftwood to hold them above the flames. We ate them with our fingers, pulling back the crisp skin to expose the meat along the spine. Afterwards we bathed naked in the surf.

The trail widened where I did not expect it. The grass to either side was flat and mashed into the sand. I knelt on one knee to see why this happened. Running my hand over the matted reeds I felt the perfect pattern of a tire tread. To the other side was the same thing. I followed it a ways.

Where the marshland began water from the inlet fanned out to soak the swale in all directions. The path veered sharply to the right to rim the marsh and head up through the dunes to the road. I climbed the nearest dune to see the sun completely free of the horizon and rising into a cloudless sky.

On the crown of the hill I turned all the way around surveying the terrain. In the distance I could see my house with smoke curling from the two chimneys. All the birds were awake, legions of seagulls scouring the beach for clams and crabs, fussing and cawing all the while.

My vantage point was quiet, too quiet. I could hear water being flushed into the marsh with the exact pulse of the distant surf. But no birds were in proximity. I scanned the dunes around me.

One of the dunes seemed odd indeed. Misshapen by a wind unseen and unnatural, it appeared a bald hump forced between two sister dunes that were higher, rounder, and green-bearded with grass. I moved down and toward it.

The topography eased me into a gully where tire tracks were clearly visible in the sand. They ended abruptly at the bastardized dune. Someone had tried to sweep the tracks away by kicking sand. It must have been too dark, or they had been in a hurry.

Sinking to both knees I thrust my hand into the loosely piled sand of the dune. I moved my arm around like someone trying to catch a fish in an aquarium. But there was no fish. I scraped and then grabbed hold of a piece of cold metal. With my other hand I started clearing away the sand while never letting go of the object with my firsthand.

It was a flat piece of black metal that curled in at the end. With both hands I cleared away scoops of sand to reveal what I already knew was under the makeshift dune. It was a license plate in a housing that had a Jeep logo across the top.

Janus Martin's Jeep was no longer in my shed. Ostros must have reasoned the cops would check all the ferries to the mainland. There was not much else he could do and still keep his promise to me.

I pulled the sand back over the bumper and got to my feet. On the way out of the inlet I did a better job than my predecessors of eradicating the tire marks.

CHAPTER TWENTY

"Where are we going?" Judith Valenti asked. It was our first date.

"Downtown. A friend of mine is playing a club."

"We are downtown. How much lower are you taking me?"

Her apartment was on Charlton Street where the West Village butted Soho.

"I mean musically downtown. My buddy's in a blues band in the East Village."

"You had to reach for that one," she teased.

I was standing outside her studio door and only caught a glimpse of the apartment before she pulled the door closed behind her. The room seemed sparse of furniture and her easel was set up in the middle of the space. We walked up to Houston Street and I hailed a taxi.

"Is your friend a construction worker?" Judith asked.

"No, music is the only thing he's got going. But he's really good."

The cab pulled out and weaved in the supper and club traffic.

"Known this bluesman long?" she asked.

"A couple of years. We came to New York the same time. Pete's from Louisiana. Wait until you hear him. He's the real thing."

Judith turned sideways to face me. Her hair hung loose to her shoulders. She wore a black sweater, blue jeans, and short black boots. Except for two tiny diamonds, one in each ear, she wore no jewelry. Her face was devoid of makeup.

"Got to love New York City," she said. "Where else would a Union carpenter hook up with a musician from the bayou? God, this is a great town. That's why I came."

"You're not from New York?"

"The State? Yes. But not the City. I'm originally from Binghamton. But we're not talking about that now. We're talking about you and Pete the bluesman."

Before we reached the club I had time to explain how Pete Franco and I met at the YMCA. He was up from New Orleans and I recently discharged from the service.

"Which branch?" she interrupted.

"Army."

"Vietnam?" It was almost a whisper.

"I missed the war. I spent the whole time doing pretty much what I do now, construction. I was with the Corps of Engineers."

"Fascinating. Where did you work?"

"Anywhere. Pulled jobs in Korea, Germany, a couple of stateside assignments. In the Army you go where they send you. It's not a question of choice and it is not up for discussion."

The cabbie nosed up to the curb and stopped with a jolt. Involuntarily I put my arm out across Judith's body to keep her from being pitched forward. She smiled.

"I'm used to New York cabs," she said. "But, thanks."

The nightclub was called Pot Belly's and it had a miniature stove over the door. A crowd milled about the entrance. The scent of reefer was in the air. I led Judith up to the bouncer at the door.

Fumbling in my wallet I produced a card Pete Franco had given me when I told him about my date. I surrendered it to the bouncer.

"We're friends of Pete Franco in the band. He said to show you this."

The bouncer took a step backward into the light afforded by a blinking beer advertisement. He scrutinized the card and handed it back to me.

"Go on in," he ordered curtly.

I held open the door with its placard demanding a fifteen-dollar cover charge. Judith went through and I followed.

"That was easy," she said with a laugh.

"In this town it's who you know."

Judith reached for my hand.

A waiter came forward and I presented the card. He recognized its worth without having to take it. Snaking through tables the waiter led us to one not six feet from the stage.

Judith ordered a glass of red wine from the waiter, while I requested a beer. Taped music was playing in the background. A Marshall Tucker tune ended and a Charlie Daniel's began. The place was trying to capture the atmosphere of the New South.

"How do you like the place?" I asked.

"It's charming."

"Not so loud. Charming is not a word we associate with blues."

"My mistake." Then, in a mock Scarlett O'Hara accent, she added, "But, sir. My Southern vocabulary is very limited. How's a belle to learn when all you boys are off to your dreadful war with the Yankees?"

That cracked me up. I was still laughing when our waiter returned with the drinks. He took small menus from his pocket and laid one in front of each of us.

"Order before the show and we serve between sets," he said. "There's no food during the show, only drinks."

I thanked him and he went to the next table.

"Are you hungry?" I asked Judith.

"I could do with a little something."

"Well don't be shy. I haven't eaten all day. Let's see what they have."

The menu went with the theme. It featured gumbo, crawdads, catfish, and things I did not recognize.

"Do you know what some of this is?" I asked Judith.

"I know what shrimp is, but that's about all."

"Same for me. Sorry. I didn't know what the cuisine was going to be."

"Don't be sorry. We're here. We're having fun. Let's be adventurous."

It was my turn to go into the act. It was a very poor Clark Gable.

"Well I declare, Miss Valenti. Where do you get your impetuous nature?"

"Is it unbecoming a lady?" she asked in her O'Hara tone.

"It's charming," I said in my own voice.

"Remember your blues, Mr. Hoffmann."

"But I'm not blue. I'm not blue at all."

We ordered gumbo and crawdads. The waiter brought another round of drinks before the show. The lighting, subdued, dimmed almost to black. A voice came over the sound system.

"Good evening, ladies and gentlemen. Pot Belly is proud to present a new blues band in its third New York appearance. The *Village Voice* has called them the freshest thing to come to blues since B.B. King. Let's give a warm Pot Belly welcome to Cajun Moon."

Spotlights illuminated the stage. The room broke into applause. Five men, Pete Franco one of them, entered from stage right. The largest of them, a portly Black man dressed all in black and wearing sunglasses, walked behind the piano on stage and sat down. A second man, also Black with a chiseled goatee but short and wiry, carried a saxophone and took up a position behind one of three microphones. A white drummer, also bearded with sunglasses, mounted a stool behind his skins. Franco and another white man carried guitars and manned the remaining two mics.

As the room quieted the piano player stroked some chords. The rest of the band picked them up. The second guitarist standing at the middle microphone started to sing. He had a voice like the sound of broken glass shook in a tin pail. Franco joined in for the chorus ending each refrain. Franco's clearer, lighter voice was the perfect harmonic counterpart to the lead's rasp.

The crowd warmed to Cajun Moon. Succeeding numbers brought louder applause. Finally people stomped their feet and pounded tabletops.

I looked over at Judith frequently. From her expression I could tell she was enjoying the show. Once she caught me looking. She smiled, reached across the table and took both my hands in her own. Several times she squeezed my fingers in tempo with the music. I felt my body get warm.

When the set was over the applause shook the place. The boys in the band nodded, waved, and left the stage.

"That was amazing," Judith said breathlessly.

"Yeah? You like blues?"

"I never heard it like that before. They're great. Which one is your friend?"

"Second guitar. The one with the poor excuse for a beard. But you haven't heard it all yet. The first set is only a warm-up." That is what Franco had always told me. I was trying to impress Miss Valenti. "When the crowd is into it and the boys have had a few whiskies and they're sweating like choirboys in church on a Sunday in July, things start to happen."

Our waiter brought the food. It consisted of steaming bowls of gumbo and a platter of Cajun fried crawdads around a dish of hot sauce. We attacked the food. It was tangy and spicy, burning our lips and mouths. I signaled for more wine and beer. We spoke little and ate lots. Our empty dishes were cleared right before the second set.

The band sank into their own groove, as Pete Franco would say. On one number the piano player kicked over his bench, stood hunched over his keyboard pounding and singing at the top of his lungs without benefit of a microphone. When he finished we thought he would collapse. Instead he wiped his face with a towel, retrieved his bench and sat like Buddha soaking in applause.

Pete Franco took his microphone and walked to center stage.

"Thank you, thank you," he repeated until the noise subsided. He introduced himself and the other members of Cajun Moon, noting where each musician was from originally. The announcement that Franco was Cajun brought the loudest acknowledgement. He waved off the attention.

"We'd like to do a new number for you tonight," Franco said. He paused and slid the metal slide onto his pinky. "The melody was written by myself. And the lyrics were written by a poet friend of mine named Karl Hoffmann."

I almost spit out the beer in my mouth. Judith was looking at me in astonishment. She was about to say something but Pete was speaking again.

"Karl's here tonight." He pointed at me. "That's him up front. Give us a wave, Karl."

My arm felt like lead. I raised it limply above my head. It brought applause from the patrons. My falling arm would have slammed the table but Judith caught it in her hands.

"Karl, you never said…" she started.

"I didn't know," I stammered. "We were fooling around. That's all."

There was no time to say more. Franco replaced his mic in the stand. The saxophonist blew a flat riff and Franco began to sing.

"There's an island in my heart
from where all my journeys start…"

I barely recognized my words. Pete Franco bent and strained them breathing emotion into the couplet. Judith was squeezing my hands so tight blood stopped flowing. Words and scenes were swimming in my head. Franco and I were at my apartment. Franco was stoned and doing progressions on his guitar. I was drunk myself. We had been fumbling away a Sunday afternoon. Suddenly I said, "There's an island in my heart." Franco snapped alert.

"Shit. That's good," he slurred. "Go with it. Work with it."

With a rush I came back to Pot Belly's as the last chorus hung in the air. People were clapping and cheering. Judith leaned across the table and kissed me lightly on the lips. I would have reached for her but she sank back in her chair. I will never forget the way she looked at me. From behind someone clapped me on the shoulder. I did not even turn around. Judith and I were staring at each other, her shaking her head back and forth.

The set ended, the guys left the stage, and the lights came up.

"Tell me," Judith said. "What other secrets am I in store for with you?"

"That's not fair. I had no idea Pete was going to do that. Hell. I'd forgotten about that song until tonight."

"He called you a poet. Is that true?"

"If it is, he's the only one that knows it. It's not like I've published anything. I write for myself."

"Not any longer."

The final set brought the tempo down a bit. The band was exhausted; the audience was drained. I moved my chair around the table to sit next to Judith. My arm found its way up and around her shoulder. She leaned into me and I held tighter. I could smell her hair and her skin. Gone were the club's aromas of booze, pot, tobacco, and cooking grease. She smelled like a deep moonless night. She smelled like a keen, crisp winter morning.

Pete Franco sauntered over to our table as most of the patrons started to leave. He carried three glasses and a bottle of Jim Beam.

"It's like sex," he said. The bottle and glasses were deposited on our table and he pulled up a chair. "God, I'm spent."

"Judith, this is Pete Franco," I introduced.

"Your band is really great," Judith told Franco.

Franco smiled at her, said nothing, and uncapped the bourbon.

"Don't think he's rude," I said to Judith. "He's always like this after a show."

Ignoring both of us, Franco poured three shots of whiskey. He slid one toward my date and one at me. He lifted his own in toast. Out came his deepest Cajun accent.

"Welcome to the blues, Miss Judith."

Judith and I lifted our glasses. We all touched rims. Franco and I drank ours down. Judith sipped a little of hers off the top. Franco replenished his and mine while she set her glass down unfinished.

"I'm sorry," she said. "I don't drink much whiskey."

"Where I come from a beautiful woman never has to apologize," Franco said. His act was thick.

That made me think of a way to change the subject.

"Why did you do our song without telling me?"

He took his eyes off Judith and looked at me with a wry smile. "Because, my Yankee friend, you would have insisted that we not do it. And as your friend I would have had to honor your wishes. It seemed simpler to just do it. Anyway, everybody loved it." He turned back to Judith. "Didn't they, Miss Judith?"

"They sure did. Have you set any more of Karl's poetry to music?"

"We have one or two in the works. But don't tell Karl that. It makes him jumpy, as you have just observed for yourself."

"Which ones?" I demanded.

Judith laughed as I fell headlong into Franco's trap.

He addressed her again. "If your boyfriend would come to rehearsal once in a while like I ask, it would probably help relieve his anxiety. He's the most repressed individual I know. Perhaps he might come if you asked him?"

"I'll make a point of it." No reaction to Pete classifying me as her boyfriend.

"Oh, Christ," I muttered.

"I, on the other hand," Franco told Judith, "rely on substances designed for such relief."

To accentuate his point, he downed his drink. Then he rose from his seat.

"You must excuse me while I rejoin my associates. It has been a pleasure to make your acquaintance, Miss Judith."

I thought he might kiss her hand. He did not.

Franco picked up the bottle of Jim Beam and his glass, bowed and then left for backstage.

"He is quite a character," Judith said.

"Pete was laying it on heavy. He doesn't have so much down home in him as he would want to impress on you."

"I never said I was impressed. Well, maybe by his talent. The rest of him is merely amusing."

"And me? Do I impress or amuse you?"

"A little of both. A lot remains to be seen."

I signaled for the check and paid our bill. Outside we walked two blocks. Several times, I tried to get her talking about her painting but she refused to be engaged on the subject. That was frustrating.

"If you won't talk about your art, how can you ask about my writing?"

"Because that came as a surprise. A very pleasant surprise. I imagine you're full of surprises and secrets."

We stopped on the corner and I summoned the only cab in sight. In the back seat I kissed Judith and she responded. Holding each other we kissed long and deep.

Too soon we were at the door to her apartment building.

"I'm not going to invite you in," she said. "Not yet. Despite what you might believe about city girls, it isn't time yet."

"One last kiss then?"

"One for good night. We both know it won't be our last."

CHAPTER TWENTY-ONE

"Did you check the shed?" Rolando asked. I had just arrived at the shop and it was the first words out of his mouth.

"No. Don Ostros is a man of his word."

"I believe that, but you better hope so all the same."

"What makes you say that?" Rolando's lack of confidence surprised me.

"The cops are back. I saw them come off the ferry this morning."

"Colonel Devon?"

"Devon was one of them. He has some troopers with him. That's not all. There's a couple of guys in suits and topcoats with Devon. You know the type. Clean-shaven, short hair, wearing sunglasses. Devon was clucking like he was trying to sell them a used car."

"What's your guess?"

"*Federales.*" He said it as if it was a curse. "Could be FBI or DEA."

"It appears Colonel Devon has made a connection between Martin and Don Ostros."

"Or he has run out of options and is fishing,"

"Maybe you should have stayed on the mainland. I'm surprised Don Ostros didn't warn you."

"How would he know? Who would have thought a proud *hombre* like Devon would bring in the *federales*?"

"Perhaps it was no longer his call. It's like the Army. Every time a project stalls the authority gets kicked up the chain of command. The brass in the State Police is not likely to let this murder roll out with the tide. The way you say Devon was fretting over our guests he must have been taken to task by his superiors. The case is probably out of his hands."

"I wish Bealer never found that body," Rolando said. "That old rummy couldn't catch a jaywalker if he bumped into one crossing Main Street. But no. He has to stumble on a murder. If he hadn't, that body would be at sea right now, sucked out with the remnants of the fish plant."

"The sea eventually gives back most of what it takes. It was only a matter of time."

"They wouldn't be here if a soggy, crab-chewed Martin had washed up on Block Island or Narragansett. This whole thing is bad luck. Bad luck for you, for me, and bad luck for Don Ostros."

"Ah," I said. "The Evil One weaving his net of maladies and misfortunes."

Rolando executed a self-blessing and kissed his finger.

"Don't waste your time or your faith," I said.

Rolando looked at me in accusation. "Stop it. What do you think you're saying?"

"This evil is in men, not the spirits, the air or the sea. No ghost killed Janus Martin. Don Ostros had him murdered. We both know that. He must live with that, as we must also, and deal with what it brings. Although I must admit Ostros is more experienced in how to handle it than we are. You should have stayed on the mainland. Ostros did."

"Don Ostros hides from no man."

"There will be no fires on the hill tonight, my friend. The soldiers have occupied the town."

Rolando crossed himself again and this time I made no comment. Let him use what he has, I thought. We all do.

Our first customer was Oscar returning the rug shampooer Gunner rented in my absence. Oscar was the Island's motor mechanic. With few cars around, his livelihood consisted mainly of boat engine repairs. His skill was considerable and he made a good living by Island standards. Oscar had a wife and two sons. The oldest attended college on the mainland, which was a source of pride to Oscar and his wife.

Oscar put the implement on the counter.

"How did it work?" I asked him.

"Did a fine job, Karl. My wife was sure we'd need new rugs. I told her it was only water stains. She didn't believe me." He slapped the machine. "A few hours with this and they look like new. Good thing too. We have a tuition payment coming up. Not the time to spring for new rugs."

"How's Bobby doing?" The college boy had painted my sheds a few summers back to earn money. He was a good kid.

"Made dean's list. Always knew he was a smart one. Gets it from his mother. She had him reading his Bible by the time he was three."

"What's he studying?"

"Accounting. He won't be scraping grease from under his nails when he comes home from work."

"And Freddie?" I asked after his younger son.

"Decent kid. Maybe too much like his old man. Can fix about anything but can't read a street sign unless you give him a hint. Shame. Be an Islander his whole life I imagine."

"An honest living is an honest living. Nothing to be ashamed of there. We all got our ways and talents."

"They say God blesses a working man. He better. Freddie needs it."

Oscar went on his way.

I checked the shampooer. A born mechanic, Oscar had oiled the brush mounts and brake cable. The man had a deep reverence for tools. Rolando returned it to the shed.

Right before lunchtime Rolando asked for a few hours off. He had errands to run for his wife. He asked if he could borrow the pickup.

"I think we've seen the only customer of the day," I said. "Go ahead."

"Need anything from town?"

"Just let me know if you hear anything about our visitors."

Not long afterward I heard Gunner Hogan's old station wagon chug up and stop out front. He came through the door with uncharacteristic alacrity. A little bounce was detectable in his stunted step.

"The shit is flying now," he said in greeting.

"You own stock in fertilizer or something?"

"I don't believe in stocks or the stock market. That's one big swindle. If I own something, I own it. I don't walk around with a piece of paper that claims I own a piece of something a thousand miles away I've never seen. No, sir. If I own something I want to be able to eat it, smoke it, drive it, sleep on it, or have some place to store it. Anything else is just fancy paperwork."

"You're in a loquacious mood today."

"Loquacious is it? I would bet there's not two men on this Island knows what loquacious means."

"Do you know?"

"Of course I do."

"Then I win by default."

Gunner laughed, went to the stove, and helped himself to coffee. I did not say anything, waiting for him to come forth with whatever had made his day. Instead of his customary stool, Gunner walked over to the counter across from me and leaned on it with one bent arm. In close proximity I could smell the ever-present whiskey on his breath though he appeared not the slightest drunk.

"The commissars have arrived from Moscow," he said.

I did not react to the remark. Gunner Hogan knew nothing about my true past. His reference was self-serving from bitter experience. When America pulled out of Vietnam he claimed our government had sold out. That they were as bad and corrupt as the communists of the USSR, China, and Hanoi. His faith in government at all was shattered. All governments to him were fascist or communist and there was really, in his estimation, no difference. He had buried too many of his buddies and lost too much of himself for any of us to argue with him about it. Gunner had paid for the right to his opinion.

"Commissars, is it?"

"KGB, CIA, DEA, it's the alphabet soup of oppression. Notice how they've always got suits and sunglasses?"

"So which is it? KGB or CIA?"

"It's the drug snoops."

He took a swig of coffee, placed the mug on the counter and fumbled in his pack for his pipe and tobacco.

"What makes you so sure?" Their agents wore no insignia, I was certain.

"I saw the ferry come in. Saw them and the State Troopers come off. You know who came off last?"

"Can't imagine. Who?"

"Captain Rudy. That's who."

Captain Rudy Ballinger was senior skipper of the ferryboat service. Been making the crossing for over thirty-five years. Everyone on Bittern Island knew Captain Rudy even though he lived on the mainland.

Gunner filled his pipe and set a match to it. I had to wait until it smoldered to his satisfaction.

"How did Captain Rudy figure out they were Drug Enforcement agents? And for that matter, why tell you?" I asked.

"When Cap Rudy was berthed he made right for the General Store to buy his cigars for the home crossing. Mrs. Ballinger has been nagging him to cut down on his smoking. Unfortunately for her, Lawler carries his brand of cigars at the store. The old Cap's got his own private smuggling operation going on, so to speak. Strictly for his personal consumption out of eye and sniff of his wife." Gunner was stretching the story and very amused with himself.

"So she put the DEA on to him?"

"I never said that. Will you let me tell the story?"

"Sorry, Gunner. Go on when you're ready."

To emphasize his control of the narrative, Gunner took a slow sip of coffee and tamped his pipe.

"Anyways, I was a bit low on medicine myself." He rapped his flask through his coat. "So I walked along with him down to the store. As we walked I asked him who the strangers were on his boat."

"How would he know they were DEA?"

"There you go again. I'm getting to it. Captain Rudy is a good and responsible man." I nodded in agreement. "Takes his job seriously. He told me the troopers never pay for the ferry when it's official business. That's the ferry line policy and Ballinger's got no problem on that score. Devon and his men were all in uniform. Rudy lets them board free of charge. The guys in suits try to follow. Captain Rudy stops them at the top of the gangway and demands the fare. Devon tries to intercede telling Ballinger they're cops too. Proof demands the skipper. Devon and the two strangers put up a beef. Captain Rudy holds his ground. It ain't his boat so he's not entitled to pass out free crossings whenever he feels like it. Any non-paying customer will be noted in the ship's log."

"That wily old sea dog."

"So like it or not for the agents, out come the badges and ID cards. Ballinger examines each one before allowing the agents aboard."

"Despite a lot of things, you've got to love this Island."

"I ain't so sure anymore. I'm not in the mood for another one of those damn inquisitions. I live here to be left alone."

Gunner took out his flask, uncapped it and tilted back a mouthful.

"There won't be any town meetings," I said. "That's not the way the DEA operates."

"How's that?"

"They like to be more subtle about things. Through interrogation and intimidation, all very clandestine mind you, they'll try and cultivate informers. These guys bring down drug empires by rotting them from within."

Gunner simulated a gasp of horror. "We got a drug empire here on Bittern Island? You're kidding me. Who do they use for couriers? Seagulls?"

"I wouldn't try that line if they latch into you. Cops have no sense of humor. And with good reason. It's a job that is seldom funny. But these guys? The DEA? They've got a sense of humor, a sadistic one. Be on your guard with these boys, Gunner."

I must have hit a nerve for he tapped his flask for another dose. I almost joined him but went to the stove for more coffee instead. He left the counter to sit on his usual chair by the stove. His story told, the energy and mirth left him. Suddenly he appeared old and sunken on the tiny stool.

"Why do you really figure they brought over the DEA?" he asked.

"Near as I can figure, they know more about Janus Martin than that he rented a chain saw and left a truck nobody can find."

Gunner Hogan was a friend of mine. I trusted him implicitly. But I had no desire to burden him with what I knew about the errant vehicle. There were, I knew, things about himself that Gunner never told me for pretty much the same reason.

"His scars aren't only on the outside," Judith used to say about Gunner. "And I don't mean wounds. He has a score to settle with himself, and with the world. I wouldn't even want to imagine what it is."

"He'll never come to grips with it here on Bittern Island," I told her.

She looked at me with eyes far away, like when she first would conceive of a painting, defining the subject in her artist's eyes.

"He'll face it when he chooses to," she said. "Or when he's forced to face it. God help him. I hope it's a fight he can win."

CHAPTER TWENTY-TWO

Judith and I went to a poetry reading at The New School on Twelfth Street. Afterwards was a reception. I had never been to a reading and was amazed at the size and enthusiasm of the crowd. The reading was Judith's idea. It was our third date. At the reception we drank wine from plastic cups.

"So? What did you think?" she asked.

"I never heard anything like it."

"Doesn't it make you want to read some of your own out loud?"

"It makes me want to go home and burn it."

"What a horrible thing to say. You're only starting out. Do you think these poets publish everything they write? I'll bet they've got drawers full of stuff that will never see publication. It's called polishing your craft."

"Mine doesn't need polishing. It needs sandblasting."

"Your pal Pete doesn't think so."

"He took some lines and made it into something he wanted it to be."

"Are we a bit sensitive about this?" Then she smiled. "That's a good sign."

"I fooled around with Franco to pass the time. The writing is for its own sake."

I took her by the elbow and led her toward one of the poets. From the table beside him I selected and purchased his book and got online to have it autographed. When it was my turn the poet opened the book and poised his pen.

"How would you like this inscribed?" he asked me.

"To Judith. And write, 'At the beginning' with the date."

He gave me a quizzical look and did as requested. Then he snapped the book closed and handed it to me. I held it only long enough to pass it to Judith. She walked to a corner of the room and I followed. She opened the book and read the inscription.

"That was sweet," she said.

"I had my reasons."

"I'm sure you do."

At her prompting we went back to my place. I did not have any wine, only a half-bottle of port left from one of Pete's visits. She said that would be fine and I poured two glasses.

"Do you know why I wanted to come here?" she asked.

"I have some hopes."

"Good choice of words. If you said expectations, I would have left."

"Perhaps I am a writer after all."

"Prove it."

After a fruitless protest I went to my desk and got out the most recent notebook that comprised my efforts at versifying and storytelling.

We sat on the couch. She had me read the work out loud. She seldom made comment; I had to look at her eyes after reading certain lines to see if there was a reaction. Sometimes her green eyes widened in surprise. A few instances they tightened and grew dark except for a pinpoint of flame at their centers.

Either way, her reactions emboldened me to throw my voice resonantly into the reading.

"Stop. Stop," she said at last, holding up her hand. She rose from the sofa. "You're all over the place. I wasn't ready for this. You're bombarding me."

I mistook her meaning and apologized.

"Don't apologize." She drained her glass and set it down on the table as if controlling herself from flinging it across the room. "I wasn't ready for this."

I came to my feet. "Ready for what?"

She looked at me in confusion, a look that simmered into defiance.

"Ready for you to be so talented, you wicked, talented man."

Her arms spread and we fell into each other locked in an embrace. I tumbled backwards, barely in control, and I guided her down with me onto the couch.

Much later we awoke naked on the floor. We kissed as if we had never stopped until the chill of the room sent a common shiver up our entwined bodies.

Judith tilted her head back. "What time is it?"

Not the exact question I could have expected.

"What?"

"It must be very late."

"Or very early."

We slowly unwrapped ourselves from each other to sit on the floor. I got up and fetched a blanket off my bed and draped it over her from the back. She grabbed the edges and pulled it over her shoulders, crossing her arms over her breasts with the blanket.

"What about you?" There was a tremor in her voice.

I suddenly realized I had been prancing about naked and felt the flesh of my thighs, stomach, and shoulders flush.

"I'm okay. Let me throw on some pants."

I grabbed sweatpants and pulled them up to my waist. I felt the flush subside from my skin. The feeling seemed to turn and blend inward through my body. Never before had I been aware of such visceral sensations. I sat back down beside Judith.

"How do you feel?" Judith asked. Again, not a question I was expecting at that moment.

"I don't know. Different. Alive. Me, but a different me." I put my arm about her shoulder. "Different in a way I've never known."

She turned her head toward mine and kissed me. Then she put her head down into my chest and I wrapped my other arm about her.

"What time is it?" she asked again. This time in a whisper.

I looked over her head toward the window. On the building across the street I could see flecks of gold and crimson. As the seconds ticked by the specks lengthened into narrow streaks.

"Almost five," I said into her hair.

"How do you know?"

"I can tell."

Judith opened the blanket to wrap me in it with her. Her body was warm and smooth and I lay my head down on her shoulder. Together we sat like that on the floor until the windows across the way, next time I looked, were ablaze with the rising sun.

From her breathing I could tell she had dozed off again. Then she stirred in my arm and lifted her face to me.

"Six o'clock," I said before she could ask.

Judith smiled and tilted her head to the side as if in question.

"I'm the son of a fisherman. I can always tell."

"Well, son of a fisherman. Do you know how to make coffee?"

"I make it strong."

"Somehow I imagined that."

Slowly we untangled from each other and got to our feet. It was still cool in the apartment and I helped her draw the blanket tighter around her bare body.

"I'll take a shower while you make some," she said.

I led her to the bathroom grabbing fresh towels from the bureau. She took the towels and disappeared inside after a quick kiss that ended with the blanket hanging empty in my hands.

I set the percolator brewing and put out cups and sugar and milk on the table. Aside from the occasional Pete Franco, she was the only guest to ever have been in my tiny studio.

Guest? The word sounded strange and inappropriate. My thought was underscored by the sound of running water in the shower. I closed my eyes and imagined her bathing. Clouds of white soap slithering along her body, water streaming her face, fingers kneading a lather in her wet hair. I felt the flush return to my skin as the water stopped abruptly.

I was pouring coffee when Judith emerged from the bathroom. She had a towel wrapped around her body below her shoulders and the other held her hair, unseen, above her head. She looked like a sculpture from the Museum of Art uptown.

"What are you staring at?" she asked.

"You."

"Haven't you ever seen a woman come out of the shower before?"

"No, and if I ever imagined it, it wasn't this lovely."

Judith smiled and let it pass. "Mmm, that coffee smells good."

She took a seat at the table and I joined her. After half a teaspoon of sugar and a dash of milk, the cup was at her lips. She blew across the top and took a sip. Judith's shoulders arched and her head rolled slightly to the side in a stretch of warmth and satisfaction.

"Mmm," she hummed again. "Very good."

"I'm glad it pleases you." It sounded lame even to myself.

She took another sip and then leveled her eyes at me.

"I have one more request," she said.

"Name it."

"Do you think next time we could use the bed? Either that or you've got to get a thicker carpet."

I laughed out loud with the memory of the two of us rolling from the sofa onto the floor, making love right there all night, and the bed not six feet away on the other side of the room.

"I mean it wasn't far even if you had to carry me," she said.

"Carry you? When we fell off the couch I wound up on the bottom."

"Oh, yes. I seem to remember something like that. By the way." Her eyes narrowed seriously. "Do you always remember the details?"

"Absolutely"

"Then don't let it happen again without protection. Promise?"

"Promise."

Judith had her second cup of coffee while I took a shower. When I came out she was dressed in her clothes from the previous night. I quickly donned jeans, a flannel shirt, socks, and sneakers. As I dressed she studied the bookshelves comprising one whole wall of my apartment. She drew out a paperback copy of *The Moon and Sixpence*.

"This is about Gaugain," she said.

"I know. Only he's called 'Strickland' in the novel."

"So you read it."

"I've read them all."

"The son of a fisherman turned carpenter and poet, who has an apartment that looks like a library. What have I gotten myself into now?"

"I guess we'll have to find out together."

"Deal. Why don't we start with breakfast?"

It was early Saturday morning and the City streets were empty. We caught a cab down to the South Street Seaport and ate omelettes at a café out on the wharf overlooking the East River and up at the Brooklyn Bridge. After the plates were cleared away we held hands across the table, lingering through final coffees.

When her cup was empty Judith sat back.

"I hate this to end already, but I have a thousand errands to run," she said.

"What kind of errands?"

"Oh, the usual. Laundry, shopping, house-cleaning, and my studies."

"I'll go with you."

"You most certainly will not. I need a little routine to settle down and regroup. My life has been rocked enough for one twenty-four-hour period, thank you very much. But you can see me home."

"It would be my pleasure," I said, affecting the Southern voice of our first date. "And as for this evening, Miss Valenti?"

"My goodness, sir," she echoed the accent. "But you are a persistent beau."

"Shall we?" I rose from my seat and extended my arm for her to take.

"And you profess to never having seen a woman leave her shower. You are the wickedest creature, Mr. Hoffmann."

Judith leaned against me with her hands in my lap for the taxi ride to her apartment. Again, she did not invite me up. I paid the cabbie anyway and sent him on his way.

"Six o'clock then?" I asked.

She smiled, nodded, kissed me on the cheek and went inside. I walked all the way home across town, past Union Square, all the way on the other side of Manhattan from her apartment.

That night we went to an Italian restaurant and a movie. Back at my apartment Judith was pleasantly surprised I had procured a variety of red wines. None were very expensive because I knew nothing about wine and had to follow the retailer's suggestions.

More comfortable with each other, less frenzied, but deeper and more considerate, we made love in the bed. I had also been to the pharmacy and acquired the promised safeguards.

CHAPTER TWENTY-THREE

Rolando Tobar did not return to the shop that afternoon. He called on the telephone around three o'clock.

"*Federales* have been nosing around the fish plant," he said.

"So what? There isn't much left of it." I had not been back to Jacob's Cove since the derelict building fell into the water. "What else have they been doing?" On a small island it was not easy to conceal your business — unless you were Don Ostros.

"They've been up and down the docks checking out boats."

"Did they board any of them?" It was mostly fishing boats but there were a few pleasure craft like the Don's own cabin cruiser.

"Not that anybody's seen. It looks like they're only writing down names and registration numbers."

"That shouldn't get them anywhere. Is Archie Bealer with them?"

"No, he planted his butt at the Sea Witch sometime this morning. From what I've heard he hasn't left. Makes no difference. He's useless to guys like this."

"Not necessarily."

"What do you mean?"

"How does one run a drug operation right under the nose of the local police?" I answered myself. "You pay them off, naturally. That's why they invented the Drug Enforcement Agency. They need an agency they hope will be incorruptible.

There's so much money involved, it's easier for the drug smugglers to make the local cops rich than try and conceal their operations."

"You think Bealer's been paid off?"

"Not really, but who knows? I figure the Don's too smart for that. He would never trust a guy like Bealer, no matter what it cost. But the Feds don't know that. Mark my words. They're going to come down on Bealer like the Wrath of God."

"But Bealer found the body. He started all of this. It doesn't make any sense for him to be involved."

I stopped listening a moment. In my mind I went back to the morning after the storm. Constable Bealer had found the body, he told me. Found it because of the smell. But?

But even according to Bealer, he had not been the first one on the scene. Fire Warden Ben Marshall had been there before Bealer. Marshall decided not to call the fireboats from the mainland. A sound decision since the plant was worthless. Besides, the storm would douse what was left in the end.

Rolando interrupted my thoughts. "What are you thinking?"

"I'm not sure."

Rolando did not press the issue. His mind seemed to switch gears.

"Do you need the truck back this afternoon, boss?"

"No, I can manage. What are you up to, anyway?"

"My wife and I got company." From his tone, he was not pleased. "Her sister came over from

Providence. *Cristo*, Karl. She's brought enough stuff to stay a year. It took two trips to haul her trunks and bags from the dock. Now I've get to set up the spare room for her."

"Didn't you know she was coming?"

"I thought it was next week. Esperansa told me but I guess I wasn't paying attention."

"So it's your fault."

"You sound like her."

"Do what you've got to do. I'll see you tomorrow."

"Thanks, boss." Rolando hung up.

I looked over at Gunner Hogan by the stove. He was whittling a piece of firewood with his jackknife. He was not carving anything, merely shaving the wood in strips to fall at his feet. Gunner did this often, sitting by the fire drawing his blade in long strokes along the grain of the wood. When he had a pile of shavings between his boots he would scoop them up and deposit them in the stove.

He felt me watching and looked up.

"What's the matter?" The knife stopped in mid swipe as a curl of wood raveled to a halt.

"Getting a little restless. Let's go to the Sea Witch for a while. I'll buy. You drive."

"Okay by me." He closed the knife and put it in his pocket. He tossed the stick onto the woodpile and put the shavings in the stove. When he stood up there was a creak in his bones and a groan in his throat.

I locked up shop and we got in Gunner's old Dodge station wagon. The back was crammed with all the odd crap Gunner collected as he wandered the

Island. There was driftwood and shells, bits of net, an old fishing reel, lengths of assorted ropes. I did not know what he did with the stuff or why he hoarded it. It was simply his way.

The old metal beast sputtered and choked but started on the third try. Gunner spun the steering wheel and we swung onto Mariners Path headed for Grace.

"What's your real mission for going to the Sea Witch?" he asked.

"I told you. I'm feeling restless."

"Don't you usually read a book?"

"Are you trying to say I'm antisocial?"

"You ain't exactly the prom king of Bittern Island."

"You're right." I gave up. "Let's not talk about it."

Gunner grunted. "Suit yourself."

He stomped the accelerator as we turned up the first ridge.

At the highest point he slowed the car and coasted to a stop. Ahead and below we could see Grace, Daretown, the harbor, and the Sound. Hogan stared out through the windshield.

"It's never going to be the same," he said.

"I know."

"Hell, it's what the State wants anyway. We're all supposed to sell off or die off. I don't think anybody cares which one, as long as we're gone. What do you think they want it for anyway?" He referred to the Rhode Island legislation barring us from selling our property except to the State.

"I've heard rumors about a maritime state park with museums and nature trails. Then there's the talk about bringing in casino gambling."

"I think it's bullshit. They simply don't want to be bothered with us anymore. We don't have all that much so they can't tax us any higher. And we're a pain in the ass to them out here. Always squawking about our utility consumption, primitive sewage, dirt roads, emergency medical evac when we need it. We refuse to be modernized and sucked into some big damn plan of theirs. That's why they've written us off and decided to let us expire one by one. Give the place back to the birds and the crabs."

It was the longest monologue I ever heard out of Gunner's mouth.

Gunner took his foot from the brake and we started rolling down toward town. I made no comment and do not think he expected one. What he said was probably true. It prompted no argument from me.

Gunner parked in the alley behind the Sea Witch and we went in through the back door. Sweeney was tending bar and we ordered drafts.

"Slow day at the shop?" Sweeney asked me.

"Regular this time of year." That discounted the business accrued from the storm. "Have to wait for the early summer traffic."

"Me too."

Sweeney waved his arm to indicate the near-empty taproom.

Two fishermen I knew were sharing a pitcher of beer at one table. Archie Bealer sat alone at the far end of the bar dealing himself a hand of solitaire from a deck of cards, whiskey glass by his elbow. He never even looked up when we entered.

"What do you plan to do with this place when you retire?" I asked Sweeney. He was in his mid-sixties, married but no children. His wife, Sophie, had taught school on the mainland but was retired with a severe case of arthritis.

"Not much I can do. Sell it to the State like they want and move south or west. I should get Sophie to a better climate. Not that she complains any. She was born on this Island and knew what to expect. Still, she'd be better off in the desert, maybe a place like Arizona."

"Wouldn't you both miss the ocean?"

"Miss the ocean?" He thought a minute. "Naw. Don't see it much any more anyway. I'm either working or staying home. Haven't even gone fishing in the last ten years. I've seen about all the water I need for one lifetime. People say the desert is pretty, and I think Sophie could use a dry spell. What about yourself?"

I did not have an answer but it turned out I did not need one for the moment. Bealer's glass was empty and he bellowed for a refill. Sweeney moved off toward him down the bar.

"The man's got a point," Gunner said. "You're still a reasonably young man. Sell off All Island and get away from here. The State would probably give you fifty cents on the dollar. I'd take it now if I were you, before the offer goes down."

"Would you come with me?"

"Now that's an interesting proposal. I don't think so, thanks anyway. I kind of want to be here when they come for me. Whoever comes first, the storm troopers or Saint Peter."

The Sea Witch's front door opened. A young man in a suit and topcoat came in. He removed a pair of sunglasses and scanned the room from the entranceway. Then he moved down the bar and took a stool in the middle. He was taller than average with blond hair and clean-shaven face. He took off his overcoat and laid it across the stool beside him.

Sweeney flipped a coaster in front of him on the bar.

"Tequila," the man ordered. "Make it two. I got a friend coming."

From the top shelf Sweeney grabbed a bottle of Jose Cuervo and poured two ample shots into rock glasses. The stranger took a billfold from his breast pocket and put money on the bar. Sweeney rang the sale and made change.

Lifting his glass, the blond man turned to look at Bealer then swung his head back around to eye Gunner and myself. The glass hovered in his hand until he turned frontal and drank off half of it. He dropped his arm and the glass came down heavy on the bar.

The door opened again and who I took for his partner entered the Sea Witch. Shorter than his associate, the newcomer had dark, swarthy features, thick limbs under his coat, and moved like a prizefighter, throwing his shoulders around as he walked. He took a stool next to the blond man and without a word threw back the drink waiting for him in a single gulp. The flash of liquor made him grunt audibly. He craned his neck in a stretch and removed the coat to reveal a dark suit like his partner.

"Is this the best joint around here?" the new arrival asked the first guy.

"Shit, Jesse. This is the only joint."

The man named Jesse did not let up. "This whole freaking Island is one big armpit."

He shoved his glass out for attention. "They should have left us in Miami."

"If you hadn't roughed up that councilman, we'd still be there," his partner said.

"Listen, Mike," Jesse said. "That was an honest mistake. Besides, you know how those Cubans are. I'll still bet a week's pay the guy is dirty."

"You're lucky you didn't get suspended."

"Yeah? What do you call this? At least I would have been suspended someplace warm."

Sweeney poured Jesse another tequila. By that time Mike was ready for another also. After putting back the bottle, Sweeney came down and drew us fresh beers.

I was watching Archie Bealer who had forsaken the cards to study the newcomers. Jesse caught Bealer gawking at him.

"What the fuck are you looking at?" Jesse yelled at Bealer.

Bealer jumped in his seat. He stood up and moved uneasily down the bar grabbing the lapel of his coat and thrusting out the badge pinned to it.

"Constable Bealer," Bealer said, pointing with his other hand to the shield. "Bittern Island Police Force."

"Constable?" Jesse barked derisively. "Constable? Where are we? Fucking England?"

Bealer, red-faced all the time, grew redder.

"I was N.Y.P.D. for twenty-six years," Bealer boasted in defense. "Detective First Grade."

Jesse turned on the stool toward the agent named Mike.

"What do they need us for? They got their own local Rambo."

Mike snickered. "Maybe he's part of the problem."

The short agent turned back to Bealer.

"What do you say about that, rum-dumb?" he goaded Bealer. "You sticking your fingers in the guacamole? You taking a little for yourself under the table?"

Bealer's hand clutching his lapel with the badge dropped to his side.

"Fuck you," Bealer mustered the whiskey courage to say.

Jesse leapt off his stool and in an instant had a hand at Bealer's throat. He pulled Bealer's face down to within inches of his own. "What did you say, rummy?"

"Let him go, Jesse," the other agent said. "We don't need trouble. Remember Miami."

Jesse released his grip, affording Bealer the opportunity to take a big gulp of air. The agent's hand went from Bealer's throat to his shoulder. He patted the shoulder.

"No harm done," Jesse said. "Just a couple of cops letting off steam. You remember how it gets. Don't you, Constable?"

Bealer nodded his head dumbly. He rubbed his throat with one hand and flattened his shirt with the other.

"Buy my friend a drink on me," Jesse ordered Sweeney. "Anything he wants."

With a hand still on Bealer, Jesse deliberately turned him around and gave a shove toward his seat. Bealer was docile and complied with the motivation.

Sweeney was already pouring Bealer a double shot of rye whiskey. Bealer grabbed the glass in a death grip and drank it.

Jesse threw money on the bar next to Mike's, drank his own drink and pushed out his glass for more. His partner followed suit. Meanwhile Archie Bealer sank onto his stool with a face of pain and shock. I would have felt sorry for him but I could not muster it.

The two fishermen at the table finished their pitcher of beer. One of them, Clive Kershaw, walked over and put the empty container and the two mugs on the bar.

"Thanks, Sweeney," Clive said. "See you tomorrow."

Jesse looked over at him. "Going home so early?"

"Early tide tomorrow," Kershaw said.

"You got a boat?"

"Yup," Clive said curtly. "Be on my way now."

As Kershaw turned to leave, Jesse posed another question to his back. "What's her name, skipper?"

Clive turned back slowly. *The Island Rose.*

"I remember it." Jesse plucked a notebook from the pocket of his suit jacket and flipped through some pages. He stopped flipping and put his finger on a page. "Here it is. *The Island Rose*. Rhode Island registration number two-six-nine-three-four. Is that the one, skipper?"

"The same," Clive said.

"Pretty thing. But a bit of a cow, wouldn't you say?"

Clive was not rising to the bait. "She's a fishing boat, not a racer. Serves right well."

"I guess it all depends on your business and your cargo."

"My business is fishing," Clive said. "Good day to you, sir."

Clive Kershaw turned on his heel and walked out of the bar. His friend followed close behind.

Jesse put away his notebook. "You got a touchy crowd here, barkeep," he said to Sweeney.

"They drink and mind their business," Sweeney said.

"Give it a rest," Mike told his partner.

"Rest?" Jesse said. "I'm just getting started."

He turned on his stool, looked past Mike, and sized me up.

"You a fisherman too?" Then a sip of tequila. "Got yourself a boat?"

"Who's asking?" I said.

The agent was not ready for the question. He was immediately back on his feet. If his partner had not risen to block him, I am sure he would have charged me. He got himself under control, reached into his jacket and produced a badge wallet.

"Jesse Mancuso. DEA," he said holding up the badge. "That's the Drug Enforcement Agency. Who are you?"

I sipped my beer before answering. "Karl Hoffmann. A.I.R."

Gunner stifled a laugh beside me.

"What the hell is A.I.R.?" Jesse demanded.

"All Island Rental. Everybody knows that."

Jesse put his badge away and sat back on his stool. "Fucking wiseguy, eh?"

"Not really. Only a working stiff like the fishermen."

In the mirror behind the bar I saw the notebook come back out, along with a pen. He wrote what I assumed was my name. He snapped the pad closed.

"I've got your number now," he said.

"No matter. It's in the book anyway."

"You are a wiseguy. We know just how to handle wiseguys."

"Give it a rest," Mike repeated to his associate.

Jesse ignored the suggestion a second time. He leaned out over the bar and peered past me at Gunner Hogan.

"Who's your friend?" he called.

I do not speak for my friends without their permission. I heard Gunner's beer mug tap down on the bar. The next sound was his stool sliding back. By the time I turned Gunner had gotten to his feet. He cleared his throat with a raspy cough.

"Lieutenant Colonel Sterling Hogan. United States Army. Retired," Gunner recited.

The introduction caught the DEA agent by surprise. Jesse's hands fumbled as he pawed around for his glass. Even Mike turned to size up my friend.

"No offense, Colonel," Jesse finally stammered. "I had no idea."

"The fact that you're clueless comes as no surprise," Gunner said.

I went back to watching the agent, who reddened a little at his neckline.

Mike tried to misdirect the confrontation.

"What corps and division?" he asked Gunner.

"Now why in the hell would you care?" Gunner said. "Want to write it down in your little book?"

"Only talking, buddy," Mike said. "No trouble here."

"For the record, agent," Gunner said. "We're not buddies. Not today, not ever. My buddy and I are having a beer. You're bothering us. If you've got a job to do, do it. Otherwise we'd appreciate being left to ourselves."

There was command in his voice. I had never heard it before. If I turned away from Mike I expected to see Gunner dressed in uniform taking the measure of an inadequate subordinate. I did not want to turn and lose the image.

Behind my back I heard Gunner regain his stool. Sweeney got both of us fresh beers. Gunner, in a placid voice, ordered a whiskey. The bar was very quiet. We all heard Sweeney's footsteps as he paced for the bottle and returned to pour the drink.

"I'll have one too," I said to Sweeney.

Sweeney gave me my drink and made one for himself. The three of us at the end of the bar raised our glasses in a silent toast and drank them down.

"What time is the next ferry?" Jesse asked no one in particular.

Sweeney put down his empty glass and looked at his wristwatch. He answered without looking at the agent. "If you go now, you'll have time to just make it."

The two agents got to their feet and put on their coats. Both men scooped all their money off the bar.

"We'll be back," Mike said as the two made for the door.

The three of us paid him no mind. The door thudded closed behind them. Archie Bealer sneezed at the other end of the bar.

Gunner said, "There's going to be trouble. That's for sure."

CHAPTER TWENTY-FOUR

By the time Judith earned her Master of Fine Arts degree, we lived together in a SoHo apartment. The arrangement took accommodating. I took a fist-full of vitamins every morning and ate less red meat. Judith learned the difference between an ERA and an RBI and went to Shea Stadium. We mutually enjoyed Mozart, Ravel, and galleries and museums.

After the University project was completed, Costa Construction kept me on building low-income housing in Brooklyn. Judith took a job as a hostess-slash-salesperson at a gallery while she circulated her resume. Her job included night hours that allowed her to paint during the day.

One summer evening I arrived home from work to find Judith rapping on our typewriter.

"I'm typing your poems," she said.

"Why?"

"Because I bought you a present."

She went into the bedroom and returned with a brightly wrapped package. "Open it."

I took the package and felt a book inside. Sliding my finger through the tape I folded back the paper. I turned the book over and read the cover.

POET'S MARKET
1200 PLACES TO PUBLISH YOUR POETRY

"What's this for?"

"Take a guess, baby, a wild guess. It's time to get your work out there for people to read."

"You think some of it will sell?"

"Publishing and selling are not necessarily the same thing. Most times you only get a free copy of the published volume. But it's a start. I've marked a few places to try."

There were scraps of paper sticking out from the book. I turned to the first one. Judith had highlighted an entry with yellow marker. It read:

GRUB STREET PRESS: published quarterly; new poets welcome; circulation 1000; payment – two copies; reporting time – one month.

"What do you think?" Judith asked.

"You think I have a chance?"

"You've got the same chance as anyone else."

"I was expecting more enthusiasm than that."

"I can't be a critic. It's too personal for me. Let's send some and see."

"What if I'm no good?"

"I doubt that. But wouldn't you want to know?"

"I'm a carpenter."

"So was Jesus Christ. And Wallace Stevens was an insurance executive." Stevens was a poet I liked from Connecticut. "What's your point?"

"Since you put it that way, I'm game."

"Good. I've already selected three poems I think you should send."

She took three sheets of paper from the stack beside the machine. "Check these out and tell me if you agree." She handed me the poems.

I had never seen these poems typed. There was a lot of blank space on the pages.

"Don't you think they're kind of short?" I asked.

"That's your style: short, clipped, concise. It's how you write."

Judith addressed an envelope to the Editor, then came over to me for the poems.

"You can mail it tomorrow at lunchtime." She licked and sealed the package.

"For luck." Judith turned the envelope over and kissed the front.

Judith had to work that night so we had a hurried dinner of grilled cheese sandwiches. When we cleaned up I made coffee and we sat on the sofa.

"There's something else I want to ask," Judith said. "I should wait until we have more time and I don't have to work, but I'm too curious."

I told her to ask whatever she liked. We never willfully withheld anything from each other.

Judith got up, went to the desk, took something from the drawer and returned to the couch. It took a moment before I realized what she was holding.

"Whose picture is this?" It was a faded black and white print.

"Where did you find that?"

"In the bookcase. It fell out of your copy of *Doctor Zhivago*. Who is she?"

I took the photograph from her hand and stared at it. I had not looked at it in years. Not even sure where I kept it. For a while it had been in a different book.

Judith Valenti's parents were dead, as were my own. I knew she was from upstate New York. Judith knew I was raised in a fishing community. Neither of us dwelt on the past.

"This is my mother. Her name was Galina."

"Where was that picture taken?" She always had the artist's eye for detail.

"Leningrad." The memory of my mother's secret stash of pictures flooded back to me.

"In Russia?"

"Yes, Russia. This was the opening night of *Romeo and Juliet* at the Kirov Theater in Leningrad. Mother said Joseph Stalin attended."

"Your mother was a prima ballerina? That's wonderful. You must tell me about her when we have time." She glanced at her watch. "I've got to get to work."

Judith took the picture from my hand.

"What are you going to do with it?" I asked.

Without answering, Judith walked across the room to her easel. She placed the picture on the empty ledge of the easel. It looked improbably small in the place where canvases normally resided. Judith turned to me.

"I'm going to paint it. It's irresistible. Now I really must run."

She collected her purse, delivered a kiss, and was gone.

When she returned around midnight the photograph was where she left it even though I had held it once more before turning into bed before she came home.

The following day, a Friday, I left for work with the *Grub Street* manuscript in my tool bag. During lunch I found a Post Office and mailed it.

"Did you mail the poems?" she greeted me that evening.

I said I had.

"Let's celebrate," she said. "You go clean up. I'm taking you to dinner."

"Isn't celebration a bit premature?"

"Nonsense. Besides, you can tell me all about your mother, the beautiful, talented, mysterious Galina of the Russian ballet."

"What makes you think she was mysterious?"

"You're here. Aren't you?"

Judith took me to Cinelli's on Second Avenue. We ate veal scaloppini and drank Chianti by candlelight. I recounted the story, trying not to leave anything out. Much of it I admitted hearing from Fargo, the agent who came to Camp Sinclair when I was dropped from the Chile team. Telling the story to someone else had a strange effect on me. It made the affair of Galina and Kurt and their desperate escape more part of me. Not a history of two people I knew, it became an extension of my very being. It was more intoxicating than the wine.

Judith felt it too. Afterwards we walked over to the river, me rambling about Bittern Island and the relationship finally forged between father and myself. I ended by describing his death by the record player.

"What an amazing man," Judith whispered into my shoulder.

"He could be hard and stubborn."

"Like father, like son."

"Me?"

"Yes. And with the strain of the poet. What a mixture. Part soldier, scholar, artist, rebel, all fermented in two generations of passion."

At the edge of the river we kissed as a tugboat churned upriver past the bulkhead.

"Have you been back?" We slid from our embrace.

"To Bittern Island? Not since he died."

"Don't you want to?"

"I've never thought about it. I've been trying to carve a life for myself instead."

"You don't carve a life like it was a piece of sculpture. It's meant to be lived, not cast. There's nothing rigid about it. You must go back sometime. Because you've changed and no doubt it's changed as well. That helps you gain perspective. It's like when you see a picture of the same place in different seasons. The location is the same, but it's different. And when the same season rolls around again, that too is different. A tree is taller, a path is wider, a boulder is gone, someone's painted a barn a different color."

"You're a philosopher."

I drew her in, folding into another kiss.

It was past midnight. We strode back to Second Avenue and stopped for coffee at an all- night café.

"The rules have changed," I said.

"What do you mean?"

"You're not getting off so easy. Now I want to hear all about you and your family."

Judith signaled the waiter for more coffee. We sat quietly while he filled our cups. At that late hour, maybe three o'clock in the morning, there was only one other patron in the café. An old man hunched at the counter nursing coffee and reading a book. The street outside was deserted. Shops across the Avenue dark and shuttered. The scene disturbed only by a passing taxi or police car.

"I'm from Binghamton and my parents both passed on as you know," Judith finally said. She nodded her head at the man at the counter. "I wonder what he's reading."

"Proust or Flaubert. That's what I read when I can't sleep. You're changing the subject."

Judith smiled, caught and guilty. Her eyes flickered a second like a firefly. She smiled again, blushed at some thought, then looked down at her cup. When she looked up the sparkle in her irises was gone. The green circles grew dark and dense like a rainforest. The gray in the very center started to smolder.

"My father, I think I've told you, was a teacher."

"You never mentioned it."

"I thought I might have. He was a professor of History at the State University. We had a house near campus. Dad was well respected by his colleagues and students loved him. Other teachers and his students were always coming by the house. My brother and I were college brats."

She had never mentioned a brother and it took me by surprise. As an only child, I often wondered what it would have felt like to have a sibling.

"In the back of the house was a den, Dad's study. He had many books. Like you. And there were busts of Marcus Aurelius, Alexander the Great, Charlemagne, and Constantine. My mother served tea in the afternoons. There were always visitors, students and faculty as well as visiting scholars.

Frank and I would be shooed outside to play. We were forever sneaking into the kitchen to filch cookies or the cakes Mom was serving. When everybody left we were called to supper. We wouldn't be hungry and Mom would know what we did."

Judith saw our waiter coming. "We should go now."

I paid the bill and followed Judith out into the street.

The merchants were beginning their day. Trucks of fresh fish, hot bread right out of ovens, cut flowers, and newspapers dotted the Avenue or pulled to abrupt stops as we walked past and their drivers flung open cargo doors to unload the delivery.

For a block Judith said nothing, holding my right arm tight with both her hands and her head tilted to my shoulder. It was as if we were walking in a snowstorm though a warm summer day was dawning.

She read my thoughts. "Binghamton can get very cold. The winters are long and dreary."

"Bittern Island could be the same. Everything seems to stop. Did your mother paint?"

"She dabbled in watercolors. With some faculty wives she did ceramics. There were pieces all over the house. She even made a tea set my father was fond of and showed off to guests. She also sewed, knitted and did crochet. Frank and I had new scarves and mittens every winter. The college had a rummage sale for charity every fall. Mom's ceramics and knitwear always raised the most money. With mills going under there were a lot of poor people in

Binghamton. You couldn't feel it around campus. We had our own little island of tranquility and plenty."

A curious analogy in view of my own circumstances.

"Let's take the train to the Battery," Judith said suddenly. "I want to watch the sun come up."

A block further was a subway stairwell. We scooted down as a train pulled into the station. Our car was empty and we sat facing the aisle as we pulled away into the tunnel.

"Dad had a massive heart attack," Judith said. "He didn't survive."

I put my arm about her shoulder.

"My mother was devastated. She was a different person after that. There were periods of depression that the winter didn't help. In the spring she was irritable and edgy. Dad's insurance was spent and the bills kept coming. The college community was friendly and supportive for a while but, as they say, life goes on."

There was no bitterness in her tone.

"Mom sold off as much as she could along with the house. We moved to Peekskill where her folks were from and Mom was raised. A sister and some cousins, all married, lived there. My mother took a job as a seamstress. Frank and I went to the local school. It wasn't so bad. But it was never the same."

We rocked with the motion of the train and I knew what she meant.

Judith sighed. "There was a bitterness in her about how it had all worked out. Like maybe Dad hadn't done his best to see we would be settled. Like maybe all the books, and teas, and honorary awards, and faculty parties weren't really all that significant after all." Judith dismissed the thought. "No matter, she died saying his name. So what's the difference anyway?"

The train pulled into Battery Park Station. We climbed the steps out into the predawn over the harbor. Ferries to Liberty and Ellis Islands were moored against each other, bobbing in the water.

We crossed the street to the iron rail above the lapping bay. Straight ahead loomed the Statue of the Lady herself, gray-green against the gray-blue of the lightening sky.

Eastward the Verrazano Narrows Bridge spanned the channel connecting Brooklyn to Staten Island. The first rays of morning glinted off the upper extremes of its twin suspension towers. Judith and I held each other. The light crept down the cables from either side. The sun rose out of the water beyond the bridge. It looked for a moment as if the suspended structure was the top of the universe dangling the sun and you could walk across the dome.

"Do you see it?" Judith whispered.

"Yes."

For a brief moment it was defined, captured, finite. And it was ours. The glow washing over our faces.

The sun continued to rise behind the gangway of the bridge, framed by the towers. It lifted beyond the bridge, defying any dome of concrete, steel, and wire. The hillocks of Staten Island and the lowlands of Brooklyn were awash in light. Somewhere upriver a ship's horn paid homage.

The harbor, before so shadowy, tranquil and vacant, suddenly teemed with activity. A ferry was inbound from the farther island. Two tugs nosed a barge to starboard into the East River against the tide. A red-hulled tanker low in the water with its belly full of crude oil came out of the morning beneath the bridge. South of us a sailboat tacked, then fluffed its mainsail as it looped the Statue of Liberty in the breeze.

Behind us, beyond the fringe of Battery Park, buses and cars revved, horns honked, and tourists made for the ferries to the landmarks of the harbor. Street vendors set wagons, started roasting fires, scooped ice, and snapped open brightly colored umbrellas in anticipation of the languid day to follow. A roadside artist set down his case, extracted a saxophone, and blew a few notes to set his reed.

"Let's go home," Judith said.

By the curb a Checker cab disgorged a family and we took their places in the cavernous back seat. We rolled the windows down encouraging a breeze. The air was thickening with the heat to follow.

Home, we stripped off clothes without talking, spun recklessly, embraced and fell onto the plain of the bed, making love furiously as salty sweat of one became the other's, slipping, groping, holding until we were beyond holding, burying our faces in all the moist feral folds of the other's body.

The bed was soaked with us when we were spent. I weakly tried to rise and remove the protection but Judith's hand on my chest was enough to sway me back down on the bed.

"Let me do that."

When she returned she brought a cool damp cloth and sponged my body. In turn she did herself as I watched, having waved off my offer with a demure smile.

The heat outside invaded the room. Our senses were beyond temporal discomfort. Drifting into light sleep, our fingers lazily brushed each other, all the feeling worthy of notice, like kids with popsicles against their tongues.

CHAPTER TWENTY-FIVE

A few days after the DEA agents left Gunner and me at the Sea Witch, the Coast Guard paid a visit to Bittern Island. No one thought it unusual as they tied up at the municipal slip next to the ferry berth. They came and went routinely. The guardsmen performed vital functions and Islanders were grateful they did them.

This time proved different. It was past three in the afternoon and kids were milling around the docks, dropped off from school on the mainland. Kids do not miss much, and they immediately noticed the sailors were armed. That was not usual. Word spread and a crowd of fishermen gathered to observe.

One was an officer, the other three seamen. Each had a .45 holstered about their waists. The officer carried a portfolio.

I had delivered a pulley rig to Oscar, the boat mechanic. After making the delivery I hung around to help Oscar set up the gear. We were in his repair compound three piers away from where the Coast Guard tied up.

"What do you suppose they want?" Oscar asked.

"I don't know. Looks like they expect trouble."

"Never been no trouble that sort around here."

When the pulley was secure Oscar stripped off his gloves and stood beside me by the winch.

As we watched, the officer selected a paper from the portfolio and handed it to one of the seamen.

Orders were given but we could not hear them. While the officer waited, the three sailors started onto the first pier with its boat slips to either side. At each dock space they stopped to read the boat's name off the transom.

Halfway out the pier we heard the guardsman with the paper shout.

"This is it, sir."

The officer walked onto the pier and joined his men.

What happened next surprised everyone watching. All four of the Coast Guard men boarded the boat. To board someone's vessel without permission was as serious a thing as you could do in a maritime community or at sea.

"I'm going to get Ben," Oscar said.

He dropped his gloves to the ground and started off for Marshall's office at the other end of the piers.

Ben Marshall, aside from being Fire Warden, was also Harbor Master. It was not a demanding job, but it had purpose.

I walked out of the boatyard toward the crowd gathered at the land end of the pier.

"Whose boat are they on?" I asked no one in particular.

"Captain Ray's," a voice answered.

Captain Ray DeGammo was a fixture on Bittern Island. In his eighties, he had not done commercial fishing in a decade. But he was still the "senior" skipper or "Commodore" of the Bittern Island fleet. A title he had the right to take to his grave before it passed on to another captain. No longer working, he puttered around his boat on days he felt up to it doing whatever it is old men do to pass time. Every spring he was propped up in Sunday best to accept the blessing of the fleet delivered by the pastor of Saint Andrews.

Two of the Coast Guard sailors came off the boat. They strode down the pier past us without paying the crowd the slightest mind. At the municipal slip they boarded their craft. Aboard, they fetched a heavy chain and toolbox.

As the pair walked by again to DeGammo's boat someone called out.

"What are you fellas up to?"

The inquiry was ignored.

Ben Marshall arrived. He was a man of placid features and attitude, and it was clear on his face that whatever was going on displeased him. Without acknowledging our group he marched onto the pier and halted astern of Captain Ray's boat, the *Betsy-Karen*, named for his granddaughters.

We heard Marshall bark, "I'm Harbor Master. What goes here? You boys better have papers."

While he waited the seamen who retrieved the chain and tools proceeded to loop the chain around the pylon nearest the *Betsy-Karen*. They ignored Marshall.

The officer reappeared on the deck of the craft. He brandished a paper in one hand while heaving himself up to the dock with the other. Squared-off in front of Marshall, he presented the paper to the Harbor Master.

Marshall took the document and read it. As he handed it back he snorted, cocked his head, and spat in a wide arc toward the water.

"Must be a mistake, Lieutenant. The *Betsy-Karen* hasn't been to sea in a dozen seasons. Her skipper, Ray DeGammo, is retired. What's your point?"

"Her keel's in the water and she's afloat," the Lieutenant said matter-of-factly. "The law is the law. Let us do our job and we'll finish up and be on our way."

"It doesn't make sense, son."

The officer shrugged and told his men to get busy. The chain from the pylon was played out and pitched to the seaman remaining on the *Betsy-Karen*. This fellow took the links and threaded them through the gunwales of the boat. Drawing up slack, he heaved the end up to his comrades on the dock. They retrieved it, wound it again about the pylon and secured both ends with a padlock.

The officer took the toolbox back onto the boat. With a hammer and tack he affixed a yellow paper to the cabin hatch of the *Betsy-Karen*. The remaining seaman gathered up the tools and the officer's portfolio and scaled up to the dock. The officer stood on deck, turned and looked up at Marshall.

"We'll be back in a day or two with a tug to impound this vessel. You can tell the owner or not, as you please."

Duty done, the Lieutenant climbed up to the dock, told his men they were finished, and led them off to their boat. The crowd let them pass unmolested.   Ben Marshall remained on the pier scratching his head and staring down at the wood planks.

Detaching myself from the group I walked to him. "What's going on, Ben?"

"Damnedest thing, Karl. Captain Ray's registration lapsed nine years ago. The Coast Guard has seized the *Betsy-Karen* for being in violation."

"That's ridiculous."

"Maybe so. But they got papers to do it. It's the law." His voice betrayed exasperation.

"It's not the damn law that's at work here." My neck tightened in anger. "It's those goddamn federal agents. They were here to stir up trouble."

Marshall took the opportunity to spit again.

"Well, consider the pot stirred," he said. "If you'll excuse me, I best be over to Captain Ray's place and tell him his boat's been shackled down awaiting impound."

Marshall moved past me. His shoulders were slouched in defeat. His normally mild countenance had turned grim. He walked off the dock, past the fishermen and kids and started up Main Street.

Rolando Tobar came toward me on the pier. I explained tersely what transpired.

"Isn't that harassment?" Rolando asked. "Captain Ray hasn't taken his boat out in years. Everybody knows that."

I made no comment.

"*Cristo*," Rolando said. "This is the kind of crap I left behind in Guatemala. Next thing they'll be murdering us in our beds."

"Easy, partner. It's hardly come to that."

"Yeah? That's what we all said back in my country when it started."

"There is something else."

"What's that, boss?" Rolando moved closer in response to my muffled tone.

"I know what they want and where to find it."

Rolando took me by the arm and turned me. "Let's get out of here. Where'd you park the pickup?"

"Over by Oscar's boatyard," I said absently. My thoughts preoccupied me.

"Come on." He dropped his arm from mine and led the way.

"What about your wife and sister-in-law?"

"They're clucking around the house like two hens. I can't stand it anymore. If one doesn't have a chore for me, the other does. I said I had to get back to work. Trust me. One woman around the house is good. Two is a curse."

I chuckled faintly at his predicament.

At the end of the dock I explained to the others what had happened. The crowd slowly started to break up. Rolando and I walked over to the boatyard, got in the truck, and drove to All Island Rental.

There was a note affixed to the shop's front door. I immediately thought of the one nailed to the *Betsy-Karen* and snatched it down.

According to the document the Environmental Protection Agency of Rhode Island had issued it. It laid claim to a violation that I had improperly disposed of oil and gas. They had reason to believe I had been dumping the fluids into the ground. I was put on notice that an inspection of the premises was to follow. I handed the paper to Rolando and unlocked the door as he read it.

"This is crap," Rolando said. We entered the shop. "You're twice as careful as you have to be. I can testify myself that I've hauled petrol waste to the docks in sealed drums so that it can be disposed of legally on the mainland. You pay some company to take it. You've got receipts."

"I don't think that's the point." I stripped off my peacoat and set about starting a fire in the stove.

Rolando flung the paper on the counter. "What is the point?"

"Martin's truck."

"Huh?"

"Think about it." With a match I lit the kindling in the stove. "They searched the Island. No truck. They did aerial reconnaissance. No truck. They've monitored the ferries. Still no truck. There's only one conclusion they could reach: it's still on the Island and well hidden."

I beckoned Rolando to follow me. In the back room I unlocked the door and flung it open to reveal the alley. "Who's got the space to hide a Jeep?"

Rolando peered past me at the four sheds across the way.

"They've got no grounds for a search warrant," I said. "This is the next best thing."

No sooner had I said the words than we heard the whump-whump of a helicopter flying nearby. Craning my head out the door I saw it hovering in the distance. It was sleek and black and without markings.

"Did you check to see if the truck is gone?" Rolando asked over my shoulder.

"It's gone."

He breathed in relief. "Whew."

"I still don't like it."

"What are you going to do?"

"Call the EPA and find out who made the charges."

I closed the door and we went back into the shop.

There was a phone number on the paper from the EPA. I dialed it to be informed by a recording that the office was closed for the day. Business hours were eight a.m. to four. I knew it was after five.

The set up had been well planned. I was certain the EPA inspectors would be at my door no later than seven o'clock in the morning. No time to head this off without a search. Someone thought they had me trapped.

I recalled Gunner Hogan's warning, "There's going to be trouble."

Rolando puttered around the shop attempting to seem busy. He swept a little though it was not necessary. Afterwards he stocked the woodpile by the stove. I filed the return receipts from the previous few days.

Topping the pile with one last hunk of wood, Rolando broke the silence.

"How much authority does the EPA have?"

"I'm not sure. But they won't find any violations."

"Maybe you need a lawyer. It ain't right for them to go poking around on phony charges. There's got to be laws that protect you."

"Protect me from what? Let them search, or whatever the hell it is they do, and then they can leave me alone."

"If they want to squeeze you, that won't be the end of it. Next it will be the Internal Revenue Service or the Immigration agents."

"Your papers are in order. Aren't they?"

"No problem here, boss."

"Let the chips fall where they fall then. It will go away eventually. I'm not looking for trouble."

Evening was upon us. I lit two oil lanterns even though the electricity was fine. Rolando fed the stove a few sticks of wood and then said he would be on his way.

"Want the pickup?" I said.

"I'll be all right. You take it home."

"I'm not going home."

"How come?"

"I'd rather be here when they arrive. Seems to me that's going to be pretty early in the morning. Might as well camp out on the floor by the stove. We've still got some gear out back, sleeping bags and such."

"Anything you want I can get you?"

"I'll be fine. Go home to your house full of women."

"Sounds better than it really is." He made for the door. "Call me if they show up early."

I waved him on his way.

Grabbing one of the lanterns I went out back to shed A for the camping gear. I put the lantern down and fumbled with the lock. A noise above and to my left stopped me. A distant drone grew louder. It was the whump-whump of a chopper. I looked up. The black helicopter was outlined against the inky blue night sky.

The bird hovered above me, still to my left, at about three or four hundred feet. From the side hatch of the aircraft someone on board switched on a powerful light. The beam swept the alley where I stood. It moved over me and toward the ocean.

Inside A I selected a sleeping bag from the dozen I stocked. Returning to the shop I could still hear the helicopter in the distance.

There was some macaroni and cheese in the cupboard that I made for dinner. Later I unrolled the sleeping bag beside the stove out of reach of cinders. With the lamp beside me on the floor I got inside the bag with a volume of Camus short stories.

Before falling asleep I fed the fire once more, dimmed the lantern and rolled onto my side. I dreamt of the desert from the Algerian stories. Everything was bright and dry. I was camped near some palms in the middle of a journey. The purpose of the journey was unclear in the dream.

I awoke about four-thirty by my estimation. Beyond my little encampment by the stove the store had grown cold with the night. I added wood and rebuilt the fire. I let it burn up a bit before completely relinquishing my sleeping bag. My body had stiffened from the wood floor and I stretched long and hard and massaged my shoulder that had been on the floor.

After using the bathroom in the back, I splashed water on my face in the slop sink. Soon coffee was perking on the stove.

It was not a long wait. The sun was up by six-thirty when I heard a truck pull up out front. From the window I saw a green van with the logo of the Environmental Protection Agency painted on the side. Two men in khaki trousers and green uniform parkas were approaching my door. They were both tall. One was bulky with a clean-shaven broad face and a gleaming bald head. The other was slight, bearded, bespectacled, and had hair down to his shoulders. While I waited for their knock, I rolled and stowed away the sleeping bag.

"Sorry, gentlemen," I said opening the door. "I don't open for business until seven. But you can wait inside where it's warm."

The bald man seemed annoyed but the other smiled congenially. As I stepped back both men entered my store.

"Mr. Karl Hoffmann?" the larger one asked. "Do you own this business?"

"That's right."

"We're Latham and Grant from the Rhode Island EPA," the broad-faced man said.

"Which of you is which?"

"Huh?" he asked.

"I'm Grant," the thin man interrupted. He extended his hand. I shook it. "We're here on official business. You should have received formal notice."

"Do you boys have some identification? I'd like to see it."

That elicited a grunt from the larger man. Grant automatically reached for his pocket. Both men produced badges and picture ID. I took them and compared the laminated images to the men before me. Then I handed them back.

"What can I do for you?" I asked them both.

"You were issued a summons," Latham barked. He had to shift his bulk where he stood in order to return his wallet to his back pocket.

"There must be some mistake. I received no summons."

"It was posted to your door," Latham said. He took papers from a coat pocket and pretended to consult them. "It was dated yesterday. Our report says it was nailed outside to your door."

"That's a dumb thing to do. It gets a might windy around here."

"Sorry for any inconvenience, Mr. Hoffmann," Grant said. "But our Department has received a complaint that you're illegally disposing of chemical and petrol waste on your property."

"Who made the complaint?"

"We only divulge that information if charges are filed based on our investigation," Grant said. "That's the law."

I decided to ease up a bit and see how bad these guys were willing to push me. "You want some coffee while we sort this out?"

Latham declined but Grant said he would be grateful for some.

"What is it exactly you have to do?" I asked.

"Inspect your grounds," Latham said. He tried staring me down. "All your grounds."

Grant lent the declaration some credibility. "And take soil and water samples for testing at our lab. If the tests are negative for contamination you won't be seeing us again. Why don't we proceed and get this over with?"

"Fine by me," I said.

Grant gulped his coffee, fogging his glasses. He put his mug on the counter and announced they needed some gear from their truck.

Latham led the way as the two went out the door. I went behind the counter and sat on the stool. As I waited the sound of a second vehicle was audible. I could hear voices but could not distinguish any words.

Presently, the door opened again as Grant walked in. He carried a large red toolbox in his right hand. In his left was a three-foot-long auger; one end the corkscrew for drilling and the other end a T-bar for gripping and driving it into the ground. Behind Grant trudged Latham, puffing as if the fat man was out of breath. He carried a similar tool chest. Latham also brought some rubber tubing with a siphon.

Neither man stopped nor turned to close the door. I could hear wind outside and the fire in the stove flared up when the fresh air rushed in. A second later Colonel Devon came through the door followed by the African-American trooper from our first encounter.

"Good morning, Colonel," I called across the room. "What brings you out so early?"

The officer stopped in mid-room and eyed me coldly with a twinge of contempt. The last thing he expected was to be received with a friendly hail. His associate stopped to close the door. Devon cleared his throat with a harsh rasp.

"We usually ride backup for the EPA," Devon said. He hesitated a moment as if undecided what to say. "In case there's any trouble."

"No trouble here, Colonel."

"I'm glad to hear that." His manner was stilted as if the words came with difficulty. "Let these men do their job,"

"Like I said. No trouble here."

Grant put the toolbox on the counter and lay the auger on the floor. He seemed calm and at ease going about his job unlike the three behind him. They were gawking and shifting restlessly from foot to foot seeming confused about what was happening or what they should do about it.

"This Island survives on well water," Grant was saying. He undid the hasps of his box. "Most of the wells are pretty deep." I was getting a lesson in hydrogeography. "Despite the abundance of rock at the surface, the ground is mostly layered in shale and clay and sand. This is a very common composition for the eastern seaboard."

"Is there a lesson in this, Mr. Grant?" I asked.

"Drainage. Excellent drainage. Take the snow for example. It's almost all gone. Really amazing when you think about it."

From his toolkit he took a glass tube with a rubber stopper wedged in the top.

"There was some flooding in town," I said.

"That's to be expected. Overdevelopment." He held the vial in front of him. "I'd like a sample of your tap water. Where's the sink?"

"Back room. Follow me."

I led Grant to the slop sink. The others remained in the store. The inspector let the water run a full minute and then stuck the test tube under the stream. He capped the sample with the stopper. From his pocket he took an indelible marker and made a notation on the vial.

"We'll test this at our lab."

Back in the shop he put the tube carefully in a rack in his box.

"Driving up I noticed you have four barns out back," Grant said. "Are the floors concrete, wood, or dirt?"

"Dirt."

"Excellent. That makes everything easier."

Gear in hand, Grant with the others in tow followed me out back to the alley. I stopped in the center of the pathway and held up my ring of keys.

"Which one?" I asked him nodding at the sheds.

"The one on the end," Devon said behind us.

We turned to see him pointing at D. Shed D was closest to the road.

"I know my job, Colonel," Grant said. "We're going to inspect them all. You're here in case I need you. This is my survey."

The nearly frail-looking EPA agent was in charge. He made that clear. Devon dropped his arm to his side, his eyes smoldering.

Grant turned to me. "Okay with you if we check that one first? Makes no difference to me but I've got to maintain some kind of relationship with the police."

"Suit yourself," I said.

The padlock on D flopped open when I turned the key.

"Let me get that," Grant said. He reached for the heavy wooden crossbeam.

He lifted it out and grabbed the handle of the right side door. I took the left handle and stepped back bringing the door with me. Devon, unable to control himself, charged up the center between us into the shed. He plucked a flashlight from his gun belt and swept the interior of the shed with its beam.

"Nothing," Devon muttered under his breath.

It was hardly nothing: a quarter of my inventory resided in D. Devon could have cared less. His shoulders drooped in failure.

"Better get started," Grant said. "This won't take long."

Latham followed Grant into the shed. Grant gave his partner the auger and the large man proceeded to bore a hole in the earthen floor at the center of the barn. Beckoning me into the shed, Grant asked me to identify the substances in different containers lodged within the facility. He checked the integrity of gas cans and oil drums. The larger powered equipment was inspected for leaks, spills, and seepage. Everything appeared to satisfy him.

Latham extracted the auger from the ground. With a pocketknife he dislodged soil from the coil and scraped it into plastic containers. Finished with that chore he used his siphon to take samples from oil and cleaning fluid drums. All the vials and containers were marked and dated.

When the agents were done I locked the shed and we moved to C. Again Colonel Devon was first through the door. A similar investigation was conducted in this barn. We moved to B. Devon's enthusiasm was waning. When I opened the door to A, Devon let the Black officer enter first.

On a shelf in A was a large unmarked plastic container filled with fine white powder. Latham and Grant ignored it but Devon grabbed it down. He unscrewed the cap and sniffed the contents.

"What is this?" he asked me.

"Nothing deadly, I assure you."

Devon cradled the jug in his left arm while wetting the tip of his right middle finger with his tongue. He thrust the free hand into the container and stabbed at the soft powder. Extracting his hand, he studied the powder adhered to his finger.

"I wouldn't taste that if I were you," I said.

"Why not? Is it poison?"

"Not exactly."

"Something else? What is it? I can have it tested."

I chuckled at the thought. This had gone far enough. Grant and Latham were packing up their equipment, ignoring Devon. Devon and I stared at each other. Him with his finger poised like a child whose mother lets him lick a bowl of cake icing.

"It's mixture of chalk and lime. People use it to make lines on the ground for baseball and football."

"What?" Devon snapped.

Latham and Grant started to laugh. The other trooper's face cringed with embarrassment for his boss.

"Out of bounds, Colonel," I said. "It's for games."

CHAPTER TWENTY-SIX

"You never spoke about Frank," I said. "Where does he live? Do you keep in touch?"

Judith shrugged. "Frank lives upstate. I don't see him much. I know that's terrible. You're going to hate me."

I reached for her. "I could never hate you."

She pulled back. Her eyes were moist.

"What's the matter?" I asked.

"He lives in a hospital. My brother doesn't even know me."

She allowed herself to be drawn into my arms. Her body quivered with sobs and she buried her face in my chest. It took time before she could compose herself and look at me.

"What happened?" I asked.

"No one can tell me. It started one day. I heard him talking. I thought he was calling me. We had an apartment in Peekskill. My mother was dead almost a year. I started college and worked nights in a diner. Frank was in high school. He just started talking to himself." The tears returned. "I tried to speak to him but it was like I wasn't there. It went on for hours. Then suddenly he seemed fine. I told him what happened and he didn't believe me. He claimed he was asleep and dreaming. He had no recollection of his ramblings."

Judith sat up in bed and dabbed her eyes.

"A few days later it happened again. A couple more days and again. Then it was happening every day. Sometimes he would be shouting. He was talking to someone, answering them, fighting them, and there was no one. I took him to our doctor. He couldn't find anything. He put Frank in the hospital for tests. Maybe it was a brain tumor, he told us. All the tests were negative. Physically Frank was fine. But the fits kept coming. Became more frequent, several times a day. Frank stopped going to school. Stopped bathing. Stopped eating. It was horrible. I didn't know what to do.

"Finally the doctor sent us to a psychiatrist. He prescribed medication, which helped for a while. My brother cleaned up and went back to school. It lasted a few months. He claimed he heard voices. Frank would wake up in the middle of the night and turn on every light in the apartment. He'd turn on the TV and blast the radio as if all the noise would banish the voices. I found him in the kitchen banging his head on the table pleading for the voices to stop. I called the doctor. He sent an ambulance and took Frank to the psychiatric ward of the hospital."

"Was Frank schizophrenic?"

Judith nodded. "He never got better. He got worse. No drugs helped. Frank withdrew so far it was as if the world no longer existed for him. He would be silent for days. Then he would mumble gibberish no one understood. He had to be fed and washed. To make him compliant, he was sedated. It became a nightmare. Poor Frank. Why?"

I had no answer.

"A few months later it appeared hopeless and Frank was transferred to the state-run facility in Wingdale," Judith said. "He's been there since. I used to visit a lot. Thought it might help. Nothing changed. He doesn't recognize me. He sits in a chair rocking back and forth talking to himself."

"How long?"

"Seven years. Seven dreadful years."

"I can't imagine how you feel."

"I've had this dream, a fantasy. My paintings sell and I buy a house with lots of grounds for Frank and myself. With all the money I'm making I hire a live-in nurse to care for him. Then maybe I wouldn't feel so guilty."

"You've no reason to feel guilty." I expected it would do no good. I would have felt the same way. That gave me an idea. "Why don't we go visit him?"

Judith brightened a little.

"Would you do that?" she asked.

"Of course."

"Just a warning, baby. It is very depressing."

"We'll have each other. It won't be that bad."

The following weekend we took the train to Wingdale. It was a bright summer Saturday. Leaving the City we started to pass farms and ponds and clapboard villages nestled in the valleys. Judith was cheery. The excursion seemed like the outset of a picnic on a perfect day.

At the Wingdale train station we engaged a taxi. Hospital visiting hours commenced at noon. It was a ten-minute drive to the hospital that Judith explained was a sanitarium.

The facility was a brick building with wide wooden front porch up some steps from ground level. Sitting chairs were scattered across the porch. Several occupied by what I assumed were patients. They ranged in age from teens to seniors. None were reading or seeming to enjoy the lovely weather. They sat, men and women alike, motionless and staring blankly. Not the slightest sense of interest or recognition came from them as Judith and I climbed the steps.

Inside the air was cooler and across the foyer was a reception desk. A woman sat at the desk in white uniform with a name badge pinned above her breast. Judith walked over to her. The wall clock above the nurse read exactly noon.

"Good afternoon," Judith addressed the lady. "We're here to see Frank Valenti."

The woman consulted her computer and asked Judith to spell the last name.

"That would be Ward Six - D," the woman said reading from the screen. "Please sign the register." She pushed a marble-covered notebook across the desk and held out a pen.

Judith signed her name and handed me the pen. I scrawled my signature.

The attendant started to give us directions. Judith politely interrupted her.

"I know the way. Thank you."

The elevator took us up six floors. The facility was well kept, clean, airy, but there was a drabness about everything. The floors were gray, the walls white. Except for the occasional red EXIT sign illuminated over certain doorways, nothing broke the monotony of the bare surfaces.

Halfway down the hallway Judith stopped at a door with a Plexiglas window. She peered through the window.

"This is it," she said. "Are you sure you want to do this?"

I nodded despite the knot in my stomach. Judith pushed open the door and I followed her into the ward.

There were a dozen beds in the room. Four beds had patients in them. Three were on the near side, one across the way. All the occupants were male. Two of them in the near beds were completely prone as if asleep. The other was propped up against white pillows, as was his compatriot across the aisle. They both had that vacant gaze like the people on the porch.

"That's Frank," Judith whispered. She took my hand and with her other unobtrusively pointed across the room.

I looked over at the patient. He appeared to be in his mid-twenties, gaunt with beard stubble on his chin and cheeks. His hair, like his beard, was dark. It was uncombed and contributed to his appearance of dishevelment. The top button of his gray pajamas was unbuttoned and the blanket and sheet were rolled down to his knees.

Judith walked to the bed and kissed the coarse-haired cheek. In a gesture fused with patience and affection, she buttoned the button.

"Hello, Frank. It's me. Judith."

His head never moved and his eyes never blinked. I had never seen anything like it. The form in the bed was oblivious to her. Judith rolled the bedclothes up to his waist where his hands rested motionless in his lap.

"I've brought a friend with me," Judith went on bravely. "His name is Karl. Will you say hello to Karl for me?"

I stepped up to the bed beside Judith. Frank did not stir a muscle.

Judith kept talking.

"Karl is a carpenter and poet. A very good poet, I might add. You like poetry, don't you, Frank?" Judith reached up to stroke his head and flattened the wild strands of hair. "Karl also likes baseball. Just like you, Frank. I'll tell you a secret. I think I'm in love with him. But don't tell him. He doesn't know yet."

"Judith," I said. We had been living together for months. Except in deep sexual passion, I had never heard the words.

"Shh," Judith said over her shoulder. "I was speaking to Frank. You weren't supposed to hear."

Judith stepped back and guided me beside the bed with a hand in the small of my back.

"You talk to him. He's being rude to me."

I was at a loss for words and said something stupid like, "How are you doing, buddy?"

Frank's head turned slightly with a jerk in my direction. Maybe it was the sound of an unfamiliar voice.

"Keep talking," Judith urged.

"So you like baseball," I said to Frank. Nothing else came to mind. "I'm teaching it to your sister. We've been to a couple of Mets games. Maybe you could come along some time. Would you like that?"

Frank started to rock back and forth. He turned to face me. His eyes were still blank and flat in their sockets. He spoke in a dry whisper.

"Are you Tom Seaver?"

Judith grabbed my hand and squeezed.

"No. But I've seen him play."

He turned his head back to look at nothing. "I thought you were Tom Seaver."

"He couldn't make it," I said dumbly. "He asked me to say hello for him."

"You're not Tom Seaver." He did not look at me again.

"No. I'm not." I wished I was.

Frank was gone. He catalogued my voice against all the others in his brain and dismissed it. Judith and I tried to engage him again. Nothing worked.

After a while it was pointless. Judith leaned forward and kissed Frank's cheek and said we were going. I patted him on the shoulder.

"Take care of yourself," I said.

Frank's eyes showed no recognition.

It felt good to be outside in the sun. The receptionist dialed a cab company for us and we waited at the foot of the porch steps. Judith's eyes were dry and her face set in a kind of resolute acceptance. Bright light gleamed off her high cheekbones. There was no anger.

"Thanks for coming." She gazed off to the road beyond the sanitarium's gates.

I put my arm around her waist and tried to draw her closer. She held her ground as if set in granite. Dropping my arm I moved in front to face her. My interposed body drew a shadow across her impassive features.

"Don't thank me. That's not what this is about. This is for you and me. Frank is not with us. Maybe he never will be. I can't change that. It's not fair, but then you know that. What I can tell you is that I love you. I love you more than anything and anyone in the world. As I am, I am for you. It's all I have to give, but it's everything."

Judith looked into my eyes. Her face went soft, the corners of her mouth turning upward in a gentle smile. The set eyes, banishing a cold vision, grew deep with small lights twinkling in the farthest reaches.

"Oh, Karl." She reached up to wrap my shoulders in her arms and pull my face down to hers. "Oh, Karl."

We kissed under the lifeless, loveless gazes of the people on the porch above us. In a fleeting, glorious wrenching of the world, I thought our passion would haul them back from the brink where they teetered so unknowingly. The moment passed. Our embrace unfolded. A breeze drifted across the lawn and the faces of the patients nearby stared on and on.

Judith and I stood side by side holding hands. We faced the road and saw the taxi come from a long way off down the corridor of trees that flanked the highway. It got us to the station just in time for the train home.

The following week, Judith set to painting the portrait of my mother from the photograph. She had to imagine colors as the print was only shades of black and gray and white. Center stage of the Kirov Theater began to appear in the corner of our apartment; the natural light from the window adjacent to the easel seeming almost like spotlights bearing down on the dance floor. Judith's style was evolving. The primitive shapes and bold flat colors softened and blended. Dissipating shadows crept in from the wings of the stage. I could see the grain in the wood floorboards where the dancer's feet pinpointed the surface as an arrow might wedge a target.

"When will you paint her face?" I asked.

The composition was several weeks in process. All that seemed needed were details of the ballerina's shoulders, neck, and face that remained an umber blur in the center of the canvas.

"When it comes to me, baby." Her session for the day was concluded. She was cleaning her brushes.

I was on the couch reading, content to spy her tenderly stripping the fine bristles of her tools with a rag. Satisfied, she stored the brushes upright in a jar and set to scraping her pallet and wiping it with a different cloth.

"You didn't write today," she scolded. Judith knew I was observing her efforts.

"Not today. I finished a piece last night while you were at work. I want to let it flush from my system before I start another."

"If it isn't flushed, how do you know it's finished?"

"It's finished. I can tell."

"Let me see it." She folded her rags neatly then went to the kitchen to wash her hands. The light in the window was fading. Long, low horizontal streams of sun reached her back in the next room.

"It isn't that finished," I called after her. "It needs to sit for a while before I can edit it."

"Is it a poem or a story?"

"A story."

"If you're not going to let me read it you might as well go down and get the mail."

Judith was back in the room. I put my book on the table, rose and brushed her cheek with a feathery kiss, my hand at her waist to stroke down across her jean-clad thigh.

"Maybe later. It can wait," I said suggestively.

She laughed. "You can wait."

In mock resignation I tramped to the door and started down the hall for the stairs to the lobby.

Just as well, I thought. The story had been about her brother and I wanted to edit it carefully before showing it to Judith.

In our mailbox were two envelopes. One was cream-colored, the other stark white. Taking them out I scanned the return addresses. My heart skipped a beat reading the first, two beats as I digested the second.

The cream envelope was from Grub Street Press. The white one bore the letterhead of Boston College.

CHAPTER TWENTY-SEVEN

Don Ostros returned to Bittern Island by week's end. He invited me to dinner that Friday night. A teenager was dispatched by the Don to deliver his message. I thought I recognized the lad from the *cantina*. When he relayed Ostros's invitation I tipped him a couple of bucks and he set off for town at a run.

Rolando came to work knowing Ostros was back but not the hospitality extended to me.

"You going?" Rolando asked.

"Of course I'm going."

Rolando did not pursue it and there was no more talking as he plodded about his chores.

Outside was a bright clear day. I switched on the radio to hear a storm predicted. The weatherman assured us it would be rain and not snow.

On the counter was a disassembled electric hedge trimmer.I spent an hour sharpening the blades and oiling the parts. When it was back together I plugged it in and switched on the power.

"Whwwrr," went the tool.

The noise startled Rolando. He had been sitting across the room mending a volleyball net. The mess of strings slipped from his fingers and slid to the floor. He cursed and bent to pick it up.

"What did you do that for?" he snapped.

"Checking I re-wired it right. How come you're so jumpy?"

He brooded a moment and said nothing. Then he gathered the net in his lap, stood up, and slipped the web back into its box. He spoke without looking at me.

"They towed Captain Ray's boat this morning."

"That was a mean thing to do. Old Ray has nothing to do with this."

"Heard from the EPA?"

"No, I even doubt I will."

"They didn't find anything wrong."

"Is that even the point? Devon wanted to search my premises and he did. Everything else is window dressing as far as I'm concerned."

"Where do you suppose it is?"

I feigned confusion. "What?"

"Martin's Jeep."

"Do you really want to know?"

Rolando looked at me across the room. His face slowly contorted in front of my eyes. The result was a look of pain. His eyes narrowed in a concerted effort to fight it down. As he won over the pain a shudder of fear replaced it.

"Come sit over here, my friend." I pulled another stool next to mine. "Talk to me."

Rolando hesitated, rolled his shoulders, and crossed the room to behind the counter and hoisted himself up onto the stool.

"Tell me what's happened?"

Rolando put his hands in his lap, lowered his head, and then raised it again.

"My wife and her sister," he began in a hollow voice, "they have no papers. It used not to matter so much, especially out here on the Island. That's why the sister came over. Nobody ever bothered anybody out here."

"Who knows about this?" Despite his bluff macho complaining, I knew Rolando worshiped Esperansa. The sister I knew nothing about.

"Who knows?" He cocked his head, his eyes filled with hatred. "People who can make trouble. That's who."

"How do you know that?"

With reluctance, as if maybe it had disappeared, Rolando reached inside his shirt and felt for the letter. He brought it out and handed it to me. I did not need to read it. One glance at the official marking on the envelope and I was sure of the contents. I handed it back.

"When?" I asked.

"Thirty days. They must present themselves in Providence at the Office of Immigration."

"That gives us a little time. We can get you a lawyer."

"I called one. A guy that helps a lot of us on the mainland."

"What did he say?"

"Esperansa's not the problem. My own papers are correct. If I marry Esperansa in the right way, in a church or before a judge, she's safe. It's her sister, Carmelina. She will be deported. They have no family left in Guatemala. Everybody's dead or emigrated. She will be all alone with nothing. My wife can't stop crying at the thought."

"Have you told this to Don Ostros?"

Anger flashed in Rolando's eyes. "Don Ostros? He brought this on us. It's him they want. They'll ruin all our lives to get him."

I made no reply. The anger drained from my friend's face. Rolando's eyes lowered to look at his hands in his lap. His body swayed gently back and forth. My hand went to his shoulder. Rolando steadied himself and raised his face to look at me.

"What am I going to do, Karl?"

"I'm not sure. We have a little time to think. That, and I suppose you ought to get married. It would solve half the problem."

Rolando nodded in recognition that he had already decided that option.

"And Carmelina?" he asked.

"Short of finding another citizen husband, there must be something."

"We've not enough time."

"We must consider all possibilities. That includes your putting the question to Don Ostros. For one thing, he has connections. For another, he'll expect it of you."

Again Rolando only nodded. All his anger had passed. There was a void where it had been. Two things fought for the vacant space. Hope and dread.

"Do you want me to speak about it to Don Ostros at dinner tonight?" I said.

"No, you're right. This is something I must bring to him. So I should do it myself."

Rolando hunched his shoulders accepting the responsibility. With a decision reached, his features relaxed into a curious calm.

"Are you all right?" I asked.

"No, but there is nothing I can do at this moment. I must wait to speak with Don Ostros. Tomorrow, maybe, after your dinner."

"There is one thing you can do in the meantime."

"What's that?"

"Take Esperansa to the mainland and get your marriage license. Anything we know we can do should be done swiftly."

I took my hand from Rolando's shoulder as he slid from the stool to his feet. His hand came up to grasp mine. We shook as partners.

Rolando donned his coat, cast me one last look of commitment, and left the shop.

I took the hedge trimmer out to Shed C and hung it back on the wall rack. Locking the door I put the key in my pocket and started down the alley toward the road. Past D, I turned off the path and started up the slope of sand of the first hillock to the south. From the crest of it I saw the ocean. To my right were large rocks, a series of them trailing off and down from the bluff. Against the sand it appeared an archipelago, obstinate islands in a sea of flat foam. I turned back to the water. An offshore wind held the breakers momentarily erect. Swirls of spray whipped from their peaks as they paused, shuddered, and folded over in a wild, crashing charge to shore. There their energy dissipated until they lapped at the extreme of the tide line.

The wind on the rise at my back seemed determined to lift me, impel me toward the brink of the shore and beyond. I held my ground, boots grinding into the sand.

Not like this, I thought. It is not this easy. There is no wind that drives a man like a ship of sail. No tide, no current he can not navigate with his will.

And if I will it so, is there a farther shore? Or is there only sea? This mirror of sky, this deepest dream.

"Oh, Judith," I heard myself say aloud. "I'm holding on until you come for me. Don't send the wind or the waves. Come get me yourself. I've no belief in signs, not a moon nor a cloud or the spinning of a compass at the poles. Only you. If that is too much to ask, then I'm a rock like these, hard and set. Am I, Judith? Am I cold and solid at the center?"

I turned to walk back. The wispy grass was bent over in the wind. A gnarled chunk of driftwood caught my eye and I stooped to pick it up. Its outer bark flaked off in my fingers. I flung it toward the top of the next dune. It landed and rolled down the side.

"Arrhk, arrhk."

A bittern appeared out of the grass cursing me in fright. I stood stock-still while it settled again, the bird's body melding before my eyes into the reeds from which it had sprouted.

Down from the bluff I walked, back to the store, through the back room where the smell of his tobacco announced Gunner Hogan.

"Where you been?" Gunner asked.

"Walking. Nothing special."

Gunner grunted he understood. He poured himself coffee. "Heard about Captain Ray's boat? Towed her away."

"Rolando told me."

"Rolando? Where is the Latino leprechaun?"

"Off to the mainland I imagine. There's a bit of trouble. He's got to get a marriage license and make Esperansa his proper wife."

"She pregnant?"

"I wouldn't know. That's not the issue. It's the other thing."

"Oh, that. At least it's something with a straightforward remedy. Not like all the other crap going on around this Island."

"It's more complicated than that."

Gunner listened as I described Rolando's predicament. He stroked his chin and sipped coffee, taking it in.

"The bastards," he cursed when I finished. "They sure know how to flex their muscles. First the Coast Guard goes after Captain Ray. Now it's my buddy Rolando's family."

"There's even more to it than that."

I recounted my visit from the Environmental Protection Agency with the assistance of the State Police.

"Bastards," Gunner said again. "What could they hope to find?"

For the moment I claimed I had no idea.

"Do you think they might taint up some evidence?" he asked.

"No."

"How can you be sure?"

"Because they accomplished what they really wanted in the first place."

"What's that?"

"Gunner, this gets pretty involved. I don't want you in the thick of it."

"The hell you say. Come on. Out with it. You and Rolando are the only friends I've got. If there's trouble, we close ranks and stick together."

"Is that an order, Colonel?"

"It's a promise from an old friend."

"Then pull up a chair, old friend. The story is longer than you think."

After feeding the stove with wood, Gunner and I sat around it while I related the history of Janus Martin's Jeep. Intermittently Gunner took pokes from his flask. I declined it the first two times and he ceased to ask. Other than that, he said not a word during my recitation. I left out the part about the truck in the dunes mentioning only that it was gone from my shed.

At the end I fell silent and stared at the flames through the grate. It was very warm in the store and I stripped off my flannel shirt, flung it on the counter, and sat by Gunner in my tee shirt. Beads of sweat dotted Gunner's forehead as well.

He took another sip of whiskey. With the other hand he tapped ashes from his pipe into the stove. Some fell onto the metal floor shield around the stove that was dotted with spent cinders. He looked up at me.

"You know, Karl? The truth is, I've never been a big fan of Don Ostros. I live alone and mind my business. Except for you and Rolando, most of my contact with the rest of the Island is a passing how-do-you-do for the sake of civility."

That was oversimplified but I let it pass. Gunner continued.

"Pretty much I like it that way. That doesn't mean I'm stupid or blind. I've had a fair idea what Ostros has been up to for years. Plodding around this Island most days and a lot of nights is what I do. I ain't nosy, but I got eyes and instincts. I've seen a few boats slip around Walls Head into Jacob's Cove and disappear by the fish plant in the dead of night when the tide's high and there weren't any moon. I knew it weren't no kids jacking for eels and crabs. And it weren't none of my business so I went on my way.

"It ain't only Ostros. I've seen more than I care to remember about other folks as well. Passed Archie Bealer's house to hear that drunk beating his wife. Seen Dan McCallum sneak out at midnight to leave a wife and six kids for a slip of a girl that waits tables at one of the summer cafes. Spied illegal nets stowed aboard a trawler or two before sunrise. It just gives me a whole lot of never-mind."

Gunner rose from his stool, took a worn blue handkerchief from his pocket, opened the stove hatch with it, and spat a wad of phlegm into the fire. There was a sizzle and a spark shower. Gunner closed the grate and sat down.

"Seems it simply doesn't pay to know anything at all," he said. "God knows I learned that lesson true enough." The flask came back out. "Not that you'd understand. You with all your books trying to cram so much into your head so it must be fit to burst. For what? You and me, we're here on the same Island and that's a fact. Not that I blame you. Judith and all. I understand it. I only wish you'd see the point. That there is no point."

This time I reached for the flask and downed a swallow. The heat from the stove and burning flash of liquor made me feel feverish. I felt sweat at the back of my neck and in the crotch of my jeans. I handed back the flask.

Gunner took it and turned it over in his hands. The eagle crest of his Army division stared up at him. "In sixty-seven I lost damn near two platoons to friendly fire. Some artillery officer six miles away got the coordinates backwards. Rained down a full barrage on my position. A bunch of good boys blown to bits and not an enemy soldier within three thousand yards of where we were dug in. What's an officer do?" He looked up at me. "They don't teach us that one at West Point."

"What did you do?"

"Got myself bandaged up and hightailed it to II Corps HQ and threw up a stink. Wanted the lame bastard in charge of artillery court-martialed. Know what they said?"

I shook my head that I had no idea.

"They said it never happened. At least not the way I knew it. Told me to my face we had been pounded by the best artillery division in the North Vietnamese Army. Bullshit, I said. I pulled out a wad of maps and aerial recon photos and told Corps command they'd lost their minds. Somebody fucked up and he was on our side. Not at all, claimed the generals. Very confused situation. But they had sorted it out properly. It was NVA fire for sure.

"To prove it they gave me a fucking medal for courage under fire and sent me home. You see? People at home were starting to get antsy about the War. Couldn't have headlines screaming about two platoons of U.S. paratroopers obliterated by their own artillery."

"Jesus Christ," I muttered.

"He wasn't there either. Anyway, they pulled a bunch of good old U.S. shrapnel out of my legs, courtesy of our keen-eyed artillery. I farted around stateside a year or so, a hospital here, desk job there, until I finally put in my papers. My wounds qualified me for disability pension.

"Moral of the story? Sometimes what you know ain't worth knowing."

"You believe that?"

"What do you think? Look at me. I was a colonel of an elite outfit. The finest men ever put in the field. Now look at me. Do you see the man who could have been that man?"

"You could have gone to the newspapers and told them the truth. Some people did about the real things going on in Vietnam. It made a difference." I regretted saying it immediately. I did not want to hurt or insult this man.

Gunner stared at the floor a moment. "I wore the uniform and I'd sworn the oath. Sometimes you hold on to the stupidest things to keep from going completely insane. By the time you figure it out for yourself, it's too late to matter any way."

He looked up at me again. "You're the first person I've told that story to in twenty years. Now it doesn't make any difference. The War is over, my men are still dead, and I'm one notch above a vagrant in a corner of the world that doesn't give a damn. Well, I don't give a damn either. Not anymore. But I'm here for you and Rolando. You're what I got left. After this it's hell or high ground. Which one? I couldn't tell you."

"Don Ostros invited me to dinner," I said suddenly.

Gunner looked suspicious. "When?"

"Tonight."

Gunner scratched his cheek vigorously, his face pursed in thought or consternation. He stood up, the chair and his cranky bones objecting loudly.

"He's reached a decision," Gunner said.

"What do you mean?"

"Ostros is a careful man. Everything he does has purpose. He's like a general in his own little world. When he makes up his mind, he acts. I don't like this, Karl. Why did he come back? He knows they're out to get him."

"Maybe he's tired of running," I mused aloud. I was thinking of the scared boy hiding in the hills shivering from fear and want of a campfire.

"Then that makes him twice as dangerous," Gunner said. Then he did a strange thing: he laughed. It was a hard, mirthless laugh from the back of his throat. He opened the door to the fire and spat again. A few cinders leapt from the stove, missed the shield and landed on the wood floor. I ground them out with my boot.

CHAPTER TWENTY-EIGHT

Judith was offered an adjunct position at Boston College. It required she teach two courses in their Fine Arts program. The first was art history dealing with Postimpressionism. The latter was "Basic Composition in Oils."

"I better brush up," she quipped.

I snatched the letter from her and read it. She had to report the third week of August.

"Now yours," she said.

I ripped the cream-colored envelope and withdrew a folded paper.

"Read it out loud."

"Dear Mr. Hoffmann," I began reciting. "Grub Street Press is pleased to accept your poem, '*A Most Patient Winter,*' for our Fall issue. Two complimentary copies will be sent upon publication. Thank you for thinking of Grub Street Press and we look forward to future submissions."

It was signed, "THE EDITORS."

"You've done it," Judith said. "You darling man, you've done it."

"We've both done it."

"A celebration is in order."

"Right. What do you feel like?"

"Champagne. What else?"

"We don't have any."

"So we'll go where they do have some. After all, you're a published poet and I'm a professor."

"And neither of us has made a dime at it."

"Don't be so plebeian. We're artists. Go take a shower."

I took Judith to a French restaurant, where we ordered champagne. Though it was the cheapest one on the wine list, our waiter opened it with flourish.

I raised my glass. "To literature and art."

"And to us."

We drank the champagne and replenished our glasses.

When dinner was over, Judith and I went to Central Park and took a carriage ride. It was a warm evening and the lights of the City came on as the day's glow slipped away. Our driver deposited us at the end of the Park near the fountain in front of the Plaza Hotel.

"Want to go home?" I said.

"Not yet."

I knew what she was feeling. The City was all around us and we a part of it. That was going to change. We had not discussed it but were aware of the implications. Judith's job was in Boston. What she did not know was whether or not I was going with her.

"Let's go downtown and hear some music," I said.

We walked down Broadway. It was as if the City existed only for us. Doormen tipped their hats. Con vendors subdued their acts in mute respect as we strode by them. Traffic lights were in synch with our progress allowing us on and down the crevice through midtown. Past the Theater District, Times Square, the Garment Center, and Chelsea we walked. The sights, smells, sounds were all familiar yet different. Changed because we changed. It was not really a part of us any longer. We were phantom returnees in later life that pause at a familiar intersection and say, "I remember this place," or pass an exhibit with the comment, "We've seen that," though neither of us spoke.

At the edge of Greenwich Village the street narrowed. There was less business and more couples cramming the sidewalks as we pressed on.

Judith squeezed my arm. "I hope Boston is like this. Will you come see?"

"You know I will. I'm coming with you. I'll always be with you."

With that we were free of it. We were not of time or place, but each other. Our feet stopped moving and we turned in an embrace. Despite the stuffy night, a wave of cool release washed over us.

"Hey, you two," a voice called.

Pete Franco stood by the curb. I had not seen him in months. I remembered thinking the last time: he's changing. The wild hair that use to dust his shoulders was pulled back into a ponytail. His beard was groomed into a goatee. An earring swung from one lobe.

"Jesus. What are you two glowing about?" Franco asked.

"We're moving," I said. "Up to Boston."

"Beantown? Did a gig up there once. It ain't the Big Apple and it ain't the Big Easy, but it ain't bad."

"What about you, Pete?" Judith asked.

"Same old same old, but it's got a new tune." He shifted from foot to foot. "Been knocking out some jazz. Brings in more work than the blues. A man's gotta eat."

"Where are you playing?" I asked.

"Round the corner at Preston's. Why don't you check it out?"

I looked at Judith and she nodded. One more part that would stay as we went on.

"Sure. Let's go," I said to Franco.

"Great," Franco said weakly. "You guys go ahead. I'll be there in a minute. I got to wait here for a guy. He's setting me up with a studio gig. I'll catch you in a couple."

There was a desperate insistence in his voice. Gone was the laidback Cajun ease. The hands trembled. I looked at Franco's face. It was pale and his lip quivered.

"Come on," I said to Judith. "He'll catch up to us."

We turned and started for the corner. I had an arm under Judith's elbow propelling her.

"What's the matter?" she asked.

"He's strung out. He's waiting to score dope."

"Oh, no."

"Don't look back. Keep walking."

As we went to turn the corner her head swung past me to look back up the street.

"Oh my God," Judith shrieked. "That man's got a knife."

I turned in that instant. A bulky man in a black vest had Franco pressed up against a building. The man had one hand at Franco's throat. In the other hand I saw the glint of steel.

"Leave him alone," I shouted. My feet impulsively started up the block in a run.

Still gripping Franco's neck, the man turned to the sound of my voice. He had a thick mustache and dark sunken eyes.

"Let him go, damn you." My arms were pumping in a dash toward them.

I was about to fling myself into the burly figure when the assailant's knife disappeared into the open flap of Franco's shirt. Franco's head snapped back and struck the wall.

"No," I screamed.

I reached out. My arm grazed his shoulder as the man spun and tucked himself releasing Franco. His left fist swung up and impacted my solar plexus. The air in my lungs came out in a whoosh. As my head drooped, the guy's closed right hand came up glancing off my left cheekbone.

I threw a punch at his midsection. His gut was taut, prepared for the blow.

"Outta my fucking way." Then he slammed both fists into my shoulders.

My strength was depleted. My lungs craved air. Wobbling from his last assault I looked up, straining for breath. The man eyed me a second, turned, and bolted around the corner.

Judith reached me. "Baby, are you all right?"

Air rushed into my aching lungs. "I'm okay." I expelled the air and sucked in more. "Pete's been stabbed."

Franco had collapsed at the base of the wall. I dropped to my knees beside him. His torso was doubled over and his arms cradled his stomach. Franco's shoulders heaved, each labored breath accompanied by a heavy moan.

"Call an ambulance," I yelled to Judith.

With my hands on Franco's shoulders I eased him back up against the bricks in a sitting position. His hands clenched the hilt of the knife protruding from his abdomen.

"Hold on, Pete," I urged him.

Pete Franco neither heard nor saw me. His mouth moved but he spoke no words, only a stricken moan. Franco was slipping away. His eyes began to narrow and his head settled down again. He coughed and blood sprayed the sleeves on my arms. Franco's body shuddered and went limp, his hands falling away from the knife to settle in the pool of blood soaking his legs.

I heard a siren. It seemed a long way away. Voices were closer, voices loud and harsh. I tried to stand up when suddenly I was pulled from behind. My body lifted and I went along with the force. I tried to turn to say I was okay when the unseen hands jerked me to my left and propelled me until my body hit the wall and my cheek and nose struck the bricks.

I heard Judith scream, "What are you doing? He's his friend."

She was ignored.

"Hands behind your head," a man shouted in my ear. "Spread your legs."

A fist drove into my right kidney. My knees buckled but a hand behind my neck held my collar keeping me on my feet.

"Hands behind your head, shit for brains."

My arms went slowly up and my fingers laced behind my neck. I felt a cuff close over my right wrist. The arm was jerked down and behind, then my left, and the other cuff was secured. Roughly I was patted down from armpits to ankles.

"He didn't do anything," Judith was yelling.

I was spun around. A short, hatless blond cop stood before me. He frisked me again from the front.

"Where's the fucking dope?" He thrust his hands into my pockets. My wallet, keys, change, and a penknife were extracted and dropped to the ground.

Numbness took hold of my body. My brain drifted cool and light. I looked for Judith. A second policeman was interposed between her and me with his arms raised, cautioning her to stay back. He was taller than the one shouting up at my face.

"Where's the dope?"

"I don't have any dope." My cheek stung from the impact against the building. I knew it stung though there was no pain. I felt my lip fattening.

"You gonna give me a hard time, asshole?" the short cop snapped.

Behind him I saw paramedics arriving. One had a kit bag and dashed to the slumped form of Franco on the pavement. My keeper watched him check for vital signs.

"He dead?" the cop asked.

The medic nodded.

The cop shook me and barked, "You're fucked now, dickhead."

"I've told you. It wasn't me."

"Shut up and save it for the detectives." He jabbed my gut. "You're under arrest."

The cop grabbed my elbow and nudged me toward a police cruiser at the curb.

"Where are you taking him?" I heard Judith demand.

"Get in," the cop at my side said.

I stooped and slid into the back of the police car. The door slammed behind me.

At the precinct I was pulled from the car and led up the steps. One cop to either side, we walked past the main desk, through a doorway and up a flight of stairs. I was pushed through an open door and jammed into a chair. The tall cop undid one of my cuffs and resecured it to the arm of the chair. Both cops left. For several minutes I was alone. My chair faced a long table. My back was to the door.

"What's your name?" a voice behind me said.

A shirt-sleeved detective passed my chair and sat across the table. He was followed by another in jeans, tee shirt, and black windbreaker. This one stood in the corner of the room.

"Karl Hoffmann," I said to the white shirt detective.

"Spell it." He had a form and was filling it out.

I spelled my name while he wrote. He asked my address, social security number, and occupation. In a monotone I supplied the answers. When the information was recorded, he laid down the pen.

"I'm Detective Brian Stiles." He jerked his head at the guy in the corner. "That's my partner, Ralph Hodges."

I nodded with disinterest.

"Tell me, Karl. Who's the dead junkie you left on the street?" Stiles asked.

"Pete Franco. I didn't leave him. Some cops hauled me away."

"Friend of yours?"

"Yes. He was."

"You don't strike me as a hop head. We're gonna check. Nice and easy now."

Hodges came out of the corner, took my free arm, undid the button, and pushed up the bloody sleeve of my shirt. He inspected my arm. Satisfied, he checked the arm shackled to the chair, careful to avoid Franco's blood.

Hodges grunted. "He's clean." He left the sleeves up and returned to the wall.

A uniformed policeman came in and took the paper Stiles filled out.

"We're running you for priors," Stiles said. "You been arrested before?"

"No."

He smirked. "Is that a fact? I'm impressed. So how come all your friends are junkies? What are you? A social worker?"

Stiles sat back in his chair, regarding me implacably.

"I told you. I'm a carpenter." I was getting annoyed. "You guys made a mistake."

"You think so? Maybe." He lifted his hands in a gesture of ignorance. "That's what we're here to find out. Isn't it?"

"Shouldn't I be read my rights?"

"Why? We're only talking. You, me, and Ralph, we're just talking."

I was not about to be jerked around any longer.

"The cop on the street said I was under arrest." For emphasis I lifted my cuffed hand and let it fall against the arm of the chair.

"Arrest is just a word to hurry things along," Stiles said. "Out on the street we've got to defuse a situation before something ugly happens. That's all it is. If you were really under arrest we'd be filling out a lot more forms, taking your picture, sending you for fingerprints."

"Reading me my rights."

"Yeah. Shit like that."

Stiles looked over at Hodges and nodded. Hodges came forward and unlocked the brace around my wrist.

"Better?" Stiles asked.

Before I could answer the door opened and the same cop from before came in. He carried a folder and placed it on the table in front of Detective Stiles. When he left, he closed the door behind him. Stiles opened the folder and read the contents. He closed the folder and slid it down the table as far as he could reach. Hodges stepped forward and picked it up. There was silence while he read it.

Stiles cleared his throat. "There was a young woman with you when you were picked up. Who is she?"

"You didn't arrest her? Did you?"

The detective shook his head. "Who is she?" he asked again.

"My girlfriend."

"Her name?" Hodges asked from the corner.

Now I really had enough. I had waited to see if they brought Judith into custody. Apparently not. That was all I wanted to know. My options got broader.

"Screw you," I said to Stiles. I turned my head to Hodges. "Screw you too." I looked at the ceiling. "Turn me loose or get me a lawyer. I have nothing more to say."

"Why the attitude, Karl?" Stiles said.

He retrieved the folder that Hodges had left on the edge of the table. He opened it. "You've got a clean record. You're a veteran. Why don't you want to help us out?"

I had made my play so I kept my mouth shut. There was a knock on the door. Hodges crossed the room and went outside. A few seconds later he opened the door and asked Stiles to join him. I was left alone.

It seemed like ten minutes before they returned. When they did, Stiles placed my wallet, keys, the penknife, and my loose change on the table without a word. I stared at my belongings, not moving to get them.

Stiles ended the stalemate. "You're free to go, Mr. Hoffmann. Patrol just picked up the killer a few blocks away. He's the candy-man from the corner where your friend bought it. We're done here."

Without uttering a word I stood up, pocketed my property, buttoned my shirt cuffs.

"If we need you we'll be in touch," Hodges said.

I walked out of the room without looking at either cop.

Downstairs I saw Judith waiting on a bench along the wall. She caught sight of me and rose as I approached.

"Baby? Are you okay? What happened?" she asked in a rush.

"I'm all right. Let's get out of here."

Resisting the urge to embrace her, I took her hand and led the way out to the street. We walked in silence, turned a corner and on the next street was a tavern.

"Let's have a drink. I need one," I said. "I'll tell you all about it."

We ducked into the pub and took stools at the bar. I ordered a shot of whiskey and a beer. Judith asked for a glass of red wine. I rolled up my sleeves to cover the dry blood. I drank the whiskey in two successive gulps.

"Did they harass you?" I asked. "I'm sorry."

"It's not your fault. After they put you in the car nothing happened really."

"What about Pete?"

"Some other cops showed up. They took pictures. One of the medics told me the Coroner was coming. I asked him where the station was and he told me, so I walked over and waited. If they hadn't let you go, I was about to call a lawyer."

"You know a lawyer?"

"One of the partners in the gallery is an attorney. I thought I'd try him."

"Good thinking. Luckily, it didn't come to that."

"Did they charge you with anything?"

"No," I said testily. I was still mad, but not at her.

In the dim light of the bar Judith examined my face. She went to touch it but stopped for fear of causing pain.

"You look like hell," she said.

"I don't usually mash my face against walls." For the first time that evening I started to feel pain.

Judith asked the bartender for ice. He served her a glass. Wrapping cubes in a napkin she held them up and tenderly placed the package against my protruding lower lip.

"I'd kiss you but you probably don't feel like it," she whispered.

"Kiss me anyway. Kiss me and say goodbye to New York. We're going to Boston."

CHAPTER TWENTY-NINE

The sun was setting when I closed shop to go home and clean up for dinner with Don Ostros. On impulse I drove past my house to the end of Mariners Path. West Beach lay before me, a red sun melting into the horizon. I turned north and climbed a dirt-packed road over the end of the ridgeline where it petered out into sand. A shallow valley followed and then the incline up to Walls Head, the cliffs that ringed the northwest corner of Bittern Island.

At the top I stopped, turned off the headlights, and got out. Jacob's Cove was below me in the darkness. Beyond I could see the lights of Grace. The lighthouse beam swung toward me, over me. The water in Jacob's Cove mirrored it like a white line bisecting a highway except it moved and narrowed toward the base of the Cove until it pointed to the wreckage of the fish plant.

Standing still I waited for the light to revolve again. In its absence, the water of Jacob's Cove was blue-black and shimmerless. There was no moon.

The beacon spun my way again. I watched it sweep the water. The mouth of the Cove was its narrowest part. Two strips of land, one the edge of Walls head, the other creeping out from the Gracetown side, almost touched but fell short where the tide rushed into the natural pocket. A duo of twinkling lights marked the tips of these extremities.

On the leeward side, the strip of light caused a flutter in the water. Briefly it appeared as a white smudge in an otherwise perfect path of iridescence. It was gone when I blinked.

I picked up the light again and followed its arc. It traversed the Cove, rose, pointed at the ridgeline, swung east out at sea beyond Grace, and disappeared only to reemerge northwest raking the Sound.

I waited. My eyes moved ahead of it, fixed on the darkness inside the Cove.

It happened again.

A white roiling dab spoiled the symmetry. It seemed to rise and fall for the instant it carried in the light. Only an instant, then the beam was beyond it, ahead of it.

This is a boat, I thought. I was sure of it. Without required running lights, it penetrated the Cove. I strained my vision to find it in the darkness. There it was. A low, sleek silhouette. Grace's light was catching the bow wake as it knifed through the water. Without the beacon, it was invisible.

But I had seen it.

I recalled Gunner Hogan recounting what he had seen, the clandestine sailings to and from Jacob's Cove on nights devoid of moonlight. And I thought of Don Ostros.

Driving home I felt a sense of foreboding taking hold of me. A lone vessel, unmarked, unlit in a deserted harbor. What was left of an abandoned enterprise hulking in desolation on the shore.

I took a cold shower. Once I was clean and dressed, I was in a better mood. Ostros's business was none of my own. He kept his word and Martin's truck had vanished from my premises. Let seagulls tell the tale if they cared to. The secrets of the dunes were none of my concern.

I drove to Gracetown.

Ostros was at a table sipping red wine. He welcomed me and offered the bottle.

"I'd prefer whiskey," I said taking my seat.

"Whatever you wish, my friend." A lift of his arm brought a waiter.

"Scotch, please," I said to the young man.

He bowed and scurried away. Ostros added more wine to his glass. I looked around the *cantina*. A fisherman and his wife were at one table. Another had four deckhands from the ferry service. Two elderly women sat at a table in one corner. They were widows I knew from the Island. One was the lady who did my laundry, Mrs. Wade. She nodded at me and went back to her meal. The rest of the tables were set but empty.

My drink was brought. I raised it in salute.

"Thank you for your invitation, Don Ostros." Ostros only inclined his head in acknowledgement. "Frankly, I didn't expect you back on the Island so soon."

"There are always affairs which need tending. How's your business?"

Times could be tough on Bittern Island, especially in winter. It was considered impolite to inquire about another's economic situation.

"The storm brought some revenue. There's another one on the way, according to the forecasts. But this time, no snow. Aside from that it's par for the season."

"You don't mind my asking?"

"Of course not."

"I'm happy for you."

"And you?"

"Obviously, I could do without this Janus Martin business. It's brought too much attention. Naturally I live here for the opposite reason."

"Things change."

"They do, but the important things should never change. They make us who and what we are."

The waiter brought two bowls of soup.

Ostros said, "I've taken the liberty of planning our menu."

"You're the expert."

The soup was a hot sort of gazpacho. Chunks of fresh vegetables swirled in a cream base. I sampled it. It was spicy.

"Delicious," I said.

Only then did Ostros start in on his own bowl. We finished the soup without speaking. I drained my scotch glass. Declining a refill, I opted for a glass of the Don's wine. He filled my glass himself and called for another bottle.

The main course was a rack of lamb roasted in garlic. Grilled potatoes and steamed asparagus came with the lamb. It was an excellent meal.

Whatever his purpose for inviting me, he did not mention and I did not ask. We spoke of nothing consequential as we dined.

When our plates were cleared, Ostros asked for coffee and cognac. The coffee was Rolando's blend. We sipped some and then picked up our snifters of brandy. This time we did not toast.

"I have something I wish to show you," Ostros said. "I acquired it in Boston."

He nodded his head at a teenage boy by the kitchen door. The same youth who had extended

Ostros's invitation that morning. The boy slipped into the kitchen. He came back bearing a flat, square package wrapped in brown paper and tied with string. He propped the package on an empty chair at our table.

"Open it," Ostros instructed him.

The lad produced a switchblade from his pocket, flashed open the blade and cut the cord. He folded back the wrapping.

"What do you think?" Ostros asked me.

"My God. I haven't seen that in years."

Resting on the chair was a painting by my wife which she had done at our Boston apartment. The subject of the painting was myself. It depicted me at the desk poring over a notebook, the fountain pen my father had given me poised in hand above the page.

"I thought the title curious," Ostros said. "It's called *The Poet*."

"I know. I remember my wife painting it. Where did you get it?"

"A gallery near The Commons. I recognized you immediately. The detail is flawless."

"Was it expensive?" I could not take my eyes from the picture. It had been years since I had seen one of Judith's paintings.

"That never matters. But since you've asked, it was over ten thousand dollars."

"Were there any others by Judith?"

"No. I asked, but the dealer said this was the only one. He knows of two others in a private collection but declined to reveal the owner's name."

"Why bring it here?"

"To show you, of course. Naturally I will hang it in my home on the mainland. My quarters upstairs here could never do it justice. I would much rather have it in my study."

I was reminded of Ostros's bizarre sculptures that adorned his lawn in the Boston suburb and the paintings in his home.

"This piece struck me in a certain way. And not because it's you," he added. "There's something about it. The composition has a distinct mood. She must have loved you very much." He indicated the picture. "The evidence is right here. Perhaps you would like it for yourself?"

"No, that's not what she wanted. No," I said again. "Besides, I have crates of my wife's work at home. Would you mind putting this one away?"

A gesture from Don Ostros brought the teenager back to our table. Ostros spoke to him in Spanish. The boy wrapped the painting. He took it back to the kitchen.

Ostros turned to me and lifted his cognac but did not drink right away. "You said there were others. How many?"

"I'm not sure. Thirty or forty."

"For goodness' sakes, man, that's a considerable trove of wealth. If you have no desire to possess them, why not sell the paintings?"

"I never thought about it. Right after Judith died I crated them up and left them in her studio. She never wanted them hung in the house."

"May I see them some time?"

"I suppose so. It wouldn't do any harm."

"Will it be painful for you? To see them again?"

"I don't know. Probably not."

The prospect excited him. "When can we do this?"

"Whenever you like. Tomorrow, if you're free."

Ostros beamed. "Splendid. Now tell me: why is that portrait named *The Poet*?"

I took another drink of the liquor. I let it roll in my mouth a moment before swallowing.

"When I was a young man I did some writing."

"I'm not surprised. Considering a man of your intellect. Poetry no doubt. Like the portrait."

"Some poetry, a few stories, whatever I felt like," I said.

"Ever publish anything?"

"A piece here and there in small literary journals. Nothing important."

"Nonsense. You're too modest. I would love to read some. Perhaps tomorrow when I view the paintings you could show me your writing."

"There's nothing to show. After Judith died I burned it all, every scrap. I haven't written since."

"How sad, how tragic. And how unlike the man I know."

"You don't know me. You only know a part. The rest is not for view. I mean no offense by that."

Ostros bowed his head acknowledging my apology.

"I'm drifting across time," he said mystically. "It's like being here with your father. Another man who lost a great love. And then? The pride, the stubbornness, the I-don't-need-anything-out-of-life stoicism. And you both ignoring a pain that drives a sword through your heart."

"You're being dramatic."

"Am I?"

"You're romanticizing an ordinary existence. There's nothing romantic about it. It simply is."

"I'm sure your wife did not agree to that supposition. No artist can."

"Ha," I scoffed. I drained my glass of cognac. "To me there's no such thing as art. What passes for art is only another interpretation of what is already there. In effect, it's pointless, if not duplicitous. Why write it if you have to live it anyway? Why paint it? Sculpt it? Why not merely get on with it?"

"Is that all it is? A weary stream of getting on with it? You didn't find that in your books. For that matter, why read at all?"

How the devil did he know about all my books?

"It passes time. Something has to," I said.

"You will die all alone."

"So must we all."

My remark caused a wave of unpleasantness to pass over Ostros's features.He grabbed his brandy, let the glass hover a moment, then drank it dry with vengeance.

The two old ladies paid their bill and left the *cantina*. The fisherman and his wife lingered over coffee. The ferry hands were drinking heavily. Their conversation grew loud and vulgar. Ostros glowered in their direction. They settled down, finished their drinks, and left.

Ostros left the table and returned with the bottle of cognac. He replenished both our glasses. With what struck me as an air of reluctance, he sat back down.

"What should I suppose you think of me?" Ostros asked.

"Whatever you like." No one else could hear us. "You're a drug merchant and a murderer. So what? It's none of my concern. That is why I can sit here and dine with you. You once told me life was comprised of little moments. This is one of them. Good food, good brandy, some talk, and nothing more. Before and after are irrelevant."

Don Ostros laughed. It started as a chuckle, gained steam, then caused him to throw his head back in full cackle.

The fisherman quickly stood up and ushered his wife toward the door. As he held his wife's coat for her, he nodded politely at Ostros, who had regained his composure.

"Good night. Come again," Ostros bellowed at the couple.

The pair smiled meekly and departed. Ostros's laughter returned. "I'm driving out my customers. And as my guest you're not paying for dinner. Some businessman I am."

It was my turn to laugh. "I guess it's one of those moments after all."

"You're *loco*, my friend. Come, let's get drunk. You're a bastard but you're the only bastard I can trust."

We finished the bottle of cognac together. It grew very late and I was impaired. When we had enough I mentioned I would walk home, being in no condition to drive.

"Nonsense," Ostros said. "The boy will drive your truck."

"How will he get home?"

"He'll walk," Ostros roared. "I pay him. Don't I?"

I accepted the offer and was driven home. Outside my house I pressed twenty dollars into the kid's hand. He thanked me in Spanish and started his hike.

Despite the overindulgence I awoke as usual an hour before sunrise. Mrs. Wade, the old widow, did my laundry for a fee. I packed two canvas bags with a week's worth. After a shower and some coffee I sat at the kitchen table and read three Hemingway stories which were set in Michigan. I thought about Michigan. Janus Martin had a Michigan driver's license, albeit a phony one.

What had Martin wanted on Bittern Island and why was he killed for it? Drugs from Don Ostros seemed the obvious answer. It had to be what the State Police and DEA believed.

Something had gone wrong. What? He had the money. Martin paid me in cash. There was the hundred-dollar bill in the black bag. The bag had probably been crammed with C-notes. Ostros had gotten his money regardless of what transpired. I was sure of that. And Ostros himself had said that Martin was a dishonorable businessman.

Stabbed in the heart: Martin had been expertly dispatched. I remember the teenager flashing his switchblade to unseal the painting. He seemed too young to know how to kill that dispassionately. Maybe it was the men in the van I had seen nights ago who probably moved the Jeep. They may have been Don Ostros's "professionals." Yet it seemed amateurish to leave the knife so Bealer could find it.

Bealer. Archie Bealer. Drunken, wife-beating, bellicose Constable Archie Bealer. I realized I hated the man. Me, who never gave two licks what another man did with his life. Who fretted not a second over how Ostros made his money. Who did not care if Ostros ordered Janus Martin put to the knife. But Bealer? I hated Archie Bealer simply for being a human being.

The phone rang. It was Rolando. He had opened shop and wondered if I was coming to work. We opened only half a day Saturdays during off-season. Often one of us took that half-day off.

"I won't be in," I said. "I've got some chores and errands. Then I expect Don Ostros to come around."

"Why?"

"He bought me dinner so I invited him. The two of us got drunk." I never mentioned the portrait or the paintings in my home.

"You got drunk with Don Ostros?" I could picture him crossing himself out of habit. "*Cristo*, Karl. How the hell did that happen?"

"I'm not sure. I told you. We got drunk."

"You're a weird one."

"Did you get the marriage license?"

"*Si*, we're all set. I called Pastor Wainwright. He'll do the service." Wainwright was the minister of Saint Andrews.

"Nervous?"

"Hell no. I should have done this years ago. I feel good about making everything right."

"And Carmelina? What about her?"

"Don't know." Then he added, "I may have to speak to the Don about her like you said. Maybe he knows someone who can help. I wish there was another way."

"Why does asking him trouble you so much?"

"I don't like being in his debt. We've always had a straight barter relationship. Or cash and carry. Nothing for nothing. This could change that."

"Only if you let it."

"Easy for you to say. You're his drinking buddy."

"I'm your friend first and last."

"Speaking of that. Will you stand up for me? Be my best man?"

"I would consider that an honor."

"Then it's settled. See you Monday," Rolando said as he rang off.

I threw my bags of laundry into the back of the pickup and set off for Grace. It was a blustery day. As I crested the ridge I saw a wispy cloud line over the low silhouette of mainland in the far distance. I switched on the radio and caught the weather as I wheeled into town. A hard blow with heavy rain was still predicted.

Mrs. Wade was a fisherman's widow. Her husband Albert had been a friend of Papa's and a partner in the fish plant. He died in a storm at sea. The body never recovered. I was in the Army at the time and Papa wrote me about it. The boat was found adrift after the storm but no sign of Albert Wade. Sometime later Mrs. Wade sold the boat and started taking in laundry to make ends meet. An empty grave in Saint Andrew's churchyard bears Albert's name and waits for her final repose.

She opened the door at my knock.

"Good morning, Mrs. Wade. Fine, bright morning so far," I said cheerily.

"Is that," she agreed. "Fine day for drying the clothes outside on the line. You picked the right time. Storm a'coming day or so. Haul in those sea bags, young man."

I lugged the bags into her kitchen and paid the woman in advance the way I always did.

"See you Monday," I said.

She put the money in her apron pocket and led me back to the door.

"Monday it is, if the good Lord's willing. A good day to you, Karl."

As I drove down Main Street I saw Archie Bealer in his police car come toward me. As he passed he nodded at me in acknowledgement. I stared straight ahead and kept going. My impassiveness must have insulted him. In my rearview mirror I saw him make a U-turn and come up behind me, flashing his red and blue lights atop his car to get my attention.

I pulled to the side but left the motor running. In the mirror I saw Bealer exit his vehicle and approach on foot to my open driver's side window.

"Turn off the engine," he barked at me.

"What's the problem, Archie?"

"Turn off the goddamn engine and get out your license and registration." He bent toward my window. I smelled the whiskey on his breath.

I turned the key and dug out my wallet from my back pocket. "Why are you being difficult?"

He snatched the documents from my hand and walked back to his cruiser. When he came back his summons book was open in his hand.

With the tip of his pen he tapped the corner of my windshield. "Your inspection has expired. I'm writing you up."

I looked at the sticker glued to the glass. Through the back I could see it had expired the last day of January.

"Sorry, Archie. I forgot about it. I'll run over to the mainland Monday and have it taken care of. I promise."

"Promise all you like, you're getting a ticket."

"It's a minor infraction. Can't we consider this a warning?"

"That's the fucking problem around here lately." He continued writing the ticket. "Nobody takes the law seriously. Well, I've decided that's gonna change."

"Just give me the damn ticket and remember you're an elected official."

Bealer tore off the sheet and handed it to me with my license and registration.

"Get it inspected Monday," he ordered. "Or Tuesday you're getting another one."

He turned on his heel and walked back to his car. I stayed still while he started up, executed another U-turn, and resumed his original direction. I put the documents and the ticket in my wallet and drove home.

Half past ten Don Ostros arrived. He was driven in a black sedan by a middle-aged man who ran the kitchen staff at the *cantina*. I invited them both in but Ostros claimed his companion preferred to wait in the car. The man, whose name was Santiago, never uttered a word. Ostros followed me inside.

"The paintings are up in the studio. There's good light up there for you. This way," I said.

Then I led him to the stairs.

I opened the studio door. Brilliant sunshine poured through the skylights and the studio seemed to glow. The easel etched fine lines of shadow onto one wall. The two crates were stacked in the corner. I lifted one off the other and placed them side by side. Each had a brass hasp but no lock. Opening them both I leaned their lids back against the wall.

From the far corner I retrieved the only chair in the room, a simple wooden chair Judith and I purchased at a yard sale. I put the chair in front of the crates.

"Take all the time you want," I told Ostros. "Call me if you need anything. There's coffee made or I can open a bottle of wine."

"You're not staying?"

"I'd rather not, but don't rush on my account. Take your time."

"I'm embarrassed, my friend; this is obviously an imposition."

"Not at all."

I turned toward the door. From the corner of my eye I saw Ostros grasp the edges of a canvas from the crate that had been on top. Without hesitation I was out the door.

In the kitchen the Hemingway stories were still on the table. It occurred to me that the studio was the only room in the house not crammed with books. Even my bathroom had two shelves full. I poured coffee and resumed my reading.

The sun was past the peak of the house and streaming in my west windows when I heard Ostros descend the stairs. He found me in the kitchen without having to call out. Ostros's face was pale but his eyes were wide in delight. He stood in the doorway regarding me a moment.

"Remarkable," he finally said. "They're truly remarkable."

"My wife was very talented."

"It's more than talent. It's brilliance, sheer genius. I had no idea. Not this many, this good. All of them."

He suddenly appeared exhausted and moved to the chair across the table from me. He collected himself as if readjusting to reality after having been transported somewhere else, somewhere beautiful and serene, only to be yanked back. Color returned to his face.

"You mentioned a bottle of wine. May I?"

"Of course." I got the bottle from the cupboard and found a corkscrew in the drawer. When it was open I poured a glass for myself as well.

Ostros accepted it greedily and took a deep swallow without the Epicurean rituals. He put the glass down slowly and studied me with fixed, resolute eyes.

"If you won't sell them, you must at least let them be seen," he said.

"Judith sold many paintings. These are only what are left."

"No doubt she kept them for a reason. *The Poet* is an excellent work, but many upstairs go way beyond that. You have no right to keep them boxed up." His voice swelled with enthusiasm. "They must be on display."

"Why? So some rich asshole who wouldn't know a Picasso from a Degas can pester me to buy them so he can lock them away in his private collection?"

"Of course not. Donate them to museums. Let the public share this treasure."

"The public?" I scoffed. I was obstinate to dampen his eagerness. He was being dramatic and hypocritical. Ostros had never impressed me as concerned for the public interest.

"I see," Ostros said. "You are testing me."

"No, I would not insult a guest in my home."

Ostros smiled accepting the truce. He took another sip of wine.

He pointed at the book on the table.

"What are you reading?"

"Short stories by Ernest Hemingway."

My voice had changed. It reminded me of my shopkeeper's voice, the one I use when mechanically reciting the features of a rental item as if I had memorized the manual.

"Ah, Papa Hemingway. Do you know he is a favorite of Fidel Castro's?"

"Along with Marx and Engels, I would imagine."

Don Ostros chuckled.

"Perhaps it's a way for Castro to thumb his nose at the U.S.," I said. "Hemingway loved Cuba."

"You're being cynical."

"Or merely unjust with regard to Fidel."

"Look at us," Ostros said. "Here we sit on this near desolate Island. The government wants us to leave so they can have it. Yet here we sit." He swept his arm around the room to indicate all the books. "Surrounded by all this profound wisdom and literature, and upstairs a great collection of paintings. You and I drinking wine in the afternoon. We're like two princes of the Renaissance taking our leisure while the world goes mad around us."

"No, my friend." I suddenly knew it was the last time I would ever call him that. "You are wrong. We are not period men. Not the royalty you imagine. We are the boats at night invading a harbor with our running lights doused. Or we are the bitterns in the marsh. Our necks quivering like reeds in the breeze."

CHAPTER THIRTY

Pete Franco's parents flew to New York for his body. I did not meet them. His remains went back to New Orleans. I learned this from a City Morgue clerk.

The detectives never contacted me. Maybe that was New York. Maybe it was how you felt if you were one of them. Another junkie had left the City for good, one way or another.

Judith and I made plans. We took the train to Boston and spent a weekend apartment hunting. There was a place near campus we liked. It had a room for Judith to paint in. The rent was more than we had anticipated, but we had some money saved. Pretending as husband and wife we signed the lease. The absence of any wedding bands provoked no question from the landlord. He was more interested in the cash we tendered.

Back in New York I rented a van. It took three trips to haul our stuff to Massachusetts. Along with furniture we wanted to keep were cartons and cartons of my books. Another trip was clothes and Judith's painting paraphernalia.

The last week in Manhattan I went to the Union Hall. I had my dues book stamped to date and requested a withdrawal card. With this I could join a union in Boston and have the initiation fee waved. My benefits would also carry to a new local.

The gallery where Judith worked threw her a party. They seemed nice and sincere and gave her gifts. I met the lawyer who might have helped me arrange bail. He and his partners were clearly men with money. They treated me nice, were sorry to see Judith go, and wished us luck.

In the morning, hauling the final load in the van, we crossed the bridges and started up I-95 for our new home.

Settling in went quickly. I was antsy about being unemployed but Judith seemed unconcerned. After locating the Union Hall, I presented my credentials. The terse letter of reference I had from Costa Construction meant nothing. What mattered were my dues being current and the separation card. By the second week I was working.

"Saturday is a 'Meet and Greet' party for faculty," Judith said. She had just come home from campus in late August. "You'll come. Won't you? It's all the teachers, deans, and spouses."

"Do I qualify?" My decision was made. No time like the present. We were starting new lives, together.

"What's that mean?"

"We got this apartment under false pretenses and now I'm to pass myself off as your spouse. When is this deception going to end?"

"If you've got something on your mind, Karl Hoffmann, say it."

"Judith, would you give me the honor and extreme pleasure, and perhaps excruciating pain…"

"Pain?"

"You could become a nag."

"And you could become a fat, hairy, belching drunk."

"You'll love me anyway."

"Then I'll have a right to nag. Get down on one knee."

Judith slapped me on the shoulder, then pushed down.

"Judith, will you marry me?" Out came the ring I had purchased before we left New York.

She looked down into my eyes. "Yes."

I put the ring on her finger as I came to my feet and we kissed. Then she backed away and eyed me with mock contempt.

"That was a lame proposal," she said.

"Nothing's lame that succeeds. And this time I have champagne."

The following Saturday I was introduced to Judith's colleagues as her fiancé. A week later, the Saturday of Labor Day Weekend, we were married in a private civil ceremony.

Judith plunged into academia enthusiastically. Her lectures on the Postimpressionists were well-prepared and she worked out exercises for the painting students. She arranged field trips to museums and galleries and was asked to sit on several faculty committees.

The Union Local I was in was strong and honest, with plenty of work. My first job was the construction site of a new children's hospital in a nearby suburb. Most of the carpenters were fathers from the area. To them the job had a "mission" quality. The project was one of the most pleasant, hard-working sites I had ever been on.

The first month Judith and I received mail forwarded from our old address in New York. There was not much. We had tied up every loose end we could think of before the move, including notifying the sanitarium where Frank resided.

"There's mail for you, baby," Judith called.

It was Wednesday afternoon and I had just come from work. Each Wednesday my wife taught one class in the morning. Home before noon, she worked in the room converted into her studio.

"Anything important?" I shucked my boots and walked to the kitchen for a soda.

"I don't know. I didn't open it. It's not addressed to me."

I popped open the soda and went into the studio. I walked up behind her and kissed her neck. She wore her paint-spattered sweatshirt, jeans, and stood barefooted before her easel. Her palette was in one hand, brush in the other.

Feeling my kiss, Judith jerked forward and drew a cloth over the canvas. "Don't look."

"Whatever you say, maestro. I'm already viewing what I want to see."

I could feel the smile part her lips as she turned. Moving forward to embrace her I was thwarted by a dab of paint deposited on my nose by a deft stroke of her brush.

"I said you have mail."

Recoiling from the paint smear I snatched a rag and wiped the glob from my nose.

"Why didn't you open it? You are Mrs. Hoffmann."

"Professor Hoffmann to you."

"More like Judith the Tease."

"It's on the table in the living room." She pointed the way with her brush. "Go see what it is."

I begged off. "I need a shower first."

Judith appraised me in my work clothes and crinkled up her nose.

"Indeed you do. However, some things, sometimes, are more important."

Her mood changed and she began to plead. "Come on, baby. I've been waiting all afternoon. Go get your mail."

Now I was curious. But a plan was a plan. I shrugged my shoulders in disinterest, turned, and trooped into the living room to retrieve what correspondence waited.

It was not a letter. The package was twice the size.

"Whew," I called to Judith. "I haven't been drafted."

"Karl," she shrieked.

"I'm getting it."

Putting down the soda I picked up the package. Its color rang a bell. I zeroed in on the return address of the cream-colored mailing sleeve.

GRUB STREET PRESS

My pocketknife came out and I slit the flap. Inside were two paperback volumes. Gingerly I drew them out. The cover of the top one read:

GRUB STREET
A Journal of Poetry & Short Fiction
Volume IV, Number 8.

Carefully I turned back the cover and pages to the Table of Contents. Scanning the page my eyes settled on the ninth entry.

"A Most Patient Winter"

Across the page of blank ivory bond was Karl Hoffmann.

My name was followed by the page number, thirteen. Stroking the leaf corners I turned to it. The poem looked up at me. Printed, bound, labored over by others to bring it to this page. No longer simply a part of me, the umbilical of mind, hand, pen to paper was cut to be itself. A published poem.

Judith came up behind me. "Read it to me."

Cradling the volumes in my hands, the top one still open to the place, I looked up into her shiny eyes and then down at the page.

I began to read and though I had recited it in my head a thousand times before, I concentrated on each word as if it was a new discovery with secrets to unfold.

"A most patient winter
approaches.
Twice fooled,
I've written her first poem
and still
she's not arrived.
It concerns me
that having traveled so wearily
she may never leave."

There was a moment of silence when I finished.

"It's beautiful," Judith said in a soft voice. "I've always liked that poem."

"So have I."

I looked back down at the page. My first published poem. Now the piece would take on new significance. Something would set it apart from anything I would write the rest of my life.

"May I see?" Judith asked.

Turning the book around I placed it in her hands as if passing a newborn. When I looked up I saw her hiding a smile at my awkwardness. She took the copy and closed it in her hands. As I had done, she studied the cover, then the Table of Contents, and found the poem on her own. She read it silently. When she was done, she kissed me on the cheek and handed it back.

"Your parents would be proud," she said.

Embarrassment flushed in me. "It's only a poem in a little magazine. How many do they print? Two hundred? Five hundred?"

"That's not the point."

She was right and I conceded it. Intending to say no more about it, I put the journals in the bottom drawer of my desk and headed for the shower.

Judith made spaghetti and I whipped up a salad.

"How was class?" I asked over dinner.

"I was audited by the Faculty Review Board."

"What does that mean?"

"Two professors from the Fine Arts Department sat in on class. They report back to the Board on how I'm doing. Don't worry. They do it to all the new teachers."

"How did it go?"

"Fine. Nothing special. It will happen many more times during the semester. They have an important decision to make before next term."

"What decision?"

"There may be an opening on the Fine Arts faculty next semester. Maybe they'll consider me."

I was confused. "But you're already a member of the faculty."

"Adjunct member. Where everybody starts. The next step is to be asked to become a full-time member of the Department. It's the first phase toward tenure."

"Isn't that what you want?"

"I'm not sure." Judith put down her fork and folded her hands above her plate. "It means I'd have to start on my Doctorate."

"You could do that."

"I probably could," she said dispassionately. "It's a lot of work but I could do it. I'm simply not sure that's what I want."

"I'm not following you."

"A Doctorate is an enormous amount of work. Hours of study, research, writing a dissertation and defending it. The process takes years."

The conflict she was grappling with dawned on me. Since coming to Boston, though we liked it immensely, Judith had growing responsibilities at the University that afforded her less and less time to pursue her painting.

"Maybe it's not for you," I said. "In fact, maybe you should cut back next semester and teach only one course. Then you could spend more time working on your own projects."

"That would be selfish. What about money? It isn't fair to you. We talked about buying a car. We talked about going to Martha's Vineyard for a week. We've got to consider the economics."

"I'm working."

"I know. And you haven't written a thing since we've come to Boston. You've been working and fixing up this apartment. It wouldn't be fair for me to cut our income now."

"Don't compare the two of us that way. I came by writing through the back door. Actually, I'm still on the back porch. But you? You've wanted to be a painter your whole life. It's who and what you are. You'll never be happy if you don't pursue it at all cost. It's the most important thing to you."

"That's not true. What about us? We're the most important thing."

There was pain in her beautiful face and soft voice.

"There's only us if we continue striving to be who we are." I reached across the table and took her hand. "Don't you think I know that? Don't you realize I respect that?"

Judith reached for my other hand so that our arms formed a frame at the borders of the table.

"I married an artist," I said. "If she wants to be a professor, an astronaut, or a circus clown along the way, that's okay too. But I know what she really is. Judith, I know who you are and I love you."

Judith's eyes grew moist and her grasp tightened. Her head tilted to one side as if she was about to doze. We sat a moment in peaceful resignation. Then she abruptly straightened up.

"A circus clown?" she squawked.

"Yes. With a big fat red nose that beeps if I squeeze it."

I released her arms and went to tweak her nose. She bolted from the table. I caught up with her in the bedroom ten paces away.

Autumn was mild that year. We explored the city on weekends, discovering museums, galleries, and libraries, and took advantage of the weather with picnics along the Charles River. Judith painted long hours in her studio, working on as many as three projects at a time.

"Come see what I've finished," Judith said. It was the day before Thanksgiving. It was a rare rainy day; my crew had knocked off early on account of the weather. School was closed for the holiday allowing the students a travel day.

Judith took my hand and led me into the studio. She had moved her easel to the center of the room. It was draped in a paint-smeared sheet, the top edges of a canvas discernible under the cover.

"Which one is it?"

She did not answer. With her hands on my shoulders, Judith positioned me in front of the easel.

"Should I close my eyes?" I said.

Judith laughed. "Of course not. What good would that do?"

"I don't know. You seem so excited."

"Wait right like this." She dropped her arms to scurry behind the easel.

With hands unseen from my vantage point, she slid the draping from the frame. Despite the dreariness of the day out the windows, the first impression I got was one of light. It drew my eyes toward the canvas. The impression was intended. It was the essence of a spotlight streaming across the painting to illuminate a face atop the arched body in the composition.

The scene was familiar. I had seen it in its various stages of development. The project was started in New York. Transported up the coast. Set aside for a while. Now retrieved, reclaimed, staring at me so perfectly complete.

Juliet, Galina, my mother.

Staring at the portrait I felt not a heartbeat, not a breath. There was a timeless, delicate preciseness to her features. Gone was the weariness and pain of degenerative disease that I remembered. What remained was alive, exuberant, defiant, sensual, and proud. A pride in the sense that all classic tragedy is proud. I could see it and say nothing.

"Baby?" Judith called from somewhere off the canvas. "What are you feeling?"

"Do you remember when I first saw you at Columbia? When I was lost and stumbled into your studio?"

"I remember."

"I feel like that. The way my father must have felt when he met her. The way when I saw you I knew I would love you until the day I die and beyond."

The sheet slipped from Judith's fingers and pooled on the floor. She came over and stood beside me, her arm about my waist. Her head tilted to my shoulder as we both regarded the painting.

"I can't imagine how you did that from an old black and white photo," I said.

"It's not always what you see. It's what you feel."

CHAPTER THIRTY-ONE

There were two paintings Don Ostros wanted. Though he would gladly take them all, two obsessed him, it seemed.

"I've told you they're not for sale," I said.

He did not argue with me. After one more glass of wine, Ostros thanked me for my hospitality and took his leave. Santiago drove him back into town.

When he was gone I went upstairs to the studio. The paintings were neatly back in their crates though the lids of the boxes were still open. I never asked him which paintings he wanted and he had not said. Peering down at the top edges of the canvases where flecks of color had spattered the narrow planes, I could not tell which was which, nor know if he moved his favorites to the front of the stacks. I put down the lids and clasped the hasps.

As I moved the chair back to its corner the sun through the skylights glinted off an object on the crossbar of the easel. I placed the chair and went over to the tripod. A gold coin was propped in the groove meant for clamping a canvas. With two fingers I picked it up and laid it in the palm of my hand. The surface bore a likeness unfamiliar to me. Its inscription I took for Spanish. Flexing my hand, I flipped the coin over and studied it more. It was from Nicaragua, bore the date 1838, and was solid gold.

Any curiosity I was feeling concerning the coin was pushed aside by anger.

"You vulgar bastard."

As I left the room I slipped the coin in my pocket, vowing to make him take it back. In the kitchen I washed the glasses and put them away. A little wine was left in the bottle. I poured it down the sink and threw the bottle in the trash bin.

My anger subsided. I still felt the sting of the insult but my mind had started to switch gears. I was groping for a plan. The problem was bigger than Don Ostros. It was this Island and what was happening to it. There was Ostros, but there was also Archie Bealer. After him, Colonel Devon. There was the DEA, EPA, immigration people, the Coast Guard, and any of the rest that saw Bittern Island as something other than what it was to the people that lived here.

Grabbing my coat from the hook I left the house, got in my truck, and set out for Grace. The shop was closed by now so I had a fair idea where to find Gunner Hogan. I was convinced he was the only individual impervious to the pressures and machinations that had been brought to bear against my community. His ticket had been punched in life and nothing would ever matter after that validation.

Gunner's station wagon was parked behind the Sea Witch. I pulled alongside it and parked. The back door of the tavern was ajar and I went inside. Sweeney saw me and nodded his head in greeting. I saw Gunner from the back; his shoulders were hunched low to the bar over a mug of beer. An empty shot glass was beside the mug. He must have heard me approach, but I was not sure how he knew it was me.

"Come to celebrate with me?" he asked without turning.

"Celebrate what?"

"I'm getting married." He signaled Sweeney to set me up and replenish his own.

"You don't say." The flash of comprehension did not jar me in the least. I knew what he meant.

"Oh, I do say. Tie the knot and the bastards can go fuck themselves."

"Will they buy it?"

"If it's fitting in the eyes of God and in accordance with the laws of Rhode Island, the Feds can kiss my ass."

Sweeney poured me a whiskey and a beer along with Gunner's pair. I lifted the smaller glass in toast.

"To the bride," I said.

"The bride," and we drank.

"Have you met her?" I asked.

"Not yet. All things in time."

"Rolando must be pleased. Was it his idea?"

"Nope. One of my own."

I clapped him on the shoulder. "A fine thing you're doing."

"Shut up and have another."

I waved off Sweeney's approach content with my beer.

"I have to go to the mainland on Monday and have my truck inspected," I said. "Why not come along? You can pick up the marriage license."

"Does she have to come too?"

"No. She only has to sign it in the presence of a witness."

"Then I'd be obliged."

The fishing fleet was in port and fishermen filled the tavern. Having been at sea since dawn they appeared raw and tired. Sweeney scurried about keeping glasses topped. Gunner at my side filled and lit his pipe.

"Never been married," he said. "What's it like?"

"It's different for different folks."

"This will sure as hell be different."

At the other end of the bar I saw Archie Bealer enter. The fishermen at the rail shuffled to one side to make room for him. Nobody greeted him. Sweeney poured his shot of whiskey. Bealer drank it and Sweeney poured another. Bealer put no money on the counter. I felt another surge of anger. My mug trembled slightly in my hand.

"What's the matter?" Gunner asked.

"That bastard Bealer. He's starting to get on my nerves."

"Starting, is it?"

From my wallet I took the summons issued me that morning. I passed it over to my friend. He examined it.

"Christ. I didn't even know he knew how to write one of these. Still, you were in violation."

"Maybe. At the same time, he should have been pulled over for drunken driving. He smelled like a distillery."

"No chance of that since he's the only cop on the Island. He starts pulling over drinkers and there won't be a car left on the Island. Do yourself a favor and forget it. There's enough trouble here already."

My anger simmered and I drank my beer.

"Are you going to tell me about it?" Gunner asked.

"What?"

"Rolando said you had an appointment with Don Ostros this morning. At your home, if I heard right. You know I ain't nosy. But it struck me as strange. You being the other recluse on the Island."

"He wanted to see my wife's paintings. He bought one up in Boston and wanted to see more. No big deal."

"Then what are you doing here? My bachelor party?"

That made me laugh. I finished my beer and Sweeney drew another. I declined more whiskey. Bealer nursed his shot and we never made eye contact. When his glass was empty he abruptly left. The men at the bar closed ranks as if he had never been there.

"I know where Martin's Jeep is," I said.

"Thought you might."

"Why?"

"That business with the EPA. Devon figured you knew something. I guess he was right."

"He's right. But for the wrong reasons. I'm not involved. I rented the guy a saw. How could I know he was using it to break into the fish plant?"

"It's not the saw and you know it. You helped stash the truck. Didn't you?"

"Not exactly. Ostros's men hid the truck. I discovered it by accident."

"Where was that again?"

"In one of my sheds."

"It's not there now. They've searched. Where did you move it?"

"I didn't. I went to Boston and saw the Don to find out what the hell was going on. He assured me the truck would be gone when I got home. It was."

"Now you've found it again."

I recounted for Gunner my discovery of the Jeep in the hastily assembled sand dune. He listened with an amused smirk on his face.

"It would appear your problems are over," Gunner said.

"Not exactly. The heat has been turned up all over the Island to solve this thing. Unless the truck and the killer are found, we'll never have any peace."

"Peace is a rare commodity, my friend. But I suppose you're right. What's on your mind?"

Gripping the handle of my mug tightly, my concerns came out in a jumbled rush.

"Present company excluded, it's getting harder and harder to trust anybody around here. Seems everybody's vulnerable to some kind of pressure. There's bureaucratic harassment. A boat's been confiscated to send a message. The INS is snooping. There'll be no end until they get what they want."

"There's more to it than that," Gunner said.

"Indeed there is. It occurred to me that Don Ostros is not poised for a fall. His men aren't, either."

"You have a plan?"

"On Monday when we go to the mainland, I'm paying a visit to Colonel Devon. I'll be in some trouble, but it won't be a murder charge."

"When did you decide all this?"

"When Ostros left me this." I took the gold coin from my pocket and placed it on the bar.

Gunner studied it a moment in silence then picked it up and examined both sides.

"Solid gold," he said. "Quite unusual. Worth a pretty penny, I suppose. Ostros gave this to you? Why?"

"It's a message telling me all bets are off. In his usual cryptic manner, it means we're even. Now it's every man for himself."

"He told you that?"

"No, he didn't have to. I got the point."

"You sure you're not reading too much into this?"

"I'm sure."

"Okay. So why Colonel Devon? Why not just show Archie where the Jeep is and be done with it?"

"Like I said. I don't know who to trust. If I had to guess, I'd say Devon is the most honorable of the bunch. A bit of a firebrand, but honest. I certainly don't want to deal with those goons from the DEA."

"Point taken."

Gunner ordered another whiskey and I joined him. My tale was told and I felt an intense weariness. Not exhaustion, it was the numbing peace of having made a decision and mustered the resolve to stick to it. Worry was pointless.

We drank our whiskies and finished our beers. Out behind the Sea Witch we said goodbye. I promised to pick Gunner up Monday morning for the ferry ride to the mainland.

"You take care, Karl. I don't like that bit about the coin. Ostros is up to something."

"I'm sure he is. But he doesn't need another dead body around here just yet."

"Mind if I make another observation?"

I told him go ahead.

"For a guy who's spent the last ten years convincing everybody you don't give a shit, you sure got a funny way of showing it."

Pulling out of the alley I cut across Main Street to park behind the General Store, as my supplies at home had dwindled.

Pat Lawler was unloading a truck over from the mainland. I pulled up alongside and helped him and the driver with the work. There were cases of canned vegetables, sacks of flour and rice, household supplies, and tins of cooking oil. When the job was done I stood by the back door of the store as Lawler signed the driver's receipt.

From the harbor we heard the blast of the ferry horn.

"You can make it if you hurry," Lawler told the trucker.

"Piece of cake." The driver shifted gears and started forward with a lurch.

"Thanks for the hand," Lawler said to me.

I was about to dismiss his gratitude when the truck passed giving me a clear view down the alley running behind the other stores.

"Isn't that strange," I said, thinking out loud.

"What's strange?" asked Lawler.

"Aw, nothing. I was thinking of something else. Sorry."

Lawler thanked me again. I followed him into the store to buy my groceries.

What I had noticed down the alley, which meant nothing to Lawler, was Archie Bealer's police cruiser. It was parked behind Don Ostros's *cantina*. And Bealer was not in it.

Back home I lugged my groceries inside and set about making a beef stew. It was a recipe Father taught me. He could make stew out of anything. In lean times it was a talent I appreciated.

After dinner I made a fire in the parlor. I took Joseph Conrad's *The Secret Agent* down from the shelf and started to read. An hour later I pulled a blanket up over me after adding more wood to the fire and kept reading. I fell asleep in the chair.

A clap of thunder woke me up. I listened to the wind. From the flue in the fireplace I could hear it overhead. Steady, then a pause, then steady again. Not the storm wind yet. The smoke from my dying fire was sucked greedily up the shaft. Steady, then a pause.

Crack.

It came again in the middle of a windy rush.

The only thunder in this world that sounds like that is the thunder of violence. Despite what the poets write, nature is neither violent nor cruel, though it can be hard. Violence is a man-made phenomenon.

I had heard a gunshot.

CHAPTER THIRTY-TWO

Judith's first show was in the spring. It followed a campus exposition where Judith's paintings outshone the others. During the expo dealers approached her from the Newbury Street art district of Boston. Frederick Aldan signed her.

A charming man, Aldan became an ardent promoter of my wife's work. His connections got the show in the papers and airtime on Public Television. The exhibit opened two weeks before the semester ended.

"Mr. Hoffmann, you must be delighted." Aldan was beaming. We were drinking champagne on opening night. "Even I did not expect such a turnout."

Two hundred people jammed the gallery spilling out onto the sidewalk of Newbury Street. I felt gawky in my rented tuxedo but Aldan's ingratiating manner put everyone around him at ease.

"It is quite a crowd. Is this typical for a first show?"

"Goodness, no. This isn't typical at all. It's an instant success. Have you heard the people talking? Your wife's a smash."

I had heard some comments. The crowd seemed enthusiastic about this new talent. I saw Judith on the other side of the room with professors she had invited. She wore a simple blue dress and looked gorgeous even from my distance.

A distinguished looking couple approached Aldan and he excused himself to attend to duties. When I looked up, Judith was not to be seen.

"Are you bored out of your socks?" a welcome voice asked behind me. "Could you find a lady a drink?"

Turning to Judith I held out my untasted champagne. She took it and leaned forward to kiss me on the lips.

"Congratulations," I said. "I think you have arrived."

"I don't want to arrive. I want to go."

"You're kidding? This is your night."

"Actually it's their night. Theirs and Aldan's. My part was done when I finished the paintings."

"You really want to go?"

Judith nodded.

Aldan came up to us smiling ear to ear.

"Darling, it's fantastic," he said. He kissed Judith's hand. "You've sold three already and we've only been open an hour. You're a hit."

My wife's reaction was to guzzle her champagne. Absently she held out the empty glass and I took it. Her hand was trembling.

"I don't know how to thank you, Frederick. And you're going to think I'm being an ungrateful bitch, but I really have to go."

"Nonsense, my dear, I understand perfectly. You're an artist. I get this all the time. If you'll forgive my decadence, it lends something to your mystique. Drives prices up. Now shoo, both of you. My car is outside. The driver will take you anywhere you wish to go. Be gone, my lovelies." He waved his hand. "I can manage here."

Aldan walked us to the door, politely deflecting the entreaties of several guests. Outside on the sidewalk he pointed to his limo, caught his chauffeur's attention, then pointed at us, nodding vigorously. The driver tipped his hat that he understood.

"Call me in the morning, darlings," Aldan instructed. "Not too early, mind you. I'll give you a full report."

Judith kissed him on the cheek and I shook his hand. Then we walked down the block, holding hands. The chauffeur introduced himself as Barney and held the door of the limousine open as we ducked in the back. Barney climbed behind the wheel.

"Where to?" he asked.

I cocked my head toward Judith for an answer.

"I don't know. How about The Common?" she said.

"I wouldn't go there at night if I were you," Barney said.

"What do you suggest?" my wife asked him.

"How about the Harbor? We can cruise along Atlantic and Commercial Streets. Check out the Wharf. That way I can be nearby."

"Sold," I said.

Barney smiled in the rearview mirror. "The bar's full. Help yourself, and ring if you need me." Then he put up the privacy partition. We sat back in the plush seats and I loosened my bow tie.

Judith sighed in contentment. "Isn't this better?"

"Much. But are you sure it was all right to leave?"

"Of course. It's the paintings they really want to see. Frederick is handling it."

Judith suggested a drink and I opened the cooler in the mahogany deck across from our seat. Three bottles of Dom Perignon were immersed in ice. I displayed one of the bottles to Judith.

"Aldan must have expected a success," I said.

"Either that or he knows how to be miserable in comfort."

I poured the bubbly into fluted glasses. "First we'll drink to your triumph."

"And then we'll drink to us."

"There's enough champagne to toast all the way out to our great-grandchildren."

"So let the lineage begin."

We kissed and drank and snuggled into the seat as the lights of Boston glistened off the Harbor. I rolled down one window and a sea breeze drifted in like a gentle tide. Passing Museum Wharf I buzzed Barney on the intercom and he pulled to the curb. We took a stroll arm in arm from streetlight to streetlight and back again. The salt air and the champagne lingered on our tongues as we shared the sensation in a prolonged kiss.

"It's time to go home, Barney," I said into the phone.

"I rather thought so," he said. I gave him directions.

The exhibit lasted three days. When it closed on Sunday evening Aldan called from his gallery. I answered the phone and after a pleasant exchange passed it to Judith. We had been playing gin rummy on the living room floor. While she spoke to Aldan, I went and made tea.

"You're kidding," I heard Judith exclaim. "I never expected anything like that."

When the tea was ready I brought it out as Judith hung up the phone.

"What did he say?" I asked.

She took a sip of tea before answering and resumed her position at the card game on the floor. She tucked her legs back under her and placed the mug beside her. Then she picked up her hand of cards.

"Well?"

"Frederick said it was a huge success." She studied her cards.

"We know that already. You spoke to him yesterday and this morning. And it was in the papers." The Sunday editions of the *Globe* and *Herald* were spread on the dining table, open to her reviews.

"He never mentioned money," Judith said. "That is, he never said anything about it until now."

Judith drew a card from the top of the deck on the floor, studied it a moment and inserted it into the middle of her hand. She seemed to shudder a second and then raised her eyes to regard me over her cards. Her eyes were wide in bewilderment.

"How much money are we talking about?"

"Oh, somewhere in the neighborhood of eighty-one thousand dollars."

I almost spit out my tea. "Eighty thousand dollars."

"Eighty-one, minus all the gallery fees and Fredrick's commission. He'll give us a full accounting when he sends the check. It will leave us about sixty-five thousand, give or take."

I was astonished. "My God, how many paintings did he sell?"

"Eighteen."

"That's a lot."

"So Frederick says. He thinks it will be even better in New York."

"You're going to New York?"

"Not me, baby. The paintings. Not an exclusive show though, not in Manhattan. We'll see."

I put my hand out to rest on her knee. "I'm very proud of you and I love you very much."

She patted my hand. "I know. Now play cards."

Scooping up my cards, I arranged the hand. When I looked up Judith was smiling and her eyes were moist and glistening.

"No you don't," I said.

"Don't what?"

"Start cheating. I didn't see you discard."

Laughing until she lost her breath, Judith flipped the Two of Diamonds beside the deck of turned down cards.

Aldan invited us to dinner the following Wednesday. We met him at a French restaurant. After a round of cocktails he presented Judith with a check. My wife examined it perfunctorily and slid it across the table to me. Without reading it I put it in my pocket.

"New York is set for August," Aldan was saying. "You'll have some new ones to add by then I expect."

"Possibly," Judith said. "First we need a vacation. School ends in another week and we could use one."

Since learning of the money my wife and I had spoken of several things we could plan. One was the week we had thought of spending on Martha's Vineyard. The proceeds from the show were more than I made in a year as a carpenter. It was more than Judith made as an adjunct professor.

"Splendid idea," Aldan said."Have you picked a spot?"

I was reading the menu, only half-listening. Then the placard nearly fell from my hands.

"I was thinking of Bittern Island. Karl was born there. But we haven't discussed it yet. We had been thinking of the Vineyard. But it's so crazy in the summer. We could use something less active." Before I could utter a word, her hand gripped my elbow propped on the table. "Couldn't we, baby? It's also not as expensive I hear."

The conversation moved off to another subject without any comment from me. Aldan was saying that after New York it would probably be wise to make some connections in Philadelphia.

"Or we could lay back and wait for the invitations," Aldan said with satisfaction. "Nothing need be decided tonight except what we're going to eat." He looked up at me. "Karl? Are you all right? You look a little strange."

"Where did that come from?" I asked as we undressed for bed.

"What?"

"A vacation on Bittern Island."

"I don't know. It just came to me. Wouldn't you want to?"

I did not have an answer. Many things went through my mind in a rush. I got into bed without saying anything.Judith slipped under the sheet beside me.

"Well?" she said.

"That's a different part of my life. All that's over now. We have something different." I pulled her close. She lay her head on my chest.

"We have each other," she said. "And that comes from who we are and what we've been. Our lives didn't start the day we met."

"Mine did."

Judith thumped her hand on my chest. "Remember that poem you wrote? The one Pete turned into a song. He sang it the first night we went to hear him play. Remember?"

"I remember."

"I've never had a place affect me like that. Even when I paint, the places are more in my head than what I actually see. I'm not geographical, if that's the right word. Somehow, I think you are. Does that make sense?"

"I'd live anywhere with you."

"I know that, baby. That's not what I mean. The island in your poem, it's not in your heart, it's you. You are my island. You're the speck of land in the mist on the horizon. I can see it. I think it's time you took me home."

My head tilted down and I kissed her hair. At that moment I had no idea what she meant but somehow it made sense. Not a sense I could explain.

A sense I could feel in the pit of my being. A sense of what I knew and was suddenly aching to share with her.

"All right. We'll go."

We fell asleep and I dreamed dreams of wild wind and thrashing sea. Later I awoke in the dark, Judith still lying across my body, asleep. My mouth was dry and I imagined it tasted of salt.

Home, she had said. Take her home. I would have said Judith was my home. But there was something else. Something that was as much a part of me as this woman I clung to in the darkness. The wind stilled and the sea calmed. I fell back into sleep, drifting on the scent of her hair and skin.

When school was over we planned our trip. I explained to Judith there were no hotels or inns on Bittern Island that I ever knew. In the main town were two boarding houses but they were for the seasonal crews of the fishing fleet and summer laborers, not places appropriate for us to stay.

"We'll make it somehow. I know we will," Judith said.

"I suppose we could pitch a tent."

"There you go. That'll be fun."

"I hope you know what you're getting yourself into."

"I have no idea. That makes it even more fun."

We went to Sears and bought a tent and sleeping bags and a variety of camping equipment. The day before we left I rented a van and packed our gear. In the morning we drove from Boston to Rhode Island and along the Narragansett peninsula to its tip.

We had an hour's wait for the ferry. We drank coffee in the diner alongside the ferry ticket office.

"I'm excited. Are you?" Judith asked.

"Yes. But it feels kind of strange."

"It's going to be wonderful."

The horn of the ferry blew one long blast. We left the diner for the van parked in line for boarding. It was a new ferry, not one I remembered. Through the windshield of the van I scanned the bridge of the vessel to catch sight of the captain. When he appeared on the outward wing of the bridge by the wheelhouse I did not recognize him. The skipper was a young man, not even my age. I drove the van onto the gangway.

"Is it a long trip?" Judith asked.

"About two hours in a fair sea."

She giggled. "A fair sea. Listen to you. You're talking like an Islander already."

I felt myself blush.

"Don't be embarrassed. It's in your blood."

We pulled into the belly of the ship and parked, and I set the parking brake.

"We can leave the truck and go on deck," I said.

Judith needed no prompting. She scrambled from the cab and I came around and joined her. There was a hatch by a stairway that led to the upper decks. We went up and out into the sunshine. A stiff breeze blew up the channel from Rhode Island Sound. Judith rushed to the rail. She peered forward past the bow.

"Can we see it?" she asked.

"Not until we clear the channel. Once we're beyond the breakwater you'll catch sight of it over that way." I pointed south-southwest.

Two trucks were boarded last. We walked to the stern to watch. One was an open flatbed laden with lumber and bags of concrete mix. The other was a forty-foot truck with no markings.

"I didn't know the ferry took trucks," Judith said.

"It has to. There's nothing on the Island that you don't have to bring over. Food, supplies, building materials, all have to be ferried over. These boats are the lifeline."

"I never thought about it. Doesn't it make you feel kind of isolated?"

"You've no idea. But you'll get use to it."

The ferry horn sounded one more blast. With a groan in her bowels, the ship nosed out into the channel and turned southward.

CHAPTER THIRTY-THREE

Must have been about three-thirty in the morning. Conrad's book was open in my lap. I put it aside and folded the blanket. All the while I listened for the sound of another shot. There was none, only the draw and rush of wind.

In the kitchen I put on my peacoat and took a flashlight from the closet. Out my back door I saw the moon setting in the west above the bluffs. It was cloudy and the pale glow was not much light. I switched on the torch.

With the shaft of light I raked left, right, and up to the crests of the nearest dunes. There was nothing to see except grass and sand. The shots I heard were farther away, even though wind could trick a man. I was certain they came from the west. Turning my coat collar up I stepped across the porch out into the night, pulling the door closed behind me.

Making my way up the crease in the dunes I played the light ahead of me. Over the rise the ocean appeared with wild surf breaks crashing and spewing white spray above their crests. When the wind whooshed, the spray feathered out in long streaks until it thinned and vanished.

There was nothing west of my position except sand and rocks and dunes that curved the tip of the Island where the beach wound north beyond my sight. Gullies and tufts, salt marshes and the nesting birds and… and the truck of a dead man.

I switched off the light and made my way down to the beach by the meager light of what stars skirted the clouds. As I turned into the wind, the remaining sliver of moon faded. I stopped and listened for sounds. Between the thump of waves there were no voices, no guttural sound of an engine in gear to bite the sand. Only the wind and surf rose to my ears. I set off in the direction the moon had been.

Strange. No birds were disturbed or distracted by my progress. The first of them should have been prowling the tideland as the water receded in its cycle. I climbed up the beach to the softer sand at the lower rim of the dunes. Here my size in the heavy jacket would not be profiled against the sea.

I came to the inlet. Heard what was left of the tide sputter into its trench then die away. Following the same trail as before, I skirted the stream where it bent and widened into the marsh ahead of me, the dunes rising at my side.

Where the misshapen dune had been remained only a cleaved hillock, its face halved and scattered. Protruding from its broad center was the dark hulk of the Jeep's engine hood, the front fenders, bumper with license plate, and the wide eyes of it headlamps blank and dark. Sprawled, half-sitting, shoulders propped against the bumper lay the form of a motionless man. His head was thrown back as if to gape at stars.

Stock-still, I waited and listened. No sound but reeds thrashing themselves mildly and the trickle of water down the stream beside me. I brought the light up chest-high in front of me and switched it on.

I saw the coat, open down the front, and the thick leather band at the waist, and knew before the beam hit his face. Archie Bealer lay dead against the Jeep.

Moving closer and shining the light down I saw the blood stain soaking through the left breast pocket of Bealer's uniform shirt. His right hand held his .357 magnum service revolver and was resting in his lap. I knelt down beside him, bent over and sniffed the barrel of the gun. From the acrid aroma I knew it had been recently fired. Regardless of what I thought of Bealer as a man, he had not gone down without a fight. I slipped my fingers around his wrist to confirm what I knew. He was stone cold with no pulse. I put the beam of the torch on his upturned face. Bealer's mouth was open. The light shined back at me from his blank eyes. Their lids were tight and required pressure for me to close them.

"You sorry bastard. What were you trying to do?"

Archie Bealer had nothing to say.

Standing up I shined the light through the windshield. I saw the blade of my saw protruding between the front seats. Still curious I brushed sand away from the passenger side window up to where it sank back into the makeshift dune. Behind the housing of the saw was the black bag Rolando and I examined in my shed.

The first rays of morning began to streak the sky above me. I turned off the flashlight.

Something had ended and something else had begun.

Archie Bealer was dead. The second violent death on Bittern Island which had not seen a murder since its earliest settlement in Colonial times. Even the Indians had forsaken the place without a struggle. The churchyard of Saint Andrews was home to deceased elders and babies who never stood a chance. Through all the wars from the Revolution to this day, not one serviceman or woman who hailed from Bittern Island had fell in battle. Excluding the infants, Judith would have probably been the youngest resident of the graveyard if she had been laid to rest in that fashion. She, like my parents before her, was part of the air, the dunes, and the sea.

I followed the eddy back to the beach. The sun rose in front of me on the walk home.

I waited until seven o'clock and called the local troop headquarters of the State Police in Narragansett. Colonel Devon had arrived and took my call.

"You better get some men and come over. Constable Bealer has been shot dead."

"How? Where?" Devon asked.

"I don't know the details, but his body's in the dunes. I'll show you when you get here. And something else. He found the truck you're looking for."

Colonel Devon was right to business. "I'll requisition a chopper and be there within the hour. Where can I find you?"

"Home."

"Right. Be there directly." He hung up.

Precisely at eight o'clock I heard the bell of Saint Andrews toll on the other side of the Island, calling the faithful to Sunday services. In mid tone the gong was obscured by the whump-whump of an approaching helicopter. I went out on my front porch and saw it clear the ridgeline to descend on Mariners Path at the edge of my property.

Colonel Devon popped the side hatch and leapt to the ground. He looked up and caught sight of me on the porch. He set toward me at a trot.

"We'll take the chopper," Devon called.

"It's not that far."

"We've got gear. We're taking the bird."

He turned around and I followed him to the helicopter. In addition to the pilot, two uniformed troopers were inside, one beside the pilot, the other in back. Devon held the door and motioned me to get in. I squeezed into the center back seat. The trooper next to me handed me the disconnected end of my seatbelt. I strapped in as Devon boarded and did the same.

"Tell the pilot," Devon ordered me.

I leaned forward and shouted over the roar of the rotor. "See that rise there?" I asked pointing. "Just on the other side." The pilot nodded. "You'll have to land on the beach. You'll see a small inlet. That's the spot."

The pilot nodded again and we lifted off. The flight lasted only two minutes. He set us down by the salt creek a few yards from the first dune.

Devon was unstrapped and out of the chopper before we completely settled. I unlatched and followed suit.

"Lead the way," Devon shouted. The blades of the helicopter revolved over our heads.

Assured the others would be on our heels I set out along the inlet to the spot. Devon surveyed the scene.

"Is this exactly as you found him?" he asked.

"His eyes were open. I closed them."

"Anything else?"

"Not that I can think of."

"Try and be sure."

"I'm sure."

Devon went forward and did as I had done, feeling the wrist of the corpse unnecessarily.

"Five or six hours I'd say," he said.

"Around three-thirty," I said.

"How do you know that?"

"I heard the shot. Actually there were two shots. One woke me up and then I heard the second one."

Devon rose and looked past me at the two troopers who had followed. The one who sat beside the pilot came up and handed his boss a pair of rubber surgical gloves. Devon snapped each down to his wrists. He knelt down and gingerly removed the pistol from Bealer's grip. He snapped open the loading guard, tipped the gun up, spun the cylinder slowly, and let the cartridges fall into his palm.

"One spent round," Devon said.

Coming erect he handed the pistol and shells to the same trooper, who had pulled on gloves as well. The guy also had a fistful of plastic bags. He put the shells in one and the gun in another.

The second trooper came forward with a 35mm camera. Devon and I backed out of the way and the officer took pictures of the scene from several angles. When he finished Devon stepped over the body around to the driver's side of the Jeep. He cleared sand from the door until it was fully exposed. It opened with a screeching noise when Devon pulled the lever. Careful not to disturb anything, he peered around the inside.

The bag proved irresistible. Devon leaned into the cab and snatched it from the back. Out from the Jeep he walked back around front beside the body while drawing back the satchel's zipper. Spreading the flaps he looked down into it. Seeing nothing he turned it over and shook it vigorously. The lone hundred-dollar bill I knew was inside fluttered to the sand beside the dead man's feet. Holding the bag in one hand Devon stooped, picked up the note with the other, examined it, sniffed it.

"Bag these, Sergeant," Devon said to his associate, the one without the camera. The trooper came up and took the items.

Devon straightened up and walked over to me, stretching his back and neck as if everything had been a great effort and he needed to relax.

"What now?" I asked him.

"The Medical Examiner and forensic team are coming on the ferry. Give me some directions. Where's the road?"

I pointed over the dune behind me and told him Mariners Path was beyond it. They should follow it to the end but stop about thirty yards before the beach. That should put them on the other side from our position.

Devon unclipped a two-way radio from the gun belt under his coat and relayed my instructions. A terse, "Roger that," squawked back at him from the box when he finished.

Devon peered up the dune as he replaced the radio on his waistband. "There should be tracks."

"Maybe," I said. "But the grass is pretty thick and we had a stiff wind all night."

"Are you saying not to bother?"

"Do your job any way you see fit, Colonel. I'm merely stating a fact."

"Which way did you come?"

I pointed along the eddy. "Up from the beach. I walked from home."

"Well the killer, or killers, probably drove. For that matter, how the hell did Bealer get here?"

I shrugged my shoulders.

"You wait here," Devon said. He turned to the others who had been joined by the chopper pilot. "You men fan out and cover these dunes toward the road," he directed. "Look for anything, especially tracks.

"Don't touch anything while we're gone," Devon charged me.

Again I only shrugged in reply.

With four or five yards separating them, the four men started up the slopes of the dunes. For the two on the end, the pilot and the cameraman, it was rough going owing to the steepness of that part and the soft dry sand. I watched until all four were over the top and gone from sight.

Standing alone in the gully, alone except for Archie's body, I heard the first birds of the morning hours late. Seagulls were cawing and a couple swooped overhead. A bittern barked somewhere beyond the rise where the troopers no doubt invaded his nest area.

Looking southwest toward the ocean through the inlet's gap I saw a cloud front forming on the horizon. Cumulonimbus, edged with sunlight, cast a dark shadow on the sea below. The wind had shifted and was bringing on the clouds toward the Island. It was a true course for squall weather. It would take a few hours, but it was coming.

I sat down at the base of the dune and propped my elbows on my knees. My eyes drifted to settle on Archie Bealer's mute form.

I revised my earlier opinion. "You dumb bastard. You were in over your head and should have known it. Now what you don't know doesn't matter any more. Does it?"

As if to answer, the constricting rigor mortis pulled Bealer's head a little to the side in objection.

"Sorry, Constable. No last word for you," I said.

"Who are you talking to?" Devon called from the top of the hill behind my back.

"I was thinking out loud."

The grunts of his effort were audible as he scrambled down the slope. He was alone.

"Find anything?" I asked.

"Not much, maybe a tire track or two. There's no vehicles. Either Bealer came here with his killer or the killer had an accomplice who removed the Constable's car. The forensic team will have to determine that."

"They better hurry. A storm's coming. Be here early afternoon." I pointed toward the front across the water.

Devon looked out to sea and cursed under his breath. Plucking the radio from his belt he barked some commands about the need for haste. I did not hear the reply.

"Do you still need me?" I asked Devon.

"What?" Devon looked from his radio to me then back at the device as if confused where the question came from.

"Do I have to hang around or can I go home?"

Before he could answer, the pilot came over the dune cautiously making his way down in the soft sand.

"Miles and O'Toole are waiting for the M.E. up on the road," he reported to Devon. "Have you looked out there, sir?" He pointed out toward the ocean. "We've got heavy weather coming in. It won't do to have the helicopter out here in that."

Devon looked at his watch and then at the flyer. His gaze drifted over to the cloud front in the distance.

"There's time yet. Be here by early afternoon," Devon quoted me.

"Whatever you say, sir." The pilot nodded in my direction. "What about him? Want me to fly him out?"

"That's not necessary," I said. "It's a short walk around the beach way."

Colonel Devon seemed perplexed and undecided. He looked from me to the pilot and out to sea again as if weighing the options. Finally he kicked some sand with the toe of his boot and looked back at me.

"Hoffmann, you go on home," he said. "And don't leave the Island. We'll be needing a formal statement from you later." To the pilot he said,

"Check the Doppler in the bird. Verify how much time we have."

The pilot approximated a salute and walked past me toward his helicopter.

"Anybody else know about this?" Devon asked me.

"Not from me. You're the only one I called."

"Keep it at that."

"Archie's got a wife in town. She'll have to be told."

"We'll handle it."

"Suit yourself."

I was glad I had no obligation to inform the widow knowing what I knew about the marriage. I was tempted to tell Devon that Bealer had been an abuser as well as a drunk but thought better of it. Hell, aside from anything else Devon was an experienced cop. He had probably figured that out for himself.

Coming out of the dunes along the eddy, I turned east on the beach toward home. The sun was high and I reckoned it around eleven o'clock. Wind whipped off the water, propelling me along at my back. I climbed the bluff behind my house and stood for a moment on the summit. Westward down the beach I could still see the helicopter squatting on the sand at the edge of the dunes. No human figures were visible.

From the harbor I heard the horn blast of the ferry coming into dock. I imagined the gruesome duties yet to be performed by Devon's team as they came ashore. A quick glance back at the sea and I calculated they had an hour and a half, maybe two hours, before the storm swept over us all.

CHAPTER THIRTY-FOUR

Judith loved Bittern Island from the moment it loomed into sight that morning on the ferry. We disembarked at the slip at the foot of Main Street. I parked the van by the General Store so we could pick up provisions for our trip. It looked the same as I remembered. Three rows of canned goods, packaged dry foods, sundries, sacks of flour, sugar, and rice in racks along the wall. Cooler for dairy products. But the butcher counter was replaced with an immense freezer stocked with pre-cut meats. I heard footfalls on the plank floor somewhere in the back of the store.

"Mister Lawler?" I called. "He's the owner," I said to Judith.

"Who's there?" a voice came back. Not the voice I expected.

"Karl Hoffmann."

A young man is his twenties came out of the back and down the aisle.

"Is Mister Lawler around?" I asked.

"I'm Lawler," the man said. "Who did you say you were?"

"Hoffmann. I use to live on the Island."

There was a resemblance in his face. He had the same wide forehead that sloped down to partially hood his eyes.

"You don't remember me," the man said. "I was still in grammar school when you graduated from Pershing High. Pat Lawler." He held out his hand.

I shook it and presented Judith. He pumped her hand vigorously.

"You aren't from the Island. I would remember you."

Judith blushed and told Lawler we had met in New York.

"You still in the Army?" Lawler asked me. "I remember hearing that's why you left."

"Not for a long time." It suddenly seemed a long time. But not this store, this Island, which became a more recent yesterday in my mind. "Your dad around?"

"Dad died a few years ago. Heart attack."

"I'm sorry. He was a good guy."

"He went quick and that's the way he would have wanted it. Dad was never one for fuss. And thanks. He was a good guy." Then he said his mother had passed within the year. We extended our condolences.

I looked over at the meat freezer, remembering the stout, ruddy-faced man with the pointed mustache that spoke German with my father a lifetime ago only now it did not seem so long.

"Whatever happened to Hans Ziegler, the butcher?" I asked.

"Retired years ago. He and his wife moved to Florida. That's the last I ever heard. I was still a kid."

"God, it's been a long time."

"What brings you back? A lot of us leave. You're the first one I know of who's come back without family still living here."

Judith explained that we were on vacation and intent on camping on the Island. Lawler was amazed by the idea and made a comment about what was our apparent penchant for places off the beaten track.

"Had enough of New York?" he asked.

"Actually we live in Boston now," I said. "But I guess a city is a city."

"I've been to Providence a few times and once to Washington, DC on a class trip. That was enough for me. You must have been around, being in the service and all."

"I've been places. Europe, Asia," I said without boasting.

"And this is the best you could do for a vacation?"

"It was my idea," Judith said.

"Well, so you're here. What can I get you folks?"

Judith and I browsed through the store, selecting items and piling them on the counter by an ancient cash register, a big brass one that I recalled had a loud bell.

We took hotdogs and bread and chop meat for burgers. Judith grabbed some canned fruits. I added cans of beans, tuna, chili, and a bag of marshmallows. From the coolers we took eggs, bacon, and milk.

Lawler eyed the pile of provisions.

"How long you guys planning on staying?"

"No idea," Judith said. "We sort of left that part open."

That was not entirely accurate. I had earned a week's vacation from my job and told the foreman I was taking a second week without pay. He was not thrilled about it but said okay. Two weeks were the extent of our plans.

Lawler rang up our purchases, making the tinny chime with each keystroke. We filled some boxes and I got our cooler from the van, filled it with ice from the store's machine, and stowed the perishables inside. Lawler helped us load the van.

"Guess I'll be seeing you around a while," he said. We shook hands. "Enjoy yourselves."

We thanked him and got in the van.

Judith said, "He seems so young to be so, so settled."

"Bittern Island is enough for some people. Come on. Let me show you around."

We drove down Main Street. As it was early summer the shops were all open. I pointed out Saint Andrews Church and told how the graveyard had stones dating back three hundred years.

"Are your parents buried there?" Judith asked.

"No." Then I told her about the bluffs at each end of the Island, the eastern one being the place where my folks had been committed to eternity.

We turned down Pearse Street, named for one of the Island's earliest settlers. I pointed to a weathered, gray-shingled house at the end of the road.

"That was our home. I sold it when Papa passed away."

Judith stared at the house in silence. A middle-aged woman came around the side of the house carrying a basket of laundry she must have collected from the clothesline strung across the yard. She stopped to regard us a moment with mild interest. She did not look familiar, not that I remembered the couple I sold the house to all that well. I put the van in gear and made a U-turn back up the road.

"Where can we camp?" Judith asked.

"Pretty much anywhere along the south side of the Island. It's beach and dunes from end to end on that side."

I drove the dirt road over the ridgeline that bisected Bittern Island since the glacier had formed it. We turned west on Mariners Path.

"Pick any spot you want," I said. We drove on about a half-mile.

"I like over there." She was pointing to a cluster of rock and sand bluffs that jutted up obscuring the sight of the water from the road.

"That's Shuman Point. The local Indians had a camp along its base."

"Are there still Indians on the Island?"

"No. They moved on ages ago. Some went to Block Island for a while, then back to the mainland."

I pulled the van off the road and we got out. Holding hands we climbed the bluff.

"That's the Atlantic Ocean," I said. "And over that way," I added, pointing southwest, "is Block Island and beyond that Montauk Point on the end of Long Island."

"I can't see them."

"You rarely can. It has to be completely clear. You need a dead calm sea and no haze. Probably only happens a few times a year."

Judith put her arm around my waist and hugged me close. "I feel like I'm at the end of the world."

"Or the beginning."

"Yes. That's it. We're at the very beginning and it's only you and me. Isn't it wonderful? All that sky. All that sea. Like it goes on forever."

"Maybe it does. On and on forever."

"And so will we."

"On and on forever."

We turned into a kiss, the wind rising, a tinge of salt flavoring our lips and we took huge breaths, holding the kiss, planting our feet firmly in the sand.

"Forever," Judith whispered into my mouth.

By afternoon we had made camp. The tent was pitched in the lee of the largest sand dune and I anchored it with pegs and rope. As Judith unwrapped the sleeping bags I set out to gather driftwood for a fire. I made three trips down to the beach and back, toting armfuls of the dry limbs that had been bleached in the salt and sun. When I came back the last time my wife was seated on a campstool, her sketchbook open in her lap. With a piece of charcoal she was making quick strokes across the page.

I gently placed the wood beside my previous loads so as not to disturb her. The sun was perched at the top of the rise extending up behind her form. Her hair hung loose and teased by the breeze. It feathered down in front of her eyes and she tossed her head absently to clear her vision. She looked up, not at me but at the twin bluffs jutting up and out beside the camp, separating us from the sea. She was as beautiful as I had ever seen her or could have imagined. Staring up at the rocks topped with waving reeds, Judith settled back on the stool and let the book slide from her lap to land at her feet. Something came to her. A shudder waved across her body starting from her legs and ending in arched shoulders as she craned her face toward the sun.

Feeling my presence she closed her eyes. "Karl, let's never leave this place. Promise me. It's all I'll ever ask. Promise me."

I went over and knelt by her side. She put her arms around my shoulders and drew my head down to rest in her lap. Leaning over she kissed my hair.

"Are we home, baby?" she whispered.

"Yes. We're home."

By sunset I had a fire going and we cooked hotdogs on slender sticks. Afterwards I took her by the hand to the top of the bluffs, away from the firelight, and showed her the stars starting to peep out in the heavens. She shivered in the chill night air and I held her close. We stared up at the bright twinkling stars and beaming three-quarter moon. Below us down the rock face of the bluff, the surf crashed against the beach. I remembered what we said earlier in the day. It felt like the beginning and the end. And it felt like the forever in between.

That first night we made love in the tent. The fading firelight outside threw shadows at the canvas wall and the wind whistled in the tent ropes. Later we clung to each other, not slackening our grips until we were asleep, if even then.

In the morning birds woke us as they fussed and foraged beyond the rim of our campsite. We snuggled in our sleeping bag, listening.

"It sounds like so many," Judith whispered.

"Hundreds of them, all kinds."

"What kinds?"

"Gulls, terns, pipers, bitterns. In the spring and fall the Island's full of migratory birds as well, eating and resting along their journey."

Judith was startled by a throaty bark near by. "What was that?"

"That's the bittern.   He barks when he's angry."

"Sounds like a small dog."

"It's his only defense. Most times he'll just stand straight and wave his neck like a piece of grass so an intruder won't spot him. If that doesn't work he barks like an animal to scare them off."

"Does it work?"

"He scared you."

Judith giggled and buried her head in my chest. We fell into a gentle sleep, feeling the sun come up to warm the tent.

"I'm hungry," Judith said awakening a second time.

"Then there's work to be done."

We crawled out of our sleeping bag and donned sweatshirts and jeans. Outside the tent, despite the bright sun, it was a cool morning. I suggested Judith collect the firewood while I prepared our breakfast. The arrangement pleased her and she set off toting a woven string bag to carry what wood she found. With the few pieces of driftwood left from the previous evening, I coaxed a flame from the embers in the fire pit.

I filled the coffeepot and set it in the fire. By the time Judith returned I was prepared to fry eggs and bacon in a skillet. She tramped into camp lugging a bulging bag of wood.

"How's it going?" Judith called.

"Only waiting for you."

She eyed what was left of my meager fire. "Waiting for me or the firewood?"

She dumped the wood in a heap, selected some stout pieces, and crossed them over what was burning. The flames immediately licked up the wood and the logs caught. Judith crossed her arms and rubbed her shoulders.

"Coffee smells good," she said. "I could use some. For a bright day, my bones feel kind of damp."

"Come sit by the fire. It's always like this in the morning. We're an Island surrounded by water, obviously. The sun has to bake us for a while."

While Judith savored her first cup of coffee I set about making breakfast. When it was ready we ate on tin plates and finished mopping up egg yolk with hunks of bread.

"Had enough?" I said.

"Enough? I'm so full I'm ready to go back to bed. We can't do this every morning."

"You'll get use to it. It's important. You'll have the whole morning to work it off. There's no such thing as lazy on Bittern Island. Here, life is a chore."

"What do you mean? We're on vacation."

I pointed to what was left of the wood she had gathered. "Look at that. We used most of it just to make breakfast. We'll have to fetch more for later." I held up the near empty water jug. "And this. We have to find a fresh water source. Then of course, we can fish if you like. Or go exploring."

"You make it sound hard, but it's not. It's all so basic, so simple."

"So necessary."

"Yes."

"So? Do you still think it's home?"

"Yes." Her tone was firm and satisfied.

"Then we'd better get started."

CHAPTER THIRTY-FIVE

My phone was ringing when I got home.

"The State Police are back," Rolando said.

"I know. I called them."

"*Qué?*"

"Archie Bealer is dead."

Rolando mumbled something.

"You can cross yourself all you want, my friend. This one isn't going away."

"No, you're right. The evil is among us." He paused and then asked another question. "Are the cops with you?"

"They're out in the dunes back by the salt marsh. That's where Archie's body is." It was my turn to pause. "That's where Martin's Jeep is too."

"You found it?"

"Yes. But only Bealer was killed for it." For some reason it did not ring true even as I said the words. "Killed for finding it or some other reason. Who the hell knows?"

"Whoever knows is never going to tell."

"That may be. But that doesn't mean the end of things. It's time I had my own talk with Colonel Devon."

In the silence that followed I heard wind rush over my house. The storm was near. A peal of thunder echoed far out over the ocean. It sounded hollow and desperate the way a man's breath sounds choked in his throat as he dies. An image of Pete Franco came to mind. The doomed, addicted musician expiring in my arms. I looked down expecting to see my shirt swathed with blood of that breath. My shirt was dry.

"Karl. Karl?" Rolando was insisting. "What will you tell him?"

Thunder came again. Louder, closer. The storm was sucking up the sea to sustain itself.

"I'll tell him the truth."

The simple declaration brought that cool calmness to my brain. I felt myself breathing deep and steadily.

"That could get... *Cristo*. That could get complicated."

"I let it get complicated. Enough."

"What about Don Ostros?"

I was thinking about the wily old bastard at that moment. He would not let it go so calmly. Even if I was ready, he certainly was not. I thought of the bleak statues rising from the snowfield in Ostros's Boston yard.

"The Don's dead already," I said. "The Devil knows it, and so does he. He's on the lip of hell and all he has left is to drag the rest of us in after him."

"You're talking crazy. You don't believe any of it. Heaven or hell."

"I don't have to believe." Suddenly I felt tired and restless in the same instance. "I once built a wall in Korea."

"Huh?"

"I said I once built a wall. A wall to keep the enemy out. An enemy that wasn't coming. An enemy that if he had come, no wall was going to stop. But I built it anyway because I was there and it was something to do."

"You've lost me, man."

"I hope not, my true friend."

I explained to Rolando what I intended to do.

After ringing off from him I took a shower. When I emerged I could hear rain falling in sheets outside. I dressed in black jeans, a white wool turtleneck sweater, and work boots. Seated at my desk I took the fountain pen from Papa and wrote a terse note to Colonel Devon explaining I had gone to town. Sticking it in an envelope addressed to Devon, I affixed it to my front door with a thumbtack.

From the peg by the door I took my rain slicker and pulled it over the sweater. Water was streaming off the eaves of the house as I secured the door behind me and sprinted to the pickup. The cab smelled damp and felt clammy but the engine barked to life with a few pumps.

When I pulled onto Mariners Path two streaks of lightning split the sky as the rain intensified. Through the windshield I peered down the road when the wipers gave me visibility. Intermittent thunder drowned out the sound of the engine.

I passed All Island Rental. Each structure discernable in the electric frenzy thrashing above them. One bolt struck the lightning rod attached to C sending a sizzling blue caterpillar of energy down its mast into the ground. The sight suddenly awash as the wind direction veered sending waves of rain across the side window. I turned back toward the road, concentrating on holding the truck down the center.

When I turned up the ridge it was if I challenged the wind that responded by attempting to lift the axles and tires from the roadbed. Stubbornly the old pickup held course as my fingers tightened around the steering wheel, feeling my knuckles whiten with effort.

Atop the hills the nose of the truck dipped, and Gracetown lay low before me. Lights were few, flickering, and scattered like ships flung pell-mell across the midnight horizon. But it was not midnight and the beacon of Grace Light was dark and unobserving.

The truck skidded once. Rainwater teemed down the gully of the road rushing along with my progress. I turned into the skid, kept my foot from the brake, and recovered. The rain was at my back. Visibility ahead improved. I could see the harbor. Conning towers of fishing boats waved violently side to side as the water below their hulls roiled with the storm tide. Low clouds of spray erupted when less-secured vessels slapped down their bows after pitching with a wave.

At the edge of town I stopped and let the engine idle. My blood was racing but my mind was clear. I had fought many a storm aboard the *Galina* with my father. The bad ones as a mere child when he threaded rope through my belt loops and lashed an end to the binnacle lest a boy be washed overboard. There always came that moment, that impervious second when the storm blanched and yawned, caught its breath, and you knew you were fighting well and would make it. The worst passed and you rode it out because you knew it, were accustomed to its fits, and could anticipate and prepare. The feeling that control had slipped back into your hands. It was what the wind and sea teach us as stern, unforgiving schoolmasters.If you studied hard, practiced firmly, you claimed it the rest of your life.

I thanked the vehicle. "Done and well done." The phrase a memory. I heard that other voice within my own.

There was a light on in the *cantina*. Out of the truck I bolted through the rain to the front door. I worked the handle as the wind took it from me and flung the door open. I reached for it, stepped inside, and jammed it shut behind me.

"Senor Hoffmann, you're soaked. What are you doing out in this?"

The voice was calm. It betrayed no surprise. I turned to it. It was Santiago, Ostros's chef and driver.

Dripping a pool of water at my feet I shucked the rain slicker and dangled it from a hook by the door.

"I've come to see the Don. Is he here?"

Santiago made a slight bow.

"He's napping upstairs. I'm sure he will want to see you. Let me go wake him."

Santiago turned and paced across the room. A moment after disappearing through the kitchen door I heard a pair of heavy footfalls climbing a stairs. I knew Ostros had a sizeable apartment on the floor above.

Another sound caught my attention. I turned to this one.

From the MEN'S ROOM in the corner came the teenager I remembered. The one with the switchblade. The one who had driven me home after

Ostros and I got drunk. He wore a stained apron, held a mop, and was pushing a bucket along the floor with his foot.

I nodded in acknowledgement. He half-nodded and looked away quickly. I knew he was embarrassed to be caught in such a menial chore. It was a different moment from when he had flashed the knife expertly and slit the string binding *The Poet*. It lacked the eloquent loyalty of obeying the Don to drive me home and hike back to town. He was washing out the shithouse and I had seen him. No doubt he was young enough and foolish enough to hate me for it. He did not know nor care that I respected any honest toil and had dipped my hands into many a bucket of soiled water.

The lad stooped, picked up the bucket, and hurried from the room without looking at me again.

All the tables in the restaurant were set for dinner. Clean napkins were at each place and unlit candles sprouted from the center of every table. I drew back the nearest chair and sat down. I heard low voices in the kitchen and the occasional clang of pots. The *cantina*'s staff was preparing for the Sunday night diners.

The kitchen door opened wider and Don Ostros blocked the light. He was smoking a cigar and did not look as if just awakened from a *siesta*. He cocked his head at the sound of thunder outside. There was intentness in his pause. With a roll of his broad shoulders and a puff of cigar smoke, he shrugged it off. He approached my table.

"This is a serious storm, *amigo*. And you have been drenched in it. Miguel," he called over his shoulder. "Bring brandy."

Ostros sat down across from me and placed his cigar in an ashtray on the table. With a wooden match he lit the lone candle between us. He looked at me with a bland, immobile face. I said nothing. Miguel, the lad who cleaned the bathroom, brought out a bottle and two glasses. They were not the usual petite brandy snifters, but short squat glasses. The kind serious drinkers keep beside their bottle in the cupboard.

I grabbed the bottle, extracted the cork, and poured equal measures. I slid one glass in front of Ostros. The other I cupped in my hand. Ostros was waiting on me and I was taking my time. It irked him a little. I could see it in his eyes. He caught me and pretended to study the painting on the wall behind me, the one of Gracetown Light.

Finally I lifted my glass and held it between us beside the flickering candle.

"One drink, Don Ostros. One last drink."

"The last one you say?" He had not picked up his own. "Why is that?"

"Because it's over."

"Over for whom?"

"For me, for you, for this bloody Island. It's over."

"How can you be sure?"

"Shut up and drink, goddamn you."

My tone, my impertinence took him back. His body heaved in the chair and slowly settled forward, a grim expression coming to his face. He reached for his glass.

"The drink of the damned," he said. "Well I've done that. Have you?"

"I will now." My brandy went down in a single swallow. I smacked the empty glass down on the tabletop.

Ostros stared at me fiercely and I stared back at him. His snarl softened and his lips went straight.

"So be it." He gulped his drink. The brandy seared his throat and he coughed it away. "You should go now. You never should have come. It is something you will regret."

"Maybe. But we started square and I want to end it square. Fair enough?"

"Your father didn't believe in fair. Not at the end."

"You've no idea what he believed. That was the difference."

"They'll crush you too."

"I didn't come here to argue the point. I've said what I came to say. You're not the philosopher you aspire to be. Not at all. You're a cold, greedy, ruthless man."

"It's a cold, greedy, ruthless world," he said to trap me. Suck me back in. Obscure the truth as I had finally determined it.

"Enough." I rose from the table. "Enough." Calmness infused with finality. I flipped his gold piece onto the table. It rolled and fell on its side.

I turned from the table without looking at him. By the door I yanked my slicker from the hook and did not put it on until I was outside in the rain with the door closed behind me.

A few minutes later I had the pickup parked behind the Sea Witch and was through the tavern's back door. Half a dozen men were drinking at the bar, all fishing fleet skippers from the harbor. They looked up when I entered, more from the noise of the storm I was leaving outside than a curiosity in my presence. Two of them waved. They all went back to their drinks. Sweeney came over as I took a stool.

"What's your pleasure, mate?" he asked.

"Just coffee."

"Fine. But hadn't you best be getting out of that dripping oil skin?"

Droplets of water were running down the sleeves of my rain slicker forming little puddles by my wrists on the bar. I looked down and saw the floor beneath me was wet as well.

"Sorry, Sweeney."

"No offense to me. Thought you might be a tad more comfortable is all."

When I stood up to remove the cloak, Sweeney wiped the wet spots from the bar with a towel. I hung the slicker to dry near the fireplace on the other side of the room and returned to my seat patting my matted wet hair.

"Hell of a blow coming through," Sweeney said. "What brings you into town? Are we going to need pumps again?"

"She'll pass through. We've seen worse."

His first question remained unanswered but Sweeney dropped it.

"Seen Gunner?" I asked.

"Not this particular day. Not yet." He looked at his wristwatch. "It's just come up on five. He's fairly regular you know."

"Like Archie?"

"Naw, not at all. No two men with the whiskey curse could be more different." Sweeney stroked his chin reflectively. "Since you mention it, I haven't seen the Constable all day. Now Bealer, I wouldn't call him regular. Him, I'd say, was faithful. I can set the clock by the routine of his tremors. 'Tis a sad thing but he gets no pity from me. I serve him whiskey on the cuff. That's my part. His soul is his own business, damn him."

Sweeney was called by one of the fishermen down the bar for another round before I could comment. I wrapped my damp hands about the coffee mug, lifted it with both, and took a sip. A shudder drew the length of my body as the hot fluid worked to dispel the damp chill at the base of my spine.

Ben Marshall came through the front door while Sweeney served his customers. He wore a bright yellow slicker and floppy Gloucester hat. Taking off the hat, he shook it out the door then hung it with his raincoat by mine. He took a stool two down from me and nodded a mute hello. Sweeney attended him and poured a bourbon with a beer chaser. Marshall took a sip of whiskey then rubbed his hands.

"It's the Devil's day," I heard him say to Sweeney.

"On a Sunday, you say?" Sweeney asked.

"It's a real prize when the Devil can snatch a soul on the Lord's Day," Marshall said.

"Aye," Sweeney agreed. "A plum on his thumb."

Marshall looked over at me glass in hand. "Bit of activity out your way this morning, Karl."

I nodded back at him. As Harbor Master he knew who and what had come ashore on the ferry. And what must have gone back bound for the M.E.'s office.

"Did you see him?" he asked.

In response I only nodded again.

"What did you make of it?"

"Murder."

The word brought a hush to the tavern. The fishermen stopped talking among themselves and turned looking past Marshall at me.

"Shot dead. Shot and left for the gulls."

"Who?" asked Sweeney and most of the captains simultaneously.

"Constable Bealer," Marshall said.

Another shroud of quiet descended on us. No one spoke. No one drank. The only noise was the crackling of wood in the hearth behind us.

"Mother of God," Sweeney blurted out at last. "What the hell is happening on this blasted Island?"

"The State Police are back to sort it right," Marshall said. "They'll probably haul us all over to the Church for another meeting. Some officer ordered me to shut the ferry service. Not that anybody's going anywhere in a storm like this."

A crack of thunder underscored his point.

"They won't have far to look," Sweeney muttered.

"Mind your tongue," one of the skippers shouted.

"I'll say what I damn well please," Sweeney rebuked him.

"That's a long lonely beach out there," another observed less forcefully.

"I'll be dying in my bed, thank you very much," Sweeney vowed.

A smattering of "Amens" came from the group.

"And I'll tell you something else," Sweeney forged ahead. "This Island was doomed long before the State wrote us off. It was doomed because we let the kind of shenanigans go on that we ought not have. You men know what I'm saying. We're a sorry lot. And Bealer was the worst, God rest his soul if He's a mind to. Called himself an officer of the law. That's what we've come to."

Sweeney threw his towel down on the bar in disgust and poured himself a drink.

"Here's to the faithless lot of us," he toasted. "May we not get what we deserve."

He downed his drink and no one joined him.

CHAPTER THIRTY-SIX

Judith's paintings sold in New York, Philadelphia, and Atlanta. We camped the summer and rented a cottage in August. Two trips to the mainland retrieved more belongings and my wife met with her agent. She resigned from the University despite their protests. I wrote my company I had found something else. The last trip we surrendered the van and purchased a pickup truck.

"What's it like?" Judith was cleaning her paintbrushes on the porch of the cottage.

"What's what like?"

"The winter here."

"Mild the most part, because of the Gulf Stream. We'll get the occasional nor'easter, maybe a blizzard once a decade, but otherwise okay."

"I can't wait."

"For winter?"

"I love winter colors. They're basic yet bold. With the sky and water I'll see shades I've never dreamed. The sand and dunes, they're beautiful too."

"You love it here."

"Mmm. It's the finest spot in the world."

"Hasty judgment. Considering you haven't seen much of the world."

I followed her inside where she set the brushes to dry. The painting on her easel was the end of Main Street where it ends in the dockyards. Fishing boats were moored, nets hung to dry. The boats in the painting were real. I recognized them and knew their names.

"Well?" I asked. "What about the art of Europe, Asia, and Africa?"

Judith looked at me and set her jaw.

"It will be painted by Europeans, Asians, and Africans. My work is here."

The matter was closed.

On a trip to Narragansett we arranged through the Realtor to keep the cottage through winter. At the Hall of Records we researched zoning and assessment maps of Bittern Island. We learned that in recent years the State of Rhode Island had bought up available parcels of the Island. There was no reference as to why.

"Here it is." I stabbed the map with my finger.

Judith leaned over my shoulder. "Are you sure?"

"Positive." I traced my finger over the map. "Here's the bluffs. See how the coast turns at this point? That's the spot."

I jotted down the lot numbers and went to the card catalog to determine ownership.

"Do you think it's for sale?"

"That might depend on our offer. The good thing is it's privately owned. The State hasn't grabbed it. Tremont Judd," I read from the card.

"Do you know him?"

"There's always been a Judd family on the Island. I went to school with a Malcolm Judd. Don't know Tremont. It doesn't matter; we'll check it out."

Back at the Realtor's office we explained our position to the agent. He promised to contact Mister Judd and say a buyer was interested in his parcel of Shuman Point. We sailed the ferry home.

"That wasn't difficult," Judith said.

"That was only the start. Suppose we can buy the land. We'll have to hire a contractor to build a house. There's a thousand details."

"Why do we need a contractor? I married a carpenter. Well, carpenter, build your wife a home."

"Are you…?" I did not finish. She was serious.

The agent called three days later. Tremont Judd was a businessman in Warwick. For the right price, the lot was for sale. The Realtor suggested we do a survey before submitting a bid.

The survey process and title search took two weeks. Judith called the agent every day. We met back at the Realtor's office the end of August.

"It's beachfront property but the market is in your favor," the agent said. He slid a piece of paper across his desk. "This is what I would offer. You could go lower but your interest might spark him to shop around for a better deal. I'm sure the State would grab it. If you really want the property, make a solid offer."

I picked up the paper. The number was in the mid five figure range. I showed it to Judith. Neither of us had any idea of relative property values.

"We can manage that," Judith said. "What are the taxes like?"

The agent smirked. "Public services barely exist on Bittern Island. Hence, taxes are minimal. Out there you're on your own."

"Make the offer," I said.

"What about the mortgage?"

"We'll pay cash," Judith said.

The words had a magical effect on the agent.

Over supper I said to Judith, "I can probably build the house. I'll need help, but that's not a problem. There's always men around the Island who can use a few extra dollars. What I really need is an architect who can lay out prints to follow."

Judith had an idea and called Frederick Aldan. Aldan's wealthy clients built houses on Cape Cod, Fire Island, and the Long Island beachfront.

"There's only one architect for you, love," Aldan told my wife. "David Beekman."

Beekman was a busy man. He was booked until late September but promised to come out at the end of the month. He did not want to hear our ideas over the phone. It was useless, he said, to take pencil to paper until he saw the ground. We would have to wait or try someone else.

Judith made sketches of our home as she conceived it, while I offered suggestions that she incorporated in subsequent drawings.

The third week of September was set for closing on the property. Tremont Judd had accepted the offer. Our only disappointment was that Judd himself would not attend the signing. By proxy, we took title to the land in Judd's lawyer's office.

It was mild enough to almost still be summer. Judith insisted we camp on our own property the night after the deal.

"Just one night. It's all ours."

I did not need convincing. We set up camp, broiled steaks on a fire, drank a bottle of wine, took a walk on the beach under the stars, and made love to the rhythm of the surf.

"We've christened our home," Judith whispered as she lay back in the tent.

As I scooped her back up in my arms, it did feel like a most natural home.

David Beekman came as promised. A short, fidgety man with glasses dressed in chinos and sweater, Beekman crammed into the pickup with Judith and myself as I drove to the Point.

Beekman stood beside the pickup and looked in every direction. "Lovely," he muttered.

He snapped a piece of reed grass, stuck it in his mouth and chewed as he walked up the bluff. At the crest he stopped and slowly spun in a circle.

"Lovely," we heard him call out.

Back down in the lee of the rocks he paced off measurements with his short legs. Then he stopped and calculated elevations by eye. By the time he was done the reed in his mouth was gnawed to a green toothpick. He joined us by the truck, shaking his head.

"Goddamn lovely. You two are lucky. Any place else this kind of view would cost you a king's ransom. Let's go back and see what ideas you've got for me."

Judith made coffee and spread her sketches on the kitchen table. Beekman picked one up. "Frederick was right. You're a hell of an artist." He picked up another one and studied it. "I'd love to see your paintings. You've really got the eye."

"Maybe as an artist," Judith said, "but hardly an architect."

"Not necessarily true. It's form and space and function utilizing the terrain without infringing on its natural beauty. The rest is math, physics, and building codes. You've done half my work already. It's simple, which I like. Makes good use of the topography. The bluffs and dunes are the real beauty. The house must fit, not impose. I think you've done that. Can I take these?"

My wife beamed. She gathered the drawings and placed them in a folder for Beekman.

"I hardly knew this Island existed," Beekman said. "No substantial wealth out here I take it."

It was not meant as an insult. Beekman designed for movie stars, authors, wealthy entrepreneurs, and Old World money. For most the address was as important as the structure.

"We're off the beaten path," I said, "and considerably underdeveloped."

"No doubt you like it that way."

My wife and I smiled.

"Have you a contractor? I know several who would do the job."

"We're building it ourselves," I said. "There's a fair amount of labor available when the fishing season ends."

"Forgive me, but do you know what you're doing?"

I briefed Beekman on my years in the Engineers and my tenure as a Union carpenter.

"Then I'd say you have a fair shot. I'll simplify the plans where I can."

"We'll take all the help we can get," I said.

"Done." Beekman rapped the table with his knuckles. "I'll have sketches for you in ten days. If you approve, we'll go from there. My office will send my contract."

We walked David Beekman to the ferry.

"I've enjoyed meeting you both," he said.

He shook hands with both of us. "I'm going to like this. I hope you will too."

Walking back to the cottage Judith said, "I like him."

"Me too."

"Karl, I didn't mean to put you on the spot."

"What are you talking about?"

"Building the house. If you think it's too much and want to hire a contractor, it's… that's okay."

"Do you think I can do it?"

"Of course I do. I have faith in you."

"Then it's settled. Come on, it's still warm enough. Let's take a swim."

We changed into suits and drove to Rose Beach on the eastern end of the Island. The name came from the wild beach roses that bloomed in the dunes above the shore.

A ways down the beach cropped up the rocky crag from which Papa and I scattered Mama's ashes. The place where I had returned to disperse Papa's. I looked in that direction but did not point it out to Judith. She was in a cheery mood and eager for the swim. She dropped her towel and sprinted for the surf.

"Catch me," she called.

The sun behind us shone gold on the water. We ran from the sun into the sea.

Frederick Aldan called a day later. He was eager for more paintings. My wife worked daily, and with completed ones brought with us, she had a fair amount. Judith and Aldan chatted on the phone. I only heard her side.

"How much did you say?" Then, "Whew. That's more than I imagined."

She signaled me for a pencil. I handed her one with a piece of paper. Judith scribbled a number after a dollar sign and slipped the paper back to me. The number was three hundred and seventy-five thousand.

"Okay," I heard her say into the phone. "I'll tell him."

"Tell me what?"

She held up her hand for patience while she ended the call.

"We love you too, Frederick. Thank you for everything. Beekman was great. Talk to you soon."

Judith put down the receiver.

"Tell me what?"

"Frederick says that we ought to get ourselves an accountant. We've made almost four hundred thousand dollars, and there's going to be tax implications. He's right. I never had that kind of money."

"Me neither. I've never thought about it. Aldan's right. We need a professional. We'll look one up tomorrow."

"Not tomorrow. Frederick's sending a van and men to crate and transport the paintings I have. You'll be busy too. You've writing to do. I haven't seen you at your desk in weeks. When we start building you won't have time or even feel like it. Deal?"

"Only if we can go out to dinner tonight."

"Dinner?"

"A restaurant, one with tablecloths and candlelight."

"That little one on Main Street? Or do you mean going to the mainland? I don't want to go off-Island."

She was acquiring the local nomenclature.

That night I took Judith for the first time to the *cantina* of Don Ostros.

Ostros was a munificent host. He greeted me warmly saying he heard I was back on the Island. When I introduced Judith he kissed her hand. Before we could study our menus a bottle of champagne appeared at our table courtesy of the proprietor.

"Does he think you're someone special?" Judith whispered.

"He was a friend of my father's. They did some business together." I did not go into the story. "He's a bit of a connoisseur." I pointed around the room. "Look at all his paintings. Wait until he hears you're an artist."

"Don't tell him," Judith said suddenly.

"What?"

She took a sip of champagne and calmed down. "I'd rather people around here not know. I don't know why for sure. It's just something I'd rather. I like the anonymity, the privacy. Do you mind?"

"Certainly not. It's entirely up to you. But if he asks, what will you say?"

"I'll say I'm a professor of art on sabbatical. But only if he asks."

"What's the matter? There's no such thing as privacy on an Island this small."

"There is if you want it bad enough."

"As long as I'm not on the outside."

"You could never be on the outside. We're a team."

"All right then. You and me."

"You and me and our own little Island."

We clinked glasses together. After the sip of conspiracy we consulted our menus.

"Anything from the sea will be as fresh as this morning," I said.

"What are you having?"

"Probably oysters and the lobster. This time of year they're large and meaty, and I'm starving"

"Sounds good. Double yours."

The waiter took the order. Judith said the champagne was too much so I asked for a wine list.

"*Pardon, senor*," the waiter said. "No wine list. It changes much. What you like?"

"Something white, cold and light," Judith said.

"*Bueno*," the waiter said. "We have this wine." He scurried away, pleased he had just the thing.

"Your friend Ostros must have spoken to him. He's charming," Judith said.

"How does it feel to be rich?"

"We're not rich. Not in the money sense anyway."

I smiled at the distinction. My wife had more to say.

"We've been lucky so far. Appreciation is one thing. Market value is another. My popularity will wane when the next one comes along."

"Does that matter to you?"

"Not a speck."

"Good. Because it doesn't matter to me. I've been poor. It feels the same."

"That's why I love you."

"I would have stayed in the tent."

"You only liked it for the sex."

"Not completely. There was that but there was something else."

"I know what you mean. It's like we're free."

"Aren't we?"

"Yes and no," she answered cryptically.

"Explain yourself, Madam Artist."

Judith drained her glass of champagne and looked past me at something not there.

"I'm a slave to my art. I'm a slave to myself knowing my brother will spend the rest of his life in an institution. The only freedom I have is you. And you're the less free of the two of us. Ironic. Don't you think?"

"How am I not free?"

"You're linked to two souls you want desperately to free. They've trapped you and you were willing. It's sad and magnificent at the same time."

I took umbrage at the notion. Before I could retort our oysters were served.

Judith changed the subject. "This is a lovely place. How does your friend manage it on this small Island? And he surely has an eye for art."

"I didn't say he was my friend. He was a friend of my father's." My tone was peevish. I was dwelling on the freedom thing.

Judith laid down her fork. "Karl, look at me."

Putting down the wedge of lemon I was squirting on my oysters I raised my head and met her eyes through the candlelight.

"We rarely argue and never fight," she was saying. "We've unlocked doors in each other's souls that neither of us ever thought would open. Sometimes it's exhilarating, sometimes painful. That is what freedom is all about. That's why it's the basis for love. I don't doubt that for one second and wouldn't have it any other way. I believe I couldn't achieve it with anyone else but you. We're the completeness for each other. That requires a bold fearless honesty. I know you feel it."

The waiter brought our wine and fresh glasses. Whatever nerve of mine Judith had tweaked relaxed. I raised my glass to her.

"Perhaps you're the true poet in the family," I said.

She lifted her own. "Loving is its own art form. You taught me that."

I could not see how but took the compliment. "This Island may not be big enough for so much love."

"The universe isn't large enough so we'll have to claim where we are. To our home."

We brushed our hands that held the glasses together.

CHAPTER THIRTY-SEVEN

"This is a somber, sober bunch," Gunner Hogan said sliding onto the stool beside me. During Sweeney's condemnation I had not noticed him enter the back door. "What are you drinking?"

"Coffee."

"Ah. That's the problem. I drink coffee before church, never after."

"I doubt anyone here has been to church today. Not that we don't need it."

"Do I detect a chink in the atheist's armor?"

"I'm not sure what we need anymore."

Sweeney reclaimed his towel and came down the bar. "What'll it be, Colonel?"

"The cup of kindness on a stormy day."

"We're out of that," Sweeney said dryly. "All we've got is sinner's stout and pity's porter."

"I see I've caught the end of the revival. Sorry I missed the preacher. He must have been a doozy."

"Sweeney did the preaching," I said. "As fair and true a bit of preaching as I've ever heard."

"Then I'd better keep it saintly," Gunner said. "Sweeney, give me something the monks whipped up."

A crooked smile came to the proprietor's lips. He turned and plucked a bottle of brandy from the shelf and poured Gunner's drink.

"You're as damned as the rest of us," Sweeney said.

A roll of thunder outside seemed to shake the room. The electric lights flickered once but held. Gunner grabbed his drink and downed it. Sweeney replenished it as Gunner put his money on the bar. Sweeney took from the pile of cash and walked away.

"He has a talent for this preaching stuff," Gunner said to me. "Even Billy Graham can't call down thunder."

When I did not answer, Gunner dropped it. The barroom got quiet again. All I heard was the wind and rain outside and the occasional hollow thud as an empty glass came down on the counter. Sweeney's service was swift and silent.

Ben Marshall had another pair of bourbons as he finished his beer. Retrieving his coat, he left without a word to anyone. I felt Gunner shift uneasily beside me.

"If this is a wake, where's the corpse?" he muttered.

"It was down on the beach, beyond my house."

"Who might that be?"

"Archie Bealer. Shot dead."

"I figured something was up. I heard the chopper fly in just before the storm. Thought I might check it out but didn't want to get caught in this foul soup."

"Smart decision."

"Who found him?"

"I did."

I would have told him the whole story but then I would only have had to repeat it almost immediately. Colonel Devon and another trooper came in with a gust of wind and spray of rain. I figured he would want to go over the facts so Gunner could hear them then.

"I found your note, Hoffmann," Devon called from the door. He shook water from himself and removed his dripping hat. "Whatever you've got to say, I'm hear to listen."

He took off his parka and sat at a table. The other trooper remained by the door after closing it. I imagined for a moment that Devon expected a confession. Could he actually think I killed Archie Bealer? He was in for a surprise, but not that one.

"Come on over with me, Gunner," I said. "You're the closest thing I've got to a lawyer."

"Preachers and lawyers and State Troopers. Jesus, Karl, all I wanted was a drink."

He followed me over to Devon's table. I pointed to the trooper on guard at the door as I sat down.

"You can tell your man to relax and dry off, Colonel," I said. "I'm not going anywhere."

"That remains to be seen." Gunner slid into a chair. "What's your business here?" Devon asked him.

"I was invited, your honor. Nothing more, nothing less."

Devon grunted disapproval but did not make an issue of it. To me Devon said, "Your note said you have some information."

Across the otherwise quiet barroom, Devon's voice rang clear. Several of the fleet skippers at the bar abruptly gulped their drinks and scrambled to their feet. Their way out the door was blocked by the trooper. A wave from Devon and the trooper let them pass. They dispersed into the storm. The two remaining captains hunched over their drinks in an effort to be soundless and invisible. Sweeney stood at the end of the bar, towel draping his shoulders, staring out the front window.

"I'm going to have a drink," I said.

"I'd rather you didn't," Devon said.

"This isn't about what you want. Take it or leave it."

Devon shrugged his shoulders.

I walked to the bar and ordered a brandy for myself and another for Gunner. Sweeney poured doubles. Instead of taking my money he grabbed my hand and shook it firmly in encouragement.

"It'll be all right, son," he said. "It's the right thing."

Back at the table I slid Gunner's drink toward him.

"Can we begin now?" Devon said.

I took a slow sip of brandy. Looking at Devon, I put the glass down. "You figured I was somehow mixed up in this from the start. That's why you searched my premises."

"I'm conducting an investigation." It was no apology. "It takes me wherever it has to go."

"And you tried to muscle me with the EPA and the DEA. Not to mention using the Coast Guard and the INS to harass my friends."

"You give me too much credit, Mister Hoffmann. Every enforcement service has its own agenda. As for me, I'm looking for a killer. As for you? Let's just say you've been around every corner I've turned. Why is that?"

"It's a small Island."

"And getting smaller."

"I did not kill Martin. And I didn't kill Archie."

"I never said you did. I've checked you out thoroughly. You don't strike me as a murderer."

That came as a relief. Devon was a sharp cop despite what one felt about his aggressive scout dog manners. He had formed a conclusion about me and was prepared to present it.

"What I think happened," Devon started up again, "is a matter of confused loyalties. Some knowledgeable people tell me that's not surprising on an Island that's so insular and intimate. But that still doesn't excuse you from the law."

"What else do you know about me?"

"I know who your mother and father were. Really were that is. I know your military service and I know your wife died from an untreatable illness. I'm sorry."

The last remark was unexpected. I believed him.

"You've made a life here on Bittern Island. It's not the life you imagined when you came back. But it's your life. I'm not judging you one way or the other. I'm only trying to draw you back from a serious mistake. A serious mistake in your judgment."

"It's not your habit to pull any punches. Is it?"

"Once or twice you tried to make me look like a fool, Karl. I don't take it personally. But let me assure you I'm no fool. I've waited. I've watched. I've poked around. I've drawn some conclusions. It's time to sort this out once and for all. You know that as well as I do. Finally."

We had arrived at the same point. I took a sip of my brandy. The two men at the bar turned sideways in their seats to watch us from the corners of their eyes. Gunner patted my shoulder. Sweeney stood tall and straight behind the bar, his arms crossed in front of him, hands on the counter. All eyes in the room were on me. All except the eyes of Colonel Devon. He was staring down at his own hand laid flat, palm on the table.

"Martin's truck was in my shed. You missed it by a day," I said to Devon.

Devon had no reaction. There was a long pause.

"I don't know who physically put it there. After I found it I went to Don Ostros and asked him to remove it. When I got home it was gone."

Devon slowly drummed his fingers on the table. "Was Ostros on the Island?"

"No. I went to see him at his other home in Boston."

"So you found the Jeep. Knew it belonged to Janus Martin. And went immediately to see Mr. Ostros. Why?"

Hearing Ostros referred to as "Mister" had a demystifying quality to it. I was about to make that comment knowing it would somehow satisfy the officer. I would have, but something happened.

The storm got very loud in the barroom. I could hear the rain pounding and the wind thrashing. It took a second before I realized that the front door of the Sea Witch had opened. Devon and I looked up at the same instant. The tall trooper was blocking the door with his sheer mass. His face was impassive, his shoulders hunched like a football player in game pads. The thumbs of his hands tucked behind the leather of his gun belt under the open flap of his parka. The trooper gave a short shallow cough and widened his eyes.

"Clarence?" Devon called.

Wind filled the room as Clarence collapsed forward. His knees buckled and he went down. Knees struck the floor, torso spasmed, and his head rolled to the side. The broad chest hit the floor with a thud.

I caught a glimpse of the pearl knife hilt protruding from between Clarence's shoulder blades. Only a glimpse. Devon was already moving. The table quaked between us. In one motion Devon was drawing his gun and lifting the table with his other arm to spill it toward me for my defense.

Then I heard the shots.

The table coming up drove me from my chair in a tight roll to the floor. I felt Gunner land beside me, his arm smacking the back of my calves.

Shots came in rapid bursts, muffled whizzing puffs of air from a silenced automatic ripping the edges of the table near my face. Four loud reports as Devon returned fire. His unsilenced gun filling the room as if thunder was beating in my head. Acrid smoke stinging my eyes, the smell of cordite in my nose.

"Back door, the fuckers," I heard Sweeney yell.

His voice was followed by a huge blast, and another, that sent shock waves through the room.

There was more smoke, the creaking of splintered wood, the tinkling of broken glass falling from shattered whiskey bottles. And then silence. The smell of gunfire and alcohol commingling in the thick air.

A few seconds later I heard Gunner Hogan grunt. Then he cursed. I pulled my knees up tight and pushed off the floor with my hands coming to my feet. Devon was standing waving his revolver back and forth between front door and back. Satisfied no more threats were imminent, he holstered his weapon and bolted to his man on the floor. He felt for a pulse in Clarence's neck and called to us at the same time.

"Who's hit? Karl? You all right? Hogan?"

I looked down at Gunner struggling to his feet. The effort convinced me he was not harmed.

"We're okay," I called back.

The place was a bloody shambles. Smoke was dissipating but the air rushing in through the two open doors was flinging tiny bits of debris around like a phantom whip.

Devon, on one knee, crossed himself over the body of his dead trooper. He stood and nudged the machine pistol away from the spread-eagled corpse beside his own man.

"Know this one?" he asked me.

I came forward and looked down at the distorted face. A bullet had pierced his face beside his right eye.

"His name's Miguel. He works for Ostros."

Over at the bar the two sea captains lay dead on the floor beside their stools. Both of their craniums were shattered. It was pointless to check for vital signs. I watched Devon calculate the scene with an investigator's mind.

"The punk thought you were sitting at the bar. He shot them first before he realized where we were."

There was a cough followed by a sneeze and then the sound of Sweeney wheezing.

"This one's dead too," he said. He kicked a lifeless form lying by the back door. "The fucker." Sweeney still held the shotgun he used to dispatch the would-be assassin. He bent a little and spat on the corpse.

Devon and I walked over.

"Know this one?" Devon asked me.

The man had taken twin canisters of buckshot full in the chest. A similar machine pistol was on the floor with a death-frozen finger looped through the trigger guard.

"Santiago. He's called a chef. He's really Ostros's driver and bodyguard."

Devon was unclipping his two-way radio from his belt. He tried to operate it but succeeded in only raising static. "Must be the storm."

"I'll try the phone," Sweeney said. He laid the shotgun across the bar and tried the phone behind the counter. He tapped the receiver button impatiently. "Dead."

Gunner wandered about the room, muttering as if taking inventory of the dead. "Worst shit I've seen since 'Nam."

"This is my fault," I said to the living and the dead.

"This was an attempted hit," Devon said. "To hit you."

"I know. I saw Ostros before I came here."

I felt all three fellow survivors staring at me. Making a slow circle I looked at each of them. Colonel Devon showed no surprise. Gunner looked confused, while Sweeney's face carried a look of disappointment.

"I'm sorry. Mistaken loyalty. Isn't that what you said, Colonel?"

I knew he did not have an answer. Not for this.

Devon paced the length of the room and closed both doors. We still heard rain pounding the roof but the wind seemed far away. Sweeney came from behind the bar and stood beside me. Gunner went behind the bar, found an intact bottle of cognac and poured himself one. Colonel Devon came up to me.

"How many men does Ostros have on the Island?"

"I don't know for sure. A couple of waiters and cooks I guess. I don't know."

"Waiters and cooks my arse," Sweeney said. "Anyone who works for him is part of his rogue army."

"How many have you got, Colonel?" I asked.

"Now it's only me." He turned to look at his fallen comrade.

"What about the guys from the beach this morning?"

"Sent them out on the helicopter ahead of the storm. The others went back to the mainland with the body. I ordered the ferry to sail. Truth is, I wasn't expecting anything like this." It pained him to confess this.

"Who would have?"

He gave himself no quarter. "I don't get paid to underestimate my adversaries. The price for that is usually blood. Now we're awash in it."

Behind me I heard Sweeney snap open the breech of his shotgun. Two empty shell casings fell out, struck the floor, and rolled away. Turning I saw him reload the barrels with fresh cartridges.

"That's right," Devon said to him. "This isn't over."

"It will be for them," Sweeney said. He jerked the breech closed. "It's Judgment Day. Those are my friends on the floor dead." He pointed the muzzle of the gun at the two dead sea captains. "There'll be no more widows made today of my friends. Not if I can help it."

Devon walked over to the trooper's body and knelt on one knee. Gingerly he removed the service weapon from Clarence's holster. Then he checked Miguel's automatic. The clip was empty. Coming to his feet he handed me the trooper's gun, butt first. I took the semi-automatic, similar to the .45s we had been issued in the Engineers.

"Remember how to use one of these?" Devon asked.

In response I worked the top slide pumping a round into the firing chamber.

"That's it. How far is it to Ostros's place from here?"

"Other end of the block, across the street."

"He probably didn't hear anything through the storm. But he won't wait long. He'll want to be gone as soon as the storm passes. Gone if we're all dead."

"Do we wait for him or hunt him down?"

"We don't know what he really has. If we wait we could be trapped here. The storm works for us. It's good cover. We can surround him. Flush him out."

Wind whipped through the bar again. The back door had opened. Devon, Sweeney, and I spun toward it with guns raised.

"*Madre de...*" the words stuck in Rolando Tobar's throat.

"Hands where I can see them," Devon shouted.

Rolando was pale with fright. Rainwater streamed down his face from his matted hair. His hands twitched and came away from his body.

"He's all right," I said. "He works for me."

"Not just for you, I've heard," Devon said.

"That's something else. He's not part of this."

Rolando was looking at the bodies on the floor. Disregarding Devon's orders to keep his hands clear, Rolando crossed himself.

"If you're wrong, you may have tipped the odds," Devon said to me.

"I'm not wrong. Trust me."

"You don't leave me much choice. We're wasting time."

Gunner stooped beside Santiago's body and retrieved the machine pistol. Expertly he ejected the clip, examined the load, and slammed it back home. He stretched the bolt and let it snap. "I'm ready."

"Got a gun for Rolando?" I asked Sweeney. Miguel's empty one was useless.

Sweeney went behind the bar and returned with an ancient looking .45 six-shooter. He checked it was loaded and handed it to Rolando.

"Ostros?" Rolando asked in a faint voice. His arm was pumping up and down to gauge the weight of the pistol.

"He started this," I said. "Sweeney says it's Judgment Day."

"Anybody out back?" Devon asked Rolando.

Rolando shook his head.

"Good. We'll circle around the block that way," Devon said. "Follow me."

CHAPTER THIRTY-EIGHT

In October Judith and I received a package from David Beekman. It contained a rendering of the house and prints. Judith examined them carefully.

"It's perfect."

I unfolded the blueprints on the kitchen table and gave them a quick once over. "Seems basic enough."

"Did he design the studio?"

"Complete with skylights, just like you asked."

Judith hunched beside me over the drawing and I traced rooms with my finger.

"I wonder what this is." I stroked a dotted line that divided part of the master bedroom. "Who'd put a wall there?"

"I suggested it. It's something we can do later."

"Why?"

"For a nursery."

"Are you...?"

"No. We're not."

"Do you want...?"

"I've been thinking about it. I thought it best we wait until the house is built, then we can discuss it. That's why I had David make it an afterthought on the print. Are you angry?"

"Not at all. Still, you've got to admit it's a novel way to broach the subject."

She reached out for a hug and our lips met as we folded into each other rocking side to side. We parted holding hands.

"What do we do first?" she asked.

"About a baby?"

"No, the house, silly. First things first."

I told her we had to make a materials list and contact suppliers for quotes. "We'll have to include the price of transporting everything from the mainland."

"Is there time? Or will we have to wait for spring?"

"The winter's often mild here. We can build through most of it."

"I'm so excited. Our own home."

I overrated my construction acumen. It was a Herculean task for my wife and me. There were permits to file, local codes to be considered, material costs negotiated. Luckily Beekman was routinely available for advice over the phone. Judith was involved in every step. On top of that, she hired our accountant and put our financial affairs in order.

The first materials arrived on Bittern Island by the end of October. The weather was fair with fresh breezes, a few scattered rains, and no snow. It was time to put together a work crew. The fishing season was almost over. Most of the younger men went back to the mainland to wait for next year. Those that stayed on-Island tended to hang around the Sea Witch tavern hoping to pick up a day's work in the boatyards where the fleet was starting its overhaul for the next season.

Judith and I talked with Mr. Sweeney, proprietor of the Sea Witch. He promised to spread the word we were looking for laborers. The terms were all cash. A day's pay for a day's work.

Six fellows showed up at Shuman Point the first day. I strung markers outlining the foundation of the house. We worked until sunset clearing the ground of rocks and wild vegetation. As the light faded I paid them from a strong box Judith brought to the site.

The next day only five returned to begin digging the foundation. These guys told me the sixth man thought it was too strenuous for the pay, cash or no cash. Judith and I provided lunch and on Friday after work we took them to the Sea Witch and stood them the first round. There was good cheer in the crew and I often caught them eyeing my wife with critical favor, but they remained gentlemen and there was no trouble.

The second Friday we did the same thing. I was drinking a beer, Judith a glass of wine, when a short raven-haired man with broad shoulders and muscular arms protruding from rolled-up sleeves approached us.

"Excuse me, *señor*. They say you look for honest labor. If that is so, I'm your man. What you think?"

"Do I know you? Have you fished with our fleet?"

"No. You don't know me. Not yet. And no, I'm no fisherman. At least not around here. *Pero*. I shrimped for a while in Texas and Florida. Came north for something else. What you think?"

"How did you wind up on Bittern Island?" Judith was at my side listening to the conversation.

"I came to see a man about a job. It turned out not what I wanted."

"What man?" I felt my wife's hand come down on my shoulder.

The man hesitated a second. "Don Ostros."

"You don't like *cantina* work?"

"Not if there's something else. I work hard. You see. What you think?"

"What's your name?"

The man squared his shoulders and locked his hands to his waist. "Rolando Tobar."

I stuck out my hand and he reached for it firmly. "Well, Mr. Tobar, I'm Karl Hoffmann. This is my wife Judith," I introduced as we shook. Our hands parted and I indicated my crew. "You follow these boys out to Shuman Point Monday morning. You give me a day's work for a day's pay and then I'll tell you what I think. Fair enough?"

"*Bueno*. That's fair." He gave a slight nod to Judith. "*Señora*." Then he left the bar.

"What an interesting man," Judith said. "Seemed sure of himself."

"I like that in a man."

"So do I. Like the first time you asked me out in front of a naked man."

"Was he naked? I didn't notice. All I saw was you."

"That's not how I remember it."

I laughed at the memory, clear as yesterday. "Let's go home. I'm dog tired."

"What's the matter? Can't keep up with these young guys anymore? Have you been taking those vitamins I lay out for you every morning? Or are you flushing them down the john?"

"If I am, I'll start taking them tomorrow."

She poked me in the ribs. We finished our drinks, bid the boys a good weekend, and drove home, Judith behind the wheel.

Monday morning Rolando Tobar was on the job site before any of us. He made good on his word. Rolando mixed concrete, nailed up shoring, and pitched in anywhere needed. The other men accepted him on the merits of his effort. The end of the day he took his pay with the others.

"Will I see you tomorrow?" I asked him.

He folded his money and stuck it in his pocket. "Sure, boss. Any day you want."

His new buddies on the crew gave him a ride back to town.

Beekman came out to the site twice during construction. He was impressed with the progress.

"How much longer?" he asked a week before Christmas.

"If the weather holds, mid-February."

He gazed from one chimney to the other at opposite ends of the house. "Where did you find that fieldstone?"

"I bought half of it. The rest I scavenged from the bluffs. One of my guys, Rolando, is pretty good at chipping it into usable pieces."

"When do you plan to run up the electrical service?"

That was a sore point with me. The power authority had been stalling.

"Damned if I know. I call them every day and they brush me off. I gave them a deposit a month ago."

"Let me make some calls and see what I can do."

He stayed for dinner and caught the second to last ferry of the night.

"What's bothering you, baby?" Judith asked. I had not been very talkative all evening, merely enough to be sociable with Beekman.

"The sum total of a bunch of little bullshit. Scheduling for one thing. I'll have to give the guys off Christmas week. They all have family on the mainland. That'll set us back a week. Not that I begrudge them the time. They've been splendid. I'm just getting impatient. Then there's the power. I can't test the wiring because I can't go live without it. David's seeing if he can do something. The roofing shingles aren't in. More excuses from the supplier. There's a couple of storm centers down south. One of them may break this way."

"Can I say something?"

"Go ahead."

"There's no schedule but the one you've imposed on yourself. Lighten up."

"If we have no materials we have no work. A couple of days with no money and some of these guys might move on."

"I doubt that. They like you. They like the work. They'll see it through. I promise."

"You know? At the start I had this wild idea we'd be spending Christmas in our new home. Crazy. Don't you think?"

"Not at all. Why wouldn't we? Listen, carpenter-man. I came onto this Island with a sleeping bag and I've still got it. If you want

Christmas in our new home, that's where we're going to spend it."

We did. With tarps for a roof and a fire in the hearth. It was crazy after all. And I loved her for it.

One week into the New Year brought an inspector from the power company. Forewarned by Beekman, I slipped him a hundred-dollar bill. That brought the inspector's boss and cost us two hundred more. The senior inspector promised an electrical main in three days. He was a man of his word.

The boys were back from their holiday and materials were waiting for them. The work went on in earnest and my mood was never better. Weather held clear and cool.

The second week of February brought the building inspector to approve a Certificate of Occupancy. I asked Beekman if money should change hands. He said to play it by ear. Some of them were not corrupt since a general crackdown in that bureau.

"Couldn't believe it when I heard someone was building out here," the inspector said. "I thought this Island had about had it."

"My husband was born and raised on this Island," Judith said. "It's his home."

He appraised the house from the edge of the road beside his car. "You did all this yourself?"

"Us and some local labor," I said.

"Let's see what you got."

The inspector started walking toward the front of the house. Half my crew was constructing the front porch. The other three were hauling the skylight panes up to the roof.

"These guys Union labor?"

"No. Is that a problem?"

"Not for me it isn't. Damn unions have all but killed the construction industry."

I was about to argue the point but thought better of it. Judith saw me tense up and sighed in relief when I kept my mouth shut. The inspector stood by the door.

"Got your permits?" he asked.

I walked over with a folder full of job permits for electrical, plumbing, sanitation approval, and the structural engineer's sign-off that Beekman had provided. The inspector glanced through the documents.

"Seems in order."

He opened the door and walked in. Judith and I followed. Inside he stepped between us and closed the door. "You think those boys can hear us outside?"

"I doubt it." I knew where this was leading.

"The State's got its eye on Bittern Island for reasons that need not concern you. Just let me say this. There's a bunch of men in Providence who'd like nothing better than for me to shut this project down. Now I don't get to Providence much myself. I like to tend my own garden as they say. Is this making sense to you, Mister Hoffmann?"

"Perfect sense, sir."

"These gentlemen in Providence have two thousand reasons to have their way. Can you think of an equal amount of reasons to have your way?"

"Absolutely. I just wasn't prepared for the argument today. Not with that many reasons."

"Pity. I don't get out this way often. Isn't there something you might do?"

"May I have a minute with my wife?"

"Of course. In the meantime I'll inspect the outside."

He opened the door, went out, and shut it behind him.

"You greedy bastard," I said to the closed door.

"What choice do we have, baby?" Judith said.

"None. He knows it."

"I can go home and get the cash box. There's enough in it if the crew will wait a day for their pay. I'll go to the bank on the mainland in the morning."

"The crew won't mind. I mind."

"This is the last hurdle. We're so close. But without a CO it's all for nothing."

"You're right. We have no other option. Go ahead and get the money. But don't bring the cash box. Just the money. The two grand. I don't want that son of a bitch to up the ante because he thinks there's more."

"Right."

Outside Judith got in the truck and drove away. The inspector came around the side of the house.

"Everything all right?" The bastard was smug about it.

"I'm not sure we have it all. But we'll have most of it." Well, I knew there was at least two thousand in the strongbox.

"Most is a relative term. I guess we'll have to wait and see."

I was a hair's breadth away from punching him in the face.

Judith played her part brilliantly. She returned and the three of us went back inside the house for the exchange. She carried a brown paper bag and spilled its contents onto the bare wood floor. I knelt down beside her and we started counting. The last thirteen dollars of the bounty was all in change. When we reached the mark, thirty-seven cents remained on the floor.

"We made it," Judith said innocently. "Thank God."

"I wasn't expecting nickels and dimes," the inspector said. He accepted the bag anyway.

"Money is money," I said. "How about that CO?"

"Deal's a deal, Mister Hoffmann. Seems like you folks got yourselves a home. The CO will be in the mail tomorrow."

I had no choice but to believe him. It did arrive on Saturday.

A few weeks later Judith and I lay in bed one night talking about the house.

"I'm glad we're so close to finishing," she said. "But I'm going to miss those boys when it's done."

"Me too. We'll see them around. They'll join up with the fleet again next month."

"You think Rolando will too?"

"I don't know. But I've been thinking about something."

"Tell me."

"I've learned a lot building this house. It's also refreshed my memory about the difficulties inherent in living out here. How even the smallest project becomes twice as hard because of the distance from supplies and equipment. I think I might have a way to make things easier for everyone on Bittern Island and make some money at the same time. If my idea works, I could use a man like Rolando."

"Let me hear your idea. Tell me the whole thing."

We talked until dawn. All Island Rental was born, at least in theory, by daybreak.

CHAPTER THIRTY-NINE

Sweeney, Gunner Hogan, and I put on raingear and followed Colonel Devon into the alley behind the Sea Witch. Rolando, toting the huge ancient revolver from Sweeney, came out last. Devon switched on a flashlight. He shined it ahead of him, saw no one, and turned it off. It was late afternoon but dark as night with thick swirling storm clouds above and chill rain pelting down.

"Don't bunch up. Keep spread out," Devon directed us. He set out down the alley. His boots made squishy splashes as he advanced.

When he was seven or eight yards ahead of me, I followed. A few seconds, I heard Gunner come after me. At the end of the alley Devon raised his hand for us to stop. The column halted while he peered around the corner. He beckoned with his hand, turned the corner and disappeared. Ten paces and I was at the corner. Around the edge of the building I saw Devon crouched in front by the street. He looked up and down the street and then back at me over his shoulder. With a nod he turned forward, stayed low, and sprinted across the street. When he reached the other side I was ready at the corner to do the same. Devon's side of the street was longer with more buildings. He crouched by the front door of Lawler's store.

I dashed across the street and ended up squatting behind him.

"What's the best way to get around back of the *cantina*?" Devon asked me. Rain was streaking his face but his eyes were calm and his voice steady.

"You don't want to go through the back. It's a maze back there. There's walk-in freezer, pantry, kitchen, laundry room. No space to maneuver and plenty of ways to get shot if you don't know exactly where you are."

"What do you suggest?"

"Massive frontal assault. There's two front windows besides the door. Gunner and Sweeney knock out the windows to give cover fire while you and I go through the door. Rolando follows us in case one of us goes down."

As I finished the scenario Gunner completed the traverse of the street to wind up behind me breathing hard through his mouth.

"All right," Devon was saying. "I like your way. Tell the others."

Sweeney came over clutching the shotgun in front of him as he ran. Like Gunner, the old man needed to catch his breath after the effort. I waited for Rolando to join us and explained the plan while Devon kept watch up the street.

"Wish I had a grenade," Gunner muttered. "That would do the trick."

"Your machine gun and Sweeney's shotgun should be fine. But aim high. Devon and I will go in low."

Sweeney and Gunner nodded in unison. Rolando blinked rainwater out of his eyes. His mouth opened in question.

"You follow us in," I told Rolando. "If the Colonel or I get hit, you know what to do."

"I'm with you, boss."

I turned to Devon and tapped him on the shoulder. "They've got the plan. We're ready."

"Stay low. Keep together this time. Keep it quiet," he ordered us. "Nice and slow and easy now."

Devon looked up the street and started advancing, keeping tight to the building line. We were right behind him moving slow and steady. Ten paces from the *cantina's* facade he held up a hand for us to halt.

"There may be innocent people in there too," he said back to us. "No way around it. You men are going to have to pick your shots."

Mutely we indicated we understood. A streak of lightning flashed illuminating our grim faces. It was followed by a long peal of thunder. It faded in a whoosh of wind.

"We're moving out," Devon said.

Another two yards and we halted abruptly. None of us expected it. The door to the *cantina* was opening. Completely open, it faced us, blocking our view of whoever was in the doorway.

I felt the automatic in my hand heavy, wet and cool. I brought it up to chest height with the barrel by my shoulder. Devon's .357 was out in front of him, trained on the door. The door started closing to expose a man remaining on the sidewalk. He was tall and dark and I did not recognize him. Not that I tried. My eyes were fixed on the long rifle he held with one hand so that its stock was up and resting on his shoulder.

Devon rose up slowly, partially blocking my view. I glimpsed the man staring straight ahead across the street oblivious to our presence.

"State Police. Drop your weapon," Devon shouted.

I came up tall beside Devon as the man turned in surprise. We both had our hands locked on our weapons, out in front, boring in on the figure before us.

"Drop it, I said."

To my amazed horror the man turned toward us slowly bringing the rifle off his shoulder. But instead of dropping it to the sidewalk, he leveled it with his other hand, barrel coming down to point at us. He had a dumb, expressionless face as if none of this had any consequence.

In the thick torpid air of the storm I saw the muzzle flash of Devon's gun a split second before the clap of its report registered in my ears.

The rifleman, still standing, looked surprised. He shook himself as if waking from a dream. The surprise turned to confusion in his features. I imagine that without any thought, he instinctively tried to raise the rifle. It dropped from his hand when I fired Clarence's gun.

"This is it. Let's go." Devon bounded toward the door, vaulting over the gunman's body crumpled on the sidewalk. He yanked open the door and entered diving for the floor to his right. I followed to the left, skidding to my knees, wildly trying to scan around the room.

"State Police. Everybody freeze," Devon yelled.

His call was immediately followed by the crashing of glass as Gunner and Sweeney smashed the windows and poked through their weapons. I felt shards of glass strike me in the back and fall away to splinter on the floor. In the same instant, Rolando was there crouched beside me, the relic of a gun in his hand waving side to side.

"Don't move. Stay where you are," Devon was shouting.

My eyes settled on the only occupant of the room. She was seated at a table, head tilted into her palm, elbow propped in support. She seemed disinterested in the controlled chaos that had exploded around her. Impervious to the menace of five guns trained on her frail body.

Devon came to his feet. "Keep your hands where I can see them."

The woman did not even blink. In fact, she yawned.

I scrambled upright and Devon and I advanced from opposite sides of the room to converge on the table. She was not even watching us. She was staring past us at a corner. I spun around, expecting an accomplice to be there, but the corner of the room was empty. Gunner and Sweeney came through the door.

"She's out of it," I heard Devon say. "High as a kite."

Turning toward the table I saw the evidence. The arm not supporting her head was stretched out across the table. Loose ends of a rubber tourniquet lay flaccid to either side of the skinny arm. In an ashtray on the table was a hypodermic needle. The serum canister was drained.

"What's your name, child?" Devon asked.

She might have been little more than a child but the ravages of addiction had drawn cruel strains across her forehead and down her cheeks.

"Who else is here?" It was pointless. She had no idea what was happening. "You men search the back. Be careful," Devon directed us.

"I'll take the apartment upstairs," I said.

"I'll go with you," Rolando said.

We followed Sweeney and Gunner through the kitchen door. They went on ahead. Rolando and I turned and went up the staircase.

The apartment contained a bedroom, bath, study, and sitting room. It was well-appointed and immaculately kept. In the study was a desk that faced the wall. Hung above the desk was my portrait, *The Poet*, by Judith Valenti. Across from it on the other wall was *Juliet*, the painting of my mother.

"Fucking bastard," I said.

"What's the matter?" Rolando asked. Still searching the rooms he had not noticed the portraits.

"Nothing. There's nobody here."

We went back downstairs. Gunner and Sweeney searched thoroughly and turned up no one. We reconvened in the dining room with Devon and the drugged lady.

The lash of the storm was filling the room through the shattered windows and open door. The wild breezes had snuffed the candles on all the tables. There was a waxy, charcoal smell in the air as if a child had blown out a birthday cake.

"Where do you think he's gone?" Devon asked me.

"Ostros?"

He nodded.

"Either high ground or his boat."

"Can't do much in a boat in this weather."

"You'd be surprised. His captains are well paid to be good. This is perfect weather for running drugs. Or escaping."

"What kind of boat does he have?"

"A forty-foot Chris Craft down in the Harbor for his personal use. Probably a mini-fleet of smaller, faster ones for his business."

"In the Harbor?"

"Jacob's Cove," Rolando said.

Devon and I looked at him. Ostros's cabin cruiser was docked in the Harbor with the rest of the Island's boats. But the drugs he ran through Jacob's Cove.

Devon tried his radio again with the same result. He hooked it back on his belt and holstered his gun. He pointed to the wretched figure seated at the table. "Anybody know this one?"

I did not truly know her though she seemed familiar. She could have been the singer that had preformed a night I had dinner with Ostros. The night Gunner had not stayed.

"Her name's Liliana," Rolando said.

"And the one outside?" Devon asked.

"I didn't check. Everything happened so fast."

I put Clarence's automatic in the pocket of my raincoat and headed for the door. The dead man lay in a heap on the sidewalk, rain glancing off him, diluting the pool of blood that had seeped from the two bullet holes in his chest. Rolando came out after me.

"He looks familiar," I said.

"Joaquin. One of the waiters, among other things."

"Let's get him in out of the rain."

We each grabbed one of Joaquin's ankles and dragged him through the doorway. Rolando went back to retrieve his rifle.

Devon had a notebook out and was writing. I told him Joaquin's name and verified he was a waiter at the *cantina*. Now I remembered him as well. It had been the same night Liliana sang. It seemed a lifetime ago.

Devon looked up from his pad. "And the two fishermen killed across the street? What were their names?"

"Donovan and Conti," Sweeney said solemnly. "God rest their souls."

I cast an eye at Rolando expecting him to cross himself. He was staring down at the dead waiter. The big pistol was wedged in his belt. His hands remained at his sides.

Devon snapped closed his notebook. "What's your bet?" he asked me. "Harbor or Jacob's Cove?"

"There has to be too many of them for a speedboat. I'd say he's taking the cabin cruiser."

"Why leave the girl and Joaquin behind?"

It was very clear to me all of a sudden. "Joaquin to make sure we're dead. The girl because he didn't care. She's useless to him. Look at her. Don Ostros has written her off."

"So why didn't he kill her? She probably knows things she can spill when we get her cleaned up."

"She's supposed to be dead by now."

"Overdose?"

"The drugs or Joaquin. Ostros is a thorough man. He'd have to be sure."

"Storm's letting up," Gunner called out. He had moved to the doorway and was looking up at the sky.

In the brief silence that followed I detected the absence of rain. The pat, pat, drip, drip noises had been constant all afternoon. The wind had also lessened considerably. Beyond Gunner's figure in the door a pale light shone from a sun setting somewhere out at sea.

"I hope you're right about the Harbor," Devon said. "We'd better get going."

"It's already too late."

The look on Devon's face told me he knew I was right. Ostros would have been set to sail the second there was a break in the storm. That second had come.

"What's the name of his boat?" Devon asked taking his radio from his belt.

"*La Fuerte.*"

The storm's static was gone from the airwaves. Devon radioed his headquarters on the mainland. The orders he issued were crisp and decisive. There had been six killings on the Island after Archie Bealer was murdered and Devon's team had departed. One victim had been one of their own, the trooper Clarence. Devon ordered a fresh squad of shooting experts be sent to the Island. He also ordered word be passed to the Coast Guard that the craft *La Fuerte* be intercepted at sea and the vessel and its party seized.

"What about her?" Gunner interrupted him. Gunner indicated Liliana in her stupor.

Devon clicked his mic on the radio and requested a paramedic for a drug overdose.

A deadening weariness took hold of me. I stumbled to a table and sat down heavily in a chair. Gunner came over and sat across from me. His flask was out, uncapped, and he set it before me. I grasped it in both hands and took a drink. When I handed it back, he did the same.

Sweeney and Rolando stepped outside into the fading light. If they talked, I could not hear them. I looked over at Liliana. Her head had come down to rest sideways on the table, eyes open and glazed staring at nothing, her long dark hair pooled on the table behind her head.

"Then I guess it's over and done with," Gunner was saying.

"What?"

"Ostros. This whole mess. It's finished."

I looked at him and for a reason I will never know I started to laugh. It was more of a chuckle than a belly laugh. Devon and Gunner regarded me with odd puzzled faces. They probably thought I was losing my mind. Some temporary lapse in sanity provoked by the immediate events. That was not it at all. At least I do not think so. Gunner had said it was over. He was wrong. I had things to do and they made me laugh. I had a traffic ticket to pay, truck to get inspected, and my laundry would be ready in the morning.

I got up from the table, went through the kitchen door and up the stairs. When I came back I was carrying *The Poet* and *Juliet*.

"I'm taking these with me," I told Devon flatly. "Don't try and stop me."

Devon stared at me and then the paintings. "Go put them in your truck and come back. I never saw them. Understand?"

CHAPTER FORTY

Our home was ready before spring. The last day of work we took the crew to Don Ostros's *cantina* for dinner then a roaring drunken celebration across the street in the Sea Witch. The boys had spent a good winter, made some money, and were ready and anxious to return to the water. All but Rolando Tobar. He sat by himself at a table drinking tequila and sulking.

"Don't be an asshole, Karl," Judith said. "Go over and tell him. If you won't I will."

"Suppose he doesn't go for it?"

"You might as well find out."

Taking my beer I went to Rolando's table. Judith watched from across the room as I sat down.

"You got a nice house, boss," Rolando said lifting his glass. *"Buena suerte."*

"I'm looking for more than luck."

"Qué?"

"My wife and I are planning to start a business. If things work out, I'd like you to come work for us." Then I mimicked his accent to amuse him, not insult. "What you think?"

"What I think?" He put down his glass. "I think you're the boss, boss."

We shook hands over the table. I leaned forward.

"Between you and me. I think my wife's the boss but we don't have to let her know that."

Rolando winked at me. "They always are."

I stood up. "Come by the house tomorrow and I'll lay it out for you."

"What did he say?" Judith asked me.

"He said he'd think about it."

She looked surprised but my smile gave it away a second later. From my pocket I took all the cash I had on me and laid it on the bar.

"Careful now, baby. Remember who's the old man."

I jerked my thumb down the bar. "He is."

I had noticed a new patron enter the bar that I did not recognize. He was older, middle age and had a slight limp. He took the last seat at the bar and ordered whiskey. After Sweeney served him, the bartender replenished our glasses.

"Who's that?" I asked Sweeney.

Sweeney leaned across the bar between my wife and me and spoke in a whisper. "New to the Island. Hogan's his name. Retired Army officer. Colonel, I think."

"Colonel Hogan?" I slurred. "Like the TV show?"

"Shh," my wife said. "Don't embarrass him or yourself."

"Not at all. Sweeney, buy him a drink on me. In fact buy everybody a drink. This is our night."

"Whatever you say, Karl." Sweeney scurried away to serve the drinks.

The man called Hogan at the end of the bar never said a word. When the drink I bought was served him, he raised his glass in a silent salute to Judith and me. We returned the gesture.

The boys from my crew wanted me to do a shot of tequila with them. Against my better judgment I agreed. When we raised our glasses, it was Judith they toasted instead of me. I felt very good about that. My wife smiled and blushed. The drink went down and the wooziness crept up.

"I think it's time I took you home to bed," Judith said under her breath so as not to embarrass me.

"Is that an invitation?"

"Always. But this time it's also a precaution."

"I love you. You know?"

"Of course I know. Now say goodnight to the boys and I'll take you home." Judith guided me from the stool.

I embarrassed myself anyway.

"Farewell, men. Hell of a job. Let's do it again some time."

There were laughs and cheers and Judith took me home. The home we had built ourselves to live in long and happy.

That summer there were two art shows of Judith's work. The first was in San Francisco and we both went turning it into a sort of belated honeymoon. The second was in Toronto. Aldan begged Judith to go because the city's Museum of Modern Art was acquiring two of her paintings for its permanent collection. She finally agreed to the trip. I stayed behind on Bittern Island. We had bought more land and the construction of All Island Rental was underway.

The property, mid-way between Gracetown and Shuman Point, had four barns on it, all that remained of a pre-Depression Islander's attempt at dairy farming. Up along Mariners Path I decided to build an office structure from which to manage All

Island, its inventory stored in the sheds behind it. David Beekman provided plans. There was a labor shortage due to the fishing season, so I hired a contractor. While the store was being erected, Rolando and I worked on refurbishing the barns.

On Sunday I drove to Boston to meet Judith's flight from Toronto. The minute I saw her coming through the door after Customs clearance, I knew she was not well. Her hair was pulled straight back and tied. Her skin was pale. Her shoulders drooped in exhaustion. She dragged her suitcase behind her.

"Rough flight?" I kissed her mouth and then her cheek, the warmth of fever against my lips.

"I'll say. I spent most of it in the can heaving or worse. Can you get me something cool to drink? My throat is so dry."

I led her to a concession stand where Judith drank two iced teas in gulps.

"You're burning up. I've got to get you home. Maybe call a doctor."

"I just need to sleep. This will pass. Could we drive home tomorrow? I really can't handle the long drive. Let's check into a motel for tonight. I really need to sleep."

"Whatever you want."

We checked into a motel near Logan Airport and I put her to bed. At a convenience store I bought aspirin, orange juice, cola, and bottles of water. Fetching ice from the motel's machine I wrapped some is a washcloth and made a compress for her forehead. She adamantly refused to go to an emergency room. She slept in fits, shaking and sweating. I sat up beside her in the only chair in the sparsely furnished room.

Around ten o'clock that night the fever broke and Judith dropped into a deep sleep. She awoke after three a.m. to find me in the chair.

"Have you been sitting there all night, you poor baby?"

"Who's the poor baby? How are you feeling?"

"Better. But I'm so thirsty."

I had the water bottles cooling in the ice bucket. She drank three of them. Then I poured her cola with ice.

"I don't know what happened," she said dreamily. "It must have been some kind of bug."

"You had me worried. That was a hell of a fever. There's orange juice if you want it."

"This is fine for now. What time is it?"

"Almost four."

She shook her head. "How do you do that? It's always amazed me."

"Never mind. I just know."

"You better get some sleep. It's a long drive and now I just want to get home."

"All right. But only a couple of hours. Wake me and we'll go."

"Come lay by me. Or do I look horrid and smell like an old dishtowel?"

"You look beautiful as always. And you usually smell of paint so this isn't bad."

When I woke up Judith was taking a bath. I went into the bathroom and shampooed her hair for her. The color returned to her face and she seemed fully recovered. While she dried herself, I took a shower.

We checked out of the motel and stopped in a roadside diner for breakfast.

"How was the show?" I finally asked.

"Besides the two for the museum, we sold eight more paintings." She nibbled at her toast. "Someone bought *The Poet*."

"Who?"

"I don't know. Some collector. He was Latin or Indian, I think. I couldn't tell. It was the last day and I was already starting to feel sick. Anyway, it's sold."

"Will you miss it?"

"Why? I've got the real thing."

On the ferry over to Bittern Island Judith asked me, "Do you miss Boston?"

"No."

"New York City?"

"No."

"Neither do I. It's good to be home. I'm not traveling any more no matter what Aldan says. I have my home, my work, and you. That's all I need or want."

We were standing on deck and I held her in my arms. A cool breeze was blowing from the southeast giving the sea a moderate swell.

"Speaking of work, how's the shop coming along?" she asked.

"You can see for yourself on the way home."

Rolando and I made several trips to the mainland to buy inventory. My associate was not only a hard worker but also an able negotiator. By the end of summer the construction was done and we were reasonably stocked. All Island Rental opened for business on September first.

"Not a bad idea," said Ben Marshall. Marshall, the Fire Warden and newly elected Harbor Master of Bittern Island, was my first customer. "A lot of us let things slide because it's such a pain in the ass trekking to the mainland every time we need tools." He signed out a sander to refinish the flooring of his home. "Good luck, Karl. I think you've got something here."

Seems a lot of people felt the same way. Business was not booming but it was enough to suit me. Judith's paintings were selling well. Money was not a problem. I used the proceeds from the store to pay Rolando and procure more machinery. If I did not have what somebody wanted, I bought it and rented it to them. The logic was simple. If an Islander needed a tool, chances were somebody else would too sooner or later. We led similar lives and were pretty much in the same boat.

Two magazines did feature articles on Judith. Her reputation in the art world was flourishing. Though she steadfastly refused to be interviewed, over Aldan's objections, one journalist did make the trip to Bittern Island in vain. From what I later read in *The New Yorker*, the reporter was surprised to discover no one on Bittern Island ever heard of the famous painter Judith Valenti. Islanders also told her that no Valenti even lived on the Island. Of course not; everyone knew her as Judith Hoffmann.

That was exactly the way Judith wanted it.

Judith's second winter on Bittern Island we had snow. The storm came in on a Sunday night and blanketed us with two and a half feet of snow. It took all Monday and Tuesday to dig out, then make it down to the shop and dig that out as well. Judith called it an "Act of God" and insisted we not be profiteers. We passed out what tools we had for free and encouraged our clients to pass them along to neighbors when they were through with them. I kept no rental receipts during the crisis but every implement came back, usually accompanied by a home-baked pie or bread or a bottle of wine.

A few weeks later Judith had several days of headaches and the fevers returned. Overruling her objections I called the doctor in Narragansett. He came over on the ferry and examined my wife. I made him tea in the kitchen when he was finished.

"Ever happen before?" he asked me.

I told him about the first bout on her trip to Toronto.

"I'm darned if I can find the cause or even if the two events are related. A fever so high can only mean infection. When she's fit to travel, bring your wife over to the mainland for tests. Meanwhile I've given her something to bring down the fever. She'll be groggy a while."

I promised we would make the trip.

The next day Judith was feeling better.

"It's probably nothing," she said.

I would not listen. She saw the determination and concern on my face and agreed without further urging on my part.

The tests lasted three days to no conclusion. The doctor prescribed medication to use if the fever returned. He also strongly suggested a trip to Providence to consult with a specialist.

"We'll see," Judith said. "It may not come back."

I knew she had mixed emotions about doctors after the experience her brother Frank had gone through to a pitiful outcome.

Judith set back to work with renewed intensity. She rose at dawn and painted until mid-afternoon. The volume of her work was prodigious. Often she would be working on three canvases at once. Along with still lifes of common household objects that were imaginative and sold well, the landscape of Bittern Island in all its seasons unrolled itself under her brushstrokes.

With Rolando minding the store I would come home for lunch most days. Judith would stop work for an hour or so and we would eat and talk. Sometimes we did not eat. Those times we made love up in the studio or out on a blanket on the beach or in the cozy bedroom down the hall from the studio.

One such day we lay in each other's arms afterwards in the bedroom as breezes fluttered the curtains and brushed lightly over our bodies.

Judith sighed. "I don't think we're ever going to have a baby."

It caught me by surprise. We had stopped using precautions when the house was finished. Not well versed in such topics, I did not know if that was a long enough time to reach a conclusion.

When I did not say anything she asked, "Are you upset?"

"No," I said honestly. "Maybe I haven't really thought about it. We've been so busy. Your work, the shop, this house, Island living. It's a lot of work. Maybe it's too much. The good thing is we're still trying even if we're not exactly thinking about a baby when we do. Some things come in their own time."

"No, I suddenly have a strong feeling about this. It isn't going to happen."

"Then so be it. I love you. You love me. We're happy. Maybe it isn't fair to ask for more."

That night I wrote her a poem. The first poem I had written in months. I read it to her by the fire in the hearth. She made me read it over and over, at least six times. Then she took it from me, folded it, and went to put it away. When we went to bed later I saw it under her pillow but did not mention it.

The season changed slowly. Judith's fevers still came, closer together, relentlessly, like a tide.

CHAPTER FORTY-ONE

Sweeney was left behind at the *cantina* to guard Liliana. The wretched woman was still semi-comatose but Devon took no chances. At the very least she was a material witness to any number of crimes. The rest of us, Gunner, Rolando, Devon and I, walked out onto Main Street.

In lines of two, Devon and I leading, we started for the Harbor. The meager light that had shone that day faded into dusk. Here and there a head popped out a doorway or a face watched us from a window. There must have been something in our faces or strides that sent a message. No one came out, called, or challenged.

"Where's his boat?" Devon asked as we entered the gate to the dockage.

"End of the main pier," I said.

Past the Harbor Master's shack we stepped out onto the planks of the pier. Devon took his flashlight out and held it in his left hand, unlit. His revolver was drawn in his right. I took the automatic from my pocket. Behind me I heard Gunner work the bolt of his machine pistol. We passed the sterns of the fishing armada tied up to either side of us.

Near the end of the pier, it angled to the right. We turned the corner. Looking straight ahead I saw a gray-blue patch of water and sky, a few stars starting to peep out in the darkness. The unobstructed view meant only one thing.

"The *La Fuerte's* gone." I slipped the gun back in my pocket.

"Let's check up there anyway," Devon said.

I shrugged and we all followed him. The flashlight came on and he worked the beam from side to side. At the end of the dock beside the *La Fuerte's* slip was a tool locker. Devon shined the light on it.

"Aw, shit," I muttered brushing past Devon.

"Wait," Devon said.

I ignored him. I dropped to one knee by the body slumped against the locker. It was not necessary for me to see the face. I knew who it was.

Colonel Devon shined his light down on the dead man. I took the corpse's shoulder with one hand and cupped the slack jaw with my other turning the face toward me. The head dipped as I released pressure. There was matted blood in the hair where he had been struck, probably from behind. And there was an entrance wound in the temple where he had been executed as he lay after the blow.

"Isn't that Ben Marshall?" Devon said.

I nodded with nothing to say.

"What do you suppose he was doing out here?"

"His job. He must have seen people on the pier. As Harbor Master he wouldn't let anyone sail out in the weather we had. Probably didn't know it was Ostros until too late. Too late for him anyway."

Gently I let the body of the Harbor Master back down to the dock. Standing up I took the gun out again and stood looking out off the pier into the darkness over the water. Unable to restrain myself I took aim at nothing out there and fired and fired until the clip was empty. The others did not stop me.

When my rage subsided I handed the empty gun to Devon. He took it without a word. I drew the rain slicker off my shoulders and down my arms.

With it I covered the body of my friend Ben Marshall.

Gunner came up and spat into the water. He looked up at the stars. "Here she comes." Gunner had heard a second before us the sound of approaching helicopters. His mind, though, was in two places at the same time. "Even now, I still hate that fucking sound."

I could see their running lights coming low and level over the water. Devon's radio started to squawk and the officer began relaying orders.

It was a long gruesome night. Bittern Island, a hard unforgiving place by nature, had never seen such carnage. An army of police and technicians descended on us from the sky and more were delivered by boat. A makeshift morgue was assembled in the parish hall of Saint Andrews. Seven bodies lay in black body bags side by side. It was a mixed roster of good, evil, and innocent. The good were Ben Marshall and the trooper named Clarence. Savagely cut down doing their duty. Joaquin, Santiago, and the kid Miguel comprised the evil. Captains Conti and Donovan brought up the innocent. Each body had a yellow tag as if the difference meant nothing in death.

Islanders clustered outside under electric lighting rigged up by the State Police. All the faces were drawn and blank except the three new widows who cried on each other's shoulders in their own little colony of grief. For the rest it was clearly unimaginable, unbelievable, and unfathomable.

For those of us who had somehow participated in the day's bloody array, there were procedures and formalities. We gave statements to the police and signed our names.

When the interviews were done Sweeney and Gunner said they were going over to the Sea Witch. It was well after midnight. I said I would join them in a while, meaning it, yet knowing I would not. Esperansa came for Rolando and led him home.

I stood in the corner of the hall with a cardboard cup of coffee the technicians supplied. From there I looked out and down at the parade of dead on the floor before me. In a while, I am not sure how long, Colonel Devon came up beside me. He looked weary but still in control. He handed me the rain slicker I had used to cover Marshall. A trooper came up requesting Devon's signature on some form. He scanned it and signed. The trooper withdrew respectfully. We stood alone, the two of us.

"Go on home and get some sleep," Devon said to me.

"Yeah, I'll do that in a bit."

"There's nothing more for you to do. My boys will finish up here."

"I said in a bit."

A lieutenant came up and drew Devon a few yards away. A serious discussion took place that I could not hear. I saw Devon's face tense, his mouth twisting as he checked his anger. The lieutenant saluted and walked away. Devon came back. His eyes were fierce and his jaw was set.

"What's the matter?"

"Dead end," he said.

"How so?"

"The Coast Guard found the *La Fuerte*. She was headed for Long Island. They must have figured they had a better shot escaping through New York instead of Rhode Island or Massachusetts. It was the longest way but I guess the smartest if you were in their shoes. An ocean doesn't leave a trail."

Devon stopped and looked at the floor then at the ceiling. While I waited, a young trooper walked over to the body bags and reverently laid a small Rhode Island State flag on the first bag. Trooper Clarence was back among his own.

"The Coast Guard arrested seven," Devon said. "No, Ostros wasn't with them. They were taken to Montauk Point and interrogated. They've got a pat story worked up. Seems there was a fight on the boat. Ostros was killed and they tossed his body overboard."

"You believe that?"

"No, I'm simply repeating what they said. Anything could have happened. They might have dropped him off somewhere before heading further south. He could be on Block Island, Orient Point, or even transferred to another vessel. Maybe one of his drug speedboats."

The coffee in my cup was cold and I drained it in a swallow. I put on my slicker

"I'm going home. One thing?"

"What, Karl?"

"When do you plan on arresting me for stalling you about the Jeep?"

"You know? I forgot all about Janus Martin. A drug deal gone bad I imagine. We'll never know.

Odd. I forgot all about how this started. Maybe you should too. Go home, Karl."

For some reason I could not bring myself to simply say thank you, so I nodded and walked out of the hall.

The crowd had mostly gone home. The harsh electric lights glared down on a few policemen taking a smoke break. One of the troopers spotted me. He crushed out his cigarette under his boot.

"Need a ride home, Mr. Hoffmann?" he called out.

"No. Thanks. I've got my truck."

"You take care then, sir."

"Yeah. You too."

Turning right I walked up Main Street in the dark past the front of Saint Andrews Church. The stores and shops coming after were dark and shuttered from the storm. I was not thinking, only moving. My truck was still behind the Sea Witch. It seemed my body knew how to get there without the slightest concentration from my brain.

A ways up the street my mental dullness was disturbed as my boots scratched over broken glass. I was in front of the *cantina* where Gunner and Sweeney had busted out the glass and some of it littered the sidewalk. The place where Devon and I had shot Joaquin dead. Not stopping, nor looking inside, on I went crushing the slivers of glass under my heel until I was past the place. Then I was at Lawler's store where we had planned the attack crouched in the rain. My body turned mechanically, pointed like a compass to a magnet, and propelled me across the street.

My first clear thought was that Sweeney and Gunner were inside the Sea Witch. I pictured them drinking whiskey held in old knarred hands. They would be silent, glad for each other's company, but not dependent on it. Two men who had lived their lives already. It had been a hard night. They had handled themselves well, done what had to be done, and though neither would sleep for many hours, I imagined them in repose. "Done and well done," I might have said. As I had known earlier, I did not go in to join them.

Inside my truck were the portraits of *The Poet* and *Juliet*. I moved them to the passenger seat in the dark of the cab, wedging the tops gently against the headrest. The truck started as if by itself. I backed down the alleyway, turned onto Main Street and drove out of Gracetown.

At the top of the ridgeline I saw the feathery finger of moonlight undulate on the ocean in the southwest. The running lights of a distant ship headed for the strip of brightness from the east. They were about to intersect when I put the truck in gear and started down the other side.

"You take care," the trooper's call came back to me.

"You take care," I said to Bittern Island. You take care, Gunner and Sweeney, Rolando and Devon, and the ship that sails through the moon.

Paintings in hand, I got out of the truck and went up my porch to the front door. There was the tack that held my message to Colonel Devon. The message that brought him to town and set the night in inexorable motion.

After I hung up my coat, I held the paintings in both hands and climbed the stairs. At the top I turned for the bedroom, stopped, looked down at the pictures, and turned toward the studio the other way.

The door opened with one hand on the knob, one holding the paintings. Darkness. Looked up. Starlight through the skylight. Still the faint old smell of linseed oil and turpentine and Judith. For a second I thought she was there crouched over the worktable meticulously attending to the tools of her art. I almost called to her to entice her to come to bed. It's late. Come lay with me. I need you so much.

"Close the door, Karl," Don Ostros said in the darkness.

I heard him rise from the only chair. Saw only a bulky shadow moving slowly on the other side of the room.

"Turn on the light. Slowly now. I have a gun. Do you?"

I did not answer. It could be over in a second. Ostros's eyes would be accustomed to the darkness. If he truly had a weapon, and I had no doubt, and if I moved forward suddenly in charge, I would be dead. The soft starlight above, the scents of life with Judith, the mute longing, would be forever.

"Do as I say. Close the door and turn the light on."

He must have realized by then I was not armed. I took a step backward and flung the door closed with one hand. With the same hand I flicked the light switch. The starlight disappeared in the sudden glare. We both blinked. I saw his gun, a small chrome semi-automatic clutched in his right hand.

He pointed with the barrel of the weapon to the pictures I held. "What have you there?"

I turned the canvases to face him.

He snorted. "Hah. You thought I was dead so it was all right to steal from me."

"I never thought you were dead. What are you doing here?"

Ostros's lips twisted in a sardonic smile. He kept the gun pointed at my midsection.

"So? Suddenly I'm not welcome?"

"I told you at the *cantina*. You and I are finished. We're even and it's over. They're hunting you even as we speak. Everybody else is caught," I lied. "Santiago, Liliana, Miguel, Joaquin, they're all in custody. The *La Fuerte* was seized at sea. The troops are here. Once again, no fire to light."

"Put the paintings on the chest and move away."

Moving to my left without turning, I placed both canvases atop the two crates of Judith's paintings.

"Now move back slowly."

I sidled to my right. "You didn't answer me. Why have you come?"

"Why else? To be of service of course," he said with a guttural laugh. "I always help my friends. Even when they are ungrateful and bite the hand that serves. I must be bigger than them, forgiving and faithful. You misjudged me, Karl. I've come to do you one last favor before I forsake this dreadful sand and rock pile. I've come to put your tortured soul at ease."

"My soul is my business. What do you really want?"

"You sorry fool. Isn't it obvious?" he asked, feigning surprise. "I want the paintings. I want them all. And I shall have them. But not for greed. No. For you. To set you free of them. They are an anchor weighing down your heart to smash your spine. They have left you unable to move, to live. And you must thank me for this."

"Why? You're going to kill me anyway."

"True," he agreed almost sadly. "But an hour's freedom is more precious than a lifetime of slavery. Didn't we once speak of moments? This moment is yours. Yours and mine."

"That's so much crap. You're a smuggler and a thief and a murderer. My life is irrelevant to you. I'm supposed to be dead on the Sea Witch floor. That was your plan. Now what? How do you intend to get away after you kill me and steal the paintings at the same time?"

"You shouldn't lie, Karl. You're no good at it, I can tell. The fact that you're here means Santiago and Miguel are either dead or arrested. But Joaquin? He had the plan. If the men did not return his orders are to fetch the last boat from Jacob's Cove and beach it here at your house." Ostros glanced at his watch. "It is after midnight. He's coming in two hours. We have a long wait. Then he and I and these lovely paintings by your wife will be gone. And you will be gone too. But not with us. Tell me. Do you wish to spend these hours enjoying your freedom, or would you rather end it now after the brief moment?"

"Joaquin is dead. I shot him. He's not coming."

Ostros smirked. "First you tell me he's arrested. Now he's dead. Like I told you, you lie poorly."

I shrugged. "All the same, it will be a longer wait than you expect."

"I'm a patient man. So are you. I will wait to escape. And you shall wait for death. A paradox, don't you think? And how will you spend your time? Reading one of your books? Perhaps writing a poem? How does one spend his last hours when one can choose?"

"You're old. You're tired. I might take you."

"Ah, the heroic." Ostros sighed. "I had not thought of that one, but I should have. Aren't all tragedies essentially about heroes? No doubt you've read that. When I have time, perhaps I shall read some too. What would you suggest? Homer? Shakespeare?"

I said nothing.

"*Pero*," Ostros went on. "You've forced me to a decision I thought you'd rather I postpone. You might indeed be a threat. I tell you this. I'm through with threats. Time to die, Karl."

I saw his thumb cock the hammer of the gun as he raised it from my stomach to my head. He was watching my eyes. I swayed back a little and he seemed to enjoy what he took for a terrified recoil. He did not see the hand go behind my back, find the switch and suddenly douse the light.

"Crack," came the first shot whizzing past my ear.

I lunged forward diving low.

"Crack, crack," in rapid succession.

Tucked, my shoulder drove into his knees. He slammed back into the chair, his weight smashing the wood as he went down. Fighting for balance with his arms, I felt the cold metal of the gun slap and draw across my cheek. I reached for his wrist in the dark; his other hand pounded my neck and back with a fist. Found the wrist, twisted it violently, hoped the hand would unclench its grip. Felt the barrel pressed to bone.

"Crack."

Burning in my shoulder socket, my arm losing feeling, other hand in his collar clawing for his throat. His wrist free, barrel staring me in the eye, glint of star stream on the muzzle.

Thunder. Again. Thunder. Lightning.

Ostros heaving backward. Gun dropped from his hand. Flailing at me with both arms to pull me down. His eyes popping out in surprise and horror. A rush of breath over my face, hot and foul. Finally falling away.

The lights came on. Heavy boots pounding the floor. Me, blinking in the glare, unable to look away from the dying face of Don Ostros. Someone's hands on my shoulders. Stab of pain where I was shot.

"Boss? Boss? It's okay. It's over."

Sinking back. Releasing Ostros. Good hand coming up to the shattered shoulder. Warm blood seeping onto my fingers.

"*Cristo*. You're hit. Hang on, boss," Rolando said. Heard him call, "Gunner, find the first aid kit."

I heard Gunner drag his lame foot across the floorboards out the door.

"How did you know?" I gasped to Rolando in a daze of pain.

"I didn't." He turned me around on the floor away from the Don's body. "Gunner came and got me. He said you didn't show up at the Sea Witch like you promised. He thought that was odd. It got him worried. So here we are."

Beside Rolando on the floor was the old six-shooter Sweeney had given him. It suddenly occurred to me that he had not shot it during the fight earlier in the evening. Because of that, the police had not confiscated it into evidence. Probably did not even know about it. The last I remembered, Rolando was tucking it in his belt under his coat in the *cantina*.

Still looking at the gun, I jerked my head back toward my shoulder. "Did you check him? Are you sure he's dead?"

Rolando chuckled grimly. "This old pea-shooter of Sweeney's would stop an elephant. He's dead all right."

"Is this the end of your Evil One?" I said through the pain.

"There's more where he came from. That's why you should pray."

He crossed himself, slid off my rain jacket and started to cut my shirt with his pocketknife.

Gunner Hogan brought the bandages.

CHAPTER FORTY-TWO

"Why do they want this Island?" Judith asked.

We had heard the State had bought up six more parcels of land.

"I don't know. There's all kinds of rumors. We'll probably never know the truth."

"They can't love it as much as we do."

"Nobody loves like we do. Maybe that's our problem. Now get some sleep."

The fever had broken. She drank some broth and ate a little toast. I could tell by her eyes she was exhausted from the fight. We had been to Providence, Boston, and New York. The doctors all said the same thing, which amounted to nothing.

"Lay down with me," she said. "But wake me when you get up. Not too long. Promise?"

"Promise. Sleep. I'll call you Judith. I'll call you Judith very soon."